(Spooky) Litigation.

Jeffrey A. Rapkin, Esq.
Attorney and Counselor at Law

(Spooky) Litigation.

Copyright © 2018 Jeffrey A. Rapkin, Esq.

Bearcub Publishing, Inc.
Fl.ID: P18000032711

Bearcub Publishing, Inc.
Fl Corp ID No. P18000032711
18245 Paulson Dr. #132
Port Charlotte, Fl. 33954

For Angela and Harry

And

I dedicate this writing to any person who has had the misfortune to find him or herself standing in a crowded courtroom and thought: "these people aren't human."
They probably weren't.

Jeffrey A. Rapkin, Esq.

Practice of law defined: The performance of services in legal matters, representing another before the courts, giving legal advice and counsel by one who possess legal skill and a knowledge of the law greater than that possessed by the average citizen.
State ex rel. The Florida Bar v. Sperry, 140 So.2d 587, 591 (1962)

Practice of "Supernatural Law" defined: The performance of legal services in supernatural matters by one who possess legal skill and a knowledge of the law greater than that possessed by the average citizen.
In re The Sale of the Amityville House, U.S. Sup. Crt. 19-2081 S.L.

Definition of "Supernatural:" The supernatural (Medieval Latin: supernātūrālis: supra "above" + naturalis "natural", first used: 1520-1530 AD)[1][2] is that which exists (or is claimed to exist), yet cannot be explained by laws of nature. Examples often include characteristics of or relating to ghosts, angels, gods, souls and spirits, non-material beings, or anything else considered beyond nature like magic, miracles, or etc..[3]"
Wikipedi

ONE

THE PRACTICE OF SUPERNATURAL LAW

FELDMAN V. FELDMAN

STANDING AT THE PODIUM IN COURT, MARTIN SANDBERG KNEW IN LESS THAN FIFTEEN MINUTES THEY WERE ALL GOING TO DIE HORRIBLY.

Martin blamed the judge, as his inexperience regarding his new responsibilities caused him to be ignorant of the gravity and of the nature of the situation.

Martin knew that the judge didn't have a grasp.

It was a problem, and there was no time to do anything about it.

Standing at the podium, trying to push back the panic, Martin took a moment to reflect.

For these types of matters, inexperience, disbelief, a lack of confidence, even hesitation would cause of the untimely death of (most) of the people in the courtroom. Martin considered throwing his shoe at the judge, but as a matter of course, judges are a stubborn lot, set in their ways and Martin decided it was probably better not to be found in Contempt of Court before his imminent and miserable demise.

Martin Sandberg and Judge Markowitz stared at each other for just a little too long, each attempting to express something to the other without putting that something into words for fear that the other would appear as though he had lost his sanity. Because he was sure that he was about to die, (excruciatingly) Martin found it difficult to concentrate on the proceeding. Because fear had broken his concentration, he had forgotten what he was supposed to do, though his notes were in front of him.

Sandberg's client, an attractive middle-aged woman in business-wear and heels that were just a little too high, stood next to Sandberg, in the almost-empty courtroom, attempting to assess the awkward moment of silence between attorney and judge.

Previously, the hearing had been scheduled for 4:45 p.m. but Judge Markowitz had sauntered into the Courtroom at 4:33

1

p.m. and announced he was starting the case, no matter what the appointed time had been.

Martin Sandberg had previously known that would be the case. Judge Markowitz was always early for everything, and of course, Martin had acquired *exclusive* information that the Judge would come in early. Martin also knew that the judge would probably be very angry when he did. In most cases, it didn't matter what the reason was, or if there was any reason at all for a judge's anger. It seemed to be a job qualification.

Though it was procedurally incorrect to start earlier than the notice stated, as to what was *about* to occur, commencing the proceedings *prior to* the noticed time could have saved them.

"Mr. Sandberg, I have read the Petition you filed on behalf of Mrs. Feldman," Judge Markowitz said, looking down at him through little glasses that sat on the end of his nose. Martin had often spent hours in court waiting for the eventual day that they slipped off.

"Normally Mr. Sandberg, " I would report you to the Bar for a psychological evaluation... After, of course, dismissing a case like this," he said. "Normally, that is."

Martin thought he detected a slight quiver of nervousness in the old judge's voice, something he had never heard before in the years he had known him.

"Yes, Your Honor," Martin said to him, standing at the podium in the Courtroom with his client, trying not to both laugh loudly while simultaneously engaging in a fit of sobbing.

At (now) *4:35* P.M. on a Friday afternoon, the Courthouse was virtually deserted. Weeks prior, Martin had almost choked on his lunch when the Judge's assistant called him on the phone, gave him the date and time, and told him to file and serve the notice of hearing. The call was a surprise. She usually left him a note in his courthouse box or sent an email.

The Judge's assistant's name was Anita (they always seemed to be named Anita), and she laughed at him when she instructed him to proceed with sending notice to the opposition for the hearing.

"You'll send him notice, Mr. Sandberg?" she asked. From her voice, he could feel her smiling on the other end of the phone. "And we can safely assume the Husband is *not* represented, correct, I mean *how* would he have hired his attorney? How are you going to give him notice, Mr. Sandberg? Are you going to use an 'Ouija Board?'"

It was at that moment, right when Anita commented on the 'Ouija Board' that she burst into hysterics, laughing as if someone was tickling her or she was at the dentist, well-gassed, about to get a tooth pulled.

"Thank you, Anita," he said, "I'll handle the notice."

"Seriously, though, are you going to print out the notice of hearing and bury it in the ground?" she asked him before descending into a fit of screeching laughter.

Laugh all you want. If you only knew, he thought.

Her hysterics only stopped when Martin heard Judge Markowitz's voice on the other end, yelling several expletives, ending with something to the effect of "go home, Anita." Martin could tell he was angry.

Her laughter stopped as the line went dead.

And now, weeks later, it was time. After Markowitz called the case, eyeballed Sandberg as he went through the recitals, the mandatory questions one must ask a Petitioner when he or she would like to be divorced, such as "are you a resident?" And: "Did you file a Petition for Dissolution of Marriage in this case?" Martin asked her a few other questions which would give the Court the necessary facts to enable the Court to issue a Final Judgment.

Martin asked his client, Annabelle Feldman, if she had been a resident for six months prior to the filing of the petition, if she alleged that the marriage was irretrievably broken, (Markowitz rolled his eyes at that one), and is she requesting to be declared single.

Martin looked around the courtroom. At *4:40* P.M. on Friday afternoon, the only people in Court were his client, the Judge, one lone bailiff named Laszlo, and the clerk.

Martin was thankful that the Courtroom was virtually empty as there were fewer people who might die with him. Though he was sure of the danger, there was always the question of *what* that danger might entail. Martin had often complained (to himself mostly) that the job was hard enough as it was without adding a supernatural horror.

The bailiff stood in the corner, smirking as always. He was a huge, well-built, meaty, muscular, monster of a man, had greasy black hair, thick, rippled, hairless arms and a thin black mustache. Martin had a casual conversation or two with the bailiff before, read his nametag, found that his name was "Laszlo," and that he had the same outlook as the rest of the bailiffs in the courthouse. Martin figured that bailiffs were forced to watch events unfold in court every day, were forced to watch lawyers argue, watch lawyers make sales pitches, *sing and dance* for their clients, and at some point, every one of the "Laszlos" just got fed up and angry. That anger quietly persisted. Faces like stone, they hid their real emotions every day as they bore witness to the daily drama.

Martin prayed that Markowitz would sign the order. Martin prayed that it would be quick. They were running out of time.

Yes, I noticed it for 4:45 p.m. and we started early. We have to be done before it's officially time to start. He might show. If her husband shows, we're doomed, Martin thought to himself, feeling himself beginning to sweat even though the Courtroom was comfortable.

Martin knew that starting early was improper, (one is legally bound to begin the hearing at the designated and noticed time) but it wasn't his place to tell a Judge *how* (or *when*) to do his job, and he certainly didn't feel like being chastised on a Friday afternoon.

4:41 p.m. Sign it, Markowitz. You have to sign it now, Martin thought, panic setting in.

"Judge?"

"Mr. Sandberg?"

"We've covered the recitals. Can you please sign the order?" Martin asked.

Martin watched, feeling despair as Markowitz sighed.

"As I was saying... I was saying that until last week, last Tuesday, to be precise, I might have even considered throwing you in jail for *filing* something like *this*. Now, I'm told everyone in this room is either *aware* of this insane cosmic inside-joke or is *oblivious* to it."

Martin watched as Markowitz looked around the courtroom.

"What are we doing here? Has the world gone insane?" Markowitz asked the world.

No one answered him.

Markowitz took a moment to look at the clerk sitting to his left, who was usually taking notes on the Clerk's minutes sheets. The notes form was blank. She was filing her nails and looking at something on her computer. Markowitz sighed again.

"As I said, I have read the Petition," he said. "I've never read anything like it."

Sign the order NOW!

(Martin, now screaming in his head.)

Is this happening?

"Your Honor, you'll find that this couldn't be a simpler matter," Martin said to him. He wiped the (now prominent) sweat from his forehead and tried to take a moment to collect himself. Still feeling panic, he felt he was out of time. "There's no property distribution, no alimony, no children under eighteen years, of age, no retirement accounts to divide, no marital debt to divide, how could it be any easier?" Martin asked.

"How could it get any easier, *indeed,*" Markowitz said as a statement rather than a question, his voice oozing with contempt. "I see you noticed Mr. Feldman through publication," Judge Markowitz said.

His tone was a mixture of anger and sarcasm.

What are you doing? Now!

(Again: head, screaming, etc.)

"The affidavit from the process server isn't in the court file," Markowitz said.

"Your Honor?"

"You didn't e-file the affidavit from the process server," Judge Markowitz asked him, pushing the glasses back from the tip of his nose before they fell off.

"The procedure is a simple one, Mr. Sandberg, you've done it a thousand times. If unsuccessful at service, *which, in this case is no surprise,* you file an affidavit of diligent search and inquiry. Then, Mr. Sandberg, the divorce is published in the notice section of the local newspaper. First, however, you e-file the affidavit from the process server which describes the efforts undertaken to effectuate service."

"I have the affidavit," Martin Sandberg said to Markowitz. He attempted glance at his watch without Markowitz noticing.

4:42 p.m. We are going to die... Or worse.

"Then why didn't you scan it and upload it?" Markowitz asked. Besides the entire situation, the very fact that Attorneys were practicing "e-law" now, as Markowitz put it, made him cringe. There was no *paper* anymore. There were no more paper files, nothing except when a signature was required, and soon *that* was going to be on tablets which meant no more paper altogether. Markowitz felt despondent at the thought of the legal system entirely abandoning the use of traditional, dependable, rational paper and *everyone signing electronic doohickeys with something called a 'stylus.'*

Markowtiz's daughter, who was now about to finish her third year of law school, had said to him, (when he tried to complain to her, which was a big mistake) "What was the world coming to?" She had replied, mocking and imitating him: "So the legal profession killed some trees, or a hundred million of them on copies and copies *and more copies* of nonsensical legalese paperwork. If it's in the interest of justice, who cares about the planet, right?"

At being berated by his daughter, Judge Markowitz felt he no longer belonged. And *now* that he had *lost his place in line,* now that he was *in on* "the great cosmic inside-joke," his feelings of isolation had become unbearable.

"I couldn't file it, Judge," Martin said.

"You're scanning machine is broken, Mr. Sandberg?"

"No. We got him *served.*"

The statement went over as well as Martin thought it would. Markowitz's eyes grew. His ears turned red.
Martin thought he might as well have told Judge Markowitz that by flapping his arms he had flown to the moon and back. Martin thought that he had a better chance of convincing Judge Markowitz that he could fly, rather than trying to explain that a process server had served *George Feldman.*

Martin Sandberg's client, Annabelle Feldman turned to face her attorney, her face suddenly drained of all color as fear came over her, no doubt thinking she heard him wrong.

"You served him? You saw him?" she whispered to Martin, her hands beginning to shake. He was unable to answer her, however, as it took all of one's concentration to endure a judicial reprimand.

Annabelle Feldman and Judge Markowitz had one thing in common. Both believed it impossible that anyone could hand papers to George Feldman and tell George Feldman: "you've been served."

"And I say 'we,'" Judge Markowitz, because *I* was *with* my process server when we got George Feldman served."

"I'm *not* in the mood for jokes, Mr. Sandberg."

"I published it on the off chance that the Court did not believe me. I have the Affidavit with me. I can file it if you like."

Martin suddenly realized that in his panic, he had lost track of time. He realized he had momentarily forgotten the gruesome fate which he was sure they were about to experience together.

"I never thought I would ever have a conversation like this in my life, much less in my Courtroom. Am I in the "Twilight Zone?" It this some hidden camera television show? Where are the cameras?"

"There are no cameras, Your Honor. We are being watched, though. It is now 4:43 P.M. and I noticed the case for 4:45 P.M. We started early..."

"That's right," Judge Markowitz said to him, cutting him off in mid-sentence, "because I knew your client's husband, Mr. George Feldman would *not* show up for this hearing to be divorced from your client.

I knew he would not be here for this hearing, Mr. Sandberg *because your client's husband, Mr. George Feldman is dead!*" Markowitz said, momentarily losing his judicial demeanor to express his dissatisfaction by yelling at Martin.

"You want me to divorce your *live* client from her *dead* husband. I would laugh if I didn't feel like crying," Markowitz said, "George Feldman's been deceased for over a year now, and you don't sign a divorce order to divorce someone from a previously *deceased* spouse!" Martin looked at Judge Markowitz. The veins in his forehead were pulsating, and his eyes had grown larger than the tiny glasses that had once again slid down his nose.

"Please, Your Honor," Annabelle Feldman said, suddenly.

"It's alright," Martin said to her, his futile attempt to help.

"You don't understand," she said, the prospects of what was happening, now making her hands shake uncontrollably as she gripped the podium. Martin hoped she wouldn't cry. He realized, however, that it was a foregone conclusion.

7

"Of course, I do, Mrs. Feldman, I do understand. I read it in your very impassioned handwritten statement in your Petition! Your marriage vows included 'love, honor,' and *all that good stuff* and then for some reason you and your *late* husband said *something* about loving and being *as one for all eternity* and apparently Mr. Feldman *from the grave* is taking *that vow* just a little *too* literally. Did I leave anything out, Mrs. Feldman?"

Martin could feel the seething frustration emanating from Judge Markowitz as he looked up at the clock on the wall, then at the door to the courtroom, half expecting something, anything, to come through the door.

4:44 P.M. Unsigned. It was a nice life, except for becoming a lawyer, Martin thought.

Feeling helpless, Martin turned to eye Bailiff Laszlo who only gave him a little smile. When he first became part of the "cosmic inside-joke," Martin had been surprised to discover just how people like him ran the universe, the people no one ever really notices, who blend into the walls, but have *all* the *real* power. The whole world around them was blind to the truth.

It is bailiffs that enforce the rules, which ensure everyone abides by the "great cosmic inside joke's" rules, procedures, and laws. Martin had thought it was madness to discover that the bailiffs were "the authority," often to be feared.

"What are you looking at, Mr. Sandberg?" You think George Feldman's going to zombie shuffle his rotting corpse into the Courtroom and argue against me signing the Order declaring the *eternal* marriage between him and his wife is over?"

"Please Judge, can you sign the order?"

"We can give Mr. Feldman thirty more seconds," Markowitz said as they watched the minute hand glide to twelve. In his head, it was like an egg timer with a little 'ding.'

4:45 P.M. came.

At *precisely* 4:45, the light changed. It was slight, but very noticeable, like colored glasses or a filter on a camera.

Reality had *changed.*

The planes of existence in Judge Markowitz's courtroom had been altered. Whether *he* had brought the Courtroom (somehow) to the darkened, rotting plane of existence, *or* he had somehow brought it *with* him when he arrived, it was very clear that now, at precisely 4:45 P.M., (the time written on the hearing notice) the *previously deceased* George Feldman was standing at the podium opposite Martin Sandberg and Annabelle Feldman.

At least he's punctual, that is, for an evil spirit manifesting physical form, Martin thought.

It was apparent George Feldman had effectuated his presence to lodge his objection to the divorce.

He was *not* a "rotting corpse," as Markowitz had put it. He wore a well-tailored burgundy suit. Martin wondered if it was the one he was wearing when he was buried. George Feldman appeared as neat and as well-groomed as he had ever been.

He was not rotting.

He was *angry.*

Martin looked at Bailiff Laszlo again who was now merely standing in his same spot. Bailiff Laszlo was smiling. Martin knew Bailiff Laszlo would be of no help.

Martin Sandberg looked at George Feldman and rubbed his eyes.

Judge Markowitz looked at the lights and sniffed the air, trying to figure out just where in the universe (or elsewhere) they were. He knew that there had been a *shift* of some kind. Markowitz could *feel* it.

Along with the feeling of falling while he was still sitting in his chair and the hairs on his arm sticking up, it was an instinctual knowledge, like yanking your hand from something hot to the touch or kicking your feet when falling into the water. This was a kind of knowledge one just *felt.*

Martin attempted to remember how he had prepared for this. He'd been here (or many similar "zones" or "realms" as some had called them) before. The black soot and the rage emanating, *bleeding* from George Feldman were growing *exponentially* as Annabelle Feldman began to cry quietly, dread setting in. Martin attempted to remember his planning.

All sense of rational thought and common sense disappears when one finds himself in George Feldmanland. (Feldmania? Feldmanville?)

This was the quintessential "out of context problem," a "great cosmic practical-joke," a situation so unimaginable that one can *never* prepare adequately.

Having had the repeated misfortune of previously experiencing some similar circumstances, Martin had prepared as

9

best as he could, knowing full well that it could take *only seconds* of idle stupidity before everyone in that room became trapped in the forever nightmare of the George Feldmanverse.

Feldmanverse. Yes. This is the Feldmanverse, Martin thought.

"Judge, sign the order!" Martin yelled at him. He raised his voice not because he was afraid, nor due to the exigent circumstances surrounding their current situation.

He screamed because the sound of rage emanating from the other podium was becoming louder and louder. The sound was horrifying. It was a mixture of a gradually increasing growl and scream, like a bomb or tornado warning.

Realizing the precarious nature of his situation, the sound of Feldman's storm filling his ears and having no option other than to take the advice of the lawyer he had been abusing just minutes ago, Judge Markowitz was flipping through the pages on his desk, looking for the Final Judgment of Dissolution of Marriage that Martin had previously prepared for him.

Glancing to his left, he could see that the clerk had vanished.

What was happening had nothing to do with her.
The Bailiff Laszlo remained stoic but was no longer repressing his menacing smile. He stood in his very same spot, teeth shining in the altered light.

The acrid, smoky, odor of rotting anger burned his throat as he tried to breathe and the pure manifestation of rage known as George Feldman swiftly developed into a kind of growing storm, Judge Markowitz began to realize that he had misjudged the new obligations of his occupation.

"I can't find it!"

Of Course.

From his file, Martin pulled his extra, unsigned copy of the order he had previously prepared.

"May I approach the bench?" Martin screamed as Feldman's growling became louder.

"What?" Markowitz asked him, confused.

"We are *required* to follow *procedure*!"

"Yes, yes! For the love of God!" Markowitz screamed at him over the deafening George Feldman tornado. Papers and small objects were flying in the air from unknown dimensions, much to Judge Markowitz's disbelief.

Martin attempted to approach the judge, tried to take a step, but he had been grabbed and felt something pushing down on him, holding him back. Martin was held fast by what he perceived to be a hand around his body. The hand was of such size it should have belonged to some giant. The thumb was on his shoulder, the fingers around his upper torso. (He realized later, of course, that it *had been* a monstrous hand that had grabbed him. He could see it by the bruises on his body in a "hand" shape. He tried to wriggle free. Martin howled as the fingers of George Feldman's hand clenched around him.

The pain caused him to go to his knees, the unsigned order in his fist.

"No," Annabelle said, still standing in place, watching the events unfold around her.

"No!" she screamed. "Absolutely not! George! Damn you George!" she screamed at him. "You leave that man alone, George! Stop this right now! Please, George! If you've ever loved me!" Martin looked back at her. Her hands had become shaking fists, hanging at her sides.

Reality moved, the air shifted, and what had been light which was the color some might describe as off-yellow, had changed to grey.

The growling sound changed.

The intermixing of love and rage transcended dimensional boundaries.

Martin swore he could see a toaster as it flew through the air past Judge Markowitz's head.

"George please! you know this divorce is the right thing. How dare you hurt that poor man! You're *done* hurting anyone, George Feldman, including me!" She screamed at him raising her fists into the air. Standing steady in the Feldmanverse, Annabelle Feldman was ready to take a swing at the shimmering figure of her angry dead husband.

For an instant, time stopped as George Feldman's face appeared inches from Martin's face. Martin could feel his heart pounding in his chest as he struggled to breathe.

"There's more of us than there are of you," George Feldman said to Martin, his breath stinking of rot and death.

11

Pinned to the floor, Martin gagged, struggling for air. "We outnumber you. When we go back to the old ways, your license to practice law won't be worth the paper it's printed on," he said to Martin, into his ears, into his head, yellow teeth clenched together as he spoke.

"Geeeeoooooorge!!!!"

Annabelle screamed at her dead husband with every ounce of effort she had. The sound she made when she pounded her fists on the podium was much louder than it should have been.

George Feldman turned to stare into the eyes of his wife. The distraction was enough for Martin to struggle to his feet and slap the order down at the very edge of the Markowitz's reach. Judge Markowitz, realizing that this might be his only chance, leaped to his feet, grabbed the order previously prepared by Martin Sandberg titled: "Final Judgment Granting Dissolution of Marriage."

As he signed, Markowitz screamed: "You, Mrs. Feldman, are now divorced and reverted back to the status of a single woman!"

Night turned back to day. The tornado vanished as papers, along with pens, staplers, garbage pails, small appliances and other objects (which did not belong in a courtroom) fell from mid-air.

Seeming disappointed, Bailiff Laszlo quietly left the room.

"Court's adjourned," Judge Markowitz said. He fled the courtroom, leaving Martin alone with his client.

Martin found it difficult to breathe through bruised ribs. He crawled, hoisted himself and plopped into one of the chairs at counsel table.

"Is it over?" Annabelle Feldman asked, standing at the podium, her hands empty and at her sides, her hair (which had been so perfect just moments ago) in disarray, her face pale, sweating, her complexion pallid.

"Those are the rules," Martin said, "I was amazed when I saw you stand up to him. I'm proud of you, Mrs. Feldman."

He watched as she gave him a smile.

"Hanson," she said, "I have my name back. It's Hanson."

"Yes, that's right. You are now Annabelle Hanson," Martin said.

"She will never believe me, but I have to tell my sister what happened here," Annabelle said. "That has to be the strangest thing I've ever experienced, but she just might believe me with everything that's been happening since George died."

Martin Sandberg was familiar.

Annabelle *Hanson* had been quite haunted.

"You can't tell her," Martin said, holding his side, still trying to catch his breath, "I mean you *can* tell her, but it will be like talking to a wall."

"What? Why? She won't believe me?"

"That's not it. I heard someone call it *a blanket of ignorance,*" Martin said, shaking his head. "She won't *get* it. She'll listen to your words, but it will be like you're talking in another language. Even if she somehow hears you, she'll forget the words right after you've told them to her, like immediate short-term amnesia."

"I don't understand."

"It doesn't matter, Annabelle. Just don't become frustrated if she looks at you like you are speaking a foreign language when you try to tell her. She won't ever understand, and if she does somehow, she won't remember. That's how this works."

"Rules for the haunted Courtroom?" Annabelle asked.

"*You* might even forget this happened."

"Not on your life," she said.

"You should go out and celebrate. You've earned it for sure," he said, wincing in pain.

"Are you alright?"

"I am now," he said. Annabelle watched as he became lost in thought for a moment.

"I thought we were all going to die, get stuck in that place," Martin said.

"Martin, should I drive you to the hospital or something?" Annabelle Hanson asked.

"No, sorry. I'm fine. I only have some bruised ribs. Thanks for saving my life, by the way."

"All I did was yell at him," Annabelle Hanson said to the young lawyer. As he sat at the table, trying to breathe, he watched as she started towards the door. She stopped before passing him and kissed the top of his head.

"Thank you," she said.

As she was about to leave, at the doors, she stopped and turned to look at him.

"Mr. Sandberg, I wasn't going to say anything. I don't know why, maybe I didn't want to sound crazy," she said, standing at the entrance.

"What is it?" he asked her.

"George wanted me to give you a message..." she stammered.

"What is it?"

"He wanted you to know... He said that they were going back to the old ways," she said, "whatever that means. He said lawyers, judges, the whole court system would all be meaningless. I guess he was threatening. That's George's way, but it also sounded like a warning."

"He told me the same thing. Good luck Annabelle," he said then watched as she walked away.

After taking some time to gather his strength and with a considerable struggle to get to his feet, Martin made his way to Markowitz's office.

He stood in the office doorway of Judge Markowitz's chambers, holding his briefcase in one hand. He carried the toaster under his arm (yet another souvenir) that had almost taken off Markowitz's head.

Now, after 5:00 P.M., the courthouse was virtually deserted.

"Come in, Marty," Markowitz said, "you need an ambulance?"

"Not this time."

"I think I might," Markowitz said. "Just a moment."

Martin watched as Judge Andrew Markowitz sat at his desk, vomiting into his waste bin. He had the office-sized waste bin sitting on his lap as he wretched. The gagging and heaving went on for much longer than Martin felt comfortable, but he stayed and waited until it was over.

Markowitz wiped his mouth with a cloth and rinsed with a bottle of scotch that looked to Martin to be very old and expensive. Martin thought Markowitz would swallow, but instead, he spit it in the bin.

They sat for another one of those awkward silences they had previously been accustomed to sharing, Markowitz rubbing his eyes and rubbing the sides of his head before he spoke, putting the bin on the floor next to his chair.

14

"How do I get out of this?" he asked.

"What?" Martin asked.

"I'm not doing this. This is a mistake. I need to get out of this."

"Get out of this? There's no getting out of this. It's apparent to me that you don't understand what's *really* happening here. "

"That's why you're here?" Markowitz asked him, "to explain to me what's *really* happening?"

"I'm going to let you in on a secret, Judge Markowitz," Martin said.

"Be quick, Sandberg. I'm busy throwing up," Markowitz said.

"You need to know *this*. It's a doozy," Martin said.

"Yes, what is it?" Markowitz asked.

"Are you sure you're ready?" Martin asked, looking him directly in his eyes.

"Martin!" Markowitz yelled, not angry as much as exasperated.

"Ok, here it is: *You*, Andrew Markowitz are a j*udge*," Martin said.

There was a moment of silence. Martin thought Markowitz would throw the waste-bin at him. Martin was especially thankful that he did not.

"Come on," he said.

"Judge, let me ask you a question. If I threw a temper tantrum in your courtroom, started stomping my feet and carrying on like a spoiled child, what would you do?"

"I'd hold you in contempt," he said, "*obviously*."

"I can depend on that. You'd pound your gavel and yell at me. You would order me to maintain composure. You might warn me once or twice, but you would demand there be *order* in your courtroom," Martin said.

"Like any other judge."

Markowitz watched as Martin Sandberg leaned in closer, considered his words.

"You had a litigant in your courtroom today who was having a temper tantrum, just like a child, yet you just sat there while he *dragged* us all the way *down*. What do you think George Feldman would have *done* if you pounded your gavel down and demanded order in your courtroom, just *like any other judge*?"

15

Martin looked into the eyes of the old judge and watched as the epiphany occurred.

"George Feldman would have obeyed?"

"Demons, monsters, alive, dead, disembodied... *All* are subject to the Court's rules and orders. It's *your* courtroom. It doesn't matter *who* or *what* is in it," Martin said.

"You mean to tell me that, that... *Whatever* it was, would have stopped all that? It would have stopped whatever it was doing?" Markowitz asked, incredulous.

"Make no mistake, the 'it' was George Feldman having a temper tantrum and he would have had to obey, otherwise the bailiff would have gotten involved."

"Laszlo? He just stood there. The world was coming to an end all around us, and he *just* stood there. I think he was smiling," Markowitz said.

"Of course, he was *smiling.* The bailiffs are in control of enforcing the Court's rules. *You* are the Court, Judge Markowitz. At any time during that insane little hearing, did you tell Laszlo to get George Feldman under control?"

"I didn't know I *could*," Markowitz said, looking a little less defeated.

"Make no mistake, Judge. The bailiffs? They are the strongest people... *things, whatever* they are, they enforce the Court's orders, *your* orders," Martin said. "Just like in any other case. If you order the bailiff to do something, so long as you are following the law, he is *obligated* to comply with your orders, just like the rest of us."

Martin watched as Markowitz took in a deep breath, exasperated at the steep personal turn his professional life had taken.

"This is just insane. It's craziness."

There was another moment of silence. Martin thought Judge Markowitz would throw up again, but he held it together.

"Craziness? I want to show you something," Martin said, putting a massive book on Markowitz's desk.

"What is that?"

"It may end up being your case; it hasn't been assigned yet. Following the rules regarding ex parte communications, I can't discuss the details with you. Even so, I would like you to *look* at it. What do you see?"

Markowitz looked at the book. It seemed the size of a very large dictionary. It also seemed very old. Martin watched as he found his bottle of scotch, unscrewed the lid, and took a mouthful.

This time he swallowed the scotch. He held out the bottle to Martin.

"No thanks, I'm driving home... Look at this *book.* Don't open it of course," Martin said to him.

You'd just throw up again.

Markowitz looked at the strange book with odd symbols etched throughout the cover.

"Is that leather?" Markowitz asked, feeling the strange covering of the book with his fingertips.

"It's *not* leather, but at the risk of you throwing up again, I'm *not* going to tell you what it's made of. That's not the point."

"Then what *is* the point?" Markowitz asked, snatching his hand away and wiping it with the same rag he had used just a moment earlier to clean his mouth as if he suddenly realized what had been used to make the book's cover.

"That book is a *'Faustian Contract.'* It's from one of my clients, and it has to be older than any other book I've ever seen."

"Faustian Contract?"

"Like a 'deal with the devil' or some other sort of madness," Martin explained holding up his fingers, demonstrating the in the "air quotes" gesture as he said the words "deal with the devil."

"I've never seen a contract bound into a book like this before," Markowitz said, "it's bizarre."

"That's the same thing anyone who's ever seen it says," Martin said, "and if you tried to describe it to your wife, Judge Markowitz, she'd look at you like you were speaking another language. If you tried to tell her what happened, about George Feldman, assuming she understood you, she would forget, just moments after you told her. You and me, we know the truth. The *blanket of ignorance* does *not* apply to people like us. *I know* you feel alone and lost..." Martin stopped a moment to meet Markowitz's eyes.

"Things like this book here? They are *just* another piece of evidence. George Feldman is just another angry husband in a divorce hearing," Martin said, watching as Judge Markowitz stared

17

into his eyes with an expression like that of a child who has just learned the truth about Santa Claus.

"I tried to set it on fire, Judge. I doused it with gas, lit it up," Martin said.

Markowitz stared at him, expression unchanged.

"It burned, you know. Then it was fine. After that, I guess because I was curious, I shot it with a shotgun, cooked it in my regular oven, my microwave oven, the toaster oven every oven I could find, and I even put it in a polyethylene container of hydrochloric acid. *Look* at it. There it is, just the same as when the client gave it to me weeks ago."

"I think I might be sick again," Markowitz said.

"This book, this *surreal* thing is *nothing* compared to what's out there. I carry it around like any other work, Judge. It's a case, just like any other."

"Just like any other case," Markowitz said, eyes becoming glassy as he attempted to adjust.

"You lost your place in line. I have come here today, to sit in your office while you throw up. I have come here to welcome you to the club. You have got do your job. You don't have a choice," Martin said, standing up, "because this..." Martin took a moment, waived his hands, indicating the experience they had just shared. "This can't happen again," he said. Martin lifted his shirt so Markowitz could see the giant bruise in the shape of a handprint surrounding Martin's upper body.

"I'm sorry. I should have said 'order in the court' or something."

"Next time," Martin said, nodding at him, walking toward the door of Judge Markowitz's office, "but this is how it is for all of us who are *in* on what did you call it? The *great cosmic inside-joke*. That's a perfect way to describe it."

He was about to walk out of the office and leave Judge Markowitz alone but stopped at the doorway.

"Your Honor," he said, "when I first started practicing law, a judge who was as impatient as he was brilliant once told me there is no *aesthetic value* attributable to the *law*. He told me that the law is *just* meant to solve people's problems in the fairest way humanly possible."

Martin met his eyes with sympathy before he spoke again.

"It's not just *people* using *our* courts to solve problems as *fairly as is humanly possible.* We are all made blind and ignorant and even though we can't *see* them for what they *really* are, every kind of monster, demon, devil-dog, hairy beast creature of myth, might and magic is *out there*, and they are using *our* laws, *our* system of justice, *our courts* to solve their problems."

"I wish I didn't know about any of this."

"Me too," Martin said.

"Has anyone like us ever been able to get his life back, go back to the way it was before becoming aware of all this?" Judge Markowitz asked. "Has anyone ever been able to get his place in line back?"

"Not that I know of, but that doesn't stop me from trying."

TWO

LIBRO DEL DIABLO

MARTIN SANDBERG STOPPED HIMSELF WHEN HE
SAW ESMERALDA STANDING IN THE KITCHEN,
STARING AT HIM, hands on her hips, wearing her best scowl.
Martin had come to know this specific expression on her face, as it
was reserved only for him.

"Hi honey," he said, knowing full well that going into the
kitchen, much less standing in the doorway was a risk to his
health.

"Don't you 'hi honey' me," she said, "are you coming in?"

"I'd prefer my limbs remain in their current locations," he
said. She gave him a well-said "humph" and her patented stare.

"Okay, whatever it is that I did, remember that I'm a man
and sometimes we do things that upset women... wives... and you
know, other people. I can tell that you're upset, and whatever I did
I'm sorry, and I promise I'll fix it, whatever it is," Martin said. "Is
it safe to come inside?"

"The danger is not from me, *Husband*," Esmeralda said.
(She always called him 'Husband' when she was especially angry
with him.) "You see this here?" she asked him.

Martin saw that his wife was pointing to the object on the
kitchen table, an object which had been the source of conflict in
their marriage from the moment it had come into their lives.
Esmeralda Sandberg had been very clear about her feelings.

"I can't believe you brought this into the house again," she
said. "I asked you to put it anywhere but here. I don't think I'm
asking for much," she said. Martin stared at the kitchen table in
disbelief. (He was sure he had left the *thing* at the office.)

This can't be happening.

Having three kids meant that the kitchen table always
contained a variety of domestic objects from coloring books and
crayons, to snacks, placemats, and all signs of family life. This
time, however, there was only one object on the kitchen table.
Esmeralda had removed everything, but (naturally) had refused to

20

touch what Esmeralda referred to as the "Libro Del Diablo," the very book he had been showing to Judge Markowitz.

The client, Martin's old friend from High School who had brought the book to Martin, had begged him to find some way to *break* the contract. Martin recognized the irony. The client had also called it the "Devil-Book."

Martin remembered at first thinking that his friend (and client) was joking when he called it the "Devil-Book," but the fear and desperation emanating from him had demonstrated his seriousness.

Due to attorney-client privilege, (and for fear that Esme would naturally be apprehensive of any item believed to be cursed) the fact that he had *also* called it a "Devil-Book" was something he had *not* shared with Esmeralda.

After spending only a few moments with the book, Esmeralda treated it as if it was radioactive, refused to touch it, and seemed to instinctively know that there was something *wrong* with it. Esmeralda, amongst many expletives spoken in Spanish, had called the item: "Libro Del Diablo." Though Martin knew only a little Spanish, he had understood perfectly.

The fact that she *had* named it "Devil-Book," (of course in Spanish) was yet another item in Martin's list of *things* that had been happening to him lately. When Martin asked her (in his opinion, nonchalantly) why she called it "Libro Del Diablo," she had launched into a loud and angry diatribe in Spanish while walking around in circles, stereotypically waiving her arms as she cursed.

Watching as she cursed and said other things in Spanish, he made a mental note, (one he had made in the past too many times to count, but still failed to follow through on) to learn Spanish if he was going to (or at least attempt to) remain married to his Hispanic wife.

The first time he had brought the book home, (while she was saying things in Spanish), she had snatched it, took it to the garage, and dropped it into a small metal wastebasket.

"What are you doing?" Martin had protested, but it was clear there was no stopping her as she had squirted an accelerant of some sort into the wastebasket with the book and tossed in a lit match. "Esme, that belongs to a client!" he had said to her as she had (with dizzying speed) performed the tasks that would ordinarily destroy *any* book. (Or so she had thought.) He had thought to himself that he *just wanted to bring a little work home,* maybe read it after everyone had gone to bed, but it seemed his life was a never-ending unachievable mission to keep from getting into trouble, to keep from anyone being angry at him, especially his wife.

He had often mused that a life's goal to keep people from being mad at him, at least in general, would be attainable, but alas, it was not. He was fully aware, of course, that he was a lawyer and with such an occupation, angry people are always going to be an occupational certainty. He thought he could at least keep his closest friends and family from being irritated with him, especially his beautiful (and yes, often annoyed) wife.

She had watched as Martin had furiously searched for the fire extinguisher, (He couldn't remember where he had hung it) pulled the pin and sprayed its contents into the wastebasket.

He had been sure that the book had been destroyed, but after wiping off the foam, he could see the book was unharmed and in its original state.

After he had taken it out of the wastebasket and cleaned it off, Esmeralda was sure that she and her husband would shortly be embarking on a long and heated discussion about the destruction of *a client's property,* but this had not been the case.

She had watched in silence as her husband had stood in silence, looking at the book. After standing quietly in the garage for several moments, considering what had just happened, (completely surprised that they weren't yelling at one another), she had watched as Martin himself dropped the Libro Del Diabo back into the wastebasket. He took the gas can used to contain lawnmower fuel, dumped a copious amount of gas into the wastebasket on top of the book, and threw in a match, actions taken which were much like his wife had taken mere moments earlier. Both had stood in silence, watching as a fire had emanated from the wastebasket, exchanging glances at one another, wondering what was happening.

Though the main garage door leading to the driveway was open, the fire gave a lingering, acrid odor. As they stood watching, their son, (and oldest child) Paul (or 'Pablo' when his mother was angry with him) opened the door leading from the house to the garage, eating a popsicle.

22

"Whatcha doing?" he had asked.

"Burning stuff," Martin had answered.

"Can I watch?" Paul had asked.

"No," said both Martin and Esmeralda Sandberg, in unison.

"Okay," Paul had said.

Neither parent watched as Paul had gone back into the house, closing the door behind him.

It took only a few moments for the fire to die down. Martin assisted the extinguishing of the flames by dumping a large amount of water into the wastebasket. Both watched in amazement as Martin pulled the undamaged book out of the wastebasket.

"It's not even wet," he said.

"What have you gotten yourself into?" Esmeralda asked him, her face suddenly pale.

"This book, it's a contract from a client," he said, "a guy I went to High School with."

"Did he give you a retainer?" she had asked him.

"Yes."

"You better give it back," she had said before going through the same door her son had gone through just a few moments earlier. Without further comment, she had closed the door behind her. She hadn't slammed it but had closed it loud enough to send the appropriate message to her husband.

Martin did not have the opportunity to explain to Esmeralda that he had already used the retainer to pay the monthly mortgage, the electric bill, and insurance. Returning the retainer would *not* be an option.

When he told her that he was not dropping the Libro Del Diablo case or handing it off to another attorney, (while rubbing her feet, of course) she had made him promise to leave the it at the office (or anywhere else) and *never* to bring it home. Esmeralda had been unequivocal.

Martin preferred to stay married. He promised her that the book would never be brought into their home again. When he made the promise, he had been emphatic, told her that "it won't pass the threshold."

It was because of this emphatic promise that she was particularly angry at her husband, (at that moment) having discovered the "Devil-Book" on her kitchen table.

"I didn't put it there," he said to her, "I swear."

"I know, Martin. You haven't been home," she said. To her, it didn't matter if he brought it home and put it on the kitchen table, if he somehow snuck it in and lied to her about bringing it home, or if the very "*Devil himself*" put it there. The fact that it was there, in her home, was simply unacceptable. "Either it goes, or I'm packing the kids and going to a hotel. You remember what happened last time?"

"Of course," he said. The last (and only) time the book had been in their home overnight, the whole family (except their youngest) had horrible nightmares, dreams so vivid and prolific, two of their three children had ended up in their parent's bed for the night. Their third child, Emily, seemed unaffected and announced at breakfast with her usual cheery smile that she had slept "fine." While Emily ate her cereal, the nightmares had been the topic of a heated family conversation at the breakfast table.

Though she didn't tell the children, Esmeralda was sure that the Libro Del Diablo was the cause of the night's discomfort.

"I swear, Esme. I left it on my desk."

"Then how is it here in my kitchen? This is where our children eat, Martin!"

She watched as he shrugged his shoulders.

"Libro Del Diablo!" she yelled at him. "quiere que lo firmes!" she yelled, amongst many other things he didn't understand due to his inability to speak his wife's language of choice when she was angry with him.

"Husband, dear Husband," she said, "*the evil* wants you to sign it, like the other fools who gave away their souls, and you will be trapped within its pages for all eternity," she said.

He looked at her in disbelief.

"Oh, come on," he said to her.

"If you didn't bring it here and put it on the table, then how did it get here?"

"I don't know," he said.

"Yes, you do, Martin."

"I do?" he asked.

"You do."

"Because it's an evil book?" he asked.

She looked at him with acceptance.

"Yes, Martin," she said.

"That's it!" he yelled. She watched as he turned the oven on "broil" and put the book inside.

"It's not going to work," she said as they peered into the little oven window, heads pushed together, attempting to watch the book as it cooked on the top rack.

Dinner that evening was peanut butter and jelly sandwiches, as the Sandberg parents were far too occupied with the attempted destruction of evil to make a regular family meal.

Twenty minutes broiling in the oven did not affect the book. Neither did scissors, (the pages could not be cut) stabbing it, boiling, microwaving, or even muriatic acid Martin borrowed from the guy next door who had a swimming pool. They sat together at the kitchen table, exhausted, staring at the book as it sat on the table, unharmed. Martin felt like it was mocking him.

"Did you read it?" she asked him, finally breaking the silence, deeply afraid of what his answer might be.

"Every time I try, I get a terrible headache. I can only get through a page or two before I have to stop because of the pain in my head. Reading it even a little makes my head feel like it's going to explode."

Esmeralda Sandberg deeply sighed, relieved that her husband had not yet read the book, though she knew his reading of its pages was a foregone conclusion.

"Drive carefully," she said to him as she got up from the table, defeated.

"Drive? Esme?"

"When you take it someplace else, you know, *right now* when you take it someplace else... Drive carefully. I'll wait up for you," she said, leaving him alone in the kitchen.

AFTER BRINGING THE "DEVIL-BOOK" BACK TO HIS OFFICE, MARTIN WAS EXHAUSTED WHEN HE GOT HOME and spent the whole drive back from his office wondering if the book would again (horrifyingly) be sitting in the center of his kitchen table when he got there. He was sure he had left it on the corner of his desk at his office when he went home. (The first time.) After Esmeralda demanded he remove it from the house, he had a great deal of difficulty trying to decide where to leave it. At first, he put it on the corner of his desk, just as he had done shortly before going to work. After staring at it in silence chewing down

25

one of his fingernails, remembering that was where he had left it before going home, (and it was waiting for him there when he got home) he concluded it would be an exercise in futility. He could spend the entire night leaving it in the same place at his office only to have it waiting for him on his kitchen table when he got home. No, he had to do something *different.* He had to find a way for it to stay where he left it.

He put the book on his bookshelf, squeezing it in between two old textbooks he hadn't opened in years. He stood for a moment looking at the books, chewing a different fingernail, before taking it back out and holding it in his hands, taking a moment to stare at it. He then put it in the center of his desk. He took everything else that was on the desk, the other files, notes, caselaw stapled together in batches and put it to the side in one pile.

Standing in silence, alone, (his assistant, Delia, long gone for the evening) he decided that the center of his desk would not work, either. Ceremoniously, Martin gently laid the 'Libro Del Diablo' onto his desk chair.

"I am going to read this tomorrow. I'm putting it in my chair, so it will be the first thing I see when I get here," Martin said out loud to no one (or everyone) feeling a little foolish but knowing that it was probably necessary. He thought he might cry (even sob a little) if he got home and it was on his kitchen table *again.*

He took a moment, sat in his car in the driveway, the engine off, breathing, wondering if it would be sitting on the kitchen table (yet again) waiting for him. After realizing he was sitting in his car for far too long, Martin went inside and peeked around the corner, through the door leading to the kitchen, as he would if he was hiding, sneaking, or looking for an intruder. He let the air out of his lungs, finally breathed, and experienced great relief when he saw that the kitchen table was clean and empty.

Stupid, crazy Diablo-Devil Evil Book.

He gingerly walked up the stairs towards his bedroom, careful not to wake anyone who might be sleeping. He could see that two of the four bedrooms were dark. Of course, Esmeralda was still awake probably watching the news.

Seeing the light emanating from the crack between the floor and her door, Martin could see that his youngest was still awake.

"There's my little sunshine," he said to the little girl sitting in the center of the bed, as he opened her door. He saw paper, coloring books, crayons and colored pencils surrounding her. As usual, it was her art that was keeping the seven-year-old awake and entertained.

"Hi Daddy," she calmly said. "Where were you?"

"I had to bring something back to my office," he explained to her.

"The *contract*?" she asked.

When she said it, Martin felt uneasy. It wasn't the *how* so much as the *why*.

Martin nodded. Emily was the only person who had properly referred to the "Libro Del Diablo' as a *contract*, and not as a *'book.'*

Indeed, it did look like a book, was the size of a book, maybe was a book in the traditional sense, but it was *not* a book. It was a *contract*, created *in writing* to satisfy the *Statute of Frauds,* and was *very* old.

For the eight months since Emily had been released from the hospital, she had been *different.* Therapists and internists alike had assured Martin and Esmeralda that their daughter had made a full recovery, but both had seen a change in the child. One minute she could be an average little girl, playing with toys, arguing with one (or both) of them that a cookie would not spoil her dinner, then the next moment she would say something *adult*, often complicated, her face frighteningly expressionless.

Emily Sandberg had spent five weeks in a coma, during which time Martin Sandberg had stayed by her bedside praying, often crying, and attempting to bargain with the universe to save his daughter.

Everyone had said it was a "miracle." She had gotten better. Even the doctors called it a mystery.

Emily had reintegrated into her life, seemingly with no problems at all, playing with friends at school, drawing her pictures, all as if nothing had happened.

However, (occasionally) she would act as if she was *not* a child, something altered, and when that happened, what she said was terrifying.

When she would blurt something out, words and phrases that didn't belong, it was not often. When it happened, it occurred without warning. Her facial expression would change from her 'little girl face' to stoic, and Emily would say something profound, emotionless, her eyes piercing. Then, as quickly as she had changed, she would switch back to a little girl, the one they knew and loved, asking her daddy if he would buy some chocolate milk when they went to the store.

Once, when attempting to wrest a little green plastic bucket from another little girl while in the sandbox, she had said (in a solemn tone of voice) "I, Emily Sandberg, daughter of Esmeralda and Martin Sandberg, 'queen supernova,' am the strongest in the universe. All *will* submit to *my* authority." Of course, Martin and Esmeralda both had been watching as the playground drama had unfolded, laughed it off. The other little girl's mother thought that Emily was merely precocious, but Martin hadn't let the situation progress any further before removing his daughter from the situation and the playground entirely. (He often wondered how the conflict would have progressed if he had left Emily alone with the girl but was sure that intervening was the correct choice.)

Martin had asked several of his contacts, some that he had met *after* he had learned of his particular situation, *what* they might *know* about Emily. Everyone he asked denied any knowledge of the child's strange behavior or what could be the cause. Martin often had the feeling that he was being lied to, however. As usual, it was like an inside joke that everyone knew, but took great lengths to keep Martin ignorant.

This evening, after bringing the "Libro Del Diablo" back to his office, he stood in the doorway, watching Emily as she worked on a picture.

"Shouldn't you be sleeping?" He asked her, watching her use a purple crayon to color the dress of some Princess. He watched as she shrugged her shoulders.

"That's very pretty," he said to her.

"I was going to use orange, but purple is better," she explained.

"How about we clean all this up, get you tucked in, and you can continue your beautiful and very impressive artwork in the morning?" he asked her.

"Okay Daddy," she said looking up at him with a tiny smile, "but only if you help."

"Such a negotiator," he said to her, realizing the 'help' was cleaning up the small mess she had made of her bed. He helped her gather up the papers and put the coloring books, papers, crayons, and pencils in their appropriate art boxes. "After you finish that picture, maybe you'll let me bring it to my office and hang it up so everyone could see what a *wonderful* artist I have in the family," he said.

"You can't have that picture," she said, now smiling widely at him.

"I can't? Not fair," he said, "please?"

"Nope!" she said, smiling, then giggled at her father. "I have a better one for you!" she said.

"It's one of a horse," she said, "*not* a lady."

"I love horses," he said, "and ladies with pretty purple dresses, too."

She giggled.

"You can have it, but I'm not done with it."

"Well then, I will take the *better one* with the horse as soon as you finish it," he said, kissing the top of her head and pulling the covers up for her. "Light on or off?"

"Off, but leave the door open," she said.

Martin took a moment to look at her, turned off the light, then turned to leave.

"Daddy?"

"Yes, honey?"

"There is no method, basis, or precedent for voiding that contract," she said.

"Emily?"

"The terms and conditions, as set forth, must be fulfilled," she said. At hearing Emily say the words, Martin stood in the doorway, speechless. He watched as she quietly rolled over away from him.

"Goodnight, Daddy."

THREE

DONNELLY V. BLACK FLAGG, INC.

Martin Sandberg stood outside of the building housing the offices of Black Flagg, Inc. He knew things were going on inside and every time he came to the building he found great difficulty mustering up the courage to walk through its doors. The building housed one monstrosity of a company, a multi-faceted machine responsible (mostly) for media, but also controlling vast electric and communications holdings throughout the world. The parent company controlled numerous subsidiaries, the extent, amount, and control, of which perhaps was even unknown to the Board of Directors itself.

Black Flagg, Inc. over the past two hundred years, had become one of, if not *the* most powerful company in the world.

Its only real competition being a conglomerate called "Barghest, LLC."

When the occasion arose, being summoned to the hallowed halls of Barghest, LLC, (usually by Abraham Cardozo, its head of 'quasi-human' resources, or something) always caused Martin gastrointestinal issues. Martin Sandberg was terrified of the place, (of Cardozo, also) and of course, afraid of the people inside. Martin thought that when used to describe the inhabitants of both buildings, the word "people" became a loosely used term of art.

Once, while Martin was waiting for an appointment, (for no reason at all, really) he searched the internet for "Barghest." As the results filled the screen of his handheld device, as the *images* came into his view, Martin was sorry had been so stupid as to look in places to which he simply didn't belong.

Putting the word "Barghest" into any search engine was just not a good idea. He wondered if collectively, the Board of Directors was being ironic.

"Mr. Sandberg, Mr. Donnelly will be right with you," said a blindingly beautiful woman who appeared out of nowhere. She had red hair, a shiny shirt, and a skirt that was just a little too tight. Martin looked up at her from where he was sitting, waiting in the busy building and could see that she was very attractive. When he looked up at her, Martin also felt terrified. She walked away to do other things, leaving Martin alone with his thoughts.

It was only a few minutes before she came back, reminding Martin of how unimportant he was, that he had to be the one to wait.

"Mr. Donnelly will see you now," she said, after placing her widest (and fakest) smile on her face.

The people in the building, (the ones working there, not necessarily the visitors) to him, all seemed *off.*

He had been trying to look at people out of the corner of his eye instead of head-on, something he did every time he entered the building. He would close one eye and look sideways at people as they walked past him. It was a challenging exercise, but every so often, every once in a while, he thought he saw something.

"Thank you," he said, following her into the office. The corner office was large and filled with expensive and needless things. Martin hated going to see William, not because of the opulent trappings, but because of the feelings he had when he was in the building. He had commented to Esmeralda that it felt the same as when he drank too much caffeine.

Nevertheless, Martin was acutely aware that William desperately needed help. Though it had been on his calendar, Martin hadn't prepared for the meeting, not because he was too busy or that the subject was too complicated, but because the work involved pain. The ache manifested itself in the form of some of the worst headaches he had ever experienced.

William Donnelly stood and shook Martin's hand. Will's desk chair was a huge, leather monstrosity, an article of furniture in which one might take a long nap.

"How are you?" he asked Martin.

"I'm stressed, but then again, so are you," Martin said.

"Where is it?" William Donnelly asked him, his facial expression the kind one might have if he or she was trying to drink straight vinegar.

Donnelly did not need to elaborate as to the "it" he had mentioned.

"I don't know," Martin said, sitting down in one of William Donnelly's extraordinarily comfortable guest chairs. He looked up at Donnelly and could see the man still wanted an answer, or at least a better one. "I left it in my office, but it could be *anywhere.* You didn't tell me everything," Martin said.

"Yes, I did. What else is there?" William Donnelly asked.

"How about the incredible pain and suffering?" Martin asked him.

"Emotional as well as physical," Donnelly said, "I told you to *watch* yourself. The Devil-Book must like you, Marty."

"It is not alive. It can't like anyone," Martin said, bitter and annoyed. Even as he said it, Martin did not believe his own words.

"If you say so," William said, smiling.

"I was serious when I said I don't know where it is, by the way. You also neglected to tell me that it goes places on its own. It likes to park itself in the center of my kitchen table," Martin said.

"Okay."

"No, you don't understand, Will. My wife named it 'Libro Del Diablo,' before I even had a chance to tell her *you* call it 'Devil-Book' yourself. It creeps her out and makes her very angry when she sees it there, just *waiting* for something."

"I'm sorry, Martin."

"I even tried to copy it, hoped the copy wouldn't give me a raging headache and plunge me into a depression."

"I warned you not to do that," William said.

"I didn't *listen,* okay? I thought 'what harm would it be to make some copies, maybe even of just a few pages?'"

"Disaster?" Will asked.

"Unmitigated disaster. It does not like being copied," Martin said, his statement a reluctant admission that he saw it the same as William Donnelly saw it. "My head hurt so badly I couldn't see."

"I told you. Why do you think I'm paying you so much? This case is not like any other you've probably ever had," Donnelly said.

"You'd be surprised," Martin said.

"When I first got my hands on it, I spilled coffee on the thing, if you can believe it. I felt it was mad at me, I somehow disrespected it, or something," Donnelly said, looking at him.

"Esmeralda and I tried to set it on fire," Martin said. He watched as William Donnelly's face lit up, smiling.

"Nothing, right?" Donnelly asked, already knowing the answer.

"Microwave oven, even acid," Martin said. "It's as invincible as it is terrifying. I'll end up needing a lawyer if I bring it back into my house, you know, for my own divorce."

"She's that mad?"

"Yes, Will, and I don't blame her. What have you gotten yourself into?"

"I got in with the wrong people, obviously..." he said. Martin watched as he sighed pensively. "I was in an impossible situation. One of the heads of Barghest, LLC., gave me an out."

"Barghest is the main competitor to this company, right?"

"Black Flagg, Inc. and Barghest, LLC. are locked in a battle for control of the world," Donnelly said.

"How important is it that someone from *your* company's opposition very conveniently offered you a solution to your problems?" Martin asked.

"I know how it looks. These two companies are always overlapping, selling to each other, suing each other, the fact that he was from Barghest is insignificant."

"You sure?" Martin asked.

"I didn't know it at the time, of course, but the book changes hands on a regular basis," William Donnelly said.

"Why's that?" Martin asked.

William Donnelly stared into the eyes of his old friend, communicating without words that the transfer of the Libro Del Diablo was by *necessity*.

"Sign the contract, *hold something* for them, keep it in *my place in line*, how bad could that be? Of course, they left some things out of the brochure," William said.

"You're housing *something* in the same space as your soul? That was the deal?" Martin asked.

"Donnelly nodded.

"What are you *holding*?" Martin asked.

Donnelly looked away. Martin watched as William Donnelly fidgeted, obviously disquieted even by the consideration of Martin's question.

Martin Sandberg realized Donnelly had been saddled with some*one* instead of some*thing*.

"Not *what*, but *who*? Will, *who* is it?"

"Can you get me out of this contract, Marty?" William Donnelly asked him, refusing to answer the question.

"Many lawyers would argue that there is *always* a way to void a contract," Martin said.

"Okay, tell me more," Donnelly said, moving closer to him.

"I'm pretty good with this sort of thing, Will, but as I said, I have to *read* it to be able to challenge it. I can't get a grip on any of the words inside. Besides my wildly unsuccessful attempt at copying it, I tried to take digital photos of the pages, I thought maybe with a program I could skew them, take out some pixels, something, so my head wouldn't hurt so bad."

"You did what?" Donnelly asked, "is that different from using a copy machine? That might work."

"It did *not*... You see the problem, right?" Martin asked. "I've been going at it as I best as I can, but it's too slow moving."

"And too painful."

"Yes, Will, but if I get what I need out of it, I can give it back to you. Reading it is next to impossible. I get cross-eyed and start to have thoughts about what it would be like to take my car up to ninety and run it into a tree. That's not like me. I don't have thoughts like that, Will."

"It puts those thoughts in your head," William Donnelly said, retrieving two bottles of water from his office refrigerator and handing one to Martin.

"For Pete's sake, I leave the thing on my desk at work, and when I come home, it's waiting for me. I bring it back. It's like it's messing with me," Martin said.

"So the purpose of this visit, I take it, is to tell me that you haven't found a way out for me," Donnelly said, taking a few swallows from his bottle of water.

"For every rule of law, there are ten exceptions. For each of those ten exceptions, there are ten more rules of law. Issues fly out of issues. I *can* do this, but I'm having a problem with time," Martin said. William Donnelly had given him a deadline. He had work to do on other cases, he desperately needed to write a brief, and several motions were overdue.

Most lawyers would say nothing about being behind (and having uncommon difficulty) and clients would wait patiently wondering what was happening. Martin wasn't that kind of lawyer, especially where his old friend William Donnelly was concerned. As a practice, no matter who the client, Martin preferred to communicate with his clients as much as possible. There was that and, of course, the pressing fact that his old friend William Donnelly was running out of time.

"I don't know how much time I have left," William said, sadly. "Do you think you *can* get me out of it?" Donnelly asked him, hope in his eyes.

"I believe I can," Martin said.

"Do you ever lie to your clients? I would like to hear: 'it's going to be okay, Will, nothing to worry about, consider this contract broken and squashed.'"

"I'm optimistic, but I'm not going to lie to you," Martin said.

"Why are you optimistic?" Donnelly asked him. "I'd like to have some optimism."

"Assuming the Parol Evidence Rule doesn't get in the way, people are supposed to get into contracts with their eyes open, with full knowledge of *all* of the facts. This way an agreement is entered into freely, voluntarily, and knowingly."

"So..." Will said, then finished his bottle of water. "The fact that it wasn't in the brochure that I would be locked in battle, losing a little of myself every day, is a reason to get the thing voided?"

"Maybe," Martin said.

"What's the 'Parol Evidence Rule?'"

"It is a rule that in certain agreements, prevents the introduction of extraneous facts, extraneous circumstances, and negotiations from being entered into evidence in a breach of contract case. In your case, the fact that the prior holder of the note and the guys in charge of the thing didn't tell you what or *who* you would be up against might be considered Parol Evidence."

"The prior holder is dead," William Donnelly said.

Martin looked at him.

"So is the person before him and the one before that. I'm going to die too, Marty, if you can't get me out of this."

"I think a Judge might agree that the risk of death is a necessary and indispensable contract term. If the Parol Evidence Rule is applied, however, we will *not* be able to use that fact as a method for voiding the contract."

"So we *are not* allowed to tell the Judge that nobody warned me before I signed?"

"If the Parol Evidence Rule is applied. Look, Will, it works like this. Let's say I manufacture shoes and you have shoe stores. You and I contract for ten thousand shoes, but when you get them, they have buckles instead of laces. You then call me all tough and rumbly and tell me that you're not paying..."

"Tough and rumbly?" William Donnelly asked, smiling.

"Angry, mad as a hatter, whatever," Martin said. "Anyway, I demand that you pay for the shoes. I argue that you know I only manufacture shoes with buckles, you say that you only sell ones with laces. We would go to court on a lawsuit over the shoes, and the judge might be faced with listening to whether before signing the contract you and I discussed laces or buckles, or if you had prior knowledge that I only manufacture shoes with buckles. However, if you and I wrote in the contract for the sale of those shoes that we both intended that the written contract would be the final expression of the terms of our agreement, then the Parol Evidence Rule would apply."

"Do people do that?" Donnelly asked, "put a clause like that in a written agreement?"

"All the time. It's a standard in Divorce Agreements."

"It seems harsh. I would think a judge would need to hear about details to interpret an agreement," Donnelly said.

"But if you didn't want to litigate a contract, spend a great deal of money and time, you purposefully put in the contract a specific clause. You put in a term that says both parties to the contract agree that they are bound by the four corners of the agreement, bound by the terms as stated, even if you might have left out details. When the written contract is clearly intended to be a complete and final expression of the parties' agreement, a judge can't consider negotiations or extraneous facts, for the most part."

"If the judge rules that the contract, that Devil-Book was supposed to be the final expression of the agreement, he's not going to consider the fact that my signature on its pages means my destruction from the *inside out*?" Donnelly asked.

"Exactly," Martin said.

"I'm not liking this 'Parol Evidence Rule.'"

"What *did* they tell you?" Martin asked.

"I was just supposed to hold him in my place, keep him *in the line*."

"Keeping him there... That's what's killing you?" Martin asked.

"It's more than just being killed," he said, "I'm being erased, a little bit more every day. I'm clinging by my fingernails... Martin, they knew that he would overwhelm me, that I wouldn't make it, that it would be just a matter of time before he ripped me apart and they would have to get someone else to sign. I'd last however long I lasted. After that, they'd get someone else to sign. After I'm gone, someone else has to deal with it, and so on. No one told me."

"I don't understand," Martin said.

"They've built jails, prison planets, *realms.* Nothing keeps *him* contained. They stopped building places for him because he kept *obliterating* everything. The resources that have been lost just trying to find a place to put him, it's staggering. Now they pass him from person to person."

"They house him with a person until he... erases them?"

"Until he overwhelms them, then they find some other sucker, like me. They didn't say: 'hey guy, we need you to house this monster in your soul-sack, but just as long as it takes for him to obliterate you. After he tears you to pieces, we'll be getting someone else to keep him until *that* someone gets ripped apart, too.' Soon as I burn out, they'll pass him on. It's been nothing short of all-out war. No one said anything about that and how it would be a death sentence."

Martin watched as his friend sighed, despondent. "They said it was just someone they needed housed," Will said. "That didn't seem so bad, for what I got in return."

"A bargain too good to be true," Martin said.

"For the life of me, I can't see how I could have been *so* stupid."

"I'm sorry, Will."

"Don't be *sorry,* Counselor. Break the contract, get me out of this," William Donnelly said.

"I'll do everything I can," Martin said.

"Please, I don't know how much longer I have," William said. He watched as William leaned in to speak, barely above a whisper. "He's getting stronger," he said. Martin took a moment to look at him. The dark circles around his eyes and his haggard expression corroborated the struggle. Martin watched as his friend stood and paced.

"Will?"

Martin watched as he pulled at this thumbnail with his teeth.

"His voice, it echoes. He has only one arm... My God, he only has one arm."

"What?" Martin asked.

"He's only got one hulking arm," Donnelly said, "well that's not true exactly, he carries the other arm around with that one arm that's still attached."

William Donnelly looked at Martin and saw his mouth was wide open. To William, it looked like Martin's face had turned pale.

"It's terrifying. He told me that the other arm was ripped off in battle. I wonder who or what could do that. He walks around swinging it. The arm. He swings it at the walls, like a club or something."

"Dear God," Martin said.

"Sometimes I can hear him pounding on the walls... My walls. He's there, *talking* to me, swinging his arm like a baseball bat. I can't hold it. When he breaks through..." William Donnelly said.

"It was a con. They knew I wouldn't last. That's why they do it this way. There's *nowhere* else to *put* him."

"I'll figure something out," Martin said.

"You don't understand, Marty. He's a force of nature," Donnelly said.

"Will I'll figure something out, I swear," Martin told his old friend.

"You promise?" William Donnelly asked him, sounding like a child.

"I'll find a way. There's got to be a way."

"You're a good friend, Marty."

"And I'm your lawyer."

"That, too."

FOUR

CALDWELL V. CALDWELL

NADINE CALDWELL STOOD IN THE DOORWAY OF THE ROOM ON SUNDAY AFTERNOON, CHEWING THE TIP OF HER THUMB. Chewing on her thumb was common when she was pensive or searching for a thought that had escaped her mind. She put her hand on her tummy, staring into the room, but not going in.

There was a long table against the wall with a large window above it. Her papers, various pens, notebooks, computer, a handheld device were strewn haphazardly on the table. The room had two desk chairs, each with wheels, but that was the extent of the furniture in the study to which a person could sit.

Bookshelves lined the walls, along with file cabinets, side-tables, piled high with textbooks, papers, and her notebooks. Piles of books were in each corner and against the shelves. On the wall, her only poster, was the infamous "Albert Einstein sticking out his tongue." Strewn about the room were dusty lamps in no orderly fashion.

Her home office was, as she put it, a "disaster area and a pig pen put together." Though it seemed as if her thoughts had been scattered, and although the office was a "disaster area," it was *her* disaster area. Pioneering a specialized (and practical) application of her theories, Nadine Caldwell was attempting to finish her postgraduate thesis and, with others at the university, she was developing technology that she thought *just might* change the world.

She felt her pocket with her hand, checking to make sure her little brown pocket-sized notebook was still in its place. The regular-sized notebooks scattered about contained ideas, notes, theorems, drawings, scribbles of all modes of thought, but the little brown pocket-sized notebook is where she kept her *secrets*. While many young women her age kept secret diaries, her little brown pocket-sized notebook diary contained formulas. At all times she held the ideas she felt were her undiscovered applications with her. Her husband had suggested that she keep them in her phone or get a pocket computer. She laughed at him, (not trying to mock him, but doing so anyway) and explained that paper and pencil with her, (at all times) was much harder to steal than something connected to the internet. She had commented (after apologizing for laughing at him) that keeping her secrets in a digital format ensured that hackers, (the digital equivalent of pickpockets), would always have access. By keeping her secrets in the little brown pocket-sized notebook, and on paper, the only way to lose her proprietary (and unique) formulas would be for someone to physically take her notebook at gunpoint and "pry it from my cold, angry corpse," she had said.

The apartment (she graciously) shared with her husband had two bedrooms. When they had first rented the place, he had thoughtfully, and without a moment's consideration, set up the room for her to complete her studies. He built the shelves, acquired everything she might need. Her husband had a menial job, but one that paid reasonably well and he supported her both financially and emotionally as she pursued her passion. Childhood sweethearts, for as long as either of them could remember, it was the two of them against the world.

Phillip Caldwell thought of his life as simplistic, uncomplicated, and that was perfectly fine for him. He turned down offers of going "out with the guys," and refused to join his friends' bowling league. Though his life was simplistic, it was his, meant everything to him, and so long as Nadine came home every day, he felt invincible. For Phillip, for as long as he could remember, he wanted to be with Nadine and would support her.

She could stay in school forever, as far as he was concerned. When they would sit together and she would tell him her latest discoveries and the specific problems of the day she was attempting to solve, he would smile and nod while creatively figuring ways to ask questions with just enough detail to make her believe that he understood even a fraction of the words she spoke to him.

For Phillip Caldwell, it didn't matter to him what she said, not that he understood her "science speak." She could speak a foreign language, and it would make no difference. He loved *listening* to her and loved the fact it was *to him* she was talking.

On this day, he saw her standing in the doorway and went to her.

"Hey," he said, putting his arms around her from behind, gently resting his hands on her tummy, and kissing her cheek, "are you thinking about finally cleaning this room?" he asked her.

"It *is* clean," she said, kissing him back, "can't you tell?"

"You are absolutely right, how could I make such a mistake. Everything is in its place, and you know where to find everything," he said, gently hugging her.

"See? You *get* me," she said.

"What about all *that*?" he asked her, indicating the piles of notebooks, textbooks, papers, and a few clipboards strewn on various surfaces of their bedroom.

"You love my piles, tell the truth," she said, but secretly, she often felt bad about the amount of space she took. Everything Phillip owned was in a side closet, (of course she had the "walk-in,") and if someone came to the apartment and didn't make an effort at searching, they might not know he even lived there.

"I do love your little piles," he said, taking the opportunity to sneak another little kiss on her cheek. "What are you up to, standing here?"

"What do you mean?" she asked him.

"You chew your thumb when you are thinking hard about something," he said, going into her cluttered study and sitting in one of the two chairs. He watched as she sighed, knowing that he *did* get her, better than anyone else ever could.

"I don't know where I'm going to do my work," she said. He watched as she went into the room and sat on the floor, began to stack one of the piles. "There's just so much," she said.

"We have time," he said.

"It will go by too fast," she said. "We will blink, and then it will be time," she said. She had almost said 'we will blink and then *it will all be over,*' instead of 'it will be time,' and was thankful she stopped herself. If she had said "it will be all over," she knew Phillip would be hurt those words.

"You don't need to give up the room, Nadine. We talked about this already. We can make it work," he said.

"We can't afford a three bedroom. We can barely afford this place," she said.

"We don't need a three bedroom. I know how important it is for you to have a place to work. Can we at least talk about the living room again?" he asked, but Nadine was shaking her head 'no,' before he even finished his sentence. "Okay, then the bedroom, a little re-arranging..." He cut himself short watching as she continued to shake her head.

"I don't know how this could happen," she said, stacking, arranging and re-arranging the notebooks and papers on the floor in front of her. When she looked into Phillip's face, she could see that what she said had upset him. She was regretful for hurting his feelings.

"I can draw you a diagram, you know, flap 'A' into slot 'B,'" he said, his tone sounding just a little more bitter than he had intended.

"For years it never let me down. I don't understand," she said, looking up at him, frowning.

He tried to think of what to say. He couldn't come up with anything that would not sound angry. He decided to say nothing would be best.

"Why now?" she asked. "I'm supposed to start my internship," she said.

"You can *still* intern. There is plenty of time and the living room..." Phillip started to say, but she cut him off.

"I'm not having our baby sleep in the living room!" she yelled at him while knocking over the pile of notebooks she had just finished stacking. He couldn't tell if she knocked the pile over on purpose.

"I can put up temporary walls, or we could re-arrange the bedroom," he said then watched as his wife started to cry.

Phillip Caldwell went to his wife, sat down on the floor next to her, put his arm around her.

"I'm going to finally *create* a hyper-kinetic graphene sheet with one hand and breastfeed with the other?" she asked him.

"You don't need to breastfeed. When you change the world, Nadine, you will be using *both* of your hands. *I* will feed the baby. I can use formula. You won't have to do *any* of that. You can connect the graphing sheet things just as you would, and you will have all the time in the world," Phillip said.

"It's not graphing, it's *graphene*..." she started to say, but decided that correcting him wasn't important. They sat together in silence for a moment, Phillip looking around her home office and imagining it as the baby's nursery.

She looked at him with tired eyes. "This isn't really about where to put the crib, is it?" he asked her.

She gave him her (specially reserved) "glad you finally used your brain" expression, complete with eyes-rolling to accentuate her meaning.

"Okay, okay. I'm sorry."

"It's fine," she said. "Phil, I'm on the verge of a breakthrough. I only need to run the simulations. I need computer access."

"The special computer is at *that* company?" he asked her.

"I can't use a PC from the local office supply store. I need *real* computing power. There are only three places *on the planet* that have the kind of power I need. One of them happens to be here, local."

"At Series Communication?" he asked.

"No, honey. I told you, Series Communication is part of a conglomerate. Black Flagg owns Series and all the other companies. That's the parent company. Right now, as we sit here on this floor, they are doing a deep background check on me, their security analysts finding out what I had for breakfast ten years ago before they let me near their servers."

She watched as he concentrated for a moment. She was fond of how hard he tried.

"Black Flagg? Don't they make like, toilet paper, things like that?"

"Yes, dry goods, air fresheners, garbage bags, things like that. Most people don't know that they also own half the media companies in the world. They have a computer designed especially from the ground up just for their needs that puts quantum computing to shame."

"I thought you were interning with Series Communication."

"Yes, Phillip, Series Communication, owned by Black Flagg, honey... Do you know I actually got a sit down with the Board's "Chair of Internal Auditing," whatever that is. His name is Marcus Whiteacre. I was so nervous."

"When was this?" he asked her, "you didn't tell me."

"Last week he came to the university to meet with us. I'm sorry I didn't mention it, but why bother?" Nadine asked him. "It doesn't matter now anyway."

"Just because we are having a baby, it doesn't mean you have to give up your dreams," he said, standing up and holding out his hand to help her.

"Doesn't it?" she asked him, taking his hand and using it to pull herself to her feet. She followed him to the kitchen. "And let's be real, Phillip. *We* aren't having a baby. *I* am having a baby."

"That's not fair, Nadine," he said.

"It's *my* ankles that are going to be swollen, *me* who's going to keep throwing up every morning, *I'm* the one who's going to have sleepless nights, any way you look at it."

"Okay, you're right, but when the baby gets here, I'll take care of everything, I promise," he said, taking a bottle of water and a can of soda out of the fridge. He handed her the bottle of water. She took it from his hand looked at the bottle of water as if he had given her a handful of garbage instead of a drink.

"Honey, I know you will," she said, watching him open the can of soda and take a sip.

"I'll do everything I can," Phillip said.

"Unless you plan on carrying *it* in your guts, there's nothing you can do," she said, putting the bottle of water on the counter, taking his can of soda from his hand and taking a few swallows. He watched as she kept the soda can in her hands, apparently hers now.

"Look. We have plenty of time before any decision needs to be made," he said.

"You mean before *I* have a decision to make," she said. He looked into her eyes.

"It's *my* body," she said.

She watched as he slumped, defeated.

He stood in the kitchen, quiet, solemn. There wasn't anything he could say that wouldn't result in an argument. A dispute between them of only *this* kind would end up with them not talking to each other for almost a day before one of them apologized to the other, neither of them caring or remembering whose fault the argument had been. The topic of conversation had caused such an argument *the last time* they had tried to discuss it.

He knew she was intent on reminding him (over and over, he felt) that it was *her* body. He did, however, agree with her about questioning *how* it could have happened, though.

How did it happen?

44

She was meticulous in taking her daily pill and keeping up with her doctors. For years she had taken the birth control pill, and she was correct, when she stated that it hadn't let her down before. Wondering if the birth control was ineffective, or she had gotten a "bad batch," (if there was such a thing as a "bad batch" of birth control pills) she had gone so far as to have her hormone level checked. Her doctor, standing before her confounded when he gave her the results had said: "there's no way this could have happened." She was angry with him (of course) and demanded he run the test a second time, using a different laboratory.

The results were the same. The birth control pills she took, on a daily basis, had worked as designed, yet she *still* got pregnant.

"I just want to ask... Can I ask one thing?" Phillip Caldwell asked his wife. She looked at him, taking another sip from her recently acquired can of soda. "Before you decide to do *anything,* you know, before you make a *final* decision, will you at least talk to me?" he asked.

"Yes, Phillip. I can do that," she said but wasn't sure that she could.

FIVE

RUBBING HIS EYES, MARTIN SANDBERG
STRUGGLED TO HIS FEET. He did not know where he was or
how he got there. There was one light above his head and a few
others scattered around what he felt might be an extensive, open-
air warehouse. There were boxes of different shapes and sizes
piled and scattered about. The vast room was mostly empty,
however. There was a noise emanating from what he thought
might be about thirty feet away. Through the dim lighting, he
could see a figure using a large, powered screwdriver (or drill of
some kind) on one of the walls. He walked to the person, careful
not to trip on the boxes in his path, to get a better look at the young
woman as she screwed metal panels into the wall.

"Oh good, can you hold this in place?" she asked him when
she saw him. She acted as if she had been expecting him, though
he had no idea who she was.

Without any consideration to suddenly finding himself in a
strange place, not knowing where he was, who *she* was, and *what*
she was doing, Martin held the large metal sheeting in its seat and
watched as the young woman put screws into it, fastening it to the
wall. The motorized monstrosity she was holding to secure the
bolts in place was loud and temporarily prevented him from
talking with her as she worked. He looked at her through the dim
lighting, trying to remember where he might have seen her before.
She seemed to be in her early twenties, was slender, had long hair,
wore a white button-down shirt, (which was dirty in various
places) baggy pants, had a tool-belt around her waist and was
wearing safety glasses. He watched as she would pull one long
metal shiny screw after another out of a brown paper bag, put it in
place, and fasten it to the sheet and the wall.

After she finished with the sheeting, he watched as she
took off her safety glasses and wiped her forehead with the back of
her arm, using her sleeve.

"That's a lot easier when you have an extra pair of hands,"
she said to him, catching her breath. He followed her as she
walked through the semi-darkness to a table and chairs in the
corner he hadn't noticed before.

"Why is it so dark in here?" he asked her.

46

"We'll fix that, but we need to reinforce the walls before anything else. If we don't make them strong enough, we are going to be in real trouble," she said, taking a bottle of water out of the cooler on the floor (that Martin also hadn't noticed before) and taking a few long gulps. He watched as she wiped her mouth with the same sleeve. Her movements were methodical, the way she handled herself, graceful.

Though he found her to be beautiful, (his being a happily married person notwithstanding) he was concerned of what might be on the outside of the warehouse, given that reinforcing the walls was of vital importance.

"I'm terrified we won't have time to make the walls strong enough."

"Where are we?" he asked her. She smiled at him, almost laughed. "What's so funny?" he asked her.

"I had expected you to ask me *who I am* first, that's all," she said to him with an innocent smile. "That's the *usual* course of things."

"You're the person reinforcing the walls in this-- dark warehouse," he said.

"There," she said, "you've answered both questions." He watched as she drank more from her bottle. "You already know where we are and who I am," she said after drinking half the bottle.

"No, I don't," he argued.

"I'm the person reinforcing the walls, and you're in a warehouse. That's a good way to describe this gloomy place. It will be so much more, so important."

"I don't know how I got here," he said nervously, ignoring her non-answers.

"I brought you here, Martin," she said, walking to the pile of metal sheeting and pulling one from the top. He instinctively helped her as she brought it to where they had finished the last one and put it in place. "I don't even know how much of this conversation you're going to remember. I need your help. I'm going to die soon if you don't help me."

"What? Are you going to die? What *can I* do?" he asked her, emphasis on the "I" in his statement.

"You're going to file a lawsuit. You're going to file a lawsuit and save us."

47

MARTIN SANDBERG SAT AT HIS DESK, TRYING DESPERATELY TO KEEP HIS EYES OPEN. He didn't remember that he had spent the night helping a charismatic young woman reinforce the walls of a dark and gloomy warehouse except for aches and pains he couldn't quite place. He looked at his hands. They were not chafed or calloused, yet they hurt just the same. The pain was a mystery.

The previous night, working with her, handling metal sheeting without gloves, he had cut his hands in several places, helping her as they talked. He didn't remember speaking with her. He knew only that his hands were excruciating, sore. Was it his imagination? He shrugged it aside, believing he must have slept wrong *on them.*

Was I talking to someone?

Sitting at his desk, searching for thoughts that he felt had escaped his mind, he waited for his 9:00 a.m. appointment.

"Hey Marty!" he heard Delia yell from the small lobby of his law office. "You're appointment's here!"

Delia Hammond always yelled through the doorway. Martin no longer wondered why Delia didn't get up out of her chair to tell him someone was there for him, or even utilize the expensive phone system he had put in. Martin had learned from the beginning that people came *to* Delia, *not* the other way around. He believed she would get up if the situation arose (like maybe her desk was set on fire or something, but probably not) and it was absolutely and completely essential. In most cases, however, she couldn't be bothered.

Martin Sandberg did *not* hire Delia Hammond to be his receptionist, had not hired her at all.

Martin Sandberg had *not* hired Delia Hammond at all.

The day after he had lost his place in line, figured out that he was out of sync, that he was forever *changed*, she was simply there in his office. It didn't appear that she was waiting for him, per se. She was sitting in the front room of his office, at the receptionist desk, (which he did not purchase) filing her long and elegant nails. There was a picture of someone on the desk, (it looked to Martin to be the photo that had come with the frame, but Martin wasn't sure) a little plant, and an appropriate lamp.

"You have three appointments this morning," she had said to him that first morning, handing him little slips from a message pad, (also not obtained by him) speaking to him as if she had been working with him for years.

"Who are you? What are you doing here?" Martin had asked her.

"I'm here to *assist* you, Mr. Martin," she had said, emphasizing the word "assist."

"I didn't hire you, did I? Did I hire you and forget that I hired you?" he had asked her, terrified he had been losing his mind. The feeling was something he had been experiencing lately. "I can't afford someone yet," Martin said, beginning to worry.

"Mr. Martin, *calm yourself*. You *will* obtain *serenity* within yourself, become familiar with the schedule I have provided you, and you *will* know that right now, at this moment in time, we *are* satisfactory, we *are* sufficient, we *are* acceptable," she had said to him with overwhelming confidence. He remembered standing before her, breathing the incense that she had lit, (the scent was calming, actually) feeling a mixture of astonished and overwhelmed.

Even so, he thought she was correct, not so much because he could trust the woman who had suddenly appeared in his office to *assist* him, but because it was what *she* wanted. It was evident that the woman was *somehow* in control of things that he had felt had previously been slipping through his fingers.

"It is nice to meet you, then," he said, attempting (and failing) to sound casual. "My *first* name's Martin, by the way, the *last* name is Sandberg. I mean, so I guess it would be 'Mr. Sandberg,' not 'Mr. Martin,'" he had said. It was the only thing he could think to say after someone had suddenly appeared in his office and announced that she worked for him.

He remembered that her reaction to his correcting her (about his name) was unlike anything he had ever experienced. He remembered the almost otherworldly, unsettling, frightening alien smile she had given him when he had corrected her. Staring into *that* smile, *her* smile, the uneasy discontent he felt, the ground beneath him tipping on its side, he felt he might explode into a thousand pieces, or fall over stiff and dead from the sight of it.

Flashes like a strobe hit his eyes for a moment, the time it took to blink an eye, the image of Delia's darkened-shadow face, blacked-out eyes, blackness radiating out from her as if it were light instead of darkness was added to the ever-growing list of things Martin would always want to avoid at all costs.

Moving forward, the very thought of her smile caused him considerable stomach upset.

"Perhaps I'll simply call you Martin,'" she said, not asking, but *telling*.

A moment had passed between the two of them where, looking at her smile, he had a sudden urge to empty his bowels and his bladder at the same time as he stood before all of its relentless glory.

"Thank you," he had said to her before quickly retreating to his office and gently closing the door behind him before he had to call his wife to bring a change of underwear to the office.

Several months had passed since Delia came into his life. Since then, he had managed to pay her a (meager, but sustainable) salary, and she seemed to have everything under control. Her presence had always remained a mystery, however.

"Send him on back!" he yelled back to Delia, through his doorway. He had learned that this was her choice of communication and if she wanted to have a conversation, *she* would tell him to go to her desk.

Martin stood when the young man entered his office. He appeared to be barely an adult, but his eyes and manner portrayed a sense of sadness, uncommon maturity, and urgency. Martin shook hands with him.

"Phillip Caldwell, sir," he said as he took his baseball cap off his sweaty head. "I need you to save my child. I'll pay you whatever you ask, and I don't have much money right this moment, but I can make payments. Please, Mr. Sandberg. Please save my kid," he said. Martin stared at the young man for a moment, trying to remember who he was having a conversation with last night, and what had been the topic. He couldn't quite remember the details, but it had something to do with saving *someone.* He remembered that he didn't want that kind of pressure, that having someone's life in his hands wasn't a kind of pressure he felt he could deal with and normally, he would send such a potential client away with a list in hand of other lawyers who might be able to help. (When any client came into the office with an allegedly life or death situation, that is.)

50

"We got married soon as we turned eighteen, just a few years ago," he said. "She's pregnant and talking about *not* having the baby," he said, fighting tears.

"Phillip, I've never handled a case like this one, I don't know if you even *have* a case. My instincts tell me that any court in which we made a challenge would remind us that it is *her* body and she can choose to house a child in it or not."

Phillip Caldwell began to frown. Martin was unaware that Phillip's wife, Nadine, had told him the same thing.

"Don't fathers have rights?" Phillip Caldwell asked.

"More today than ever before," Martin said, "the law certainly has evolved in that respect, but I'm not sure we're even going to get past a motion to dismiss if we filed for some unclassified injunctive relief. You're not a father *yet*. You anticipate being a father, but you are *not* a father as of this moment."

"Will you at least try?" Phillip Caldwell asked. Martin noticed the man's eyes were turning glassy as he fought back tears.

"I don't know," Martin said. "Can I ask a stupid question? Have you tried to convince her not to go through with it?"

"Of course!" he said, obviously in agreement that the question Martin had asked him was indeed, stupid. "She's not listening to me. Nadine's listening to *someone else*. Other people are talking to her I think. I can't stop them. I can't stop her from listening."

"That's her name? Nadine?" Martin asked.

"Yes, Nadine Caldwell," He said, then watched as Martin wrote the name on his legal pad.

"I guess my next stupid question is... are *you* sure you want to be a father? You are so young, what about college? A baby means you're busy all the time. I'm not trying to say that your life is over when you have a baby, but suddenly, everything you do is for your child."

"I'm not going to college. Nadine and I both *want* to have a baby. We *talked* about it. She doesn't want it *right now*, though. She's getting her degree and thinks that it will interfere."

"That very well may be the case. What is she studying?"

"Science, Computers... Physics? All that I think."

"You can see how it might be difficult to raise a baby while trying to get a degree in such complicated fields of study."

51

"Yes, but I told her I'd do all the work," Caldwell said.

Martin stared at him for a moment, skeptical.

"Caring for a baby is hard work," Martin said.

"I'm ready. I have to be," he said.

"How long have you been separated?" Martin asked him.

"We're *not* separated, Mr. Sandberg. Except for this one subject, we get along on *everything*," Phillip Caldwell said.

"I'm sorry, forgive me, Phillip," Martin said putting his pen down. Most people who come in here and are having issues of this kind have usually separated."

"Not us," Phillip said.

"You said you've talked about having a baby. Besides her studies, is there anything going on that's caused her to change her mind?"

"I don't know. I think it's *more* than her school. Nadine? She can do *anything,* Mr. Sandberg. Nothing has ever stopped her. She's on the verge of a breakthrough discovery. I understand where she's coming from, I guess."

"Are you sure she still wants to be a mother *at all?* She could have changed her mind about being a parent."

"I know that's *not* what's happening here. Please, Mr. Sandberg," Phillip Caldwell begged, "my child is special."

"Phillip, everyone's child is special. Listen, your case might be something for another attorney. Maybe you could talk to a lawyer who specializes in injunctive relief. I can give you some names..."

"No, Mr. Sandberg," he said, cutting Martin off mid-sentence. "It has to be you," he said.

"Why me?"

"Because *she* said you'd care, that you would *know.*"

"Who said that? Not Nadine, right?"

"No, never mind," Phillip Caldwell said, shifting in his chair.

"Phillip, who referred you to me?"

"It's not like that. She said you might know because you were doing a project together, building something?"

"I'm not building anything," Martin said, "I barely know how to use a screwdriver. Please, tell me who you're talking about."

"I can't tell you that," he said.

Martin stared at him for a moment. The conversation had gone from confusing to not making any rational sense.

"Okay, so I'm going to write down the names and telephone numbers of three attorneys I know who handle injunctive-type cases," Martin said, writing on his legal pad.

"It has to be you. *You* have to be the one to represent her, Mr. Sandberg," Phillip Caldwell demanded.

"Represent her? I thought you were the one who needed an attorney," Martin said.

"Yes, I mean, both of us?"

"Phillip, who is this person you're talking about? Is it a girlfriend?"

"Oh God, no."

"Who do you need me to represent?"

"This isn't going right," Phillip said.

"I agree," Martin said, "seriously, spit it out already."

"I don't know if I can. I don't think so... I can't."

"I don't represent anyone who hides things from me," he said. "If you're not going to tell me why it is that *I have to be the one* if you won't tell me who's this woman telling you these things, I'm not taking the case, Phillip. Why isn't this something for a different lawyer? Surely it is not because of my experience in these matters. I've never filed a petition like the one you're describing. What's going on here?"

"Only you can do this. She said."

"Who?"

"My daughter!" Phillip yelled.

Martin stared at him, confused.

"Do you have a different child?"

"No. My daughter. The one in Nadine."

Martin watched him as he sat in front of him, suddenly appearing very small, fragile and let a moment pass, while he considered the ramifications of what the young man in front of him, sitting in one of his client chairs was actually saying. Phillip Caldwell was telling Martin that his unborn child recommended him for legal services. Even if this were somehow true, Martin wanted no part of it.

"Your unborn daughter recommended me?"

"It's not like that."

"Like what?"

53

"You are her only hope. You have to trust me."

"Your unborn *daughter's* only hope is an attorney, one who is not very experienced for injunctive cases, who doesn't want the case? One other thing, you keep referring to the fetus as a 'she.' If you know the sex of the child, you might be too late anyway. No judge is going even to consider what you're asking if the child is viable," Martin said.

Martin eyed Phillip Caldwell as he wiped his forehead, stammered.

"She's been pregnant for six weeks," he said, barely whispering. They stared at each other.

"She's already talked to you," he said, barely audible.

"What?" Martin asked.

"She's already *talked* to you," he said.

"Your wife?" Martin asked him. He was still confused.

"Oh my God," Phillip said, then groaned in frustration.

The "she" Caldwell was referring to could *not* be his unborn daughter, or so Martin thought.

"No, not my wife, Mr. Sandberg. You've been talking to *her*."

Martin stared at him.

"Who?"

"My daughter." Phillip Caldwell said to Martin, angry.

Without saying a word, Martin stood up and closed the door to his office. It made no difference if Delia heard the conversation, (she always knows everything) but Martin felt more comfortable.)

"Think hard," Caldwell said. "She told me you would have trouble remembering or that you might not remember at all."

Martin Sandberg stared at the young man, tried to remember having a conversation which would have been *out of place.* He looked at his hands, rubbed them where they had been cut while he assisted with the reinforcing of the warehouse, somehow, someplace, sometime. Like "Deja vu," it was thoughts, memories, just out of his reach.

"She's special, Mr. Sandberg. My daughter is going to change the world," he said, "you don't remember her at all? You talked with her while you worked together."

"I'm building something with your unborn daughter?" Martin asked him.

"She's doing the construction. You are helping her."

Philip Caldwell watched as Martin once again began to write on his legal pad in silence.

"What are you doing?" he asked.

"I'm *not* going to give you three names of other lawyers, Phillip. I'm writing down three names of mental health professionals who work on a sliding scale and would be happy to meet with you," Martin said.

"I don't need a shrink," Phillip said.

"It is my learned opinion, that you do not need a lawyer and you do not have a legal problem. You need a therapist," Martin said. "I can't help you."

Philip Caldwell stood and cursed at Martin before walking out of his office, slamming the door. Without knowing why Martin followed him to the front room and watched him leave.

He stood next to Delia's desk in silence.

"That sounded like it went well," she said. Her tone was usually sarcastic. This day was no exception.

"Are you sure you are not going to help that man?" Delia asked.

"Positive," Martin said, looking at Delia's desk.

Delia's desk was empty except for the scant few objects she kept. Spread out next to the little plant and the frame with the pictures that were in it when she bought it, Delia was playing solitaire with an old deck of cards. She had the rows of cards spread across her desk. Martin looked at her cards, then looked at her.

"My computer's down. I'm having to do everything manually," she said.

"Very funny," he said.

SIX

MORENO V. SCALFANI

"ALIVE, DEAD, EITHER WAY, STALKING IS A CRIME," Martin said, "Haunting and stalking are really the same thing." He eyed the young woman sitting across the desk from him. She looked back at him, wide-eyed, anxious. "I looked it up, you know," Martin said, "to *haunt* someone means to torment them, disturb, trouble, burden, worry, plague..." he stopped himself, took a moment. "Stalking someone means to harass or persecute someone with unwanted and obsessive attention... So... Haunting and stalking, synonyms..."

"How much did you say the consultation fee is?" she asked him, frowning at him.

"It depends," he said, then watched as she rolled her eyes at him, making no attempt to hide her dissatisfaction. Her attitude and specific issues caused Martin to rethink how to handle the conversation.

He sat across his desk from the young woman in silence, wondering how it was that he had received another one of "those" cases.

She stared at him.

He stared back, wrote nonsense on his legal pad.

She continued to stare.

"I don't know if you can help me," the young woman said, finally breaking the silence, sitting sheepishly in one of the chairs across from Martin's desk. She seemed to be holding herself, hugging herself a little, like she might be cold. "I don't know if this is a matter for a lawyer," she said.

He waited a moment before speaking.

She wondered if he would say something profound. She concluded that it would be astonishing if he did.

"There's a Shaman down the street I can refer you to," he said.

"Really?" she asked, straightening up in her chair, her face lighting up.

"No," he said.

56

"   Oh," she said, slumping again, resuming the act of hugging herself, her facial expression returning to disappointment as she became apprehensive.

He concluded trying to make a joke about a shaman was in poor taste.

The consultation was going swimmingly.

"How old are you again?" Martin asked her.

"Twenty-one," she said.

"Drinking age," he said. After making the statement, Martin was instantly regretful that he had somehow lost the ability to think *before* he spoke. Being unable to consider one's words prior to saying stupid things to potential clients was a trait most detrimental for an attorney, whether *or not* his life goal was to keep people from being mad at him.

"Mr. Sandberg, if you're implying that I'm hallucinating these things because I've been drinking or something, let me assure you that is *not* the case," she said, angrily.

"No, no, I wasn't suggesting *that* at all. The reason I mentioned it is if you do *not* drink, maybe right *now* would be a good *time* to *start*," he said.

After offhandedly mentioning that she was at drinking age and then attempting to cover by making yet another statement twice as stupid, Martin decided that he would end his lousy day by perhaps calling a therapist and asking if there was a such thing as "anti-insensitivity" pills.

"Sir?"

"Charlene," Martin started to say, but she cut him off.

"Charlie," she said, correcting him.

"Fine, Charlie... You have an angry stalker Italian poltergeist. Given the precarious nature of your situation, I was suggesting alcohol, but only joking, of course," Martin said, writing 'angry stalker Italian poltergeist' on his legal pad.
In his mind, Martin congratulated himself for telling her he was joking, though he knew that "I'm only joking" was something all idiotic men say when they are trying to get themselves out of trouble.

"What did you just write down?" she asked him.

"Nothing important, just the 'angry stalker Italian poltergeist' thing," Martin said, reluctantly answering her question.

Martin hated when clients asked him what he was writing, but he answered her, nevertheless.

"Why does it matter that it's an *Italian* poltergeist?" she asked, "*I'm* Italian."

She looked at him.

He looked back at her.

"Because statistically, most ghost stalkers are Italians," he said, again cursing himself for not thinking before speaking.

He knew the reason he was nervous to the point of saying stupid things was because he was sure if she did have a poltergeist, she brought it with her. That was the nature of poltergeists. They don't haunt houses, contrary to popular belief. They choose a person and then follow that person.

Delia promised that she had taken measures to "keep the office safe," but poltergeists were slippery and seemed to come inside whenever they wanted. He made a mental note to ask Delia (respectfully) not to schedule any more "ghost stalking" cases. She should refer those out.

The whole conversation was making him nervous. He often found himself making comments that (in his mind) weren't meant to be insulting, but when spoken came off as insulting.

"Really?" she asked, on the edge of believing that poltergeists consisting mostly angry Italians.

"No," he answered, "but that would have been a good reason though, right?" Martin asked her, watched as she stood up out of the chair and put her purse over her arm.

"I *don't* think you are taking me seriously, Mr. Sandberg," she said.

"I'm sorry, it was just meant to be descriptive. I didn't mean to offend you. Please sit down. Please," Martin said, pleading with her not to leave. "I had no reason to add the 'Italian' part. I promise I'm not racist," he said, "I love Italian things. I love pizza."

She looked at him, seething.

"Why? Why am I saying such stupid things?" he asked her.

"I was about to ask you the same thing," she said.

He stopped himself, took a deep breath.

"It's not you."

"Really?"

"Ok, look. I'm scared, Charlene," he said.

"Charlie," she said, again correcting him.

"I can't get a break here," he said.

"Why are you scared?" she asked, point blank, her hands on her hips, her eyes piercing.

"You have a poltergeist," he said.

"That's what I've been trying to tell you," she said.

"If I say the wrong thing..."

"Don't want to get smacked by flying objects or hit by a stray bolt of electricity? Welcome to my club, " she said.

"Last time I had a client in here with a poltergeist, I said the words: 'don't worry, I'll take care of everything,' and it put three staples into my hand," he said, pointing to the tiny scars on his hand. "If we were old friends, I'd lift my shirt and show you the hole in my shoulder where I got stabbed by a pencil."

"You'd better not be joking," she said.

"No, I'm not, and I don't have any pencils," he said. He watched as she reconsidered leaving the office. "Please. I'm sorry," he said.

He watched as she put the purse back down on the floor and gingerly re-took her seat. Of course, she sat down with a little sigh and the continued obligatory eye-rolling.

"I don't mean to be flippant or lackadaisical. I'm taking your situation very seriously. You can see how it would make me anxious. Point of fact, one of *these* almost killed me in court recently," he said.

"Almost killed you in court?"

"A ghost who thought he was still married to his wife almost killed me," he said, "I drafted the petition and filed a divorce to free his wife from him."

He watched as she stood up again, let out a sigh of frustration, put the purse back over her shoulder.

"You're a jerk," she said, "I hate lawyers."

"No, wait, it happened."

"*This* is serious!"

"Yes, I'm sorry. I'm taking it seriously."

"No, you're not," she said.

"Here, just give me a moment," he said and watched as she looked at him, frowning. "I'll prove it."

"Fine, " she said, letting out a huff, "you prove it, but I am *not* paying you a consultation fee."

"Right," he said, tapping numbers into his phone then setting it down on the desk in between them.

They listened to it ring (on the "speaker" setting) and waited. A woman answered.

"Hello?"

"Hey, it's Martin," he said.

"Hi, Marty! How are you?" the woman on the phone asked.

"I'm fine, more importantly, Annabelle, *how* are you?" he asked her.

"I'm free! And loving it! Thank you so much, Marty," she said.

"Yes, you are very welcome," he said, "is this a good time to talk for a moment?"

"Sure," she said, "what's going on?"

"I have a young woman in my office. She's being stalked."

"Oh?"

"Like you were," he said.

There were a few seconds of silence. Charlie Moreno looked back and forth from the phone to Martin.

"Are you still there?" he asked.

"You said you might need help some time," she said, letting out a sigh. "I didn't realize it would be so soon. No need to worry. I'm *ready*."

"Annabelle, there's no reason to expect that what happened last time will happen again. That was unusual."

"I'm okay. I want to help. She's sitting there with you right now? I'm on speaker?" Annabelle asked.

"Yes," he said.

"I know you don't know me..."

"Charlie."

"Charlie, yes, my name is Annabelle Hanson. I used to be Annabelle *Feldman* until Marty helped me. If you can wait for me I'll be there at Marty's office in about a half hour, forty-five minutes, tops, and we can meet. Can you do that?" she asked.

"I'm afraid to go home," Charlie said.

"Don't worry honey, Mr. Sandberg *and I* are *both* going to help you. It will be alright," she said.

"That's hard to believe. He's a little weird," Charlie said to the phone, looking directly at Martin as she spoke.

"Oh honey, he's not *just* a *little* weird. He's *very* weird, but you have to be, a little odd, I guess, to practice what did we call it Marty? "Strange Law?' 'Scary Law?' Yes, I remember, we called it 'Supernatural Law. Yes, Marty is a lawyer specializing in 'Supernatural Law.'"

"I don't know how a lawyer's going to help me with this situation," Charlie said.

"He *saved* me," Annabelle said. "You'll see, you'll be free forever, and your ex will be gone and forgotten like he's supposed to be," Annabelle Feldman said.

The temperature in Martin's office suddenly began to drop.

"I'll do everything I can," Martin said, "One trip to Court and I will get him out of your life *forever.*"

When he said the word: "forever," Martin's phone lifted and levitated from its resting place on his desk, flew through the air and hit him in the forehead, knocking him and his chair back and into the bookshelves behind him. It caused various items (put there mostly for decoration) to fall on him.

MARTIN SANDBERG HELD A CLOTH TO HIS HEAD, NOW SOAKED RED FROM THE NEW CUT IN THE MIDDLE OF HIS FOREHEAD, caused by Charlene Moreno's "angry stalker Italian poltergeist."

"Delia, I thought you said *this* couldn't happen. You said you made this a *safe* place," Martin said to Delia. She was standing over him with gauze and alcohol. He was amazed that she had actually gotten out of her chair to come help.

He made a mental note that Delia would get up out of her chair if someone were bleeding, and maybe crying a little.

"I'm sorry, Mr. Sandberg, but you believe me *now,* right?" Charlie asked. Martin could tell that Charlie was not sorry, that the little demonstration of the phone spontaneously flying into his face served only to accentuate the fact that *this* was *indeed* happening to her. Also, Charlie wasn't skilled at hiding her emotions and enjoyed seeing Martin hit in the head by a floating phone.

"I always believed you," he said.

"I'm sorry you got hurt," she said, though Martin did not believe her.

"It's not your fault. 'Angry stalker Italian poltergeists' and such things are not supposed to be able to get into this office," Martin said, looking at Delia.

"Now Mr. Martin, you will understand that I have taken complete control of the situation, the space surrounding this place, everything obligatory, required, imperative *and* necessary. Be aware that right now, at this moment, you are especially *superlative,* you are safe, *we are all* sufficiently satisfactory, and *I have* taken care of the complication. *This* one got by me, slippery and slick, but *not* again. Nothing will harm you again. You are undeterred, appropriate, absolute, admirable, and *we* are *all* copacetic. *You* are assured and reassured," Delia said, forcibly taking his hand from his forehead, replacing the rag with an alcohol-soaked wad of gauze.

"Ok Delia. She likes reading a thesaurus for fun and practicing with new words," Martin said, looking at Charlene Moreno.

After giving him a look for the "thesaurus" comment, Delia held the back of his head with one hand and pushed the gauze into his forehead with the other. He found Delia's medical treatment to be disquieting and would (almost) prefer continuing to be smacked by Charlie Moreno's poltergeist.

"He might need stitches," Charlie said.

"Nonsense, child," Delia said. She watched as Delia removed her hand from Martin's now-scabbed-over forehead and gently pulled the gauze back to examine the wound.

"That looks incredible," Charlie said, eying the wound on Martin's forehead. "Like it's been healing for a few days," she said.

"The wonders of alcohol," Delia said to Charlie with a little wink.

As she left the room, Delia turned to Martin.

"Thesaurus?" she asked, then smiled at him. It was a tiny smile and only for a moment but it was one of her *special* smiles, explicitly made by Delia when she wanted to accentuate a point.

She must have decided that her employer needed further education.

"Oh no," Martin said, looking directly into Delia's face.

No one screamed, but Martin could hear someone screeching in his head. For only a tenth of a second, the world became inverted, negative, and the air smelled like it was on fire. Martin thought he was going to throw up.

"Delia," Martin said, "That's not fair. I asked you not to do that anymore."

"Fish gotta swim," Delia said, leaving Martin's office and closing the door behind her, still smiling.

"I've never seen anything like that," Charlie said, "Oh my, I have to go to the bathroom... I think I might be sick," she said.

"The bathroom's that way," Martin said, pointing in the direction of the bathroom, "but don't worry, it will pass."

SEVEN

SMITH V. STATE

MARTIN WAITED IMPATIENTLY IN ONE OF THE
INTERVIEW ROOMS AT THE PRISON. After finishing the
lengthy meeting with Charlene Moreno and Annabelle Hanson,
who arrived shortly after Martin was hit in the forehead by his
own phone, he had yet another appointment. This one was a
"house call."

Martin was exhausted, which for him was becoming a
common condition. Going to the prison to meet with any client
was Martin's least favorite activity as an attorney. The odor, a
mixture of sweat, human funk (un-showered humanity) cheap
disinfectant and floor wax always lingered with Martin long after
he had left the prison, always causing him to be in a depressed
mood for much of the day. Sitting, waiting, he wondered, (as he
had several times in the past) if it was possible for the people
working in such a place to sometimes forget that a lawyer was
there.

He wondered if the people working in the prison would
ever leave a lawyer trapped, or worse yet, just decided *not to
worry about it.*

Fears of being forgotten (and left in prison) always plagued
his visits, and he did his very best to refer prison clients to other
lawyers if it was possible.

Martin's evenings had been spent with the charismatic
young woman, reinforcing the walls of the strange, empty and
seemingly meaningless warehouse. He had no memory of
spending time and working with the woman but was tired just the
same. Exhausted, waiting, Martin knew he had done *something,*
only he couldn't remember what it was.

Delia had been insistent that Martin go to the prison and
visit a man named Theodore Smith. Martin didn't know what kind
of powers, gods, or voodoo that Theodore Smith employed to
cause such a reaction in Delia, but she was unequivocal that
Martin would be visiting Smith, assessing his case, and then doing
everything *in the realm of possibilities* to help him.

64

"You will utilize your legal skills to assist that man," she had said. Martin found that ignoring Delia on the matter was not going to be an option.

For Theodore Smith, legal assistance was *required.*

"Good morning, Mr. Smith," Martin said as casually as he could when witnessing what he assumed was his new client being ushered in by the prison guards. Theodore Smith was a man of thin build, Martin figured that he was maybe in his early 40's. He wore the usual orange scrubs which seemed uncommonly dingy, had neatly combed hair and looked to have what some might refer to as permanent dark bags under his eyes.

"You can take those off please," Martin said to the guard, referring to the obligatory handcuffs that Theodore Smith had been forced to wear.

"I could if I felt like it, Counselor," the guard said before exiting the room, smirking.

"It's alright," Theodore Smith said, holding his shackled hand out to shake Martin's hand. "Thank you for coming."

"No problem... Delia insisted," Martin said.

'Yeah, she's a sweetheart."

"A sweetheart, yes," Martin said. "So. What are you in for? I tried to look up your case in the database, but didn't find anything."

"You won't," he said, "unless you look in actual paper files or microfiche."

"Microfiche? Why's that?" Martin asked, failing to recognize *the only possible reason* Theodore Smith's records were *not* in electronic format.

"I've been here a while."

"Right. Delia said you want to file a petition to have your sentence commuted. Tell me about that."

"I have been here a *very* long time, I mean a very, very long time."

"I see. How long is 'very long?'"

"Mr. Sandberg, I've seen this prison change names twice, I saw the end of the inmate leasing system, I've seen construction and destruction of buildings, worked in the farm, the license plate factory, laundry, kitchen, everything, seen racism from segregation to radical tyranny, to the current state it is now... I've seen the construction of death row, and I've seen more people get stabbed by home-made implements, beaten, forced hangings, more singular and purposeful murders than probably any other person on earth," he said.

"That is a long time," Martin said, of course stating the obvious, considering the occupations Smith mentioned. "License plate factory?" Martin asked, "Are they *still* doing that?"

"Not anymore, not for *years. That's* what I'm trying to tell you."

"I see," Martin said, (but did not see) and the two men exchanged glances.

"No, I don't think you do," Theodore Smith said.

"Mr. Smith, why don't you start with the *first* question I asked you," Martin said, laying his legal pad on the table and writing the current date on it and the man's name.

"I'm here because I caused the death of a young woman. At the time, she was the daughter of a high-ranking government official. I was sentenced to what they so eloquently called 'life without the possibility of parole,' and back then, life meant *life.* Back then, when you got life without the possibility of parole, you didn't get a sentence and a few years later get paroled and it didn't mean twenty-five years to life, or anything resembling a period with an *expiration* date. Life meant you were here until the *end* of your life."

"Are we looking to re-open the case for a mistake in law, an illegal sentencing, or maybe some new evidence has surfaced? What do you think might be the grounds for getting you out of here?" Martin asked.

"I want you to file a motion, or some kind of petition, or *whatever.* I want you to ask the Court, Governor, *whoever* to *let me out.* I've had more than my fair share."

"I'm not sure it's up to you... I mean it's not up to you as to what constitutes you're 'fair share,' as you put it."

"I'm not sure that the Court understood the *ramifications* of a life sentence for me," he said. "For me, the punishment doesn't fit the crime. It doesn't fit," he said.

"Mr. Smith, again, I don't think it's up to you whether the sentence *fits,* whether you think it's too long, or appropriate, whatever," Martin said. He then watched as Theodore Smith ran a hand through his thick black hair, his other hand in tow due to the aforementioned obligatory handcuffs compelling his wrists to stay near one another.

"Mr. Sandberg, I'm told that you are aware of certain... *things.*"

Martin sighed.

"Unfortunately, these days, I feel like I'm aware of *everything.*"

"Then I can talk to you, I mean, really *talk* to you. I can tell you things, and you will remember them? You will understand?"

"Sure," Martin said, nodding his head.

"You won't forget our conversation the minute you leave my presence, right?" Theodore Smith asked.

"Oh," Martin said, somewhat annoyed with himself that he hadn't recognized Theodore Smith was asking whether or not he was snug and warm under the *blanket of ignorance.*

"I'm not like them," Martin said, "if that's what you're asking. I'm awake. Someone pulled off the covers, and I'm out in the cold, just like you are, apparently."

"That is a relief," Theodore Smith said.

Martin thought for a moment of asking who it was that told Theodore Smith about him. Does Delia know Smith personally? What does she have to do with anything?

He thought of asking Theodore Smith how it was that he knew Martin had *lost his place in line.* He thought of asking who told Smith that Martin *now* knew more than he ever cared to know, trapped in a perpetually untenable position.

"My back is against the wall," Martin said.

"It could be worse," Smith said.

Martin looked at him, looked at his clothing, his handcuffs. "Point taken."

The two men sat together in the prison interview room, sat together in a moment of uncomfortable silence. Theodore Smith stared at him before he finally spoke.

"I've been here since 1920, Mr. Sandberg," he said.

"I see," Martin said. Then he started to write on his legal pad.

Theodore Smith, out of extreme curiosity looked on as Martin wrote: *Life sentence for someone who doesn't age? Can't die? Is an immortal vampire?*

"I'm not a vampire," Theodore Smith said, smiling.

"Next, you're going to tell me vampires don't exist and how I'm the crazy one," Martin said.

"Don't be silly," Smith said back to him, still smiling.

Martin took a moment to try and do the math in his head. *If he was here when he was eighteen? Even so how long I wonder...*

"I see the wheels turning," Theodore Smith said, "Don't strain yourself, Mr. Sandberg. Before you take off your shoes so you can count on your fingers *and* toes, my appearance is that of a forty-year-old person or so. I appear the *same* as when I was put in here, ninety-eight years ago."

"You don't look a day over eighty-five," Martin said without smiling, the compulsive note-taker in him escaping and causing him to write sentences of little value on his legal pad. Theodore Smith observed in silence as Martin took notes.

"Okay, except for how long you've been here, I'm not going to ask you *how old* you *actually* are," Martin said.

"I'll tell you if you want," Theodore Smith said.

"No, *please*. I don't want to know. Nope," Martin insisted, raising a hand as he would if he was standing in the middle of the highway, intent on stopping traffic. "I'm also *not* going to ask you *what* you are."

Martin stared at him.

Smith stared back.

"I don't want to know that, either," Martin said.

Theodore Smith watched as Martin scratched the side of his head, questions lingering.

"Even if you can't help me, thanks for coming out to see me at least. It means a lot. The fact that you understand is of great relief, Mr. Sandberg. You don't know what it's like trying to tell someone *about myself*, and about this *situation.* "

"Maybe you do know," Smith said, after taking a second to consider.

"Let me guess. You tell them that you're not in the system, that there's a mistake. You say: '*hey take a look at me, I haven't aged,*'" Martin said.

"They either laugh at me, tell me I'm crazy... Once, I got the Warden to listen to me. He listened when I said that there was a problem with my sentence. I didn't tell him more than that, hoping being vague might *work*, maybe he'd remember, understand, and at least try to *find* my case."

"How would that help?" Martin asked.

"I don't know. I'm desperate, willing to try anything. Maybe if he found it on his own, counted on his fingers and toes like you were about to do, maybe talk with me about the time, itself. I could give him a little, just enough information for him to maybe consider doing something."

"That didn't work, did it?" Martin asked.

"I thought maybe he'd discover some truth, even a little of the truth and help me."

"How did that work out?" Martin asked, but he already knew.

"I'm still here."

"I see that. I'm asking how did your plan work out, of side-loading the fact that you're an immortal demon monster into his tiny brain?"

"I'm not a demon monster."

"You know what I mean."

"He said he was going to look on the computer but then never came back. The next time I saw him, it was as if we never had the conversation, like we had never spoken about it at all."

"A judge I know who recently lost *his* place in line called it a 'great cosmic inside-joke.' I guess if you aren't *in* on that 'inside joke,' people forgetting you, not knowing, not being aware, things like that are going to happen," Martin said.

"I can see you're not of *my* kind. Are you..." Smith started to ask, but Martin cut him off.

"No, no, I'm a regular person. I'm not a demon monster, either, except in the morning before I've had my coffee. I'm a person, you know, no horns, beaks, claws, scales, or tails. I lost my place in line." Martin said. He watched as Theodore Smith nodded.

"How does that feel?"

"That's an interesting question," Martin said, "you know how it feels like when you feel like you forgot to do something, but it's really important, but can't remember what it was?"

"Sure."

"It feels like that all the time. I feel like I'm lost when I'm in my living room, like when you leave the house, and you're halfway to work, but could swear you left the television on, the water running, a cake baking in the oven, and the front door not only unlocked, but wide open."

69

"Uneasy," Theodore Smith said.

"Nothing looks right. Nothing feels right."

"What happened to you?" Smith asked him.

"My wife and I tried to save our daughter. She was dying," Martin said and met Theodore Smith's concerned eyes.

"She's okay," Martin said.

"That's good."

"I guess you could say we tried to do some side-loading of ourselves. I don't think I get any of this," Martin said.

"I understand," Smith said.

"I think you do," Martin said, looking at him. Above the bags under them, Theodore Smith's eyes were kind and concerned.

"I'm with you, Mr. Sandberg. I've been trying every way possible to get someone to understand that this isn't *right.* I've tried hinting, giving half-truths, beating around the bush, every trick in the book. Folks either stare at me stupidly, *listening,* but *not hearing* what I'm telling them, not understanding, or they forget the moment the conversation is over. I once told someone my real age. The guy forgot moments after I told him."

"I suppose it might be only a small comfort to you, Mr. Smith, that I am 'part of the club' so to speak. I won't forget you."

"Do you think there's hope for me?" he asked.

"There is always hope. I won't give up if you don't. Do we have a deal?"

"I'm in."

"As to strategy, I'm going to have to think about that. A life sentence has different consequences *for you* than it would be for someone who ages, grows older."

"That's what I'm saying," Smith said.

"I have one question, though, from a purely mechanical point of view. You tell me you were sentenced to life *without the possibility* of parole, right?"

"Yes, the Judge obviously didn't understand *who* I am... or *what* I am."

"Even so, the *legal sentence* is life. If the Judgment of Guilt which was originally entered says what you've told me, what would be the difference between someone who did *not* age versus someone who would *die* in prison of old age?"

"Life doesn't mean *life,*" Smith said, "not for someone who is like me."

"But doesn't it?" Martin asked, "I know it sounds like semantics. Think about it for a moment. Life *does* mean *life,*" Martin said. "You *are* alive, are you not?"

"I fit that definition," Theodore Smith said.

"Heart beating, blood pumping, oxygen exchange?"

"The whole nine yards."

"Then, for so long as you are *alive,* you're supposed to be *here.* Isn't that the nature of the *Legal Sentence*?" Martin asked him.

He watched as Theodore Smith scratched his chin.

"Point taken," Smith said, his facial expression exposing to Martin that he was beginning to feel defeated.

"It's 'ipso facto.' You live, therefore you must be incarcerated," Martin said.

"There has to be an exception, some kind of loophole. Isn't there anything you can do?" Theodore Smith asked him.

"That's the beauty of the law. in almost every situation, there's *always* something that can be done. Like I said, though, I'll have to work on this one," Martin said.

The two spent a moment in silence, each considering what he had learned from the other.

"The irony here is that I've died a number of times while being here," Theodore Smith said, breaking the silence.

Martin looked at him, his eyes wide with excitement.

"Now that's a different story," he said, "go on."

"I've been stabbed a few times, beaten to death, I was even forcibly hanged once."

"How does that work?"

"For me, for *what* I am, I die for a little while, rigor mortis, the whole thing. Then I come back. Most of the time I wake up in the morgue. After I wake up, they all look at me as if nothing's happened."

"As the ignorant do," Martin said. "You actually die, heart stopped, all biological functions cease?"

"My heart stops. What do you mean by 'biological functions?'" Theodore Smith asked.

"Gastro-intestinal system, that oxygen exchange I was talking about, the things that define living."

Theodore Smith looked at him in silence.

71

"Never mind," Martin said. "Heart stops. I got it. Then you end up in the morgue for a while?"

"Yes, then they think I'm an inmate wandering around and they bring me back to population."

Smith watched as Martin furiously scribbled notes on his pad, curious as to what he was thinking. Martin looked up and saw.

"Life means life? If life means life, if you died, wouldn't your so-called 'debt to society' be paid? I think a valid legal argument can be made that if you died at least once, then you have served the life sentence ordered and are to be released because your sentence has been fulfilled."

"That sounds like it might be a strategy."

"We look at the sentence in its basic form: Life, without the possibility of parole. Once *the life* has ended, your obligation to the state has been fulfilled, has it not?"

"Sounds right," Smith said.

"Then that would be the argument, I think. At the moment, I can't think of any other angle. I can draft a petition along those lines. Should we try?" Martin asked.

"Yes please, Mr. Sandberg. I can't stand the thought of spending eternity in this place."

"Then let's get you out of here."

EIGHT

ARTIFACTS

MARTIN SANDBERG SAT AT HIS DESK, STARING AT THE WORK PILING UP, THE ANGRY GHOST STALKING CASE, THE IMMORTAL MAN IN PRISON, AND ESPECIALLY THE DAUNTING LIBRO DEL DIABLO ALWAYS INVADING HIS THOUGHTS. Martin wondered how he would read it, much less find a way to render it void. His daughter Emily's admonishment notwithstanding, Martin desperately wanted to help William, and if he could convince a judge, maybe William might be saved.

"Hey Marty!" Delia yelled from the front lobby.

"I see Cordozo walking up to the office," she said. From the front window, she could see Abraham Cordozo walking towards the office and knew a warning might be in order. "You want me to tell him you're not here?" she asked.

"Thanks, Delia, but he would know, anyway. Just send him back," Martin said and let out a groan.

"Go on back," Delia Hammond said to Abraham Cardozo, without looking up from filing her nails. She refused to look at him unless it was absolutely necessary.

"Thank you, Ms. Hammond," he said.

"Did we have an appointment today? I don't have you on my calendar," Martin said, standing up from his chair to shake hands with him.

"Mr. Sandberg, we have a standing appointment. It is anytime I feel the need to speak with you," Abraham Cardozo said with a smile.

Martin noticed that Abraham had walked in carrying a briefcase. The briefcase, in and of itself, to Martin, was a work of art. The briefcase was covered in soft leather, its buckles shiny and golden. It was no surprise to him that Cardozo would be carrying a fancy, expensive briefcase. He always wore suits worth thousands. His briefcase appeared to be in the same class as Cardozo's clothing.

"I'm swamped," Martin said while slumping back in his seat. Cardozo eyed the Libro Del Diablo as it sat innocently in the

73

center of his desk, pretending that it was just another bound volume of pages.

Martin watched as Abraham Cardozo, a man (seemingly) in his early sixties, with a moderate build, finely combed white hair, clean shaven, and in a finely pressed suit sat down in the chair in front of Martin's desk.

Martin watched as he gently placed the briefcase on the floor next to his chair.

"Still hard at work trying to break the contract?" Cardozo asked him, trying not to look at the book himself, but failing miserably as his eyes drifted directly to it.

"It won't let me make copies of its pages, and every time I read it, or try anyway, my head feels like it's going to explode."

"Well, good luck with it," Cardozo said, failing to suppress the smirk on his face.

"Yes, thank you. Can you please tell me what I can do for you?"

"In a moment, you and I are going to go into your conference room. Once there, I'm going to show you how to remove the southern facing wall to reveal a safe I've had installed."

Martin stared at him, frowning.

Abraham Cardozo smiled.

"When did you have a safe installed? I'm here every day. I haven't seen any construction."

"I had it installed during off hours so as not to disturb your work," he said, but Martin felt he was probably hiding something.

Abraham Cardozo was always hiding something.

"Mr. Cardozo, this is *my* office. If I wanted a safe installed in the southern wall of *my* conference room, I would have done it myself," Martin said.

"My company owns the building," Cardozo said.

"You own Eureka Management Partners?"

"Eureka Management is a subsidiary," Cardozo said.

"Barghest, LLC. owns Eureka? Is there anything you don't own?" Martin asked.

"I did not come here to discuss my company's assets."

"I didn't need a safe. I never take in enough money for it to be an issue and I go to the bank regularly. You can go ahead and take it back *out*," Martin said knowing that he installed the safe for his specific (and nefarious) purposes and it would not be removed

74

unless Abraham Cardozo wanted it removed. "Now, if there's nothing else," Martin said, standing from his chair to lead Cardozo out of his office.

"Mr. Sandberg, you know very well that the safe is not for you," Cardozo said, then watched as Martin slumped back into his seat, resigned that Cardozo might be there a while. Before we go into your conference room I need to ask you a question: do you know what an artifact is?"

"I guess," Martin said.

"The standard definition of an artifact describes an item that is sometimes of cultural or historical significance."

"And I'm to hold some of these historical items in my new safe for you?" Martin asked.

"You are."

"Mr. Cardozo, I know I'm indebted to you..."

"You are very indebted to me, Mr. Sandberg," Cardozo said, interrupting him.

"Nevertheless, I will not house stolen items in my office, not for anyone, not at any time."

"No, Martin, I would never ask you to do such a thing, and I apologize for giving you that impression," Cardozo said. "I do not engage in criminal activity, and would certainly never condone it."

"Why use my office? Surely there has to be a better place to store *expensive items of cultural significance.*"

"While in most cases, I would agree. However, that's not the case here due to the uniqueness of the items. The adage about keeping all of one's eggs in one basket holds true, pertaining to artifacts. The Board of Directors has now implemented a system for storing artifacts in various locations."

"One of them, being my office," Martin said.

"It is out of necessity that we keep artifacts separated, in separate locations, throughout the world. At one time, we did have them housed in a centralized, secure facility. For a great deal of time, this was a good system, a secure system..."

"You don't need to explain further," Martin said. "There's always someone trying to break a code, defeat a lock."

"And before our current system, that's what happened. Someone stole the entirety of our... *collection.*"

"How did you get the items back?" Martin asked.

"We haven't... yet. We are currently in the midst of relocation. The task has been costly, cumbersome, and quite frustrating. When we find items, we store them in one of our *new* locations."

"Like my office?" Martin repeated himself purposefully, annoyed and confused as to why Barghest, LLC. would choose to hide any item of great worth and significance in the wall of his law office.

"Martin, your office is an excellent location."

"But what about security?" he asked. "I'm not going to have security guards standing in my lobby."

"Of course not. You will not be disturbed, I assure you. The safe is biomechanical. There is no code or combination, no handprint, no iris scanner. It opens by way of identifying the person requesting entrance and will open only for an authorized user."

"Maybe I can live with that. I can pretend it's not there, and I don't need to worry about it," Martin said, believing that he would *not* be one of Barghest LLC.'s "authorized users."

Sadly, however, by the expression on Abraham Cardozo's face, Martin could see that this was not going to be the case.

"Mr. Cardozo, I am a lawyer, *not* a museum curator," Martin said.

"I'm not giving you a new job," Cardozo said, but that was precisely what he was doing in Martin's eyes if he was required to be responsible for items of worth belonging to someone else.

"Rest assured, the intrusion will be minimal," Cardozo said.

He watched as Martin sighed deeply and slumped further in his chair, defeated.

"So, what is it?" Martin asked.

Abraham Cardozo looked at Martin quizzically.

"The briefcase? You've obviously brought something in that briefcase to be put into my new museum. Is it some golden cup an Aztec king used to drink hot chocolate? A piece of some jewelry worn by a member of some royal family? What do you have in the briefcase, Mr. Cardozo?" Martin asked him.

"It's not what's *in* the briefcase, it's the briefcase itself," Cardozo said then put the briefcase on the desk in front of him.

Abraham Cardozo watched in horror as Martin Sandberg reached out to touch the briefcase.

"No, don't touch that," Cardozo said, almost yelling, pushing Martin's hand away as if Martin were a child going into the cookie jar. (Raising his voice was something that Martin had never seen him do, *ever.*)

"Why not?"

"Mr. Sandberg, as usual, you did not give me a chance to explain the true definition of 'artifact,'" Cardozo said, relieved that he had prevented Martin from touching the briefcase.

"Oh no," Martin said.

It had suddenly dawned on him what it was that was sitting on his desk.

Cardozo watched as Martin Sandberg suddenly turned pale, his face expressing a mixture of realization, surprise, and fear. Though he truly did try to resist, Cardozo could not help himself but display the tiniest of smiles at Martin Sandberg's reaction. These little moments, a facial expression of surprise and fear on anyone, primarily when he, Abraham Cardozo, was the cause of such emotion, were often the brightest spot of Cardozo's day.

"Why use the word *'artifact'* to describe these items?" Martin asked, his expression of fear changing to an expression of anger. "Everything you say always has a hidden meaning. You talk in riddles, innuendo, never completely giving me the whole truth. You should have started off being honest."

Martin tried unsuccessfully to stare him down.

"Martin, really," Cardozo protested, but Martin could see that Cardozo found entertainment value in the sudden panic Martin was feeling.

"I mean it. You should've started off explaining to me that your Board of Directors has decided, in its infinite wisdom, to house *cursed objects* in a safe and in *my* law office. You should've started out by calling them 'haunted objects,' or, for that matter, call them items that are created to ruin a person's life, trick people, maim people, kill people, cheat, destroy souls. No way. Nope. You have to be joking."

"I could have started off calling them 'cursed objects.' The term 'artifact' does not do justice to what these items are. They are so much more," Cardozo said.

"These things are a blight, they are the scourge of humanity," Martin said.

"Oh, come now, be serious," Cardozo said, no longer smiling at Martin's discontent.

"Let me guess, you've got a piggy bank that gives the owner as much money as he wants, but then he gets arrested by the IRS or something. Or maybe you've got a magic cup that always quenches thirst, but makes the owner have to pee all day. I bet you have a genie in a bottle which always grants wishes the wrong way like if someone wished for long life, the genie would turn them into a redwood tree or something," Martin said, feeling his heart beat faster, almost raising his voice at Cardozo. "There is no way you're housing devil objects in *my* law office," Martin said, defiantly.

"You're overreacting," Cardozo said.

"Am I, Cardozo? Don't these things call out to you, play with your mind, force a person to use them?"

"Hence, the safe. Once an item is in our *specially prepared* safe, you can go about your day."

"The safe keeps the objects from calling out to people?"

"It has been specially prepared," Cardozo said.

"Then why do I need to have access or *authorization* as you put it, to open this Pandora's box you are shoving down my throat?"

"Because, Martin, I might need your services in connection with an object."

"I knew it," Martin said. "You *are* making me a curator. Why don't I just put up a sign that instead of saying 'Law Office of Martin Sandberg,' says: 'Sandberg's Museum of crazy, cursed, trip-you-down-the-stairs devil-objects?'"

"You're being melodramatic," Cardozo said. "Myself or someone in my stead will put the objects in the safe for you. Besides, only objects which have *minimal* influence will be brought in. It's not like I'm going to put the cursed diamond in there or that ancient box with ghosts flying out of it or something. If you don't touch the objects and you leave them alone, everything will be fine.

"How am I supposed to deal with these things if I can't touch them?"

"I'll do the touching."

"What if I wear gloves or something?" Martin asked him.

"Yes, of course, Mr. Sandberg, a pair of gloves will keep you from falling victim to the artifacts," Cardozo said.

"The sarcasm is unnecessary," Martin said, "you came to me, remember? Now, how do I hold these things?"

"Emotional maturity, spiritual fortitude. I can mentally prepare myself, just so long as I know what it is I am dealing with. Martin, you must not touch any object brought here for storage."

"You say you can mentally prepare yourself so long as you know what it is? What if you thought this was just another briefcase?" Martin asked.

"I have been caught by the influence of these things before. Breaking free was... costly. Let's go to the conference room, and I'll show you the safe. Let's get to it now, shall we?"

"No, Mr. Cardozo. It's bad enough that I have this Devil-Book in my life. I leave it here on the desk then go home after work, and it's waiting for me on my kitchen table. No, you can't do this," Martin said.

Martin Sandberg watched as Abraham Cardozo's facial expression went from calm to angry. His voice changed, and he spoke barely above a whisper.

"When your wife *ripped a hole in reality*, having no idea what she was doing, and you went through? That should have been the *end* of *all* of you. When you went through to get your daughter, do you remember what happened to you?"

Cardozo wasn't speaking anymore, so much as he was growling.

"Yes," Martin said, barely above a whisper.

"I don't think you do. You were lost, kicked, beaten. Do you remember? Do you remember, Martin Sandberg?"

"Yes."

"There is no way you would have come out *without me*," Cardozo said, his teeth gritted together, angry. "You and your precious little Emily would have been trapped there forever without me. You should still be there. I was supposed to leave you, and I chose to pull you both out. It's been ages since I've done something so stupid."

Martin looked at him without saying anything. He was unable to look away.

"I paid for that indiscretion. You *owe* me, and you have not even begun to pay me back."

"I'm sorry," Martin said, "I understand."

"No, sir, you do not," Cardozo said, eyes ablaze with anger. "I bring people in, Mr. Sandberg. I drag them, kicking, screaming, begging. I bring them to hell, Mr. Sandberg, *not* the other way around."

"I'm sorry. I didn't mean to upset you," Martin said.

"What I did for you? Unheard of. I *paid* dearly. I'm still paying, Mr. Sandberg. Now *you* must pay *me*."

Cardozo took a breath and looked at him.

"These were the choices you *and* I *both* made. We must now abide by them, both of us. When I request your services, you don't tell me no."

"I'll watch over your things. I'm sorry," Martin said, though he was much more afraid than sorry. He watched as Cardozo's face relaxed as he took in another deep breath, regained composure.

"Martin, please allow me to introduce you to Connor's briefcase," Cardozo said, holding up the briefcase. "As long as you don't touch it or *allow yourself* to consider what it might do for you, you won't be called to it."

"What happens if I think about using it, or take it out of the safe?"

"First you will suffer, and then you will die, Mr. Sandberg. It is the same with most artifacts."

"Suffer and die," Martin said, repeating him.

"The lawyers who have had the misfortune of owning this briefcase win all of their cases," Cardozo said.

"That doesn't sound so bad," Martin said.

"They get verdicts worth millions of dollars, they represent the richest people, judges, and juries always rule in their favor."

"What's the catch?"

"In this case, everyone that owns the briefcase ends up having a better career practicing law than they could've ever imagined, while, of course, their private lives and everything around them crumbles," Cardozo said. "The last man to own this briefcase became a millionaire almost overnight. Clients with lawsuits worth millions came to him and insisted that *he* be the one to represent them. Celebrities, industrialists, politicians, all wanted him to represent them in their legal matters. At the same time, however, family members became sick. Long-time friends died from accidental, but suspicious circumstances. For the last man who owned the briefcase, his house burned down, and he ended up killing himself.

"That's horrible," Martin said.

"As always, Mr. Sandberg, you have a flair for the obvious. It *is* horrible, but it is the *law* of *exchange.* If one uses extraneous means to compel the forces of chance and probability for a specific positive result, what you would commonly refer to as 'good luck,' for example, there must be an equal exchange of what you might call 'bad luck' for the universe to remain balanced. The specialists working on these particular items have traced the original owner of the briefcase to a small-town attorney who owned it a long time ago."

"He made a big? Had lots of money and cars and whatever and then stepped in front of a bus?" Martin asked, only half-joking.

"No, quite the contrary. The lawyer's daughter gave the briefcase to him as a Father's-day present. She loved her father dearly, had saved her money to purchase it for him. Unknown to her, the lawyer's daughter had certain *gifts.* As you can imagine, the briefcase was precious to the lawyer, who thought of her every time he carried his things in it. He never went anywhere without it. The lawyer and his family lived modest lives. He didn't have a lot of money, Mr. Sandberg, like you, he couldn't get out of his own way to be more successful than simply making his bills and maintaining that modest lifestyle. There was a hitch for this lawyer, though."

"There always is," Martin said.

"The lawyer had a penchant for forgetfulness. On occasion, the lawyer would be standing in the courthouse, holding his 'Father's-day briefcase' and realize he had forgotten paperwork he desperately needed. He would find himself panicking, remembering he had left his briefs, law, things he needed for the case on his desk instead of bringing it with him to court. Clearly remembering he had left these items behind, he could close his eyes, think of what he had forgotten, reach into his briefcase and miraculously, his forgotten things would be in the briefcase waiting for him. Quite literally, he never had to bring his files, briefs, anything to court. Anything he needed would always be waiting for him in the briefcase."

"What about the million-dollar cases? What about the fame and fortune?"

"This particular lawyer *refused* to take those cases no matter how much or who was involved. He was an idiot 'do-gooder, took only cases where he thought he could help someone. He did not make a lot of money. Sometimes he was barely able to pay his bills. This didn't bother him, though. He felt that he was helping others and to him, that was worth more than anything else..."

Cardozo stopped for a moment to eye Martin, gauge his reaction.

"You see, Martin, in most cases the *original owner* of an artifact is *not* cursed by the object per se. The object is converted solely for that first individual. Those who become victims of an artifact are the hapless individuals who end up owning the artifact *after* the original owner. The original owner of Connor's briefcase had a long career. He prospered not in money, but in helping others.

The lawyers that owned the briefcase after him, ones who purchased it at a secondhand store, a garage sale, estate sale? Those poor souls are the ones who have been its victims. Now that we have it, we can take it out of circulation and prevent anyone else from becoming a victim. It's important to do that."

"We get it out of circulation, store it in the wall of my conference room," Martin said, a statement rather than a question.

"To prevent others from being victimized. Something you should know, Martin, is that the more an artifact is used, the more powerful it becomes. You were correct when you said that these items are a blight on humanity," Cardozo said.

"If I leave it alone, just leave it in the safe, I'll be okay?" Martin asked, "it won't call out to me, mess with my head?"

"If you leave it closed, sealed, and if you remain mindful, it won't affect you."

Abraham Cardozo looked at him and could tell Martin was still uncertain.

"You must know that I would not house dark and powerful objects in a safe in the wall of your law office if I didn't know for sure that you, Martin, have the emotional fortitude to refrain from using them. Contrary to my earlier scorn, I do believe in your willpower and strength of character. I know you see keeping these objects here as some sort of punishment, but it is quite the contrary. It is a compliment that the Board of Directors and I feel secure in keeping these items here," Abraham Cardozo said.

To Martin, however, the tone Cardozo used made him feel that Cardozo's feelings were opposite. He had been uncertain before, but Martin was beginning to think that Abraham Cardozo hated him.

NINE

MORENO V. SCALFANI

MOTION TO DISMISS

CHARLIE MORENO SAT AT COUNSEL TABLE NEXT TO HER ATTORNEY, WHO SHE THOUGHT WAS FIDGETING A LITTLE TOO MUCH. She sat still. The room was much colder than it had to be, the effect of tall hairy men in business suits deciding the optimum temperature for a courtroom. She looked around, listened to the sound of the air conditioning as they waited for the judge to arrive. Aside from the clerk and *that* bailiff with a mustache standing in the corner, the only people in the room was her, the other lawyer, and Martin.

"I still don't understand this," she said.

"I can't remember if I explained it to you. I thought we talked about it. Did we?" Martin asked.

"Yes, but I still don't understand what today is about."

"Some of these procedures can be very confusing."

"It's all right. If you don't mind, can you tell me again what this hearing is?" she asked.

"The other lawyer, his name is Robert Murdoch. Somebody hired him, I don't know, the family, someone to represents the interests of the opposition."

"What?"

"He represents the other side," Martin said.

"The lawyer represents who?" she asked.

Martin sighed.

"I think your dead angry stalker ex-boyfriend found a way to hire a lawyer and that lawyer, Mr. Murdoch, is here today on a motion to dismiss our Petition for Injunction for Protection Against Domestic Violence."

"Tony hired him? How did he do that?"

"Maybe his family?"

"No, Mr. Sandberg. The family wouldn't hire an attorney. The family has been helping me through this."

"Someone must've hired him," Martin said.

84

It only took a moment for Martin to realize that the "legal-speak" he often used, was probably very confusing to everyone who was not an attorney. Martin made a mental note, one he had made several times in the past and had forgotten, to speak in plain terms for his clients to understand him.

Together, they listened to the hum of the air conditioning for a few seconds. Martin knew that she was still confused. He was as well.

"Hey Bobby," Martin said, "who paid you?"

Robert Murdoch was in the middle of chewing off the nail of his middle finger, when Martin interrupted the activity, reminding him of where he was and what they were about to do. Snapping to attention, Robert Murdoch looked at Martin with a stunned and surprised expression.

"The respondent," Martin said, "he's dead. Usually, those people, in general, have cash flow issues. I'm curious as to who retained your services for this proceeding."

"That's privileged," Robert Murdoch said, the expression on his face still one of surprise, but never wavering as he pulled the top part of his fingernail off.

"No, it isn't," Martin said.

"Yes, it is."

"Bobby, it's not."

"It's not?"

"No. The identity of the source of funding for any litigation is always discoverable," Martin said.

"Is that true?" Murdoch asked him.

"For Pete's sake, Bobby."

"Fine. The deceased ex-boyfriend did *not* hire me, *obviously.* I didn't go to purgatory and have him sign a retainer if that's what you think," Robert Murdoch said, although I'm told that's not beyond the realm of..."

"Bobby," Martin said, interrupting him, hoping to get an answer before the judge arrived.

"Whatever. His secretary hired me. I never really met her though, just talked to her on the phone. We used email, and she direct deposited my fee."

"Tony had a secretary?"

"She said she did some work for him now and then, was related to a cousin or something."

85

"Never saw her in person at all?"

"Nope. She wasn't specific, but I think she's out of the country," Robert Murdoch said.

"See, that wasn't so hard," Martin said.

"Don't be smug, Sandberg," Robert Murdoch said.

Martin Sandberg sat back in his chair, satisfied, another mystery solved. He put his hands behind his head and leaned back.

He glanced at Charlie Moreno. She appeared confused. Martin believed she was trying to figure out who the secretary was. She seemed more nervous.

"What's the matter?"

"Tony never had a secretary," she said.

"Did he have cousins?"

"Lots."

"You did tell me that the family was on *your* side, that they knew what he did to you. Maybe it was someone just trying to preserve Tony's interests, whatever those may be."

"I suppose you're right," she said. He watched as she took in a deep breath and tried to calm herself. "Maybe it was his aunt. She was always a little flaky," Charlie said.

"All rise," Laszlo the bailiff said. Martin looked into his client's eyes and nodded to her, ignoring Laszlo as he did his "court in session" routine, same as he had a thousand times before.

She nodded back to him, signaling that she was all right. Martin watched as Judge Markowitz sauntered across the floor to his big, plush chair and plopped himself into it.

"I just love Injunction Court. Okay, let the perjury begin. Mr. Murdoch, it's your motion," Judge Markowitz said.

"Thank, you, Your Honor," he said, "may it please the Court, counsel. I have filed a motion to dismiss in this matter..."

Markowitz rolled his eyes, but Martin figured he was the only one who saw. Murdoch was reading his carefully prepared script, an activity that annoyed Markowitz, like most judges. Markowitz had once commented that it wasn't "time for a bedtime story," and that a lawyer "shouldn't read to him" as if it was.

"I've read your motion," Markowitz said, interrupting him, "but frankly I find it lacking in an explanation as to why Miss Moreno's Petition should be dismissed. You say that this Court does not have jurisdiction."

"That's correct, Judge."

"But your analysis, or lack thereof, fails to explain that *lack* of jurisdiction."

"My apologies Your Honor. To put it concisely, and I can't believe that I'm saying this, the Petition filed by Mr. Sandberg seeks a restraining order against a deceased individual."

"And?"

"And..." They watched as Robert Murdoch stammered a little. "That's just not how things are done," he said.

Judge Andrew Markowitz looked down his nose through his little glasses at Robert Murdoch, who stood at the podium as if he was standing in a long line for the bathroom after downing a two liter bottle of soda.

Markowitz looked at Martin and the two exchanged glances at one another.

"Son, do you still have your place in line?" Markowitz asked him.

"Sir?"

"*Your place in line,* the thing that keeps you stable and stuck in your very own place in the universe and reality. Do you still have that?"

The expression on Robert Murdoch's face was not unlike the face he might have made after escaping a cardboard box only to find out that he had been drugged and mailed to some far away nation.

"Never mind," Markowitz said.

A moment of silence passed as Murdoch, Sandberg, and Markowitz each took turns looking at one another as if they were in some old Western wondering who was going to shoot first.

"The statute does not permit this type of action," Murdoch said.

"It doesn't?" Markowitz asked, "enlighten me, Mr. Murdoch."

"Your Honor, the Petition seeks injunctive relief against a person who is 6 feet underground."

They watched as Markowitz sighed, rubbed his temples. The span from argument to headache was becoming shorter, yet he persevered.

"Mr. Sandberg?"

"Yes, Judge. Mr. Murdoch is correct in that we set forth a restraining order against my client's deceased ex-boyfriend or any other *hostile anachronistic entity* which has been recently committing acts of violence against my client."

"Well, there you have it," Markowitz said.

"Your Honor?"

"Done, and done."

"Judge Markowitz, at no time while I was in law school did any professor mention filing a case against a ghost or whatever it is that Mr. Sandberg just said, 'hostile anachronistic spirit...'"

"Entity," Martin said.

"What?"

"Hostile anachronistic entity," Martin said.

" I don't care what you call *them* Sandberg. You can't sue ghosts."

"Mr. Sandberg, your opposition poses an interesting legal issue."

"Judge?"

"I don't suppose you have a copy of the statute handy," Judge Markowitz asked Martin, knowing from experience that Martin always had his statute book with him.

"Of course, Your Honor," Martin said.

"Mr. Murdoch?"

"I didn't think I needed to bring it," he said.

"Mr. Sandberg, please provide your statute book to Mr. Murdoch so we may resolve this very intriguing legal issue as to whether a Court has Jurisdiction over a non-living respondent for the purposes of issuing of an Injunction for Protection Against Domestic Violence," Judge Markowitz said.

Robert Murdoch might have thought that Judge Markowitz was joking except for the pained expression on the old man's face.

They waited in silence, (made tense because Markowitz seemed genuinely aggravated) as Robert Murdoch flipped through the pages. Both Robert Murdoch and Martin knew that Judge Markowitz had a dog-eared copy at the bench. Compelling Murdoch to look for the rule himself was Markowitz being overly dramatic, as usual, when he was trying to make a point.

"Okay, here," Murdoch said.

"Go on," Markowitz said.

"Domestic violence means any assault, aggravated assault, battery, aggravated battery, sexual assault, sexual battery, stalking...."

"Yes, yes, Mr. Murdoch, we *know* the definition of Domestic Violence," Markowitz said, "move on."

"Yes, Your Honor... For the definition of 'domestic,' that means spouses, former spouses, persons related by blood or marriage, persons were presently residing together as if a family or who have resided together in the past as a family, and persons who are parents of a child in common, regardless of whether they've been married.

With the exception, of persons who share a child in common, the family or household members must be currently residing or have in the past resided together in the same single dwelling unit."

"Let's address that," Markowitz said, "Miss Moreno, please stand and raise your right hand..."

Martin watched as Judge Markowitz swore her in. She made a visible effort to keep herself from shaking.

"Now that you've been sworn, I'm going to ask you a couple of questions and give the attorneys an opportunity to ask you some questions as well. You've alleged Domestic Violence," Markowitz said.

"Yes," Charlie said, her voice barely above a whisper.

"Before we get to that, can you please tell me: did you live with your, what was it? Ex-boyfriend or ex-spouse?"

"We weren't married."

"Boyfriend then?"

"Yes, sir."

"Did you live with him?"

"Yes."

"And the last time something happened to you that you would classify as an act of violence when was that?"

"Yesterday."

When Charlie Moreno said 'yesterday,' Markowitz first looked at Murdoch, then looked at Martin. Though he was skilled at keeping stoic, Markowitz's emotional response was conspicuous.

"What happened yesterday?" Markowitz asked her.

"I woke up in the middle of the night."

"And?"

"My bed was on fire," she said.

A moment of silence, which Martin would classify as a deafening moment of silence, passed between the people in the courtroom as everyone looked into Charlie Moreno's eyes, glassy, afraid, but not crying.

"Do you have a good faith belief that you are currently living with someone or *something* that is currently attempting to do you harm?" Markowitz asked her, breaking the silence.

"Yes, sir."

"Mr. Murdoch, any questions based solely upon the courts questions?"

"No, Your Honor."

"Mr. Sandberg?"

"No questions, Your Honor."

"Gentlemen, we have the household member requirement met, do we not? Miss Moreno lived with her boyfriend and is currently living with someone or something that set her bed on fire while she was sleeping in it... and a whole host of other horrible things if I've read her affidavit correctly... What else, Mr. Murdoch?"

"Judge?"

"The statute, Mr. Murdoch."

"Sorry... The statute says any person who is the victim of Domestic Violence or has reasonable cause to believe he or she is in imminent danger of becoming the Victim of any act of Domestic Violence, has standing in the Circuit Court to file a sworn Petition for Injunction for Protection against Domestic Violence..."

"So far, the threshold requirements have been met," Markowitz said.

"One second... Okay, it says a person's right to petition shall not be affected by the person having left the residence... The case can be brought by family or household members. The cause of action does not require either party be represented by counsel... Nothing herein affects the title to any real estate, and the petition can be filed in the circuit where the petitioner currently or temporarily resides, where the respondent resides, or where the Domestic Violence occurred. There is no minimum requirement of residency to Petition for an Injunction for Protection..."

"Is there anything else?" Markowitz asked.

"No, except no bond is required for the entry of the order," Murdoch said.

"Mr. Murdoch, how are we so far?"

"The Petition was sworn, residency has been established."

"Correct. While one could argue residence is an issue based upon the residence of the respondent, it is *not* an issue as it pertains to the *Petitioner*, Miss Moreno, here. Her address is on the Petition, and clearly, she resides within the circuit."

A few seconds of silence passed in the courtroom. All parties were looking at Robert Murdoch who suddenly made a realization.

Murdoch's facial expression was priceless in Judge Markowitz's opinion. One might call Robert Murdoch's sudden understanding, sudden realization, an "epiphany."

"You've got to be kidding me," Robert Murdoch said, gently setting Martin Sandberg's statute book on the council table in front of him.

"Please look at my face, Mr. Murdoch. While some have called me cold and emotionless, you can see that I find absolutely nothing humorous about all this."

Charlie Moreno looked at Robert Murdoch, who appeared puzzled and confused. She then looked at Martin, who was relaxed and comfortable. Her eyes went to Judge Markowitz.

He looked at her and could see her confusion.

"Miss Moreno, you appear puzzled. Though it is not within my province to give legal advice or explain the law to any litigant, quite frankly it's the opposite, I'll explain exactly what's happening here."

"Thank you, sir."

"The law is a system of 'no's' and 'thou shall not' types of rules. This is something you inherently know. For example, Miss Moreno, there is no law anywhere that says you may not wear a blue shirt while in a courtroom," he said, pointing out that Charlie was wearing a blue shirt. Martin settled into his chair. It was going to be a classic Markowitz dissertation.

"Since there is no law anywhere on any books that says you may *not* wear a blue shirt in a courtroom, right now, at this very moment, are you allowed to wear that blue shirt?"

"Sure."

"And, Miss Moreno, by wearing that blue shirt, are you committing a crime or some civil infraction?"

"No," she said, giving a smile.

"Taking it one step further, if a young and inexperienced attorney, say, someone like Mr. Murdoch were to file a charge against you for wearing that blue shirt, would he prevail?"

"You mean win because nothing is saying I can't?"

"Correct."

"No, he couldn't."

"No, he would not prevail because there is no law which says that wearing a blue shirt in my courtroom is illegal. This leads to why Mr. Murdoch blurted out, unprofessionally I might add, the words: 'you have to be kidding me.' He has made a realization. You see, the statute is very specific about the requirements which must be in existence, prior to a court issuing a restraining order."

"Yes," she said, her face indicating that she was still confused, but also still giving a smile.

"There is a venue requirement, there is a requirement of violence, imminent danger, or a rational fear, and the requirement, in your case, that you and the perpetrator either reside in the same household or have in the past. The statue would also apply if you were married, or had a child in common, but we don't have those things here, and they are not needed."

"Yes sir," she said, eyes wide.

"You see Miss Moreno, there is no requirement, listed anywhere in the statute, or anywhere for that matter, that, for you, the survivor of Domestic Violence, to obtain an Injunction for Protection against your abuser, that the abuser must be *alive*," Markowitz said.

They watched as Robert Murdoch slumped into his seat.

"I won't fault Mr. Murdoch for making the logical assumption that the respondent must be alive, but I would respectfully request that if he knows of any statute, any precedent, ordinance, administrative code, or piece of legislation written on a fast food napkin that states that you are not permitted to obtain an Injunction for Protection against Domestic Violence against your abuser who is now deceased, please produce it."

They turned to Robert Murdoch, who shrugged his shoulders. It was clear that he had enough.

"I'm sorry I spoke out of turn," Murdoch said.

"What? When you said the words: 'you've got to be kidding me?' Mr. Murdoch, think nothing of it. When I came to the same realization as it pertains to some of the work I now do, I said things which were much worse."

"Do you think that the legislature did that on purpose?" Murdoch asked.

"What? Purposefully *leave out* the requirement that the respondent be alive in order to obtain a Restraining Order?" Markowitz asked.

"Yes."

"I don't know, Mr. Murdoch, but the statutes are very specific. You will find that very little is written in them which not on purpose."

"I'll prepare the order," Martin said, as it was a matter of course for the attorney who prevailed in any motion to be the one to draft the order and present it to the judge for signature.

"That's okay, Martin. I'll do it. It's the least I could do," Robert Murdoch said, meeting the eyes of Martin Sandberg's client. While he would not apologize for doing his job, the eye contact between the two of them was Murdoch's acknowledgment.

"Court adjourned," Markowitz said, then walked out of the courtroom.

"I don't understand," Charlie Moreno said, "what just happened."

"The judge just denied their motion to dismiss. Your injunction stands and is still in full force and effect, at least for the time being. Now comes the hard part," he said.

"The hard part?" she asked.

"We have to serve process."

TEN

BARGHEST, L.L.C. V BLACK FLAGG, INC.

ABRAHAM CARDOZO, VP OF "SPECIAL PROJECTS FOR BARGHEST, LLC." SAT ALONE ON THE PARK BENCH, a brown bag of birdseed in his lap. Taking a moment (or a few) to self-reflect in the park while tossing birdseed on the ground was an (almost) daily ritual for him.

He watched as a man who appeared to be his own age, wearing a modest grey suit sat down next to him, pulled his bag of seed from his jacket pocket and joined him. The man in the grey suit had three finely-dressed men with him, complete with the mirrored sunglasses, the earpieces, and bulges under their sport-coats where their firearms were holstered. They followed behind the man in the grey suit, faces intense as they scanned the area around their charge. Cardozo saw the three security men and wondered: besides the three he could see, how many were scattered throughout the region, presence unknown, searching for possible danger?

The two older men sat on the park bench in silence. They appeared to be two civilized older gentlemen enjoying a day in the park. In reality, they were both something very much different.

"Mr. Marcus Whiteacre, Chair of Internal Auditing of Black Flagg, Incorporated, what brings you to *my* park bench on such a pleasant day?" Abraham Cardozo asked him.

"It seemed like such a waste to spend the whole day indoors," Marcus Whiteacre said.

"Tell me, Marcus, what does the 'Chair of Internal Auditing' actually do at your company?" Abraham asked him.

"Aside from sluffing off poorly-made jokes at my expense, you know, because of the acronym 'CIA,' it is my job to make sure everyone else is doing his or her job."

"Sneaking around and getting into everyone else's business, with your job to be the 'CIA' of your company? I don't envy your new position," Cardozo said.

"My predecessor was needed *elsewhere*," Marcus said, 'I certainly didn't ask for the position or the problematic obligations it entails."

"The position suits your skill set, Marcus," Cardozo said. He meant it as an insult.

"I suppose," Marcus said, not noticing the jab.

There was an uncomfortable, palpable silence between the two. Finally, it was Cardozo who spoke and broke the moment of silence that lasted just a bit too long.

"Unlike myself, *you* did not come here to feed the birds," Cardozo said.

Marcus nodded. The statement was true. He had come to talk, but the subjects were complicated and challenging, and Abraham Cardozo's temper was unmanageable. It wasn't that Marcus was afraid of him, it was that should something set him off, it would be impossible to have a conversation with him, and Marcus hated wasting time.

"Do we need to discuss the William Donnelly problem?" Cardozo asked.

"It's not a problem, *yet*. Did you know William Donnelly calls the contract a 'Devil-Book,'" Marcus said, "of all things."

"Of all things," Cardozo said. Both men spent a moment in deep thought on the same subject: the impending doom of William Donnelly.

"He'll be overcome by that one-armed monstrosity fairly soon," Marcus said.

"Yes, and we *have several* new hosts ready and willing to take his place," Cardozo said. He watched as Whiteacre appeared pensive, despondent.

"There's no other place to put *him*, is there?" Whiteacre asked.

Cardozo suddenly turned towards Whiteacre, his face intent.

"Do I need to remind you of the entire *realms* he's destroyed? It makes me physically ill to think of the backbreaking labor, the resources, only to watch his anger destroy everything... Whole *realms*, Marcus. The contract is the only way to keep him contained."

"I know, I know..." Marcus agreed, despondent.

"Abraham, is the continuing conundrum of this *monster* the only thing we agree upon?"

"We agree on much more, don't fool yourself. Even I see the *indecency*, the *cruelty* in housing that beast with someone only to watch him destroy, devour body and soul," Marcus said.

"I take a specific amount of pity on William Donnelly," Whiteacre said, "as well as pity on all others that have had the misfortune to sign name to the 'Devil-book,' and have been bound by contract, forced to hold him, at least until he tears them apart..."

"I lean on the legal doctrine of *caveat emptor* to keep myself from feeling sorry," Marcus said.

"The doctrine of 'buyer beware?'" Abraham Cardozo asked, incredulous.

Whiteacre looked away.

"Now it's *you* fooling yourself, Marcus. No one who signs the book has any *real idea* of what is going to happen," Cardozo said.

"William Donnelly signed the book, and I have provided what he wanted, a great job, lots of money, anything he wants for as long as he can survive. That's the deal," Whiteacre said.

"Until William Donnelly is ripped apart, then it is my turn, and I find someone to sign and give them the life he or she wants... I'm fully aware of our alternating yet *shared* continued responsibility."

"I wish you, and I shared *ideology* as well," Marcus said. He watched as Cardozo looked away from him, scoffing.

"Marcus, we are *aware* of your collaborative's activities," Cardozo said to him, attempting (and failing) *not* to sound threatening. He nonchalantly threw a few seeds in front of himself and watched as the birds pecked.

"My people are aware of *your* group's machinations as well," Whiteacre said dryly.

"Though we are still the majority, I will *not* be so bold as to predict an outcome," Cardozo said.

"Of course, *nor will I...*" Whiteacre drifted off, lost in thought for a moment before speaking again.

"Don't you find the continued efforts taxing?" he said.

"An understatement," Cardozo agreed.

"I lay the pieces in place, use incentives, yet none of these *people* seem to do what is needed. The monotony, the tediousness, it's overbearing."

"That's the way people *are*, Marcus. They make their own decisions, often unexpected," Cardozo said.

He watched as Marcus Whiteacre sighed in frustration.

"It can be a matter of *utter* importance... It makes no difference. They go east when I want them to go west. It's infuriating. Even a *rodent* knows enough to go to the strawberry when it's laid in front of him. People these days go in the other direction and then say, 'oh crackers, everything's in shambles, I'm lost. Poor me. What do I do now?'" Marcus Whiteacre said, a mocking statement more than a question. His tone was sarcastic, but clearly, he was angry.

"Though I don't agree with your ideology, Marcus, I certainly *understand* it. We lay a perfect road for them, and they choose to wander lost in the woods. We sometimes even take the time to *tell them* that it's for their own benefit, but no one seems to be listening. It's frustrating."

"Maddening."

"I will say, recruiting Nadine Caldwell to work for you was brilliant. Does she have any idea *who* she's working for? Does she have any idea *what it is* she's pregnant with?" Cardozo asked, already knowing the answer to his question.

"It would appear not," Marcus said, "but she's still on board."

"Be sure to follow the law, Marcus."

"Don't lecture me. Nadine Caldwell makes *her own* decisions."

"I'm sorry how that sounded, Marcus," Cardozo said. Marcus nodded but was still mad. "The pregnancy. Does she know?" Cardozo asked.

"What? That her uterus houses someone, some*thing* none of us have ever seen? Something, someone who can *forever* change the universe for *everyone*? Of course not. We've worked very hard prevent Nadine Caldwell from *hearing* her. It's taken all our resources to keep her *disconnected*. I wouldn't want to risk disturbing the fact that she's listening to *us*."

"Her husband knows. He's been talking to it... He's been talking to her," Cardozo said. The statement wasn't meant to enlighten. Cardozo knew that Marcus had as much information on the subject as he did. Both Marcus and Abraham were aware that Caldwell was *talking* to his wife's *pregnancy.*

"Phillip Caldwell is a dolt," Marcus said.

Cardozo did not argue.

"His wife, however? She *is* brilliant."

"Yes."

The men fell silent for a moment, realizing that notwithstanding the conclusion that Nadine Caldwell was a genius, both *actually did* agree on more subjects than either dared to admit.

"You were correct earlier, Abraham. I did not come here, disturb your little ritual of bird-feeding just because I wanted to sit in the park," Whiteacre said.

"Then enlighten me so I can continue on with the rest of my day."

"We know about Martin Sandberg. He is, after all, representing William Donnelly," Marcus said, then suddenly began to smile.

The big smile was unusual. Only the two of them were aware of the inside joke, of Martin Sandberg thinking it was possible to void the contract. He couldn't help but start laughing.

"Don't make me laugh," Cardozo said, but the statement regarding Martin's representation of William Donnelly was enough to turn two very serious old men, who were having a serious conversation, into laughing children.

Both men uncharacteristically (for both) laughed together for a moment.

"He's going to file a breach of contract... He thinks he might have a chance of getting Donnelly out of the contract!" Whiteacre said, then burst out in loud, hideous laughter.

"He thinks he has a chance!" Cardozo said, joining in the laughter, "He's not even a *competent* lawyer!"

"The sheer idiocy!" Whiteacre said, "If they make it to court for a hearing, that's a hearing I'm going to watch with drinks and a bucket of popcorn."

"I'll join you," Cardozo said.

It took several moments before they calmed down.

"But seriously, though. We know *she's* been talking to Sandberg," Whiteacre said.

"Yes, yes. Though we know about it, there's nothing anyone can do. She's been *talking* to Sandberg since inception if you can believe it... apparently talking to him almost every night, too. Did you know she is *building* something?" Cardozo asked.

"Building something? *Where? How?*" Marcus asked, suddenly very concerned. The Chair of Internal Audits clearly did *not* like discovering that there were things he didn't already know.

"I'll confess I don't know the details. We've never seen such power, such sheer, raw power. Nadine Caldwell's unborn child is simply the most powerful *thing* I have ever seen," Cardozo said, clearly experiencing the same discomfort from not already having all the facts. "We have no idea what she's building, but things have been disappearing from all over," he said.

"Things are starting to make sense. Some of our best reinforcing tools have gone missing," Marcus Whiteacre said. "I chalked it up to theft, but security has been unable to track down any of the missing materials.

"She took them, Marcus, I guarantee it," Cardozo said.

"It's been *very* long since I have been surprised by *anything*," Marcus said.

"Eons, probably," Cardozo said, "It's unnerving. What in the world could she be building?" Cardozo asked.

"Your guess is as good as mine, but rest assured, it's going to be very sturdy with the materials taken," Whiteacre said.

A moment passed as the men tried to consider the possibilities. Finally, Marcus broke the silence.

"I have to know, Abraham. Why?"

"Why? Why what?"

"Why Sandberg?"

"Why what?"

"Why did the Board of Directors choose Sandberg? I'm not saying he's stupid..." Marcus started to say, but Cardozo cut him off.

"It's ok, you can say it. Sandberg is, at best, below average, unintelligent, severely lacking in imagination," Cardozo said.

"Then why did you choose him? Why did the Board of Directors choose Martin Sandberg to represent Nadine Caldwell's unborn child?" Marcus asked.

Abraham Cardozo stopped feeding the birds, turned to meet Marcus Whiteacre's eyes.

99

"We didn't choose him," He said. He was bitter, almost laughing.

"What?" Marcus asked, suspicious of Cardozo's motives.

"You heard me correctly, Marcus. The Board chose *another*. We did *not* choose *him* to represent her."

"No?"

"Of course not, but it doesn't matter now. *She* chose him," Cardozo said.

"No, no. That can't be right," Marcus Whiteacre said, shaking his head, "It can't be true."

"As unfathomable as it is, it's true. To protect Nadine Caldwell's pregnancy, we picked a genius. We chose a lawyer with a passionate legal mind to represent her, the best lawyer we've ever seen. It doesn't matter now. Nadine Caldwell's pregnancy has been talking to Sandberg since the premise began. *She* chose *him*."

"Abraham do you think her choice has anything, you know..." Marcus started to ask, then uncharacteristically stammered.

"What? With the fact that I defied the law to save *that* idiot? It wasn't for Martin Sandberg."

"Esmeralda," Marcus said.

The men fell silent.

"The worst mistake ever," Abraham Cardozo said.

"What's done is done. Either way, I don't understand *why* the pregnancy retained him. Nadine Caldwell's unborn child has been talking to Martin Sandberg since inception, she's retained his services to represent her, *and* she's building something, most likely for him," Whiteacre said. "I feel like a fly about to be swatted. Does that about cover it?"

"I'm in the dark as much as you," Cardozo said.

"We were sure *all of you* chose him. We were sure there was a *reason.*"

"Why would we choose him for the most *important* case *of all time*? Of all lawyers in the world, him?"

"I don't know, that's why I'm here with you on this bench. That's why I came here."

"We didn't *choose* him, and we *don't* have high hopes for his success," Cardozo said, "there's your answer."

"No way for you to have someone smarter than him step in, at least for the hearing?"

"*She's* the client. Nadine Caldwell's unborn child has the right to choose her lawyer."

"Unbelievable," Marcus said.

"Yes," Cardozo said, then waited for what he thought was the right amount of time before speaking again.

"Marcus, I would be remiss in not broaching the subject with you, maybe one last time," Cardozo said, but Marcus was already shaking his head.

"We can discuss it ad nauseam, until we are both blue in the face from screaming at one another. If there were a middle ground of any kind, my kinship and I would happily pursue it. I don't see a middle ground," Whiteacre said.

"It's all or nothing?" Cardozo asked.

"Wouldn't you agree?"

"Yes, yes, I know."

"There are the *old ways*, and there is our current system. It's either *freedom for us*, or we continue following *humanity's laws*. It *is* one or the other, nothing in between. From the beginning, following humanity's laws been unseemly, undignified, don't you see how out of place it is?" Marcus asked, almost pleading.

"It is *necessary*," Cardozo said.

"Necessary, Abraham? Don't you remember what it was like? We could do what we wanted, take what we wanted. We could walk across the land, *stepping on them* all as if they were mere insects and we could grind to dust any who vexed us. I can't believe you don't long for the way things were when we could be who we truly are, where the only confines were our very natures themselves. I long for the impunity of ages past, for the old ways. Don't you?"

"Of course, Marcus, yes. I feel as repressed as you, but as *humanity's laws* have pontificated, you have to conduct a cost-benefit analysis, you have to look at the good the system does for the world, for *us*."

"For us? What has any stupid, mouth-breathing *human* done for me?" Marcus Whiteacre asked, animated.

"Look *around you*. Are you blind?" Cardozo asked him. "Are you?"

Marcus Whiteacre watched as Cardozo reached into his pocket. A large-muscled man stepped forward, intent on seeing what it was that Cardozo was fishing for in his pocket. Marcus Whiteacre lifted a dismissive hand without even looking at the guard. The man stepped back.

"You see this?" Cardozo said, cradling his device in his hand, holding it out for Whiteacre.

"Your phone, yes, everyone has that cheap model, Abraham."

"You can't call this a phone. When Alexander Graham Bell stole Elisha Gray's method of acoustic telegraphy, when he used the device to call his assistant in the next room, in his most vivid of dreams, he could not fathom the device in my hand. The fact that it is a phone is incidental to what this small device can actually do. It opens doors, takes amazing pictures, it allows me to discover the answers to questions I might have, tell me the weather forecast, I can create or read any document with it, and I have instant access to business affairs. Oh, yes, I also use it to pay for breakfast."

"Your point?"

"My point, Marcus, is that it was those *stupid, mouth-breathing humans* who *invented* this amazing device I am holding in my hand. The imagination, the creativity, the emotional and physical persistence it took for a device such as this to come into existence is inconceivable. Do you think that one of *our kind*, could *ever* create such a thing?" Cardozo asked him.

Marcus was silent. The fact that he refused to answer Cardozo's question gave him the answer.

"Marcus, the very thing *you* use to communicate, and keep your calendar, and discover the world around you, was created by these people. None of *our* kind, our 'kinship,' are even remotely capable. You get that, right?"

Marcus reluctantly nodded.

"It's the creativity," Marcus admitted.

"A trait none of us will never possess. With that, I ask you, how would humanity move forward and into the future if *our kind* is grinding them beneath our heels, forcing us to worship them, killing them by the thousands if they should get in the way of our stupid, petty conflicts? Without the system in place, without using the human legal system to resolve *our* disputes, humanity would be living in straw and dung huts with no running water, just trying to keep from being destroyed by *our kind,* never mind inventing anything like this amazing device I'm holding. Tell me I'm wrong, Marcus. Tell me that my miraculous yet inexpensive phone could be invented by humans *even if* we were allowed to tear them down and *set them back* every time they tried to take a step forward."

"Abraham, for the sake of *innovation, we* have to continue to live like *this*?" Marcus asked.

"It's been a very long time since you could take what you want without paying for it, Marcus. You should be used to it."

"We must continue to deny our very natures, all of it, insanity, the tedium day in and day out, humanity embroiled in some kind of sick, long-running 'Rube Goldberg' machine, *our side* laying tracks while *your side* lays roads, *our side* putting up obstacles, and *your side* providing the methods for circumventing them? And all the while we subsist in frustration, pent-up, insanity-creating uncommon rage as we continue pounding the ground, cursing at the sky, *singing about the walls,"* Marcus Whiteacre said. Cardozo watched as Marcus looked at the sun for a moment.

"Doesn't all of this madness diminish us?" Marcus asked.

"I never claimed it was *not* madness. I know the Board would certainly prefer to focus on *other* matters. The constant corporate espionage, as it were, causes such considerable economic waste. Consider the alternative, though."

"We have," Marcus Whiteacre said, "We've discussed it until members walked away in disgust. The miracle of *wireless technology* notwithstanding, how can our existence like *this* be better?"

"Marcus, you and your friends are very powerful as it pertains to physical manipulation of the world around us. It is because of your *power,* of course, that you want to go back to the old ways, to play 'king of the hill,' schoolyard bullies forcing anyone and everyone around you to bend to your will. Before the system's order, you were at the top; consequences delivered only by the few and far between and only on rare occasions. I understand the allure, the desire to go back to a bygone era where those who are like you would be worshiped by the populace, not for love and devotion, but for fear of destruction."

Marcus Whiteacre scoffed.

"We have evolved. We wouldn't go that far, Abraham."

103

"Wouldn't you? It was one of *us* that defined the very nature of power to corrupt. You would have a tool and not use it? Would you own an automobile and not drive it to work? Would you buy a house, but choose instead to sleep in the dirt? Come now, Marcus," Cardozo said, "let's not fool ourselves."

Whiteacre sighed.

"Our impasse is defined once again. Even though you obviously do not deny the pent-up frustration, you also have to see that there *will be* a breaking point. I feel a war coming. Even humanity needs a *riot* or a *war* now and then to blow off steam," Marcus Whiteacre said.

"Let's not go down the slippery slope of comparing *us* to *them*."

"Yes, sorry, I agree we cannot make *that* comparison. My point is that nature abhors a lack of expression. You have to see that there *will be* a breaking point."

"A point where *we* riot? Where *we* explode, where anger and rage take over, the blanket of ignorance pulled apart thread by thread as we howl at the sky, tearing into each other, as you *and he* said, pounding the ground, *singing of the walls?*"

"Exactly."

"That's why *she's* here," Cardozo said, "that's what *she* is for."

"Nadine Caldwell's pregnancy? You seem so sure," Marcus Whiteacre said, a statement of fact, not a question, his face appearing as if he just bit into a lemon.

"You *know* what she *will* do," Cardozo said.

"I know the promise, but I also know rage, uncommon."

"As do I, Marcus. The Caldwell child's appearance is timely," Cardozo said.

"Yes, and why do you think we're attempting to resolve *that* issue *before* it becomes an issue?" Whiteacre asked, the question rhetorical. "We have all even considered going out of bounds to prevent its birth. The thought of Nadine Caldwell giving birth to that *thing* is most unsettling. "

"Not for me. I want to see what it does," Cardozo said.

"Ridiculous," Marcus said.

"You are free to believe what you like, of course, but I am soon out of bird seed. I am now getting up to leave," Cardozo said, eying Whiteacre's security, clearly informing *them* that he was

104

getting to his feet, ensuring he did not surprise them and experience unnecessary strife. "Given the impending," Cardozo said, "this may be the last conversation we can have. Before I go, I would like you to consider for a moment that the pregnancy, that girl inside of Nadine Caldwell is the *real* thing."

Cardozo stopped for a moment while Marcus scoffed, even laughed a little at the notion.

"Hear me, Marcus. Humor me and for just one moment, consider that she is what we all *think* she is. Wouldn't you want to see her born, grow, do the things we know she will?"

"Not if it means we would be thrust further down the dark hole. There is no light. The feeling of being trapped has become unbearable."

"Consider her power. Some say she would take the pain away for *us,* even our kind. Can you imagine? Isn't that worth at least exploring?" Cardozo said, straightening, turning his bag over and dumping the last of his seed on the ground, putting the empty paper bag in his pocket.

"Being myself, living as I want to, eating what I want, taking what I want, *that* would take away the pain. I don't need *her.*"

You always seem to forget one fact," Cardozo said.

"I'm sure you'll enlighten me."

"You always forget this is *their* home. We are merely guests," Abraham Cardozo said. Marcus Whiteacre scoffed, but Cardozo was already walking away.

ELEVEN

LASSITER'S GOLF CLUBS

MARTIN SANDBERG SAT AT HIS DESK, LOOKING AT THE WOMAN SITTING ACROSS FROM HIM, TRYING TO GUAGE WHAT KIND OF TROUBLE HAD JUST WALKED THROUGH HIS DOORS. When making the appointment, she said her problem was unlike any other and she didn't think there was anywhere else she could go for help. She had said she was desperate and needed to see Martin as quickly as possible.

She appeared to be in her early to late 60's, was very well dressed, perhaps too well-dressed for an attorney consultation. Her makeup was tastefully applied, her hair perfectly tied back, and she wore eyeglasses with thick frames complemented by tasteful jewelry.

"This is an extraordinary situation. In all my years, I've never been to a lawyer before, besides, of course, our family attorney who came to *our* house when needed... It was always my husband and my father who took care of things... I don't *know how* to start," she said, nervously rubbing her delicately manicured hands together.

"I can see that you're nervous, Miss Yancy, just tell me what brought you here today, and I'll try to help," Martin said.

"I read that you do mediations," she said.
"That's correct, I'm a certified mediator."

"I thought of using our family attorney for this, but I believe he's too *close* to us. I think I need to hire someone to mediate between my two boys," she said, "I don't necessarily need anyone to go to *court* or to file a lawsuit. This is an odd problem."

"I've been mediating for a few years now, and I've resolved some very tricky situations," Martin said, "tell me about your boys."

He watched as she smiled nervously.

"I call them 'my boys,'" she said, smiling, "but they're both adults. They have been fighting and arguing most of their lives, as brothers sometimes do. In the past, they've always worked things

106

out together, most of the time *without* any intervention by their father *or* me."

"Your husband?" Martin asked.

"Passed away just a few years ago. For the most part, my boys have been 'thick as thieves.' I would say sometimes they have even been each other's best friend."

"That's good to hear," Martin said, "I often hear about siblings who won't even speak to each other."

"No, no, not my boys, *ever*. They always talk, and when they're not talking to each other, they are yelling at one another. *We* don't do the silent treatment in our house," she said with pride.

This sounds normal enough. Is it possible I have just a regular case? Martin thought to himself.

"Can you tell me what the source of the conflict is? Was there an incident? Are they arguing over something specific?" He asked.

"Exactly, yes. That *is* the case, Mr. Sandberg. It's only been a few months, maybe three or so, but it has been *unbearable*."

"Do your boys live with you?"

"Before the fighting began, they each lived in their *own* homes with their wives and children. Both have moved back with me. I have plenty of room, and the house has several bedrooms... Don't get me wrong, I don't mind them being at the house with me, but both of my son's wives have thrown *them* out."

"*Both* are having marital difficulties? At the same time?"

"Oddly enough, yes. Both are experiencing marital discourse at the same time."

Martin watched as Marlene Yancy shifted uncomfortably in her seat, still nervous.

"You see, I was cleaning."

"Cleaning?"

"Lassiter's things... That's my late husband's name... It was time finally for me to begin, at least, removing and disposing of my late husband's things. The boys each took some clothes, a jacket here and there, neckties, some old wristwatches, the usual."

"Did they argue over their father's things?"

"No, *not* at *all*. Amongst themselves, *the boys* decided *who* would take *what*, resolved any issues they had between themselves, as they have for years. For example, there was a particular tie that my husband had purchased in Las Vegas. It was loud and obnoxious, Mr. Sandberg, a dreadful, awful thing. Quite frankly, I never used to let Lassiter wear it. The boys both wanted it. They argued at first, but then they *horse traded* with one another, trading a sport coat, a billfold, I think, and Bradley took the awful Vegas tie while Brandon took some other things."

"It sounds like your sons get along pretty well," Martin said.

"Normally, yes. The trouble started when we came across a set of golf clubs. It was the strangest thing, Mr. Sandberg. Lassiter owned *several* sets of clubs. When he passed, the boys divided them up amongst themselves without a problem. Just recently, however, while we were cleaning, my boys and I, we found a locked box. It was in the back of Lassiter's closet. It took some considerable effort, but the boys managed to pry it open. We were very curious as to what could have been inside, why Lassiter would take such pains to lock something and hide it away."

"Yes, go on," Martin said, intrigued.

"It was a set of golf clubs inside. They weren't fancy, just ordinary clubs. It was puzzling, Mr. Sandberg, a mystery. The boys went into the pockets of the golf bag expecting to find jewels, rare coins or something, anything to explain why their father would go to such lengths to secure an ordinary golf bag. My husband didn't do anything without a purpose," she said. Martin nodded.

"I was curious as to why Lassiter didn't keep *this* set of golf clubs with *all t*he others. He had many, Mr. Sandberg, always trying out the latest advancements in *golf club technology*," she said, emphasizing the words "golf club technology," then smiled a little.

"In the end, I concluded, as did Brandon and Bradley, that perhaps this *particular* set was his favorite... Though I can't remember ever seeing him use them."

Martin watched as Marilyn Yancey looked straight ahead, her eyes becoming glassy, lost in thought.

"They've argued over the golf clubs?" Martin asked.

"Yes," she said, her facial expression darkening, "those clubs are the sole subject of their disagreement. Invariably, as these things sometimes do, the clubs gave a kind of birth to disputes that they hadn't had before."

"What do you mean?"

"Instead of trading with one another, in justifying *who* should get the golf clubs, Bradley will argue with Brandon that he got all their father's attention, that he was their father's favorite, and that it's only fair for *him* to keep the clubs. Brandon will argue *similar justifications* that *he* should be the *one* to keep the clubs..."

Martin watched as she paused, an expression of sadness and frustration on her face.

"To the boys, it seems as though there is nothing worth trading to exchange the clubs. It is as if those horrible golf clubs are worth more than *anything* in the world, much less my late husband's belongings... The main argument over them ends with screaming and yelling about things that happened when they were children, Mr. Sandberg."

"Can I ask a question?" Martin asked her.

"Of course," she said.

"Aside from the 'horse trading,' as you put it, can you explain why they won't share them? Take turns?" Martin asked her.

"At first, that's exactly what they did. It's important that you understand Mr. Sandberg, neither of my boys was a particularly *vested* golf fanatic. Each played the game on occasion, and both like the game, but neither of them particularly preferred playing instead of engaging in other hobbies."

"Playing golf, they could take it or leave it?" Martin asked.

"That's the way it used to be, for the most part..."

Martin waited patiently as Marlene Yancy seemed lost in thought.

"Brandon has a boat. It's rather small with just a few cabins," she said.

Martin wondered to himself how a boat could be *small* with "just a few cabins."

"Brandon almost always would prefer to go on the water, take his wife and children on trips *rather* than play golf."

"But that changed?" Martin asked.

"Brandon's wife was the *first* to throw him out of the house. The source of the marital discourse between Brandon and his wife was *not* the argument he was having with his brother over the clubs. It was that Brandon had suddenly become *obsessed* with golf. Brandon's wife, Linda, and I are very close. She told me she could put up with his obsession with playing golf or having a

109

hobby, but she said that for Brandon, it had suddenly become as if *nothing else* in the world existed other than playing golf. When he was home, he wore his golf shoes indoors until she told him that she would leave with the children if he didn't take them off.

"You mean the shoes with the metal spikes on the bottom?" Martin asked, "you'll have to forgive me. I have never played. I've seen them before, there are metal spikes on the bottom, and they are very loud when you're not walking on grass. Those shoes, right?"

"Exactly. Linda told me that Brandon seemed always to have one of Lassiter's clubs in his hand, practicing his swing, he was always fiddling with the bag, putting things into it and taking things out."

"Couldn't it have been that he just became interested in playing better? Maybe he realized that he liked the game more than before. My understanding is there is a lot of men who have become obsessed with golf but can maintain perfectly normal lives."

"He stopped going to work, Mr. Sandberg. The trading *firm* fired him for not showing up. He'd been fired for weeks, but he didn't tell Linda."

"She thought he was still going to work?" Martin asked. Marlene Yancy nodded.

"When he was not at the driving range, he was looking for a golf course that had an opening. It's a good thing that we have money. Otherwise, I would not have been able to pay the mortgage for Brandon and catch him up on his bills."

"It sounds like an addiction," Martin said.
"That's exactly how I would put it, too. I've never seen anything like it, Mr. Sandberg. My boys have never been overly consumed with anything, in fact, they've been the opposite. Every time someone wanted a hobby, say a musical instrument or sport of some kind, I indulged them. For example, both went through a guitar phase, but by the time we had purchased the guitar and hired someone to teach them, they were both onto playing basketball... They moved from hobby to hobby while growing up... This is very unusual, Mr. Sandberg. Linda said it got to the point where she couldn't even have a *conversation* with Brandon."

"Mrs. Yancey, it's not uncommon for a husband to tune out his wife while watching a game or concentrating on something."

"I am very *aware* of the average man's limited attention span," she said, smiling, "as a woman, we recognize our men can become preoccupied on occasion. This? It's something different, entirely."

"It *is* as bad as an addiction then?"

"Linda said that she had finally had enough when she had to convince him, practically beg him to go to bed. What's happening is very uncommon, Mr. Sandberg. Linda is lovely," Marlene Yancy said, then sighed, sadly. "While they were in bed together, he refused to take off his golf glove."

"I can see how that would make her angry," Martin said.

"She said she couldn't take it anymore, and quite frankly I don't blame her one bit."

"What about Bradley?"

"It was pretty much the same thing. Bradley's wife, Nadia, is a quiet woman, and I don't have the same relationship with her, but we are *very* amicable. She told me that Bradley was supposed to pick the kids up from school but went to play golf instead."

"That's bad," Martin said.

"The school, of course, called her and though she had another appointment, she skipped it and picked up the kids instead. I think, for her, the end was when Bradley took their son to soccer practice and left him there *alone.* They were lucky that they had been friendly with the parents of the other kids on the team. One of *them* brought him home."

"Bradley left his son on the soccer field in the middle of practice?"

"Like he had forgotten his son was there at all. It was his obligation to look after him and take him home. My son actually left his son's soccer field to go and play golf. He went to the driving range," she said.

"Did your son's have golf clubs of their own?" Martin asked her.

"Yes, but neither use them anymore. As I said, in the beginning, the boys were *taking turns* with Lassiter's clubs. It was the *only* solution. Each would have one week at a time. That worked for a concise time before each started keeping the clubs longer than his designated week, longer than his turn. One brother taking another's turn regularly caused quite the conflict."

"When one was in possession of the clubs, what happened to the other?" Martin asked.

"What do you mean?" Marlene Yancey asked him.

"When Brandon had given the clubs to Bradley for Bradley to have his week with them, how was Brandon without them? If it was Bradley's turn, did Brandon stop obsessing over golf or vice-versa?"

"You mean was it an 'out of sight, out of mind' situation? Did my boys go back to being their non-golf-obsessed selves when the clubs were in possession of the other? No. In fact, Marlene told me that Bradley was *worse* when he didn't have the clubs in his possession. She said he paced, seemed nervous and shaky, and drank too much. Mr. *Sand*berg, my boys aren't like this. I was very lucky with them while they were growing up. Neither of them has what you might call an 'addictive' personality."

"How did they play?"

"With Lassiter's clubs? They played better than they ever have, better than the professionals. Each has gotten a 'hole in one' more than once since using the clubs," she said.

"Mrs. Yancy, I think I know what this might be, but first I would like to rule out any other possibilities. Is it possible that there's an attachment to the clubs because the brothers feel that the clubs were precious to their father? I'm wondering if this is less about golf and more about cherishing their father's memory by holding onto those clubs, which were precious enough for your late husband to put into a strongbox and hide away from everyone," Martin said after taking a moment to consider the situation.

"Mrs. Yancy, I don't want to offend you, but this sounds like it might be something for a therapist. Do you think that the obsession with your late husband's golf clubs might have something to do with your sons' unresolved issues regarding their father?"

After he asked the question, Martin watched as she took in a deep breath. She was exasperated.

"I have considered that might be the issue. Already I've tried two mental health practitioners, one as family therapy. Neither said that it was what you just suggested, and quite frankly I had the same notion as you. I wondered if it might be unresolved

112

issues. After going to the therapists, both agreed that it was the same as you concluded earlier."

"Ma'am?"

"That it is an *addiction.*"

"I'm not sure what a lawyer can *do*, Mrs. Yancy."

"I don't know, either, but I'm out of options. Maybe you could mediate between them. Make an official agreement for them to follow."

"Like a custody agreement, only with Lassiter's golf clubs?" Martin asked.

"Perhaps."

"I don't know," Martin said, "this problem might not be worked out with a contract of some kind or *legal intervention.*"

"You couldn't weigh them down and drop them in the ocean?" he asked.

Martin looked at her.

"I meant the clubs, of course, not your sons," Martin said.

"I thought of that, too. I think I could handle them being angry with me. I couldn't take them searching for the rest of their lives to find wherever I hid the clubs."

"Is melting them down an option?" Martin asked.

She gave him a wide-eyed look.

"I had to ask," he said.

"Mr. Sandberg, you are *not* the first attorney I have consulted on this matter," Marlene Yancy said. "My coming to see you is the result of a referral from a friend of mine. She told me that you could help me with a kind of situation that seems... out of the ordinary."

"Ma'am?"

"Annabelle Feldman is a member of my club," Marlene Yancy said.

"Hanson," Martin said, correcting her, "she's back to her maiden name now."

"That's right, I forgot. I understand she has *you* to thank for that."

"Did she tell you about that case?" Martin asked.

"She was very vague. When she recommended you, she told me that *you* were the person to see for unusual situations... I disregarded her advice, tried everything else, then remembered that she had recommended you. Was she wrong, Mr. Sandberg? Can you help me?"

"I think. Maybe."

"You said you thought you knew what this was. Is this type of situation something you've seen in your practice?"

Martin stared for a moment, considered his options.

"Have you ever heard of artifacts?" he asked.

"You think my late husband's golf clubs are cursed," she said, frowning at him.

"You did do your research."

"I told you, I've left no stone unturned. I can't think of anything else to do, anyone else who can help me. Can you help me?"

"I am willing to try. Can you tell me where the clubs are, right now?"

"In the trunk of my car," she said, "I've been driving around with them."

"Wow," Martin said.

"You have no idea," she said.

"Alright."

"I don't know what else to do with them. I don't dare bring them in *here*."

"Why?" he asked.

"I told you when I came here, Mr. Sandberg, this is a very strange situation. The last lawyer I saw, who was of no help at all by the way, behaved *badly*."

She paused for a moment, saw that Martin was waiting for a further explanation.

"I brought the clubs into his office *with me* when I went to see him... He was fine until he *handled* them. It was innocent enough. While we were talking, he took out the putter. It was as if the man had suddenly realized for the first time that he was alive, Mr. Sandberg. That lawyer wanted me to *give* them to him. All he had to do was touch those clubs, and he became just as obsessed as my boys... I had to practically pry them from his hands, threaten to call the police to get them from him. So strange," she said, "but my research on these 'artifacts,' these 'cursed objects' indicates that this is how they tend to work."

114

"That *is* strange," Martin said. It only took a moment, then Martin wondered (somewhat angry at himself) why it took so long for him to make the connection.

I have a safe.

"Mrs. Yancy, I have an idea."

"I'll try anything."

"I have a specially lined safe in my conference room," he said, "I think it may just solve everyone's problems."

"A safe?" she asked.

"Let's go to the conference room. I'll show you."

THE DOORS TO THE SAFE HAD JUST CLOSED WITH LASSITER'S GOLF CLUBS INSIDE AS BRADLEY AND BRANDON YANCY STORMED INTO THE FRONT DOOR OF MARTIN SANDBERG'S OFFICE. The doors to the safe had once again become the back wall of Martin Sandberg's conference room.

"Sir, please, you can't go back there!" Delia yelled, but she might as well have been talking to herself.

They ran past her as if she wasn't there.

Standing in the conference room, exchanging glances with one another, both double-checking the wall for fear that the two angry young men might see that it was a hidden safe, Martin Sandberg and Marlene Yancy were both nervous.

"Mom, what did you do with them?" Brandon asked. He wore a peach golf shirt, (complete with new armpit sweat stains) matching pants, his golf glove, a nondescript white baseball cap, and, of course, golf shoes with the noisy metal bottoms.

"Seriously, Mom, what is this?" Marlene Yancy's other son, Bradley said. He was dressed in a similar fashion, though his clothing was red and cream, and in addition to armpit sweat stains, his back was matted.

"Mr. Sandberg, I'd like you to meet my two sons, Bradley and Brandon," she said. Marlene Yancy managed a light smile as she introduced them. Martin Sandberg was sure even the best Poker players would lose if they had the misfortune of playing against Marlene Yancy.

"Pleased to meet you," Martin said.

Martin shook each of their hands in turn, took the opportunity to examine what a person looked like when he was deep within the clutches of an artifact's power. They were noticeably nervous and high-strung, not unlike an addict who was experiencing the first stages of withdrawal. Each had bloodshot eyes, was sweating, (head, face, and armpits, etc.) and spoke just a little bit louder than a person should when in a conference room with their mother and her lawyer.

"Yes, can you please tell me what my mother is doing here?" Brandon Yancy asked Martin.

"How did you find me this time?" Marlene Yancy asked her sons. Both looked at one another, the shame obvious.

"Well?" Marlene asked her sons using her best motherly tone.

"We tracked your phone," Brandon said.

"I thought I turned that off," she said.

"Bradley turned it back on when you went to bed last night," Brandon said.

"You told me to!" Bradley yelled. "I wouldn't have done it if you hadn't!"

"What, like I'm the mastermind? Did I somehow hypnotize you into betraying our dear mother's trust?" Brandon said, "I can't help it if you have so little respect for the woman who carried you within the hallowed walls of her uterus."

And just like that two grown men began to argue as if they were children on the playground.

"Boys!" Marlene Yancy yelled.

"Gentlemen!" Martin yelled, even louder than her, sneaking a glance to her, and giving her an ever-so-slight nod.

The boys looked at him, wide-eyed.

"I'm afraid I'm going to have to ask you to leave," Martin said.

"You can't do that," Brandon said.

"Where are they, Mom?" Bradley asked.

"Sit down, Gentlemen," Martin said. Neither of them sat down. They looked at one another, then at their mother in silence, shocked. Neither of them was used to someone telling them what to do. The experience was all but foreign to them.

"That wasn't a request," Martin said.

"I don't know just who you think you are, but you don't talk to me..." Bradley started to say but was interrupted by his mother's angry voice.

116

"That's the only man on this Earth who knows where the golf clubs are. I suggest you show some respect," she said.

If Martin wasn't sure before, he was sure now. Marlene Yancy had to be an expert Poker player, (if she played Poker, that is) demonstrating the ability to lie to her sons with ease and conviction.

The looks on both their faces was unnatural desperation.

Silently, the two men wearing golf clothing sat down at Martin Sandberg's conference table.

"I have the golf bag in a safe place."

"Where?" Brandon asked.

"I just told you. They are in a safe place," Martin said.

"You can't do that. I'll call the police. That's theft."

"You can't steal our clubs!" Brandon said, pounding his golf-gloved fist on the table.

"They're not *your* golf clubs!" Martin yelled back.

They were silent, confused.

"I see *that* got your attention. They belong to your mother, not you," Martin said, making sure to point to Marlene when he told them that the clubs belonged to her. This time he knew her smile was for real, even though he could not tell the difference between then and before.

"Now wait just a minute," Bradley said.

"No. Stop talking, Mr. Yancy. Stop talking and listen to me," Martin said.

Martin took a moment to look into each brother's eyes in turn, to be sure that he had their full attention.

He had an idea.

"I would give you a recitation on marital property as it pertains to your mother being the true owner of the clubs, and I would provide an explanation as to the concept of a 'bailment' as it pertains to my having temporary possession of the clubs, but I'm sure it would be a waste of my valuable time."

Bradly pushed air out of his nose, much like a bull before it charges at someone with its head lowered in its effort to gore someone.

Brandon said "ugh," or "uck," or some other gagging angry sound, Martin wasn't sure.

"Your mother doesn't know where the clubs are, but I do. She told me that they were ruing your lives."

"Oh, come on," Brandon said.

"I know what's causing this obsession," Martin said.

"What obsession? We're not obsessed. What are you talking about?" Bradley asked, taking the appropriate moment to adjust his golf glove, pull it tighter on his hand.

"Never mind," Martin said. "I'm going to tell you where your golf clubs are."

"Thank you!" Brandon yelled at him, again pounding Martin's table, and again using his golf-gloved hand.

"Your golf clubs are currently the property of the U.S. Postal service. They are on their way to Fresno."

"What?!" both brothers yelled, almost in complete unison.

"My mother-in-law lives in Fresno. I've sent her money so that when she gets the big heavy box containing your golf clubs, she can ship it to my cousin in Cleveland. She's not going to even open it, gentlemen. She's just going to turn it around and send it out again. Louise, that's my cousin in Cleveland, is going to ship it to Yonkers..."

"This is not funny," Bradley said.

"It's not meant to be funny. It's meant to help you," Martin said.

"I don't get what kind of game you're playing." Brandon Yancy said, staring at Martin with hatred in his eyes.

"This is what we call a 'time-out.' You are both parents, so I'm sure you're familiar with the concept. I have relatives and friends all over..."

"This is unacceptable!" Bradley Yancy yelled.

"I'd be very careful about your behavior, gentlemen. My wife has relatives in both Puerto Rico and in Cuba. I'd be happy to send your golf clubs on an extended tropical vacation." Martin said.

After taking only a moment to collect himself, Martin spoke again when he was sure that both Yancy brothers would hear him.

"It might take a couple of months for the golf clubs to complete the circuit I've devised. In that time, you are not permitted to play golf, you may not go near a golf course, you may not think of golf, you may not even say the word golf! You will go back to your mother's home, change out of that ridiculous clothing, and go to your wives on your hands and knees begging forgiveness!" Martin yelled.

A moment of silence passed.

Brandon and Bradley Yancy looked at Martin.

Martin stared back.

They looked at Marlene Yancy.

"Don't look at me. You brought this on yourselves," she said.

Brandon Yancy stood, put his face inches from Martin's.

"I hate you," he said, then turned and walked away.

Bradley Yancy looked Martin up and down, then followed his brother out of Martin's office without speaking.

After the boys left, Martin slumped into one of the conference chairs, breathing heavy, relieved. Marlene Yancy joined him, sat at the table next to him.

"That was amazing," she said.

"Just following your lead," Martin said.

"No, I mean it Martin. They would have gone to your home, ransacked this office, done anything they could to try and find those horrible golf clubs."

"When my son misbehaves, my wife mails his video game to her sister. Then she mails it back. The round trip is a week, give or take. This way, he can give us all the crocodile tears he wants, it makes no difference. His punishment is in the hands of the Postal Service. I was just taking a little something from her playbook."

"I love it," she said, "I wish I knew her while they were growing up... I hope they follow through. I hope they get better."

"Mrs. Yancy, I know what's happening to them. You know, too. Those clubs are in my wall safe to stay. You should also know that I'm almost positive that the longer you leave them in *that* safe, the less they will want to play golf. I can't tell you how or why I know it, but I do. That safe is going to solve this problem."

"I hope you're right, Martin. I'm out of ideas."

TWELVE

OWEN HOOPER

CHARLENE MORENO, THE VICTIM OF THE ANGRY STALKER GHOST WAS IN MORTAL DANGER AND IT WAS GETTING WORSE. She had told Martin that fire being set to her bed while she slept was only "the latest." Much worse things were happening. She had tried unsuccessfully to hide the bruises.

Martin had to find the only person who might be able to help. He had to find the one person capable of doing that one thing needed to save her from the angry stalker ghost.

Charlie Moreno was almost safe.

One thing needed to happen first. Martin Sandberg needed a Process Server and the angry ghost stalker had to be served.

Martin had to find the one person who could serve the Restraining Order on the angry stalker ghost and Martin knew that the man would not want to help.

Without someone to Serve Process, the Injunction for Protection would remain ineffective. A lack of court intervention meant the hostile entity would be free to continue its path of abuse, ending in the young woman's untimely demise.

Martin knew only one person who could do it. He had served the divorce papers on George Feldman. If he was capable of serving that monster he could help Charlie.

There was one problem, however.

After he had served George Feldman, he had told Martin not ever to call him again, that "this last one was the last one." He said that after he "knocked" he had almost become *lost,* and that he was "far too old for this kind of lunacy."

Charlene Moreno wouldn't survive if she didn't get help. Martin knew that without help, Charlie would be found hanging from someplace in her house, or sitting in her garage with the engine on, or she would be found some other way which would (most certainly and stupidly) be classified as a "suicide." Martin would know that suicide would not be the case, but there would be nothing he could do after it was too late.

He knew he would find Owen Hooper in the diner. Martin would have preferred to go anywhere else (except maybe to the

120

illustrious offices of Black Flagg, Inc.) than to go to the greasy spoon where Owen Hooper spent much of his time.

The locale was more of a meeting spot than a place to eat. Having failed several health inspections, Martin wondered how it was that the place was still open. He saw him sitting alone at a corner table. Standing in the doorway, considering the limited options, Martin realized that he had no choice but to go and sit down with him. As a waitress (who appeared to be very tired and cranky) was pouring him a cup of coffee, Owen Hooper met Martin Sandberg's eyes with a definitive frown as he walked towards him.

"Can I buy you dinner or whatever meal this is?" Martin asked, looking at his watch. Owen Hooper nodded to and thanked the waitress as she finished pouring his coffee and hobbled away. Martin sat in the empty seat in front of him.

"I don't recall asking you to join me, Counselor," Hooper said.

"Please Owen, I have to talk to you," Martin said.

"You don't need to talk to me. What you 'have to do' is leave me alone as I asked you. Go find somebody else," Hooper said, his voice low. Martin looked around nervously, and even though the diner had only a few patrons, he leaned in to speak.

"No one else can do it," he said.

"You mean no one else who shares my particular skills and afflictions."

"Please help me," Martin said.

"I'm not going to say that it's not my problem or that I don't care. I know how important your work is, at least anything we've done in the past, but the last time needs to be the last time," Owen Hooper said.

"I have a client..." Martin started to say, but Owen cut him off by giving him the universal "time out" hand sign.

"Nope, don't tell me, don't want to hear it," he said. "You were just about to leave, and I have plans for the evening."

"Plans?"

"Yes, I have a *life,* you know. I was just about to eat a cheeseburger with bacon, moldy cheese and probably some rat droppings, go home, throw up, and go to bed. As you can see, I'm very busy with important things."

Martin watched as Hooper took a swallow of coffee and grimaced.

"The coffee's okay?" Martin asked.

"Tastes like rotten lemon juice mixed with battery acid," Hooper said, "just the way I like it."

"Let me join you, at least buy you a piece of pie?" Martin asked.

"The pie *is* passable. Unfortunately, I'm not allowed to eat sugar anymore, so you have to go. Have a nice life, Counselor."

Martin looked at Owen Hooper, the bags under his tired eyes, his traditional military haircut, and two day's growth of beard on his face. Before becoming a Private Detective and process server, Owen had been in the military, had been a law enforcement officer, a "Special Agent" for some agency or another, and had held many high paying, high-danger jobs. Owen had told him that he had become a Private Detective for the sole purpose of keeping himself busy during his retirement. Martin had commented that Owen was far too young to retire, but Owen had explained that a life filled with "the constant introduction of 'fight or flight' adrenaline into a person's nervous system" makes a person older than they actually are, whether they to live a life filled with danger *or not.* Owen had made it clear that he was *finished* with stress. Owen had explained that he was "embracing the mundane."

Hooper had a skill set which made him a commodity. He could get papers to *anyone*, especially a respondent who was attempting to dodge Service of Process.

And, of course, Owen Hooper could *knock* and gain entrance.

"Her ex is stalking her," Martin said. Owen slammed the spoon on the table that he had been using to stir milk into his coffee. He knew the milk would do little, if anything, to improve the flavor, but had to try anyway.

"I didn't ask. Do you remember what happened *last* time?" Owen asked, this time *without* worrying about how loud he was speaking.

"Keep your voice down," Martin said, looking around nervously, "I still have nightmares."

"Quit whispering to me like we're on a date, Sandberg. Nobody in *this* place cares," Owen said, though he didn't believe it himself.

"It was necessary for him to be served. Due Process would not have been satisfied, otherwise. He would still be making his ex-wife miserable if you hadn't helped. I never filed your affidavit, though. I think Judge Markowitz would have committed suicide if he read what you wrote," Martin said.

"Committing suicide would be an improvement for Judge Markowitz," Owen Hooper said.

"Do you still have your badge?" Martin asked him.

"My brother is the *chief,* what do you think?"

"Martin met his eyes.

"It doesn't matter anyway because I'm not doing anything for you."

"It's a Restraining Order," Martin said.

"So that's why you need a *badge.* You need a Law Enforcement Officer to serve it," Owen said, needlessly reminding Martin of the law that only Certified Police Officers could serve an Injunction for Protection. In almost all other lawsuits, a private Process Server is permitted to serve any litigant on any type of case. Only certified Law Enforcement Officers were allowed to serve Restraining Orders, however.

"You're the only one I know who can get *through.* You are the only one, Owen, much less any *regular* cop," Martin said, and then watched as Owen smiled.

"Can you imagine taking it to the Sheriff's Department, and trying to explain that you need to serve papers on a *hostile anachronistic entity?*" Owen Hooper said, laughing. Owen Hooper referred to *almost all* of Martin's opposing parties as "hostile anachronistic entities." Martin was pretty sure Owen Hooper had conjured the term himself.

"If I brought this to a beat cop he would lock me up in a mental institution for sure," Martin agreed. The two of them smiled at the thought of trying to explain what it was Martin was trying to accomplish, and what the expression on what a young Law Enforcement Officer's face might be when confronted with *what it is* that is stalking Charlene Moreno.

Martin watched as the man sighed deeply, signaling to Martin that he was beginning to thaw, starting to wear down, or at least considering the situation. Hooper had sympathy for anyone who was the victim of continued violence, and Martin was one of the few lawyers that Owen did not want to immediately grab and forcefully drown in a toilet.

What had initially impressed Hooper had been Martin's pursuit of the idea that lawyers are supposed to help people and are supposed to leave clients in a better position than they had been *prior to* the initial consultation.

"That last one was *bad,* Marty," Owen said. "I got *lost.*"

"I know, but that's *not* going to happen this time. Owen please, I'll get down on my knees right now on this greasy floor and beg if I have to," Martin said.

Martin made a concerted effort to stare into Owen's eyes.

"It's going to kill her, Owen."

"You'd catch an incurable disease if you got down on *this* floor," Owen said, gliding past Martin's impassioned plea, "If I do this, are you going with me?"

"I'll go *as far as I can go* until someone or *something* stops me," Martin said. "If you're done with all this, why are you in *this* particular restaurant where all the monsters come to eat?"

"I'm not sure that I would call this place a restaurant, so much as a place to commit suicide by cheeseburger."

Owen had inadvertently made the statement (of course) just as the waitress brought his bacon cheeseburger and fries to the table.

The waitress set the dish in front of Owen, (gave it a little drop instead of gently setting it down) gave him a nasty look making sure she met his eyes, then waddled away without asking Martin if he wanted anything.

"I don't know, Martin."

"Can I just..."

Owen cut Martin off before he was able to speak.

"I don't think you truly understand what it is you're asking of me," Owen said. Martin watched as he leaned in to speak in a low voice. "Once you knock on *that* door, you're stuck with the job, and there's no turning back. There is *no way* to say 'so sorry sir, to have disturbed your eternal restlessness, please don't reach into my *guts,* take hold of my soul with your icy grip, rip it out and stuff my worst nightmares down *my own throat.* I just have some papers to hand you, sir.'"

124

"I went with you last time," Martin said, sitting back, beginning to accept the fact that Owen might not help him, "don't forget."

"Those hostiles had no idea what *you* were," Owen said, "It was a good system we ended up with. I was as surprised as you."

"It happened at the final hearing, you know."

"What, the whole courtroom?" Owen Hooper asked, suddenly interested.

"Everything, all of us. Judge Markowitz literally pooped his pants. I thought we were all going to die. I named it the 'Feldmanverse.'"

The Feldmanverse," Owen said, "I like it. Very creative, Marty."

"Thank you."

"What was Laszlo doing?" Owen asked, but already knew the answer.

"He was standing there, smiling, letting it happen."

"Pretty mean-spirited," Owen said, smiling, taking a bite of the meal the waitress had just brought and instantly regretting doing so.

"Alright," Owen said, looking Martin in the eyes.

Martin tried unsuccessfully to hide his relief.

"Looks like a poltergeist, but I'm not sure. The client's just a girl, and it's *hurt* her. It hit me in the head with my own phone when she came to see me, knocked me back. I'm scared."

"I can see that," Owen said, putting the burger back on the plate, pushing it aside, telling himself that he deserved to die of food poisoning if he was stupid enough to walk into the diner again.

"Your client..."

"Yes?"

"*What* is she?"

"A person."

"Human?"

"Just a *regular* girl."

"Regular?"

"She still has her place in line, Owen. I want to keep it that way. She deserves a life."

"She's completely ignorant?" Owen asked.

"Clueless and terrified."

"If she only *knew,*" Owen said.

"She doesn't understand what's happening to her," Martin said, "but knows enough to be terrified."

Martin watched as Owen Hooper sighed deeply, picked up the old-style, glass sugar dispenser and began dumping it into his coffee, ignoring the fact that he wasn't supposed to eat sugar, signaling that Martin had succeeded in manipulating (and convincing) him to help.

"Two pieces of pie, please, and I'll get the check," Martin said to the waitress.

THIRTEEN

SERVICE OF PROCESS

ABOUT TO ENGAGE IN AN ACTIVITY THAT COULD CAUSE SUFFERING, (OR DEATH, OR DISMEMBERMENT) MARTIN SANDBERG, OWEN HOOPER, AND ANNABELLE HANSON, FORMERLY ANNABELLE FELDMAN, STOOD OUTSIDE THE MODEST TOWNHOUSE OF CHARLENE MORENO, THE YOUNG WOMAN PLAGUED BY AN ANGRY STALKER POLTERGEIST.

Sandberg handed Hooper a thick envelope and watched as he pulled the papers out.

"Signed by Markowitz, ready to be served," Martin said, "three copies."

"I'm surprised he hasn't been admitted to the mental institution yet," Owen said.

"He's hanging onto reality by his fingers," Martin said, "but still hanging."

"As are we all, my friend," Owen said.

"This is Annabelle Hanson," Martin said introducing them.

"Nice to meet you, Mr. Hooper, I've heard good things. It's my understanding you helped Mr. Sandberg with my case as well," she said.

"That's right ma'am," Hooper said, shaking her hand.

"You've been working with the victim, Miss Moreno?"

"Best I can," Annabelle said.

Martin watched as Owen Hooper sighed deeply, obviously taking one last moment to tell himself that he was going inside instead of running screaming from the front lawn of a house inhabited by an angry poltergeist stalker.

"Ok, here's how this is going to go," Hooper said, taking charge. "Annabelle, you're on client duty. You have to try and keep her as calm as you can."

"Can we wait outside?" Annabelle asked.

"She has to be inside if this is going to happen," Owen said.

"Right."

127

"Your job is more important than you think. If Miss Moreno becomes emotional, that's going to cause a flare-up. Annabelle, it's essential, you have to leave your emotions at the door," he said. He looked at Martin. "both of you do."

"A poltergeist turns *any* house into a 'haunted house.' Keep a grip, don't get into your heads, don't let *it* get into your heads."

"What do you mean it turns every house into a haunted house?" Annabelle Hanson asked, her nervousness showing.

"Look, if you go through the door to the bathroom, but end up in the kitchen, try not to be alarmed. These things, for the most part, are self-contained. If something looks out of place, out of time, or just plain wrong, don't focus on it. Don't give credibility to anything that's been corrupted."

"It's alright, Annabelle. You can stay outside. You don't have to come," Martin said to Annabelle, sensing her fear.

"Yes, I do," she said, looking Martin in the eyes.

"Counselor, you're going to run interference, like last time. It will be angry with you, but you can't let it get to you. Get me all the way in so I can *knock*. Once it sees me, I'm not going to give it a choice and it will have to let me in. The hostile entity itself will be my responsibility..." Owen's voice trailed off as he thumbed through the pages. "I will serve process on... Tony Scalfani... That name is familiar," Hooper said. "How do I know that name? I could have sworn I've heard that name before.

The order restrains Tony Scalfani or other 'individual' entity or otherwise, stalking, harassing, intimidating, harming, or otherwise committing illegal acts upon the Petitioner, Charlene Moreno... Martin, you have this restraining Tony Scalfani *and* any *other* entity? Are you uncertain whether it's Tony that's stalking her?"

"I added the '*other individual*' part because I'm not so sure it's him. *She* says it's Tony. He used to abuse her, was arrested a few times, but the charges were always dropped. He passed away several months ago under suspicious circumstances," Martin said.

"She killed him," Annabelle said, barely above a whisper, leaning in to speak softly to the two men. She watched as they looked at each other, became silent, faces betraying both surprise and fear. "I thought you knew, Marty," she said, "does *that* matter?"

128

"Ma'am, *that* makes *this* much more dangerous... *Revenge entities* are much more *volatile.* Knowing that it's after retribution make a big difference. If the *hostile* was bound to the house and *not* bound to Charlene Moreno, I'd be already setting explosives on the house. I'd blow it up and be done rather than go in there. Revenge entities are like your ex-husband, Annabelle. They are not your *average* angry, as far as angry goes."

"She never told me, Annabelle," Martin said, "I didn't know."

"She never actually told me either, not in so many words, but that's what happened," Hanson said. "When it happened, he had thrown her against the wall, hit her face, broke her nose. She ran into the bathroom to hide and closed the door."

"Why do they always run and hide in the bathroom?" Owen asked, "there's no way out from there."

"She had grabbed his gun from the nightstand before going into the bathroom and locking the door behind her. From the things she told me, I pieced together that he was beating on the bathroom door, screaming how he was going to kill her. She panicked, shot at the door with all the bullets in the gun," Annabelle Hanson said, ignoring Owen's "running to the bathroom" comment.

"One of the bullets went through the bathroom door and killed Tony Scalfani?"

"That's what happened."

"I didn't read about this in the paper," Hooper said.

"Tony Scalfani's Uncle Jerry is a police sergeant," Annabelle said.

"Jerry Scalfani. *That's* where I've heard the name," Hooper said.

"My understanding, at least piecing together what she told me, is that Jerry Scalfani and the rest of the family knew he was beating her and let it happen," Annabelle said.

"In the cop gossip rumor mill, I remember hearing about a sergeant's kid or family member who beat his girlfriend so bad one time she couldn't open her eyes, this is her, then?" Owen asked.

"Yes, Mr. Hooper, and Uncle Jerry and the family felt so bad, so remorseful that he, as *she* put it, *took care of everything,* making sure the police didn't charge her, making sure it was kept

129

out of the news except for one excerpt about a man who accidentally shot himself while cleaning his gun."

"Only that's not what happened. His girlfriend, Charlene Moreno, shot him, instead of it being a suicide like the police reported?" Martin asked, but it was more of a realization other than a question.

"Obviously," Owen said, "The folks in the Department know better."

"Jerry Scalfani helped her through everything. She says that Jerry's wife is now one of her best friends and the two of them have a standing lunch date."

"That's very thoughtful, but maybe they should have helped her *before* all the abuse."

"I believe Jerry Scalfani would agree with you," Annabelle said.

"Martin, you said you're *not* sure it's Tony who's haunting her? What makes you think that there's a different *entity* involved?"

"Just something she said, Owen. She said: 'it feels like he's sorry and asking for forgiveness,'" Martin said.

"It's him," Owen Hooper said with confidence. "Even after everything, he's still abusing and manipulating her. It's textbook. Dead or alive, he's *not* getting forgiveness. She needs counseling."

"She's seeing a therapist but what she needs is to finally be free from this, from *him*," Annabelle said to Hooper, her tone of voice not angry, but stern.

"The most important thing in there is to follow my lead, okay?" Owen asked them, "once this gets served, the 'no-contact' provisions go into effect, the rules and laws regarding contact apply, and Charlene Moreno will have peace. Then you take care of the lawyering, Martin."

Martin sighed, nodded. An Injunction for Protection against Domestic Violence operates the same way for Charlene Moreno as it would for any Petitioner, whether he/she is seeking a Restraining Order against a living abuser or *something* else.

Martin had spent time explaining to Charlie the legal strategies he was going to employ to protect her. After explaining that the term "Injunction" and what people referred to as a "Restraining Order " are synonymous, he described the process of obtaining an injunction, having the Temporary Order served, then having a final hearing.

After Martin's long (but thorough) explanation of "Due Process," as it pertained to Restraining Orders, Charlene Moreno had considered the idea and concluded that it was absurd. He was a *poltergeist now,* after all.

Martin recognized how she could consider the whole thing an exercise in stupidity, seeing as she was a *regular* person. After all, her place in line was still intact, the blanket of ignorance still covering her as it covered most of humanity.

He asked her to consider what they were doing as a sort of "spirit cleansing" service. He asked her to have an open mind. In his attempts to justify the absurdity of taking a poltergeist to court, he simplistically asked her if what was happening to her qualified as abuse, violence, stalking.

Having books suddenly thrown across the room at her, having her shower suddenly turn scorching hot, (or freezing cold) having her keys thrown at her, her computer shorted out, and occasionally feeling that someone was pushing down on her so hard that she could not get up or breathe, certainly qualified as Domestic Violence.

Martin had told Charlene Moreno that she was entitled to live free without being harmed and terrorized. "When you have a problem, you go to court," Martin had said, "to have the problem solved."

Just as in Annabelle's case, serving a respondent, such as the angry stalker poltergeist Tony Scalfani, posed its own unique and challenging obstacles. As in most "regular cases," serving a hostile spouse, ex-boyfriend, no matter the case, was (and always is) a dangerous proposition. Law Enforcement Officers who routinely serve Restraining Orders are particularly mindful for the hazardous nature of the task.

Owen Hooper recognized that serving a "hostile anachronistic entity" posed its own set of dangers, both extraordinary and common alike.

Owen Hooper often mused that Law Enforcement officers who are serving Restraining Orders on "regular common folk" have no idea how much *worse* the job could be. Owen had once overheard a couple of cops complaining about being assigned to serve Restraining Orders and wanted to tell them that they should "try serving an injunction on an enraged poltergeist, then come talk to him." Of course, he had said nothing, feeling jealous of the cops with their "normal" lives.

"Are you ready?" Own asked both Annabelle and Martin. They looked at one another. "Okay let's go," Owen said.

SITTING AT CHARLENE MORENO'S KITCHEN TABLE, MARTIN SANDBERG, ANNABELLE HANSON, OWEN HOOPER, AND CHARLENE MORENO DRANK CHARLENE'S POORLY MADE INSTANT COFFEE. All were in various states of apprehensiveness about what was about to take place.

"I'm sorry," Charlene said after taking a sip from her mug and tasting the bitterness.

"Not to worry, we're not here to socialize," Owen said. "Is there anyone else here?"

"Just us. I mean we're the only *people* here," she said, looking at him.

"Did he do *that*?" Hooper asked, eying the bruises on Charlene Moreno's neck.

She had hand-shaped bruising around her neck which was turning green and purple, as bruising does when it is in various stages of healing.

"At least once or twice a day something tries to strangle me," Charlene Moreno said. "I don't know how long I can fight back. I feel so weak."

He could see dark circles under her eyes.

Owen Hooper was angry at himself for not immediately complying with Martin's request to help her. He hated himself because he almost refused.

"I know you're tired, but don't give up," Hooper said.

"I'm freaking out. How is this going to happen?" she asked, "I mean, I know you're here to *serve* him, to perform your *legal magic,* but where am I when that happens?"

"Annabelle is going to take you to your bedroom and close the door. If you see him, don't pay attention to him, Miss Moreno. It's very important that you don't talk to him. Can you do that?"

"I think so," Charlene Moreno said, nodding.

She turned to Annabelle.

"Thank you so much for being here," she said to Annabelle, taking her hand.

"We can do this, Charlie," Annabelle said.

"I mean it. If he shows up, you can't respond to anything he says, you must look right through him as if he's not there. Look away if you have to. Don't connect," Owen said.

"After we start, Owen, what happens if she talks to him?" Martin asked.

Owen shook his head at him, frowning, then turned to Annabelle and Charlie.

"The two of you should talk about shoes, or dish soap, or potpourri, or whatever it is women talk about. Look at each other instead of him. Don't engage. Alright?"

"There's no turning back?" Charlene Moreno asked, fear washing across her face.

"You won't get another chance. He'll follow you wherever you go," Martin said, "you know that, right?"

"I guess," she said, "I know I have to do this."

"No matter what you hear happening, do not open the door to the bedroom."

"Just keep your eyes on me, Charlie," Annabelle said, still holding her hand, leading her to the stairs.

"When the bedroom door is closed, we'll start. You remember what I told you last time?" Hooper asked Martin.

"Interference. Got it."

"Stand your ground, Counselor," Owen Hooper said, as obvious a warning as it was necessary. Martin nodded, watched as Owen Hooper took two of the copies of the order and handed him the third.

On the second floor of the townhouse, Martin and Owen heard Charlene Moreno's door gently close.

Owen Hooper nodded at Martin, who held the order in his hands. While Martin read, Owen would *knock*.

In a loud voice, Martin spoke.

"Service of Order for Protection against Domestic Violence and Stalking," Martin said. He spoke loudly, as if he was reading to a filled auditorium. "Caption. In the Circuit Court for this Honorable Judicial Circuit. Charlene Moreno, Petitioner. Anthony Scalfani, and/or hostile force, Respondent.

Martin and Owen's eyes met. Day turned to night at a speed just quick enough for Martin to realize his heart was thumping in his chest.

"That was fast," Martin said.

"Read!" Owen yelled.

The light in the townhouse changed. Because he had been afraid, Martin hadn't seen Owen performing his unique service which would allow him to ensure Due Process. Through the front window, Martin could see that the sky was now dark red, almost burgundy. It felt to Martin as if the temperature had dropped at least thirty degrees, and he could see his breath in front of him as he read the contents of the order. There was a loud hum coming from all around them, like electricity, almost deafening. The air moved around him as if several high-powered fans were blowing at him all at once.

Martin remained standing in place, though his spot in the room had quickly become unbearable.

"The Petition for Injunction for Protection, pursuant to State and Federal Statutes has been filed in this Honorable Court... and having reviewed the facts and circumstances set forth in the affidavit, this *Honorable Court* hereby finds, *rules,* and *Orders* as follows..." Martin said as loudly as he could, almost screaming.

"Oh no you don't," Hooper said. Martin could not see who it was that Owen had spoken to. Nevertheless, Owen had yelled at *someone.* "Stay on it," Owen said to Martin and ran up the stairs towards Charlene Moreno's bedroom. Though Owen had run up the stairs, Martin did not hear any of the doors open or close.

As Martin read the Petition aloud, the sound of electricity was gradually increasing in volume. Just below where he had rolled up his sleeves, Martin could see the hairs on his arms stand, not because of the cold, but because of something else. He felt the urge to run away, hide, but he also knew that Service of Process was dependent on him staying where he was, remaining on task.

"It is intended that this Protection Order meet the requirements of 18 U.S.C. Section 2265 and therefore intended that it be accorded full faith and credit by the Court of any other State or Indian Tribe and enforced as if it was the Order of the enforcing State or of the Indian Tribe," Martin said.

What's that smell? Martin thought as he read the protection order. The scent of perfume filled the air. Pungent, sweet, and overpowering, it burned Martin's nose and throat.

He tried not to breathe through his nose.

A bolt of lightning appeared out of nowhere to strike the wall behind Martin with a deafening crash.

"Get out of my house!" Martin heard a man scream. It wasn't Hooper's voice.

Cold sweat dripped down Martin's back.

The television in the living room fizzled. Sparks flew out of the back.

The screen shattered. Pieces fell off onto the floor.

Martin continued reading.

"Petitioner and Respondent are instructed that they are scheduled to appear and testify at hearing regarding this matter," Martin said.

"You *will* accept!" Martin heard Hooper yell at someone.

Martin was sure that Owen Hooper was *not* talking to him. Owen's instructions to Martin were for him to stay in place and to keep reading. Martin wondered who (or what) it was that was on the other end of Hooper's yelling.

His voice sounded distant.

It had an eerie echo.

Hooper's voice did not come from upstairs as Martin had thought it should. The last time he saw Hooper was when he went running up the stairs. It was as if Hooper was standing right next to him. Martin nervously looked to his right and saw the upper half of Hooper's body, transparent, an apparition, as if Hooper had become intangible.

Martin felt his heart beat faster as fear gripped him.

"Owen!" Martin yelled.

The ghostly apparition of Owen Hooper, in the middle of an otherworldly struggle, turned to Martin.

"Read!" The ghostly form of Owen Hooper yelled at him.

Is that perfume? Martin thought to himself, trying desperately not to gag on the sickly-sweet odor.

"At hearing in this cause, this Honorable Court will consider the facts and circumstances alleged by sworn affidavit. If either the Petitioner and, or the Respondent fail to appear at the scheduled hearing in this cause the Court may, upon the Court's

135

own motion, continue the hearing, issue orders, or dismiss, at the Court's discretion..."

At the very moment when Martin read the words "Court's discretion," a woman appeared in front of him.

She appeared from nowhere. The woman was middle-aged, well-dressed, and had surreal blackness surrounding her eyes.

"You *leave* my son alone," the woman said. She exuded the odor, now making it difficult for Martin to breathe.

While he watched, the woman's eyes melted into black sockets. The blackness bleeding off her, radiating out all directions was the opposite of a light shining, overwhelming the space around her.

"Who are you?" Martin asked her.

"Read!" Hooper screamed, his voice coming from nowhere and everywhere at the same time.

Martin forgot where he had left off. In the dim, abnormal, burgundy-red light, Martin found it difficult to see the words on the pages written in the Order in front of him.

His hands were shaking.

He felt the electricity in the room, stronger now, increasing.

He was surprised at how much the electricity was beginning to hurt his whole body and how he hadn't noticed it all around him, *growing.*

He struggled to find where he had left off as the middle-aged woman shifted, screaming at him. The electricity hum was expanding. The air rushed past his ears, a windstorm surrounding him. Through the sounds, Martin could hear the creaking of the townhouse as the foundation cracked beneath it.

Martin Sandberg struggled to stay in place.

He was losing.

He remembered he had promised.

"I am a *mother,*" the middle-aged woman with the black eyes and sick odor said.

The smell enveloped the room, forming a dense, pungent fog. She was standing directly in front of him. Martin gasped and struggled as he tried to breathe the freezing-cold, polluted air.

From nowhere Martin could see, Owen Hooper jumped over the couch from behind Martin.

This time Owen Hooper was in solid form. Though the light was dim, Martin could see that Hooper's right shirtsleeve had been ripped off and blood was oozing down the side of Hooper's face.

The middle-aged woman let out a scream that snowballed like a hurricane warning. It was unlike anything Martin had ever heard. Before his eyes, insects and rot came out of the woman's mouth as she howled. The Order in Hooper's hand spontaneously caught fire.

Martin watched as Hooper threw the unnaturally burning Order on the ground and stomped it out.

"I have another," Hooper said, pulling his second copy out of his back pocket.

Hooper went after her.

Lightning flashed as Hooper and the dark woman faded. Martin found himself alone again as the entire contents of Charlene Marino's living room lifted several feet off the ground. Martin's feet were the only thing still touching the ground as he fought to stay in place. It was as if Martin was the only thing in the room still obeying the laws of physics and gravity.

Blinking, he tried desperately to find the place where he had stopped reading. Furniture, magazines, remote control devices, keys, a phone, the entire contents of the living room, now uninhibited by gravity, bobbed and moved through the swirling air.

Far too surprised by what he was seeing, Martin failed to read from the order he gripped in his hands. With the sight of numerous items floating around him, he had stopped looking for where he had left off.

"No, please!" Martin heard Charlene Moreno scream from upstairs.

"Leave us alone!" Annabelle Hanson yelled from behind the bedroom door.

At the pleas coming from upstairs, Martin forgot what he was supposed to be doing, forgot he was supposed to stay in place.

Instinctively, he felt the need to help.

As Martin started towards the stairs, the couch deliberately moved into his path. He watched in amazement as the various items in the living room piled in his way, unseen hands moving the objects with purpose.

Realizing that his opportunity to make it to the stairs and hopefully to Charlene's bedroom to help her and Annabelle was rapidly ending, the Order for Protection now in his closed fist, Martin scrambled on top of the items, crawling on his hands and knees to the stairs.

Toasters and other small appliances exploded behind him.

Climbing up the stairs on all fours, the universe tipping sideways, Martin watched as the now-ghostly apparition of Owen Hooper, engaged in his supernatural struggle, came out of one side of the wall and disappeared into the other.

Martin Sandberg threw open the door to Charlene Moreno's bedroom. Inside he saw Annabelle and Charlene huddled together in the corner of the bedroom. He saw various items, pens, a comb, a pair of scissors, all embedded in the wall above their heads. Directly in front of Charlene and Annabelle, kneeling, palms outstretched, Martin saw the figure of Anthony Scalfani.

"I'm so sorry," he said, "I didn't mean to hurt you."

Tony Scalfani saw Martin standing in the doorway.

"I didn't mean to hurt her," Tony said to Martin. "It's my fault. All of it was my fault. I have to be able to take responsibility."

Martin watched as Tony looked at Charlene, sadness in his eyes.

"I'm so sorry, Charlene. I am sorry that I hurt you," Tony said.

"But you still are," Martin said.

"What?"

"This, all of this, you have to stop," Martin said.

"*This* isn't *me*," Tony said.

"There's a woman downstairs. Her perfume makes it impossible to breathe," Martin said.

"I can't stop her," The apparition of Tony Scalfani said, "I've been trying. She's too angry. She's going to kill Charlie. She's going to kill her, and I can't stop her."

"That perfume... That smell? Oh no," Charlene Moreno said, still huddled on the ground, in the corner, her face clearly expressing unmistakable terror.

She made the connection and realized who the woman was.

Charlene Moreno began sobbing.

"Charlie?" Annabelle asked, hugging her.

"No, oh no," Charlie said.

"Tony, who is that?" Martin asked.

"It's my mother," he said.

A small kitchen appliance appeared from nothing, flew through the air, and shattered on the wall behind them.

"I never did *any* of this, I mean *after*. Before, I was a bastard. But after, it's been Mom," Tony said.

"I understand you now," Martin said to the figure. "Charlie is listening now, Tony. Tell her what you came to tell her."

"I just wanted to tell you that I'm sorry," he said to her, "what I did to you, all of it. I'm sorry."

Charlene looked at Martin.

Martin nodded.

"Thank you, Tony. Thank you for apologizing," she said.

They watched as Tony nodded his head and faded.

He had never sought forgiveness, only a moment to apologize.

"That's all he needed. Now he'll go, and you'll never see him again," Martin said.

"No!" Joan Scalfani, the apparitional mother of Tony Scalfani screamed, coming up from the floor, dragging Hooper by his head as she flew upwards. "My boy's gone! You made him go away!" She said, pointing at Charlene.

With both now solid, Joan Scalfani threw Owen Hooper across the room. He landed with his back against the wall.

Martin watched as he rolled over, groaning.

As Joan Scalfani's darkness grew, Martin kneeled before Owen Hooper.

"You have to get up," Martin said, pulling on his arm.

"You're supposed to be downstairs. How come no one does what I ask?"

"I forgot, I think."

"I need your copy of the Order," Hooper said.

"What happened to yours?" Martin asked him.

"She set it on fire," Hooper said.

"I saw that, I was there! You had two copies."

"She burned up both copies! For Pete's sake, a little help would be greatly appreciated," Hooper said.

Martin handed him the papers and turned just in time to see what appeared to be hundreds of knives, poised and ready, floating in the air beside the menacing figure of Joan Scalfani.

"It's all *your* fault. My poor boy," she said to Charlene, "my poor, poor boy. You did this to him!"

Martin watched as Hooper leaped, pushed the handful of papers into the chest of the now-solid Joan Scalfani. She turned and looked at Hooper, enraged.

Her eyes became red fire.

"You've been served, ma'am," Hooper said.

The knives fell to the floor as Joan Scalfani disappeared. Night became day and the sky was blue again.

Many of Charlene Moreno's belongings that had been floating in the air, and had amazingly gone unnoticed, dropped to the floor.

Owen Hooper fell to his knees.

"You were supposed to keep reading," Hooper said to Martin. He had cuts and bruises all over his body, but Martin could tell he was relieved.

"You're joking," Martin said, "did you see the toasters coming at my head? Hey Charlie, how many toasters do you actually have?" Martin asked.

"Just the one," Charlene said, still sitting on the floor.

"Not anymore, there's about eight or ten of them down there. Somebody's been throwing toasters at me," Martin said.

"Is it over?" Charlene asked.

"Seriously, where are these toasters coming from?" Martin asked.

"They're gone now. You're safe Miss Moreno, but your lawyer, Mr. Toaster here, seems to be a little crazy," Hooper said to Charlie, "you might want to retain alternate counsel."

"We're safe? I'm safe?" she asked.

"You're safe."

FOURTEEN

NADINE CALDWELL, GENIUS OF MATH, CHEMISTRY AND PHYSICS, PREGNANT, WORKING ON WORLD-CHANGING PRACTICAL APPLICATIONS sat at her kitchen table, chewing her thumb. In the past, she had made a mental note to *not* chew her thumb as it was a "tell" of some kind. She had let that mental note slip away. She had far too much on her mind. On the kitchen table in front of her was an envelope and one sheet of printed paper.

Moments earlier, she had been pouring through her little brown pocket-sized notebook, the only place she kept her most important theories and formulas. It was where she held the "math that worked."

The little brown pocket-sized notebook was where Nadine Caldwell kept all the secrets, *her* secrets. She knew the contents of the notebook, her pencil-drawn diagrams, and formulas, erased and rewritten over and over, were beyond anything previously considered. She was sure that the contents of her little brown pocket-sized notebook would change the world.

Though she was confident most of her colleagues, including her peers and instructors alike, would be dumbfounded by its contents, she was always worried that someone would take her little brown notebook from her. It was the physical manifestation of her young life's work. It was the solid form of her strategizing, creating, calculating, reworking and recalculating, over and over, almost every day, nearly every moment, the culmination of creative scientific ideas artfully fabricated into scientific fact.

She always kept the notebook with her, brought it into the bathroom with her, brought it with her when she went to sleep, ensured she wore pants with pockets and always kept it in her right front pocket. At night, she held it on the bedside table just in case an idea or the resolution to a complex set of calculations presented itself while she slept. The little brown pocket-sized notebook was the *most critical* thing in the world to her.

Sitting at her kitchen table, after scanning through the pages, (as she did several times each day) she had read the mail and found the letter.

It was a "once-in-a-lifetime" letter. Nadine felt she should not have been surprised, but there it was. Having one's dreams put into writing brought shock and bewilderment, no matter how intelligent the dreamer.

She had read the letter several times. Ordinarily, the document's contents would have her ecstatic, but her current situation, (and condition) presented itself as a "thumb-chewing" scenario. Phillip came through the door, two large grocery bags in his arms, his keychain in his mouth, keys dangling on his chin. She watched as he looked at her and put the groceries on the floor. He would typically have placed them on the kitchen table, but there was a piece of paper which was apparently causing concern, and he did not want to cover it with bags of fruit, chips, and soda.

He looked at her as she sat at the table, one envelope and one piece of paper in the center of the table in front of her. The way she sat, coupled with her frowning and thumb-chewing told him that there was something profound on her mind.

She looked at him and nodded. She watched as he dug the recently purchased frozen pizzas out of the bags and put them in the freezer. He grabbed two cans of soda (now full of sugar, but minus the caffeine, a compromise of sorts) and handed her one.

"Thanks," she said. As she took the soda from him, Phillip stole the opportunity to kiss her on the cheek. She smiled as he sat down next to her.

"May I?" he asked, reaching for the paper. She nodded and watched his face as he read the letter's contents, his brow wrinkled, lips moving as he tried to understand. "Longinus, Inc.? This is great, right?" Phillip Caldwell said to his wife. "Hyper-kinetic... full funding, a lab at your disposal to develop, and profit-sharing, this is amazing."

Phillip looked at his wife as she chewed her thumb, nodded. She didn't say anything.

"Who is Longinus, Inc.? I've never heard of them."

"It's Black Flagg. Everything's Black Flagg," she said. "One of their many subsidiaries. I wonder if there is anyone at Black Flagg corporate whose job is to create and disassemble shell corporations. Black Flagg seems to be at the heart of everything and it appears they have taken a special interest in my work."

"Black Flagg is where you're doing your internship, right?" he asked. He watched as she nodded, took a long swallow from the can of soda.

"You remember last year when I applied? There was a huge meeting. A few friends and I met with everyone, then there was another meeting, where we met individually with members of the Board. After that, I ended up having a meeting with Marcus Whiteacre. Even though he said he was 'Chair of Internal Auditing,' whatever that is, I got the impression that he's in charge of *everything*."

"And the Chair of Internal Auditing loves your work," Phillip said.

"He said he was impressed with my proposal and after the Committee met, I might expect something like this," she said, pointing to the letter.

"Does this mean you'd be going to work full time? You won't be going to school, finishing your degree?" he asked, suddenly afraid that she would quit school. She was so close to having what she called "alphabet soup" after her name, quitting now would be an unmitigated loss.

"Oh no, they want me to finish. They've even offered to sponsor me. I'll have my own resources... Everything."

"They're going to pay for school?" he asked. She looked at her husband. She knew that with the rising costs of tuition, the money would be his primary focus.

"Full scholarship, but Black Flagg gets a percentage of my discoveries, or rather, I should say, I get a percentage of my discoveries, and Black Flagg owns everything."

Phillip Caldwell took a moment to consider the information. He recognized the fact that she wasn't jumping up and down and screaming with joy at the news she had just received.

"Are you going to take it?" he asked.

"I don't know, Phil. I hadn't thought past getting my hands on their supercomputer," she said.

"Black Flagg's computer?"

"Black Flagg is the only one with a supercomputer, at least locally, capable of running my simulations."

"This all sounds like good things," he said, testing the waters of giving her an opinion based on his limited understanding

143

of Nadine's work. He looked at her face as she became momentarily lost in thought.

"It does sound like good things," she said.

"Is this about the baby?" he asked.

Without speaking, she gave him her special "yes, of course, my poor dim-witted husband" facial expression (complete with eyes rolling) then drank more soda.

"This tells me that their people have gone through my theories, checked my math, and they think I'm onto something," she said.

"Okay," Phillip said, "you already know you're onto something," he said.

"There's a difference. Knowing *myself* is one thing. It's something different entirely to have the biggest company in the world throw large sums of money at me for development. It's a reaffirmation, Phil."

"Free school, salary, reaffirmation?" he asked but didn't give her a chance to answer. "It's awesome," he said, "What am I missing?"

"What you are missing is that I told Marcus Whiteacre I was pregnant," she said. "It's not exactly something I could keep to myself."

"That's none of his business. It's not his concern," Phillip Caldwell said to his wife.

"It is *completely* his concern. He's a businessman who doesn't want to dump large sums of money into a person who's going to be disappearing for maternity leave, trying to work through sleepless baby-crying nights, and distracted by... snot bubbles and daycare."

Phillip Caldwell looked at his wife for a moment, looked into her eyes.

She watched as he stood up from the table and started to put the groceries away.

"You're *not* going to be a *single mother.* I'll take care of the baby. I can do it. We've been through this," Phillip Caldwell said.

"No, *you've* been through this," she said.

"With this offer? I can't see how your life won't be anything short of perfect," he said, putting the rest of the groceries in the refrigerator and maybe closing the door just a little too hard. He sighed.

"Nadine?" he asked her. "What did he say? What did Whiteacre say?" Phillip asked her, though because of her somber attitude he was pretty sure he already knew what Marcus Whiteacre, "King of Auditing and Money things" had said to her.

"He said that my timing was *off.* "

"Did he say that they'd take away the offer if you had the baby?" he asked.

"He didn't come right out and say it."

"But *that's* the deal then," Phillip said, a statement rather than a question. "You have the baby, and you're out? *Fine.* No one needs Black Flagg," Phillip said, putting boxes of crackers (he was hoping she would be using in the next few weeks to settle her stomach) in the pantry.

"Maybe he's right. Maybe right now isn't the right time," she said, looking at him.

"I can't believe this," he said.

"And I don't understand you," she said.

"Me?"

"We talked about having a baby sometime in the future, but *after* school. You always agreed that it would be something for a little later," she said.

"So?"

"So, can you look me in the eyes and tell me that you're *ready* to be a father?" she asked him.

She watched as he sat back down at the table, defeated.

"No. I am *not* ready to be a father," he said.

He knew if he tried to lie and told her that he *was* ready, she would see through it.

She could always see. Phillip knew it was best for him not to bother trying a half-truth.

"Then what is it?"

"What do you mean?" he asked.

"Why have you been so preoccupied with *this* pregnancy? I've never seen you push so hard for anything."

"You mean you've never seen me *not* agree with you," he said.

"That's not true, Phillip. Even if it was, and I am not saying that's the case, there's something *else* going on with you," she said.

"No, there isn't," he said but cringed after the words came out. He felt he sounded like a child who had lied to his parents about breaking a lamp, and Phillip knew she had realized he was hiding something.

"You keep acting like you know something I don't," she said, "tell me."

They sat in silence as she looked at him. He looked away.

She scooted her chair closer to him, attempted to meet his eyes.

"Phillip, you've never kept anything from me... At least until this," she said, "what is it?"

"There isn't anything," he said, making one last feeble effort. He knew Nadine didn't believe him and there was no point in trying to hide anything from her.

"Out with it."

"Nadine, our baby's special," he said.

"Any baby we have will be special, Phillip."

"*This* baby, Nadine. This *particular* baby."

"What's so special about this baby?" she asked.

"Now I'm going to sound like a stupid, crazy person, but I know she's going to do amazing things. Our daughter's going to change the world."

"Daughter?"

"I know it's true, Nadine," he said. Nadine stared into her husband's face.

She waited.

"I dreamed it," he said.

"It's alright to dream," she said.

"Don't talk down to me. It's not like that."

"How do you know?" she asked him.

"Because this was different. *She* is different."

"You dreamt it was special and it was a girl. That's alright."

"*It* is a *her*," he said, "you called her an 'it.' *It* is a girl."

"You've imagined the cluster of cells in my guts is female and becomes an amazing person. This explains why you've become obsessed? Phillip, you are going to be a great father to *any* child. You know that, right?"

"Not *any* child. This girl, Nadine, this one," he said.

"It's too early to determine if it's a girl or a boy. We could be having a boy."

146

"We are *not* having a boy," he said. "I've been *talking* to her," he said.

She looked at him, silent.

He knew telling her was a mistake. He hated himself for not being more careful, for not keeping his mouth shut.

"I'm not explaining this right," he said, hitting his forehead with his fist. "Okay, you know how you were on the pill?" he asked Nadine.

"It is not a divine miracle that our birth control failed," she said.

"Okay, but the things she says..."

"I'm wondering if I should be concerned, Phillip."

"Don't make this about me. I'm trying to tell you that this girl is special, once in a million years special."

"I get that," Nadine said, then went to him and hugged him. "And I love you for it."

"I know she can get through *to you* if you let her," Phillip said. She looked at her husband who was now appearing deflated and lost.

"You can see this from my point of view, right?" she asked.

He nodded.

"You say the pregnancy is special and you're dreaming about it. You are having conversations with it. You are aware how that sounds."

"Yes, I know, like I'm a crazy person," he said.

"I'm telling you that this opportunity, for me, this job, this money, it's once in a lifetime. You know that. If I pass on it, I won't ever have a shot like this again."

Phillip Caldwell sighed.

He knew he had lost; maybe he could at least stall a little.

"Can you promise me one thing?" he asked her.

"What's that?"

"Don't decide yet. We have time. Just think about it a little, ok?"

"Of course."

"And if you decide, well, you know, promise me that you won't go and do it *alone*," he said.

"Phillip..." she started to argue, but he stopped her.

"That's not too much to ask," he said.

"Fine. I promise," she said, though deep-down Nadine did, in fact, feel that it was "too much to ask."

STRUGGLING TO REMAIN AWAKE, AIR CONDITIONING AND MUSIC BOTH AT FULL-BLAST, MARTIN SANDBERG DROVE HOME ANGRY. He was angry because he had come far too close to having an argument with Delia about a potential client that would not seem to go away. Just as Martin had gathered his things and was about to leave work for home, Phillip Caldwell had stormed into the office after repeatedly calling him throughout the week. Martin had dodged his calls, told Delia to tell him he was in meetings and not there. As he was about to leave, Phillip Caldwell showed up in his waiting room, sweaty, greasy, more desperate than he had ever been.

"We are out of time," he said with his hands balled into fists at his sides, shaking as he stood there in the waiting room, staring Martin in the face.

"Phillip, I told you there's nothing I can do," he said. "You have to stop calling me and showing up," he said.

"Please, Mr. Sandberg," he said.

"You have to accept that I am *unable* to help you, the law can't help you. I understand how you feel," Martin started to say, but was cut off.

"No, you don't. You don't understand *anything* about this. I was told that you did, that you are *like* me. But you don't know anything," Phillip Caldwell said. Defeated, his head low, Phillip Caldwell turned around and walked out of Martin's office, leaving him wondering.

Martin turned to see Delia Hammond sitting behind her desk, filing her nails. During the argument he had just had with Phillip Caldwell, she hadn't intervened, hadn't said a word. During the argument he had with Phillip Caldwell, Delia Hammond hadn't even looked up or stopped filing her nails, hadn't acknowledged the presence of anyone else in the room with her.

"Some help *you* are," Martin said to her.

"You think I should have asked that poor misbegotten young man to leave, *Mr. Martin*?" she asked him, not looking at him, still looking at her nails as she filed.

Martin Sandberg knew he was in trouble with Delia when she wouldn't even look at him. He cursed himself for not merely wishing her a good night and walking out.

"Well, yes," Martin said to Delia, "as a matter of fact I do think you should have asked him to leave."

"I gave you my opinion, Mr. Martin," she said.

"Unsolicited," he said. It was enough to get her to look at him. He looked at her frowning face and was sorry for the comment.

"Whether you *solicited* my opinion or not, I informed you, Mr. Martin, I advised you, communicated rationally, thoughtfully, enlightened you, and I was clear... But if you don't want to consider my prudence, my wisdom, I guess that's that," Delia said, again turning her attention to her nail filing and refusing to look at him.

Since he had met her, Martin had listened to Delia Hammond's advice on (almost) *everything*. The reason Martin had always followed her advice (except when it came to Phillip and Nadine Caldwell) was that she had always been correct, at least since he'd met her. Delia didn't give advice often, nor did she give him a kind word, or talk to him in a voice not patronizing as if he were a child. In the past, when she did volunteer a suggestion, it had always been the best course of action for him to take.

When it came to Phillip Caldwell wanting Martin to file some sort of Injunction, Writ, or some other inadequate cause of action to ask the Court to issue an order which would compel his wife to have his baby, to *not* end the pregnancy, Martin had stood his ground. Martin had been adamant that he was 'obligated to only file cases that have merit,' and file only cases he thought there was even a slim chance of success. Martin had been unequivocal that he would *not* be taking on Phillip Caldwell's cause.

Martin had said that there is a word for cases when there is no chance of success: frivolous. Martin prided himself on legal ethics, his intellect, and refused to file a "frivolous" action of any kind.

"Stupid Phillip Caldwell. Stupid!" he repeated to himself, wondering how he was going to get the young man out of his head. He made a mental note to bring doughnuts to work the next day for Delia. Maybe if she were eating, that would keep her from smiling at him. Martin shivered at the thought.

149

FIFTEEN

EMILY'S TEA PARTY

"WOULD YOU LIKE TO COME TO MY TEA PARTY, DADDY?" Emily had asked her father. Believing that it was going to be her little table surrounded by stuffed animals in chairs, each with a little cup and saucer in front of them, Martin Sandberg took his daughter's hand. Martin Sandberg had forgotten the notion that his daughter had remained ageless for thousands of years somehow, somewhere, and when he and her mother had given everything to bring the girl back, she had brought back with her a palpable rage.

ANOTHER TIME, ANOTHER PLACE, MARTIN SANDBERG *STANDS* ON THE HOT SAND. He can feel the heat coming from the ground through his shoes, improper for a desert as is the rest of his clothing when he had entered Emily's room for a tea party.

What now? He thinks to himself. He stares around him, looking at the lifelessness of an open, bright, sandy desert. The sand is almost white. The heat is shimmering from it. Suddenly the sun feels powerful to him, almost laying a hand of heat onto his back. He thinks to himself as the heat begins to grip him that he hadn't ever really noticed the sun before. He begins to sweat. He rubs his eyes, unable to understand where he is. He and Esmeralda both had been ignoring the reality of what had happened to the three of them, each playing a part in defying the laws of the universe, life and death, and, of course, reality in and of itself. What Martin Sandberg and his wife had accomplished had never happened before (not in the history of humanity, anyway) and even though Martin had known the consequences, it was his daughter, and he would break any law, defy any natural order, any law, *any universe* to save her.

Standing atop a desert plateau, staring out into the endless span of sand and rocks, not a hint of green to be found, wondering how his life had suddenly become a series of strange, unforgiving incidents, Martin remembered the moment where it all had changed.

In the hospital, waiting in desperation for a doctor to talk with him and his wife, someone had been screaming, people were running. Someone had yelled "code" or "stat" (Martin couldn't hear very well, as he was watching Emily die, lying lifeless in the hospital bed) and there was a loud electronic sound seemingly coming from *everywhere*. First watching his daughter, then as the people ran past him in slow motion (as life-changing moments sometimes do) Martin turned to see Esmeralda's face. She was frowning, looking into him, concerned as she held him by his shoulders. He could see tears welling up in her eyes. A person in scrubs had put them both outside, but through the window of her hospital room, they could see doctors and nurses working on Emily, an exercise in futility to save her tiny lifeless body.

"Are you sure?" Esmeralda had asked him.

He was amazed. She was fierce.

"What?" Martin asked her. The sound the machines made when someone is dying had filled his ears, surrounded him. The world around them began to slow as they had begun to step out of it. Confused, he had difficulty understanding her. He had trouble holding onto the world around him.

Esmeralda had *already* started.

"Martin, are you sure?" she almost yelled at him because of the loudness and overwhelming nature of sound once it is unnaturally slowed.

"Esmeralda? he asked again.

"It has to be now," she had said, her face inches from him as the two stood in the midst of every parents' worst nightmare.

Martin had nodded.

"I'll keep it open. You have to hurry," she had said to him, "bring our baby home."

That had been the plan. Without words, using her fingers, Esmeralda pried it, ripped it open, held it open while Martin went through to look for Emily.

Unfortunately, she had severely underestimated the quickness and ferocity the universe employs when correcting itself.

In defiance of the law, Martin had gone *in*, walked past Esmeralda, their eyes meeting as he slid past her through the opening. Stuffing down the apprehension, the fear, Martin had gone through Esmeralda's makeshift doorway from the hospital through time and reality to get Emily and bring her back.

Waiting for him to come back, her strength weakening, Esmeralda had held the tear open as if it were a heavy garage door.

It had felt like an eternity for Esmeralda, with time unmeasurable, standing in-between moments, the world completely stopped as she stood alone, holding onto the thoughts of her husband and daughter. She pushed through everything she had, everything she was, and might someday be, *just* to keep her self-made door from slamming shut. At first, when she had pulled reality apart, her feet on the bottom of the opening while her hands pushed the top, she had held it above her head, her hands on the entryway as a bodybuilder would hold up a massive weight to demonstrate the feat of sheer strength and determination.

Nature will always return to a state of order. In her timeless, makeshift moment, Esmeralda had not anticipated the speed at which this would occur.

In the sideways moments, time stopped to the world around her, the "garage door" had become very heavy, very quick, faster than she had thought it would. It was not long before Esmeralda found the door no longer in her hands, but across her shoulders as she struggled to remain upright. Her feet across the bottom as it dug into her, she could feel blood soaking her socks inside of her shoes. Her body in between the opening, her shoulders across the top, legs trembling, blood now oozing out of her nose from the pressure, her hands and shoulders bleeding from holding the edges of the opening, Esmeralda had screamed the scream of someone trying to push against something far too heavy.

With her pained screams soundless to the stone-grey world around her, she trembled under the weight. With her legs shaking, she had begged her husband to hurry, a whisper that she knew he would never hear, but words she had to say, nevertheless.

She knew she had to keep the door open or she would lose both her husband and daughter forever. Esmeralda Sandberg defied the laws of nature only as any mother and wife would to protect her family.

As reality struggled to correct Esmeralda Sandberg's ultimate feat of defiance, invariably, she had been *noticed.*

She knew it was a calculated risk. She also knew the odds were great that performing such an act would cause those who lived outside the scope to see her as she struggled to hold the doorway open for her husband and child.

She refused to give in. The increased weight and strain from holding the opening caused the heels of her shoes to crack. Alone, she was the only one to hear that sound as she strained against the closing of the doorway.

Gripping the opening with her bleeding fingertips, shaking under the strain, Esmeralda had been at the bitter edge of sadness and despair, losing her grip when Abraham Cardozo, the Hellhound who wore an expensive, business suit had *stepped in*. She had been looking at the ground, at the bottom edge, far too exhausted to lift her head, but seeing his expensive shoes in front of her, she had summoned the strength to lift her head, looked into his face to realize he had been watching her. She hadn't known it at the time, but the look of respect and admiration written on his face was as alien to him as it was to find a human woman, by herself, holding open a doorway to Hell.

She would never know how long it had actually been since the figure standing before her had worn the facial expression of a man experiencing pure and unadulterated *astonishment.*

In attempting to accomplish the impossible, Martin and Esmeralda Sandberg had been *noticed*. A responsive action was required.

Esmeralda met Abraham Cardozo's eyes. Meeting her eyes with an expression of acknowledgment, of her superhuman accomplishment, as well as recognition of her unmatched emotional endurance, with the slightest of nods and for only a tiny timeless moment, he stood before her. Watching her, head tilting to the side, (like a Beagle deep in thought) Abraham Cardozo decided that instead of *kicking her in* through the hole she had created, he would do the opposite; he would help her.

Of course, (and as always) for Abraham Cardozo to take such an action, there was a cost that would have to be paid.

154

SIXTEEN

SOMEWHERE, SOMETIME, MARTIN SANDBERG *STOOD* IN THE DESERT, WIND BURNING HIS SKIN AS HE SEARCHED THE HORIZON. Martin desperately *tries to forget* what happened when he and Esmeralda fought to rescue Emily.

No matter what he does, the memories always come back. They leak through his thoughts, like a song stuck in his head, playing over and over in the back of his mind.

Martin kneels, picks up a handful of sand and lets it run through his fingers. He'd never been to any desert before. Eyes squinting from the brightness, the experience becomes overwhelming. He wonders why he is in the desert, of all places, as there is nothingness as far as his eyes can see. He hears something from behind him. He turns around and sees that behind him is the opposite of what is in front of him.

In front of him is vast nothingness. Behind him *is much more* than any oasis. He wonders if he is dreaming as he sees the green grass field, a span of impossibility in the desert. Fruit trees, fields of vegetables, waterfalls, all in the middle of the desert, seemingly replacing the lifelessness with impossibility in a speed that is unnatural for such plant growth.

He sees people talking, laughing, all working the land. He steps towards the green and beneath his feet, he sees where sand ends and the blackest, richest soil begins. There is water everywhere. He feels a cool mist in the air and is thankful.

Martin Sandberg, who thought he was in Emily's bedroom having a tea party with her wonders if he is having a nervous break from reality. He wonders if the desert world around him is merely the construct of a stressed and broken mind. At the edge of the expanding sea of green, there are flowers growing, blooms of all shapes, sizes, colors. The scent fills the air as he kneels to look at yellow, white, red roses, seemingly growing from nature itself with a random perfection. He kneels to touch one, pricks his finger on a thorn, feels the slight pain as a drop of blood forms on his finger. The little prick of pain and the taste of his blood as he puts his finger in his mouth tells him that this is real, though he is still apprehensive.

Beneath his feet, crawling at a slow and deliberate pace, the sand is replaced as the green itself seems to crawl along the sand, changing it as it moves outward. He starts walking towards the people. This is the way to go, towards people instead of lifeless desert, of course.

He is slow as he walks, unable to make sense of what he is experiencing.

People are handing bags, gardening tools, buckets, wheelbarrows, hoses, and other implements to one another. Some gather fruit, while others shovel and rake. At the center of it all there is someone giving directions on how to best work the growth around them.

He stops when he recognizes the young woman giving directions. They all go to *her* for guidance. She is the young woman who has been helping him convert a warehouse into a reinforced stronghold. The young woman that Phillip Caldwell had named "Ariel" looks the same as she does when she and Martin are reinforcing that warehouse.

Her hair is thick but sweaty. She is wearing a dirty white shirt, nondescript baggy pants and her ever-present tool-belt around her waist. Someone talks to her but is too far away for Martin to hear what is said. The young woman laughs. The people hug one another, laughing, then continue to work. The sun beats on his back, a fist instead of a hand, and Martin realizes he is still on the plateau. He thinks of calling out to the woman, but his voice is lost, his throat dry and cracking, and he knows she won't hear him if he tries to call out to her.

Suddenly from far off, he hears something loud, engines that don't belong in such a tranquil scene. Men in jeeps, military, reinforced vehicles are speeding to the growing span of green. Martin sees the vehicles coming quickly and feels his stomach become a rock, a knot in his chest at the prospect of disaster which he is sure is soon to occur.

No matter what it is, when something miraculous appears, there are always men with guns to come and claim it.

Martin watches as the drama unfolds. The men, women, and children tending to the land run to the young woman, trying to warn her of the military presence which has suddenly appeared, though it is evident to Martin that she already knew. The numerous trucks, jeeps, vehicles of all shapes and sizes stop at the edge of the green. It is an unnatural sight as the green grass seems to grow out from her, sliding beneath the stopped military vehicles.

The young woman walks towards the men as she waves to the gardeners and townspeople to stay back. She stops several yards from the vehicles. She says something to a man, who, by his clothing, position, and stance, is apparently the leader of the fighting force, Martin thinks is probably a general or something. Though he can hear their voices, the wind and distance prevent Martin from understanding what is said between them. The general raises his hand and says something incomprehensible to Martin.   The men, dressed for battle, exit the vehicles and aim their weapons at the helpless group of people who, moments earlier, were gardening and gathering fruit.

Martin feels like he might throw-up when he sees the general say something, retrieve his sidearm from its holster.

He watches helplessly as the general empties his sidearm into the young woman with the dirty white shirt, baggy pants and tool-belt.

Martin manages to croak "no," even though his mouth and throat are dried out. He might as well have whispered the protest, watching in horror while the general shoots.

Her white shirt turns red as he fills her with bullets. She steps back as the bullets reach the intended target. Martin can smell the smoke from the gun as the unforgiving wind continues to blow in his face. Like the people who had been gardening with her, Martin falls to his knees in despair as the leader of the fighting force shoots her. The man refills his weapon with loud mechanical clicks and snaps, then empties it again into the young woman.

The people who had been working with her call out in despair.

She remains standing. She walks with deliberation towards the man as he continues to shoot at her, his gun in both hands. She is only a few steps away from him when, weapon still outstretched in front of him, he continues to shoot her.

Now empty, it clicks over and over. Martin Sandberg, along with the people who had been gardening only a moment earlier, and the leader's men watch, dumbfounded, as the young woman holds her hand out at the leader, palm upwards.

Though Martin can't hear what she is saying, her meaning is clear. As a mother demanding that a child relinquish the cookie the child stole before dinner, she requires that the general, the man who shot her, place the gun in her hand.

Martin Sandberg hears the leader of the fighting force yell at his men to fire at the beautiful young woman wearing a now-bloodstained and dirty shirt and a tool-belt containing various gardening tools.

All the men fire their weapons at her.

Martin feels tears on his cheeks as he watches helplessly, the deafening sound of gunfire surrounding him. Dirt, sand, smoke fill the spot where the woman had been standing. Because of the destruction, with ammunition of all kinds, she becomes invisible as the men empty their weapons into her. In scant seconds that feel like an eternity, their guns stop firing, as they all must do when there is nothing left to fire. As the smoke clears, Martin sees the impossible.

Appearing as if no one had shot her, she stands before the men, holding out her hand, palm-up, demanding. She says something to the leader. Martin curses the wind and distance because he can't hear what she is saying. Although he can't understand the words, her meaning is clear to him, her tone of voice, demanding.

Martin watches in horror as the leader walks to the back of the jeep and takes out a long, barrel-shaped weapon. The people behind her scream and back away as he puts it on his shoulder. Martin watches helplessly as the general fires a rocket at her.

The sound is deafening. Dirt, smoke, explosion fills the very spot where she had been standing. It takes a moment before the smoke clears. Green life and dandelions grow before Martin's eyes, under her feet on the spot where she has been standing. The effects of the explosive weapon dissipate.

For a moment, her hands on her hips, she calls something out to the general. The men stand around, fidgeting, unsure of what is happening. The general takes a sword of some kind from the jeep. He runs to her, screaming, the sword above his head. Martin watches as she catches it in her hand, breaks it in half, takes it from him, tosses it on the ground next to her. The leader, the general, stands before her, eyes wide, defiant. She holds her hand out, palms up repeats whatever it was she has said previously to him over and over. The leader, exhausted, screams again, gives her a kick from some martial arts stance, punches her face, punches her chest, screaming while he yet again tries to harm her.

He stands before her, breathing heavy, eyes wide.

She stands before him incredulous, defiant, unharmed.

The general and the young woman's eyes staring into each other, Martin wonders if the man is going to resort to continued violence. He starts shaking and falls to his knees.

She puts her hand on his shoulder.

Overcome with emotion, he finally complies with her repeated demands and he hands her the gun he had had been using moments earlier, attempting in futility to destroy her. As everyone within the field of view watches, she takes his gun apart as expertly as if she had built it herself, tossing the pieces onto the ground.   She says something to the military force, orator to captivated audience.

The men stare at her, fidgeting, uncertain, watching as their leader is on his knees before her. They can see she is as unharmed as when they arrived. They watch in wonder as she touches the leader's face. The hardened man begins to sob like the young boy who was caught defying his mother.

With the general on his knees before her, Martin has no idea what she will do to the general, but then he is angry with himself.

He should always know.

She hugs him as the general falls into her arms, sobbing as a lifetime of anguish is finally acknowledged. She says something to the man as she holds him. She gently rubs the top of his head, talking to him. Martin watches, astounded, as she calls out to the military force, to the men still carrying their empty and useless weapons. He watches as she lifts the leader of the men to his feet.

He says something to the men. Because of the wind, Martin cannot comprehend the words spoken but can hear from the inflexion that the general is repeating what she is saying. Martin, still kneeling on what was once lifeless sand, but is now green mixed with flowers, watches the men take apart their weapons.   One at a time, she steps to each of the men as they disarm, taking to them, shaking their hands, touching their faces, shoulders, hugging them as, right before Martin's eyes, each man changes.

They change from soldiers to something different.

159

Some of the men begin to cry like the general, nodding their heads as she talks to them, each in turn. Some fall to their knees only to be taken by the hand or shoulders and lifted back up again. Some of the men strip off outer uniform shirts and toss them to the ground. Men in white t-shirts and army pants form a line before the gardeners who, with unrequested forgiveness begin to once again hand out rakes, shovels, and bags of fertilizer and seed.

Some of the men, including the leader, join in working the land while some climb into the vehicles, driving away in the direction from which they had come.

It appears that the people are gardening again. It is almost as if the whole scene had not happened. Martin watches as the young woman walks towards him a little, picks up a rifle that someone had dropped. He watches as she expertly takes it apart.

He watches as she slowly lifts her head.

She sees Martin.

She looks at him, acknowledging his presence as Martin meets her eyes. She stares directly at him through everything and looking through him, she nods her head.

Her silent acknowledgment is deafening.

MARTIN SANDBERG FELL BACKWARDS AWAY FROM EMILY'S CHILD-SIZED TABLE AND CHAIR SET. He suddenly realized had been kneeling on the floor. Surrounding the child-sized table were stuffed animals in chairs and before each was a tiny teacup and saucer.

"More tea, Daddy?" she asked him, pouring imaginary tea into a teacup that was sitting in front of a stuffed bear.

Covered in sweat, his shirt matted and sticking to him, breathing heavy as if he had run some distance, eyes wide, Martin was on the floor before his daughter as she arranged her tea set. Martin Sandberg crawled on the floor away from the table. Seconds passed as he tried to catch his breath, at one moment on all fours on the floor of her room, unable to stand.

There was silence.

He looked and saw that Emily was standing, now motionless at the table.

Frowning, she was looking at him as he crawled to the wall behind him to lean on it. Still catching his breath, unable to stand, covered in sweat, he sat on the floor against the wall.

160

The tiny cut on his finger where the flower's thorn had pricked him was still there, a subtle reassurance.

Epiphany washed over his face as he met the eyes of his daughter. She continued to stand motionless, still staring at him.

"Why?" he asked.

"*Why?*" she asked him back, scowling, angry as if he had insulted her.

In silence, she walked towards him, bent just a little for her face to be inches from his face as she spoke to him, barely above a whisper. "You hide under the covers like a scared child. Wake up... *Father*. Do your job," she said to him through clenched teeth, anger in her eyes.

He watched as she turned and walked back to her tea party table and picked up a tiny toy tea kettle.

"Daddy, would you like *two* spoons of sugar?" she asked, smiling, eyes bright as if none of it had happened.

Esmeralda watched from the kitchen door as her husband stomped down the stairs, covered in sweat, the color drained from his face.

"Weren't you going to a tea party?" Esmeralda asked him as he walked past her.

Martin met the eyes of his wife for just a moment, then ran to the downstairs half-bath where, bent over and kneeling, he emptied the contents of his stomach into the toilet.

When he finished, he looked up at his wife standing in the doorway to the bathroom, still holding the dishtowel she had been using in the kitchen moments earlier.

"I remember," he said, standing to his feet, shaking. "Everything... I remember everything," he said to Esmeralda, to no one, or to everyone, as he turned on the faucet. He used his hands to cup water from the faucet. She watched as he drank, splashed water on his face, still trying to catch his breath. He took the dishtowel from her hands without her objection and used it to dry his face. "I remember everything. I *know* everything," he said to her, sitting on the closed toilet.

A mixture of remorse and sadness washed across her face as she stared into his eyes.

"Lo Siento mi Amor," she said. Though his grasp of the language was lacking, he knew what "I'm sorry," was in Spanish. (It was the first Spanish he had learned, knowing that a husband

161

needs to be well versed in the language of apology if he wants to remain married.)

"No es necesario," he said, telling her that an apology to him was unnecessary. "We did it together... All of it..." he stopped, deep in thought, eyes glassy. Esmeralda Sandberg watched as her husband struggled to find words.

"What have we done, Esme?" he asked.

"No cost too high," she said, "for our Emily. For our family," she said.

"After spending thousands of years *there?* I didn't remember. You don't know because I couldn't remember. I never told you. I couldn't tell you because I didn't remember..."

"What is it, Martin?"

She was in *charge,* Esme. Emily ruled over all of them... All of it, everything, it was hers. She had taken it, had taken *all* the power... our little girl. There were millions, Esme and they were worshipping our daughter, they were bowing at her feet," Martin said, standing, his hands shaking.

Martin stared into Esmeralda's eyes as he spoke to her. "Something is happening," he said.

"I know," she said.

"I have to do something... *now,*" he said.

"Now?" she asked.

"I'm going to my office. I have to get ready," he said. She could see the fear in his eyes.

She watched as her husband left.

Esmeralda walked to the foot of the stairs.

"Emily? You get down here right now! You come down and tell me what you did to your father!" she said, calling from the bottom of the stairs.

SEVENTEEN

SPITTING OUT THE LASZLOS

FIDGETING BECAUSE TIME WAS AGAINST HIM
AND HE HAD BEEN MADE TO WAIT, MARTIN SANDBERG
SAT ON THE UNCOMFORTABLE BENCH IN THE LOBBY
OF BLACK FLAGG, INC.

As was usually the case, he was there to visit William
Donnelly. For most people, Martin required clients to come to his
office to speak with him. For Donnelly, however, Martin was
cognizant of Donnelly's hectic schedule and as a favor to his old
friend, Martin had made the trip to meet with William at his office
several times. Each time Martin went to visit William, when he
had sat in the lobby, watching people come and go, Martin had
told himself that *this* was the last time he would be going to
William's office, that from now on, William would have to go to
him. As Martin sat waiting, he hated himself for not remembering
that rule he had set for himself.

Sitting in the lobby of Black Flagg, Inc., Martin felt
uneasy, disturbed.

It was the same feeling he had when being shaken awake
from a nightmare only to realize he couldn't remember what had
happened in the dream. It was the same feeling Martin had when
there was something he needed to do for work that had a deadline
of dire consequences, like a statute of limitations issue, or a
discovery requirement, but could not remember what it was he was
supposed to do. It was the feeling he had when he shuffled
through his papers in his office trying to figure out what it was that
had an imminent deadline but could not remember.

He sat in the lobby, watching the people come and go. For
no reason, he fixated on the security desk. Tired, he stared at the
security desk until he had tunnel vision, until the lone security
officer, oblivious to Martin's presence, was the only thing in
Martin's field-of-view.

Martin slowly, while remaining fixated on the security
officer, turned his head sideways (not his eyes) then attempted to
view the security officer from the corner of his eye without
looking directly at him. For a few moments after forcing himself
to look away from the security officer, as tunnel-vision began to

hold, while looking directly at the security guard through the corner of his eye, Martin thought he saw something.

He thought he saw something immense, solid, dark, horrible, but then it was gone.

Martin rubbed his eyes, shook his head, and looked back up, directly at the security officer.

What?

"Laszlo?" Martin asked aloud, not really to anyone. The security officer, who had been a slight man with blonde hair and blue eyes was now tall. He had black, neatly combed greasy hair, a neatly trimmed mustache, and was a hulking figure, built similar to men who competed in the Olympics for bodybuilding.

It was Bailiff Laszlo.

Martin walked to the security desk, scratching himself behind his ear.

"Laszlo?"

Laszlo the security officer was taller than Martin, he had to look up at him as he spoke.

"Sir?" The security officer said.

"It's me," he said, "what are you doing here? shouldn't you be at the courthouse?"

"Yes sir, you'll be called when your appointment is ready," the security officer said, not looking at Martin, writing on a pad of prefilled forms which were attached to his clip-board.

"Laszlo? Hey. Talk to me," Martin said, still staring.

It's him.

"Sir, the name is Forrester," he said to Martin, not looking at him.

"No. Your name is Laszlo, and just yesterday we had a long conversation about where to go to get the best deep-dish pizza. I had this conversation *with you* while we were in court waiting for the judge. Come one, Laszlo," Martin said, incredulous.

"No sir," the security officer named Forster said, taking a moment to look at Martin instead of his paperwork. "My name is Forrester," he said, pointing to his name badge, his tone not loud, but annoyed, "and we have never met. I don't know what your game is, but I'm not in the mood. You may go and sit down, sir."

"Where's the other guy?" Martin asked.

"What 'other' guy?"

"The security guy here a second ago? He's much shorter than you. He has blonde hair and blue eyes," Martin said.

"I'm the only one here until my shift partner comes back from his break. He has *black* hair. He is African-American. The *only* blonde hair, blue-eyed security on shift, *is me*," Forrester said.

What?

Martin stood motionless, staring at him.

After a moment, he laughed.

"The only blonde hair, blue-eyed security guard on shift as you?" Martin said it as a statement more than as a question.

"Sir? What is wrong with you? Why are you asking me that?" Forrester said, still holding his clipboard, still under the misimpression that he would be able to work with Martin standing in front of him. He could not finish his paperwork with Martin asking pointed questions, (which made no sense to him) and refusing to sit down though he kept requesting as politely as he could.

"I ask because *you* do *not* have blonde hair and blue eyes, *Forrester*. You have black hair, black eyes, and a mustache, like always. Did you lose your bailiff job? Are you moonlighting? I won't tell anyone."

Martin was becoming angry. Not only was he sure that Laszlo was playing a sick game, but he was feeling considerably uneasy, more than when he usually visited Donnelly.

"I don't mind if you go stand in traffic and tell anyone anything you like. I am not Laszlo. I am Forrester."

"This isn't funny," Martin said.

"On that, we agree, sir. I'm trying to fill out my status update and you're interrupting me. Just have a seat, alright? Someone will be with you shortly."

The man who introduced himself as Forrester stared at him with his piercing black Laszlo eyes.

"Normally I would," Martin said to the officer, but really to himself, "I usually chalk it up to temporary insanity, or that I've made a mistake on my end. I'm so quick to tell myself that I'm wrong but this is the point where I say I'm not the one making the joke. I'm *not* wrong. I know you. I talk to you all the time at the courthouse. I thought we might be friends, or at least getting there. When I came in here, a security guard was standing exactly where you are standing right now. He has blonde hair and is shorter than you."

"Sir, I'm considering calling my supervisor and escorting you from the building. This is stupid. I'm not going to argue with you."

"You must have an identical twin named Laszlo who is a bailiff at the courthouse," Martin said.

Forrester (finally) put the clipboard down on the desk next to the computer monitor. He looked at Martin.

"What are you?" he asked.

"What?" Martin asked.

"What are you?" Forrester asked again, his teeth gritted.

"I'm a lawyer. What are you?" Martin asked.

"I look at you. I can't smell anything else."

"How are lawyers supposed to smell?" Martin asked.

"Go and sit down, sir," Forrester said. Another security guard came sauntering in, let himself behind the security desk next to Forrester. He was carrying a brown paper bag. Martin looked at him as he walked, eyes wide, astonished. For only a moment, Martin thought he was having a nightmare.

"I brought cookies," the security guard holding the brown paper bag said.

"What's happening to me?" Martin asked.

"You are about to be escorted out of the building, *that's* what's happening," Forrester said.

"Who's this?" the security guard with the bag of cookies asked Forrester.

"Never mind who *I am*. *You* are Laszlo, just like *he* is Laszlo," Martin said, pointing to them each in turn.

"What's a Laszlo?" the guard with the cookies asked, taking one out, putting the whole thing in his mouth at once and chewing with his mouth open.

"I think this gentleman is having a mental break," Forrester said, " he thinks I have black hair and a mustache."

"Really? What do I look like?" the officer with the cookies asked, smiling and chewing with his mouth open, happy to join the party.

"Just like him... black hair, tall, a mustache."

The security officer with the cookies frowned, stared at Martin as he ate his cookie.

166

"I look like the white guy," he said, pointing to Forrester.

"*You* are a *white guy*," Martin said.

Forrester and the man eating the cookie looked at one another and laughed.

"Man, I am black," the officer with the cookies said, still eating and laughing, "my name is Lewis."

Forrester reached into the bag, took out a cookie and started munching.

"You are as white as I am," Martin said.

"Here. Have a cookie, go sit down, relax. Someone will come and get you for your appointment," the officer who had introduced himself as "Lewis" said. He held out the bag for Martin. He could see the cookies inside. They looked delicious.

"He won't go, even if you give him a cookie. He's busy having an episode," Forrester said, picking his clipboard back up in a futile attempt to finish the report.

"No thank you," Martin said, even though he wished he had taken a cookie. "Please. I'm not here trying to cause trouble. I would just like an explanation," Martin said.

"An explanation for what?"

"For why he's seeing Laszlos everywhere," Forrester said, looking at his clipboard as if to pretend Martin wasn't there, "*I'm* Laszlo, *you're* Laszlo, that lady over there with the pink hat, *she's* Laszlo, *we* are *all* Laszlo!"

"I'm Lewis, didn't we *just* go over that?" Lewis asked, pointing to his name badge, in the same manner as how Forrester had pointed to his nametag a moment earlier.

"But... "

"Don't even try," Forrester said to Lewis, who was about to continue arguing with Martin.

"Mr. Sandberg?" a voice said from the elevator entrance. It was the red-headed woman who had brought him upstairs before. She was still frightening, though Martin didn't know why.

"Oh, thank God," Forrester said, "This guy's been driving me nuts."

"See, that's a woman with red hair," Martin said, "but you *both* are Laszlo."

"Please go, sir," Forrester said.

"Fine, I'll go, but we are not done here, gentlemen," Martin said.

"Whatever you say, sir."

While on the elevator with the redheaded woman, Martin remained silent, did not speak to her for fear that she might spontaneously turn into another Laszlo.

Martin made a mental note to himself that as soon as the appointment was over, instead of going back to his office, he would either go to the courthouse and try to find his Laszlo, perhaps get an explanation, or he would seek out the first psychiatrist he could find.

"Have a seat right there, sir. Mr. Donnelly will be with you in just a moment."

Martin sat down on yet another uncomfortable bench. This was the usual course of things when he went to see William Donnelly. He would first wait in the lobby; then someone would bring him to another waiting area near William's office to wait further.

I don't have the time for this, Martin thought to himself. When Donnelly had called him, Martin had almost told him that he did not have the time to visit, but couldn't deny his friend, especially when he sounded so desperate. It was only a moment before William Donnelly appeared. Martin was shocked by his appearance. In all the years that Martin had known him, Donnelly had always taken great pains to look clean, neat, and fashionable, three things which were lacking.

William Donnelly always wore the latest clothing, had neatly combed hair (with heavy use of hairspray) and always appeared as if he was ready to go out on a date at a moment's notice.

Today, however, William appeared disheveled, there were scratches down his face, bags under his eyes, and he had enormous sweat stains. As they walked, Martin could see his friend was sweating, nervous, like he was suffering, like he'd caught a virus, or had food poisoning.

"What happened..." Martin started to ask, but William made a hand motion, shook his head, indicating to Martin that he should stop talking and follow him. Martin waited until they were in the hallway alone, out of earshot of anyone before speaking. "What happened to you?" Martin asked.

"Oh, this?" William asked, pointing to the scratches on the right side of his face, "I think I tried to pull my face off this morning."

"What?"

"It's unbearable, Marty. I'm breaking."

"I'm sorry this is happening."

"He wants *out*. He knows he's got to go through me... He's *going* through me. He's killing me."

"I didn't know it was this bad."

"Tell me you've found a way to get us to court, defeat that contract," he said.

"The Petition's on my desk, ready to go," Martin said, lying to his friend. It was true he had drafted the pleadings, but they weren't *ready to go*. Martin couldn't go more than two pages through the Libro De Diablo without wanting to claw at his eyes and scream.

"How long to get a court date, then?" William asked him. His tone was clear that he didn't believe Martin.

"Not long, Will. I'll work on getting a date the minute I get back to the office. I'll call you in a couple of hours, ok? Just hold on."

"He knows who you are," Donnelly said.

"What?"

"He *knows*. He calls out *your* name sometimes as he beats on the walls, swinging his severed arm. He says *you* can't do *anything*."

"I promise I won't let you down," Martin said, knowing that it might already be too late.

William Donnelly nodded.

"My company might have a way to help me, at least that's what they indicated."

"Black Flagg can help?" Martin asked as they walked down the hallway.

"They didn't come right out and *say* it, but it was *hinted*. The Board of Directors wants to see *you*."

"Me? Why do they want to see me?"

"I don't know."

"Alright, we can schedule a meeting..." Martin began to say, but Donnelly cut him off.

"Now."

"Now?"

"Yes, Marty."

"The Board of Directors wants to see me..."

"Right now, Martin. I'm to bring you up to the top floor. This is *their* elevator."

"Will, I don't know," Martin started to protest, but glancing into Donnelly's eyes, seeing his friend's desperation was all that was needed.

"Alright," Martin said, nodding as he followed William Donnelly onto the elevator, "but only because you said they might help you."

The ride in the extravagantly decorated elevator was an uncomfortable silence, as Martin still had no real way to help William. Martin was sure William knew, as his face displayed an expression of fear and despair, unusual for him. They walked together to the Boardroom. Donnelly opened the double doors for Martin. The conference room was much more ostentatious than Martin could have imagined.

Adorned with priceless artwork, meticulous furnishings, plush carpeting, leather chairs, and a vast, beautiful table with refreshments, Martin couldn't help but feel impressed. Men with expensive suits and white hair sat around the table, staring at William and Martin as they entered the room.

"Thank you, Mr. Donnelly. That will be all," Marcus Whiteacre said, standing at the head of the table.

"Sir?" Donnelly asked. The expression on Donnelly's face indicated that he had thought he would be staying with Martin for the meeting.

"Yes, I'll take it from here," Whiteacre said, looking at Donnelly, eyes piercing.

"Wait," Martin said to Donnelly as he turned to leave, "Sir, I came *here* to see *him*, shouldn't he stay?" Martin said to Whiteacre.

"Mr. Sandberg, today you did *not* come here to see *him*. You came to see *us*," Marcus said, displaying a smile that was just a little too bright and cheery. Martin's apprehension grew.

"That will be all Mr. Donnelly," Whiteacre said. Everyone in the room watched in silence as Donnelly nodded his head. Defeated, he left the room in silence, closing the doors behind him. Martin stepped slowly further into the room and noticed the security personnel.

"Mr. Sandberg..." Marcus Whiteacre said, but Martin uncharacteristically, (and somewhat rudely) interrupted him, put his hand up as one would when telling someone not to speak.

"Hold that thought," Martin said, not looking at Marcus, but standing in front of one of the security guards, staring him in the face. Martin knew that he was standing too close to the guard, was in his "personal space," but did so, regardless.

Martin's back was to the table and the Board of Directors as if they weren't there. He hadn't noticed them. He was looking into the guard's eyes.

"Mr. Sandberg..."

"One second," Martin said sharply as if he might be scolding a child, again preventing Marcus from speaking. Being told to *be quiet* was an unusual experience for Marcus Whiteacre.

He did not like it.

Marcus Whiteacre couldn't remember the last time a *measly human* had dared to *ask him* to shut up. He also recalled what he had *done to* the human when he had. That was a long time ago.

"I don't know why you've summoned me," Martin said, still studying the guard as if he was examining a piece of rare artwork.

"I'm interested in anything you have to say, but I have a question, first," Martin said, turning around to face everyone in the room.

"Mr. Sandberg?" Marcus Whiteacre asked.

The Board of Directors stared.

"What's with the Laszlos?" Martin asked.

He watched as, while seated, the men's heads moved, swiveling as they exchanged glances with one another.

"Excuse me?" Marcus Whiteacre asked.

"You see, this? Martin asked, almost yelling, pointing to the security officer. "This, this, this..." Martin stammered. He took a deep breath, let it out.

The Board of Directors continued to stare.

"*This is Laszlo*," Martin said, having difficulty, but ultimately finding the words. The Board watched as Martin quickly went to another security officer. The guard was standing in the opposite corner of the enormous room.

The security officer poised to take action as Martin, (who appeared menacing) walked quickly, almost running, approached him. The officer met eyes with Marcus Whiteacre, who shook his head, the universal expression of the word "no."

Having received the nonverbal instruction from his employer, the officer took an "at ease" stance and stared straight ahead as if Martin wasn't there.

"*This* is Laszlo!" Martin said, pointing to the guard, now standing with his hands behind his back and staring straight ahead in the military "at ease" stance.

They watched as Martin pointed to the guards in the room, one at a time, voice loud, almost yelling at them.

"He's Laszlo, he's Laszlo, that guy there, *he's* Laszlo," Martin said.

"I don't understand what you mean, Mr. Sandberg," Marcus Whiteacre said. His tone was calm and even.

"I mean that I met two of your security personnel downstairs. They were pleasant enough, but they looked *exactly* like Laszlo. These guys here?" Martin said waving his hands around, "are all Laszlo..."

The Board of Directors seemed entertained as they silently watched Martin's tirade.

"You're Donnelly's boss, right? He mentioned you to me once or twice. You're Marcus Whiteacre, right?"

"Yes, Mr. Sandberg. I am pleased to meet you."

"And you as well. Am I crazy?"

"'Crazy' is a vague, nondescript, concept," Marcus said.

"But they all look the same. How can that be?"

Marcus just stared at him, emotionless, taking a moment to consider his options before answering.

"The man you are referring to as 'Laszlo,' the bailiff, was the first of his line. His mother spat him out first."

"The first?"@@@

"As he was the first one spit out, the rest, of course, is just like him. That's how their species works. You saw the others. Now you see what's underneath that, but you can't see *underneath* the underneath. You see only the underneath," Marcus Whiteacre said.

"Underneath?" Martin asked.

"Yes."

"I can see underneath the underneath?" Martin asked.

"No, just underneath," Marcus said, "you can't see underneath the underneath."

Martin sighed.

"You don't see them as having any other designated imprint. Though each of them, whole the litter, looks the same, most people see all races, shapes sizes. You see underneath that layer of cross-cultural multitudes, Mr. Sandberg. You see the first, the template, which is the bailiff Laszlo," Marcus said.

"This meeting is going much better than I had thought it would since I heard I was going to have it... less than five minutes ago," Martin said. He looked at the men. He looked at their faces.

They all knew something. No one was going to tell him, though.

It was yet another inside (great cosmic) practical joke Martin felt was at his expense. He was starting to get used to feeling he was on the outside.

"I don't think I'm seeing clearly, sir, quite the opposite," Martin said, (surprising even himself that he was) finding the courage to speak.

"The security officer downstairs, Forrester? He thinks he has blonde hair and blue eyes, but when I looked at him, I saw Laszlo. All I saw was Laszlo. The other one, Lewis? He *says* he's a black man, but that's not right. He's Laszlo, too. These men here..."

This time it was Marcus Whiteacre's turn to interrupt Martin.

"Yes, yes, I get it, they're all the same," Marcus said.

"Am I losing my mind?" Martin asked.

"No, Mr. Sandberg. As I was trying to explain, you must have met the *first*, and I suspect that you are adjusting. You met Mr. Laszlo at the Courthouse. He was the *first* of the litter. All that was spat out are the same, maybe with small differences, but the same, nevertheless."

Whiteacre looked at him, into his eyes. Martin might have been mistaken, but he thought he could see understanding, maybe even sympathy, though he wasn't sure.

"You can't have the same running all over town. Some are then blonde hair, blue-eyed, while others appear African-American. All different face, races, body types."

Martin watched as just then, a food-service worker in a skimpy black dress came into the room, pushing a cart which contained muffins and other baked goods, a pitcher of water, glasses, mugs, and a coffee urn. The food-service worker wore black heels, pantyhose, and the typical (underdressed) service uniform.

The food service worker wore women's clothing.

The food service worker, (alas) was a Laszlo.

"Oh, come on," Martin said.

"Fascinating," one of the Board members said aloud.

"Indeed," said another.

"He sees them all, but not us?" someone asked.

"Gentlemen?" Marcus said to the table. The word "gentlemen" was his way of telling them to stop the small-talk.

"You see this young lady?" Marcus asked.

"That's no lady," Martin said, "that's Laszlo."

Martin stood, stunned, staring at the large, muscular, mustached man wearing the skimpy women's waitress uniform.

"No offense, ma'am. I'm sure you're lovely. It's me. It's not you," Martin said to her.   She acknowledged Martin with a head-tilt and continued her duties serving muffins and pastries to the men at the table. The food service worker was Laszlo in an ill-fitting dress.

"Mr. Sandberg, we have a pressing matter to discuss," Marcus said.

"No."

"No?"

"I'm feeling a bit overwhelmed. Can we meet another time?" Martin asked.

"I'm afraid we require expediency, Mr. Sandberg. Please," Marcus Whiteacre said, "It will take but a moment."

"When I look at them, they are regular people. Under *that* they are Laszlo."

"And underneath they are who they are," Marcus said.

"Underneath the underneath?" Martin asked. "To everyone else, they are blonde-hair, blue-eyed people of all races, anything and everything. But underneath, they are all Laszlo? Underneath is *something* else.
"

Martin stared at him for a moment. He stared back. Martin looked at the impressive table. He looked at the people who were sitting there. They were looking at him. The room became quiet for a moment.

"If you saw him for what he *is in reality*, you'd most certainly go mad," Marcus Whiteacre said with the most sympathetic voice he could muster.

"Go mad?" Martin said, "Just how far is *that* distance?" Martin asked him, but Marcus could see he had directed the question at himself. They watched as he wiped at his sweating face, unable to hide his emotions. "Sometimes I could pretend, maybe even forget for a little while," Martin said.

"What?"

"That I know what we all are," Martin said.

The men still stared, eating pastries. It was simple to conclude that they wanted something from him. Making such an assumption wasn't a stretch. As to what they wanted, he would have to hear what Marcus had to tell him.

"We are all civilized businessmen, trying to have a quick meeting and I'll get right to it, Mr. Sandberg. We have an offer to make."

Martin looked at him, the expression of confusion still on his face.

"We can offer you anything you want."

"What does that mean?" Martin asked.

"There's no other way to say it. Anything you want means just that. It's not complicated. Do you want riches? Fame? whatever it is, we are offering it."

They watched as Martin stood, staring at them.

Marcus thought Martin appeared deflated, like a pile of sad, dirty laundry.

"Whatever I want?"

"What do you want, Mr. Sandberg?"

A moment passed as they looked at each other, two chess players trying to determine what the other was going to do.

"Anything I want?" Martin asked.

"Tell us."

"I want him to be okay," Martin said.

"You want *who* to be okay?" Marcus asked.

"My friend, William Donnelly. I want him to be okay," Martin said, "he's dying."

The room turned cold. The men had been smiling, enjoying an entertaining meeting. It was apparent to Martin as he looked around the room, eyes pleading, that they had become angry.

175

Martin didn't understand why they were staring at him. He looked at each of them, their faces. He could see they were infuriated.

He assumed (incorrectly) that the Libro De Diablo was a source of contention and discourse and the mention of releasing someone from the contract was taboo, perhaps.

"Did I do something?" Martin asked.

"Not at all," Marcus said, appearing uncharacteristically nervous.

Martin didn't know it at the time, but the source of the Board's outrage, the reason that he had suddenly became the object of seething hatred was *what* he had asked from them.

Presented with a priceless opportunity, Martin did not ask for unimaginable wealth, power, or fame. Martin hadn't even asked for a new car.

Martin had asked them to give him *something* that was for *someone else.*

The Board of Directors was enraged.

"Come now, Mr. Sandberg," Marcus Whiteacre said.

"That's what I want," Martin said, "you said anything."

"You don't want, say, your student loans to be paid? A bigger house? A car that doesn't need repairs once a month?"

"My car runs fine," Martin said.

"No, it doesn't," Marcus said.

"You're right. I'm surprised it still gets me to work."

"How about a brand-new car? Or fifty of them?" Marcus asked.

"Fifty cars," Martin said. "How would I drive fifty cars?"

"Anything. Think about it. Whatever it is that you want," Marcus said, "for you."

The Board of Directors watched, still frowning, impatient, as Martin stared.

He looked back at them.

"And what would you like in return?" Martin asked, "what's my end of this deal?"

"Yes, something straightforward," Marcus said.

Martin stared at him.

"I'd like you to skip a hearing," Marcus said.

"Sir?"

176

"Stay at home or in your office instead of going to court. Skip a hearing."

"You want me to throw a case?" Martin asked.

"I want you to throw a case," Marcus said.

"I took an oath. I'm supposed to fight for my clients' rights.
"

Marcus Whiteacre and Martin Sandberg stared at one another.

"Throwing a case violates that oath," Martin said.

"We understand the personal cost as well as the potential risks posed to you. Of course, that is why we agree to provide whatever it takes in return," Marcus said.

The entirety of the room looked on as Martin Sandberg made the connection.

"The Caldwell case?" Martin asked.

"Stay home that day, Mr. Sandberg."

"If I didn't go, that kid Phillip Caldwell would be in Court by himself with no lawyer. He'd lose for sure."

"We are aware of that."

"The law is against me," Martin said.

"We are aware of that as well."

"I'm going to lose, anyway. No court is going to rule in my favor, no matter whether I stay home or not."

"Mr. Sandberg, we are fully aware of *that* as well as anything and everything else."

They watched as Martin studied their faces.

"We know everything," Marcus said.

"No, I don't think you do. You're worried about *her.*"

"Nadine Caldwell's pregnancy is unfathomable," Whiteacre said, though he was reluctant to make the admission.

"She is unfathomable," Martin said.

"You understand the issue."

"You don't know everything. It's alright," Martin said, "I'm scared too, but..."

"For Pete's sake," someone at the table said.

"Unbelievable," someone else said.

"Ridiculous!" Someone said.

"You don't have to be afraid, any of you," Martin said.

He experienced them scoffing at him.

"You want her gone," Martin said.

177

Marcus didn't respond. The Board of Directors was seething.

"You're just monsters, all of you," Martin said.

"Mr. Sandberg, please," Marcus said.

"Every one of you. Underneath the underneath, you are all monsters," he said. Still frowning, they laughed at him.

"I can smell the evil on all of you. All of you," Martin said, then turned for the door.

"Sandberg!" Marcus yelled.

Martin turned.

"Our agreement?"

"You never actually said you'd help William. You said I could have anything I want, but you never said you'd do it."

"Sandberg..." Marcus began to argue, but Martin interrupted him.

"No, I don't want to know anything," Martin said, refusing to allow Marcus to finish his sentence.

"It is unwise to refuse us," Marcus said, but it was too late. Martin was leaving.

"Mr. Sandberg!" Marcus yelled as Martin walked towards the door. Martin refused to turn, knowing that if he didn't take the opportunity to flee, he might not receive another.

"Mr. Sandberg!" Marcus yelled. Martin shivered at the sound of Marcus Whiteacre's growl. Shaking, he felt he might be sick, but kept walking. Trembling, Martin Sandberg walked out of the boardroom without looking back.

EIGHTEEN

NADINE CALDWELL, GENIUS IN THE FIELDS OF
PHYSICS, CHEMISTRY, AND MATHEMATICS STOOD,
STARING STRAIGHT AHEAD, REFUSING TO LOOK AT
HER HUSBAND. She held the petition he had filed in her hands,
had read it several times.

"Are you mad at me?" Philip Caldwell asked.

"I'm not mad," she said.

"Not even a little?"

"Do you want me to be mad?" she asked him.

"No."

"Because I am about to get mad, not because you're suing
me, but because you keep asking me if I'm mad."

"Sorry," Phillip Caldwell said.

"Are we supposed to get separated now?" she asked.

"I don't know," he said.

"I think something like this usually means that a couple is
screaming at one another, you know, throwing things, and
whatever."

"That's not us," Phillip said.

"It's not," she said. "I wish we could've resolved this
without going to court."

"I didn't know what else to do," Phillip said, "I feel
helpless."

"I don't know how it happened, but here we are, in
different places," she said. Nadine held the papers in her hands,
looked down at them. The words on the pages seemed strange and
alien to her. "You think that I should have a baby now and I don't."

"It's not that simple," he said.

"It never is," she said.

"I don't want to argue about it again," Phillip said.

"We agree to disagree? Now some judge makes the
decision for us?"

A moment of silence passed between the couple as each
carefully considered what to say to the other. Phillip Caldwell ran
a hand through his greasy hair, sighed. He felt sadness, a rock in
his chest.

"Usually people aren't together, living separate when things like this happen, I think," he said.

"That's how it usually goes. I can't imagine even a day without you." she said. She took a moment to put her hand on her pocket, the place where her little brown pocket-size notebook sat. "You're the only person I want to talk to at the end of the day. I know you don't understand most of what I tell you," she said.

He looked at her, caught her attention.

"You listen anyway," she said.

"I love to hear you talk. Please, I'm sorry, Nadine. I can't lose you," Phillip Caldwell said.

"Yet, here we are, going to court."

"I wouldn't be doing this..." He started to say, but she interrupted him before he could finish the sentence.

"If the pregnancy wasn't some *miracle of the universe*, you wouldn't be taking me to court? If it was just a regular baby, you'd be okay with me not keeping it?" she asked.

"I don't know," he said, "I only know about what's happening now."

"That's another reason I fell in love with you," she said.

"The fact that I don't know?" he asked.

She met his eyes.

"You admit it."

"In the entire time I've known you, I've only had one secret that I kept from you," he said. She sat down next to him.

"That you're talking to her," she said.

"Do you believe me?" he asked her.

"I don't know," she said, "like you, I don't know."

He watched as she paused, deep in thought.

"What is it, Nadine?"

"I know there's something," she said.

"What?"

"I've been feeling something. I was trying to ignore it, but I can't."

"What is it?" Phillip asked, desperate to find hope.

"I can't explain it," she said, holding her tummy with both hands.

"I tried to explain it," he said.

"You did," she said, "There's something else, besides what I'm feeling."

"What is it?"

"Out of the blue, everything I want the world seems to be falling into my lap. The world doesn't work that way."

She watched as he took a moment, looking straight ahead, deep in thought.

"When we sit and you're going a mile a minute, telling me things, some things that I couldn't possibly understand, I'm *not* just nodding my head and smiling," he said.

"I know that," she said, afraid she might have offended him.

"It's like you're Albert Einstein, explaining the *big* science to a second grader... most of the time. I'm not *just* listening. It's more than listening to you."

"You *hear* me. I couldn't see it before."

"It took a really long time, but I get it, Nadine. I get it."

She looked at Phillip and she knew. She hadn't realized how much effort he put into *hearing* her.

"You have to know, I'm not saying because you're my wife and I love you... I know what you've *created.* I know what it took out of you, from you. I believe in you. Please believe me, even if I never met you, I'd believe in you. It's amazing."

"Amazing?"

"Nadine every single person in the world, talking, no limits, sharing ideas, reaching one another. They'll make posters of you."

"Phillip that's nice for you to say," she said.

"I'm not trying to be nice. It's true. It won't matter what dark corner in any part of the world a person is trapped in. It will be just like flipping on a light switch," he said.

He watched as tears came to her eyes.

"Hey."

"I thought I was alone. I've been feeling so alone."

"You're not alone."

"You knew," she said, her eyes becoming glassy.

"It wasn't easy," he said, "I get it. You see?"

He hugged her.

"How did we end up here?" she asked.

"I don't even know where here is," he said, "and though neither of us want it to be now, here we are. I thought I'd have a few years to put some savings together, have a little bit of a cushion, have us in a nice house, in a nice neighborhood, you know with the white picket fence and a backyard that's just a little too small."

She watched as he sighed. He looked tired.

"I wanted to have a dog first," he said.

"We can still get a dog," she said.

"I'm going to be a father. The dog can wait. For me, everything can wait. Your job is to see this through."

"I have to, Phillip."

"I'll make sure you get there, one way or another."

"And that feeling you've been having?" he asked.

"I know," she said.

"I'll take care of her and I'll take care of you," he said.

"Yes, you will."

He looked at her, hope in his eyes.

"Are you sure, Nadine," he asked.

"You're with me. I'm with you," she said.

She put her head on his shoulder as he hugged her.

"We have to cancel court," he said.

"We are still going to court," she said.

"What? Why? Why would we do that if you're going to have the baby?" he asked.

"Because no one tells me what to do with my body," she said, "whether I want to house a baby inside of me is *my* decision."

"Understood... You have a lawyer," he said, "I saw in the papers."

"Compliments of my employer," she said.

"Don't you think that's a little weird?"

"Actually, I do."

"Why is your boss hiring a lawyer for you? Why does your boss have a vested interest in whether or not we have this child?"

"He said he wants me to focus on the work. He had said I can't devote all my attention to a child and still have the appropriate amount of time to put my theories into practical applications. That's what he said, but I feel like there is something more going on with him," she said, "Marcus Whiteacre is hiding something."

"It's all weird."

"I don't know what it is, but I feel something," she said, "I'm not going to ignore it anymore."

182

He watched as she cradled her little brown pocket-sized notebook in her hands.

"I feel the same way I feel when I my numbers *work*, when it all... Balances.

He looked at her.

"It's my math, Phillip. When it works? I feel like that. I know. I just know."

"You'll tell the Judge you changed your mind?" he asked.

"After I tell him that no man is going to tell me what to do with my body."

"The hearing is in the afternoon," he said, "late in the afternoon."

"I'll go to work, have a difficult conversation with my boss and meet you at the courthouse."

NINETEEN

POPPA CAVEMAN GOES TO THE MOVIES

MARTIN SANDBERG STOOD INSIDE OF THE NOW-REINFORCED IMPENATRABLE STRONGHOLD. He watched as the young woman, with great effort, was polishing the smooth metallic walls around them. The warehouse, which had been so open, was now significantly smaller because of the layered reinforced panels they had installed.

Martin touched one of the walls, was maybe a little frightened at first, but then ran his hand along the smoothness. It looked like steel, felt like steel, but there was something different about it. He would not be able to describe it if someone asked him.

She had her back to him. He knew she was aware of his presence.

It was in the way she moved, the way she tilted her head. It was as if she was always tuned in. Bright lights had been embedded in the ceiling and there was no longer any part of the room that he could not see. There were no dark corners. The room was rounded now, corners replaced by polished reinforcements and the floor was painted white.

The young woman was wearing her regular white shirt, baggy pants, and tool-belt. There were several boxes next to her, packed as if someone was moving from one home to another. As he walked to her he could see she was intently rubbing a cloth along a part of the wall, polishing metal that seemingly did *not* need polishing.

"You are a perfectionist," he said to her.

"Last touches," she said, without turning around to look at him.

"We're done then, I mean with this place?" he asked her.

He watched as she nodded, continued her work, intently, deliberately, and with great effort. The room was empty, even the table and chairs which had sat in the corner were gone.

"Ariel," he said.

"That's what Philip Caldwell has decided to call me," she said.

"You mean your father?" Martin asked her. Though her back was mostly to him, he could see her smiling at the comment.

184

"It's a good name."

"He thinks it has significance," Martin said, "that it has meaning."

He watched as she stopped for a moment, hands on her hips, looked around the room, surveying her completed project.

"He is a kind young man. He is in over his head," she said as she walked to the opposite wall and worked the wall, running the cloth in circular motions. "You will continue to help him, won't you?" She asked.

"Yes."

"Even after?"

"I want to be a person who does the things he says he is going to do," Martin said.

She smiled, her back still to him, kept working.

"You know, you never told me..." Martin began to ask, but then stopped to consider his words. "You never explained what this is."

"Didn't I?"

"I don't think so."

"It is a "safe room.'"

"But I don't know where we are. I don't know how I keep getting here, and what is this 'safew room' supposed to keep me safe from? A safe room is maybe a place you go when disaster strikes. How would I get here?" He asked then watched she turned to meet his eyes, still cleaning a wall that he thought did not need to be cleaned.

"This is the last time you will be standing *inside* of this room," she said.

He looked at her. She stopped working, stared him in the eyes.

"Anytime you are here, you will be standing *outside*. This place? It's not to keep danger out. You called it disaster prevention? Very well-put. This place is to keep disaster *inside*."

Martin sighed, exasperated.

"I feel like I don't understand anything," he said. "I still feel like nothing makes sense."

She continued to wipe down the prison walls.

"Primates began to diverge, separate from other mammals roughly eighty-five million years ago."

"What?" he asked. He watched as she went back to work.

"Neanderthals, that is Homo sapiens neanderthalensis can be traced from four hundred thousand years ago. They became extinct about forty thousand years ago. They made stone tools, were hunters, there's evidence that they used fire."

"You're talking to me about cavemen?"

"Cavemen, Martin. They didn't have computers," she said. He laughed.

"No, they didn't," he said.

"Imagine for a moment that the cavemen and cavewomen are hanging out in an indistinct group, living in caves. They are doing whatever it was that cavemen do. Imagine one day, you go and pick up Poppa caveman in your minivan and take him to the movies," she said.

"What are we talking about?" Martin asked, laughing at the notion, "okay, now you're just having fun at my expense."

She kept working on the walls.

"It doesn't matter which movie," she said, ignoring him, "You put Daddy caveman in his own chair, and have him watch a movie, you give him snacks, popcorn, soda, the works."

"All I needed to do was take a Neanderthal to the movies. Now all my questions have been answered," Martin said.

He watched as she looked at him, gave him her signature stare.

"You bring Papa home to his family after he's seen a movie for the first time, eaten nachos, hot dogs, popcorn, candy, drank soda, all the stuff they sell at the movies. He tells the other cavemen and cavewomen, that he has just gone and had the most amazing experience. 'What happened, Papa?' They ask him..."

"Okay, I get it. I'm as stupid as a caveman You wouldn't be the first to say so," Martin said.

"I was not calling you stupid," she said, frowning at him. She took a moment and he thought she was staring through him. He realized she wasn't trying to stare him down when she walked to the wall behind him, crouched and ran the cloth along the hardened wall closest to the ground. "How would he do it?" She asked Martin.

"How would who do what?"

"How would the caveman describe to his friends and family *what it was like* to go to the movies? How would he describe someplace beyond their imagination?"

186

Still working, she turned and smiled at him as she spoke, as a mother smiles to her child while she prepares lunch.

"How would our caveman patriarch describe a strange and alien place such as a movie theater, to see something that none of them had ever seen before, eat things none of them had ever eaten, to sit in a theater chair?"

"I guess he would do the best he could," Martin said.

She stopped running her cloth along the metal, stood up, looked at him, and smiled.

"*I'm* Poppa caveman?" he asked.

"Finding a way to explain what is perhaps *incomprehensible,* presents challenges," she said, running the cloth along the ground next to him.

She watched as Martin sat on the ground, leaning against the rounded wall next to where she was working. She could see he was deep in thought as he sat in uncharacteristic silence.

"This is the last time I'm going to see you," he said.

"As I am now," she said.

"I have to tell you something," he said, "I wasn't going to tell you."

"About Emily's little tea party? She should not have done that," she said.

"You know about it?"

"Emily was doing what she thought was necessary."

"In the desert, is that really you?" he asked.

She smiled at him, a teacher demonstrating to a child how to write his name for the first time.

"I haven't been born yet," she said.

"My Emily. I can't believe what she's become. What have I done?" he asked. She stopped her work and looked at him.

"You're a good father, Martin," she said.

"Emily is all wrong. She's going to grow up all wrong. I wonder if it's even *her* anymore." he said.

"Of course, it's her. That's *your* daughter, nothing else. It's Emily, through and through." She said, smiling, then continued cleaning walls that had no need to be cleaned.

"Sometimes she seems *different.*"

"You and Esmeralda got her back sideways, she brought it with her. She is rage personified... in a cute pink dress. Keep doing

187

what you're doing and remember that beneath it all, she's still your Emily."

"My daughter, queen of hell," Martin said, despondent.

"You are always trying to help people, sometimes the cost is high. Why would your own child be any different?"

"There are thousands of people out there trying to help others, just like me."

"It's one thing to help others, to do what's right. *Bleeding* for it is something different entirely," she said.

"I'm going to lose," he said.

"Maybe, but you're my best chance."

"Can't you talk to her?" Martin asked, "Can't you talk to Nadine?"

"I have. It's not a question of *talking* to her. It's a matter of her wanting to listen... I won't force myself on her."

"Yes, but if she knew..." Martin started to say, but she cut him off.

"She knows."

"Maybe I can ask Abraham Cardozo to help me," Martin suggested out lout to himself.

"Don't bother the dogs," she said.

"What does *that* mean?" he asked her.

"The Japanese call them Inugami, or Okuri-inu. The Chinese call them Panhu or Tiangou. They're called Cerberus, in Greek Mythology, and in Scandinavian folklore, they're called 'Church Grims.' America's tribes have wolves and shapeshifters... And don't get me started on the English. They have 'Black Shuck,' 'Cwn Annwn,' 'Yeth,' 'Hell-hound,' and, of course, in Yorkshire, they have the legend of the "Barghest.'"

"Abraham Cardozo is a dog?" Martin asked her.

"Don't you find it odd that every single culture in the world has its own version of the same thing? Everyone knows of them yet can't quite describe them accurately."

"Abraham Cardozo is running the most powerful company in the world. He wears a suit worth more than my car," Martin said.

"Lunch at a fast food restaurant is worth more than your car," she said.

"Very funny. You know what I mean, though," Martin said, then watched as she again gave him her patented stare. "I remember what he did for me," Martin said, "I remember what he did for my family."

She sighed.

"A *puppy* is still a *puppy*, even if you put it in an expensive three-piece suit and call it 'sir.'"

A moment passed while he looked at her, the walls around them. She looked at his face and saw the expression.

"What is it, Martin?"

"I was wrong."

"Wrong? About what?" she asked.

"I'm *not* Poppa Caveman. *You* are. You went to the movies. I'm the ignorant caveman, sitting at a campfire, eating bugs while you're trying to explain what happens when you go to the movies."

He watched as she stood, looking at the confined space around them, satisfied with the work.

"This is done," she said, "you know what to do."

"I do?"

"Trust what we have built here, Martin, and when you go to court, I know you'll do your best. What client could ever ask for more?" she asked.

He opened his eyes. Though it was the middle of the night, Martin Sandberg showered, dressed, and went to his office to prepare.

TWENTY

STANDING OUTSIDE OF HIS OFFICE, MARTIN
SANDBERG SPOKE TO PHILLIP CALDWELL.

"You could have called," Martin said. Phillip Caldwell had
been waiting for him when he arrived.

"This is important," he said.

"Talk with me while I get my things out of the car. What's
going on?"

"Nadine might be changing her mind," Phillip said.

"That's fantastic news... Wait, 'might' be changing her
mind? You're not sure?" Martin asked, opening the back of the car
and taking out his briefcase and an extra (comfortable) pair of
shoes.

"I think when we go in for the hearing, she's going to tell
the judge that she's, you know, alright."

"Phillip, has she made the decision or not?"

"Last night we talked about it. She said she would have the
baby, but I'm never sure of anything anymore."

Martin took a moment to consider Phillip's new (but vague)
information.

"I have to tell you. Most people in your situation aren't
staying in the same house or going to sleep in the same bed."

"I know. She said the same thing last night when we
talked."

"It's promising that you two are communicating with one
another, but listen Phil, if you are not absolutely sure that she's
changed her mind on this, I have to prepare as if we are having our
hearing. She has a lawyer who's going to fight hard. That means
right now, I have to go into that office and get ready to fight."

"Do you think we could move the hearing? Maybe give her
some time to think about it?"

"Not this time. With the situation being what it is, and time
being such a factor, we're having that hearing today. I can ask for a
continuance, but the judge will most surely deny the request."

"Will you ask anyway?" Phillip asked him, sadness in his
voice. Martin felt sorry for the stress Phillip Caldwell was feeling.
Martin knew firsthand how difficult it was to be a 'father-in-

190

waiting.' It had to be that much more difficult for Phillip Caldwell, who had this insane Court case to go along with it.

"We'll see when we get there. I do need to go in and prepare now, though."

"I'm sorry, I didn't mean to disturb you," Caldwell said, nervously.

"No, no, you didn't bother me. I'm glad you told me what's going on. The more information I have the better. If you hear from her or learn anything else, call me or come by. Are you going to see her before the hearing?"

"I don't know. She's at work. If she's changed her mind, which I think she has, she's probably having a hard conversation with her boss."

"There's all sorts of protection for people having babies," Martin said, not realizing that it was Marcus Whiteacre that was the 'boss' to which Phillip was referring. "There's maternity leave, the family medical leave act, all sorts of good stuff."

Phillip Caldwell watched as Martin looked towards his office, took in a deep breath.

"We can always cross those bridges when we get to them. I'm going to go and get ready. Make sure you're early, ok?"

"Don't worry, Mr. Sandberg. This might be the most important day of my life."

MARTIN SANDBERG, NERVOUS AND SWEATING WALKED INTO HIS OFFICE FOR FINAL PREPARATION BEFORE THE CALDWELL HEARING. Delia Hammond was standing next to her desk, holding a file, waiting for him.

"Good morning," he said to her. Though he had intended to walk past her and go into his office, she stood in the doorway, blocking his path.

Seeing her standing caused an already nervous Martin Sandberg to feel his ears turn hot and red. He had never come to work and found her up out of her chair. The instances in which she was standing were few and far between, but, of course were as necessary as they were mundane. He had seen her walk to the bathroom, walk out of the door at the end of the day. Her standing and waiting for him meant that there was something important to her that involved him, and he simply didn't have the time to be distracted.

"You have to go to the prison this morning," she said.

Martin remembered Theodore Smith, the immortal sentenced to an endless life in prison. Martin also remembered that Delia had recommended Martin for the case. He had never asked her what her relationship was to Theodore Smith, nor did he ever think it was necessary to know. Martin was very busy, however, experiencing more stress in his professional life than he had ever felt, and Theodore Smith could wait an extra day or two. He had, after all, spent almost 100 years in prison.

"I'll go tomorrow," he said.

"This morning," she said.

"Delia, the motion is done, I just need to have Mr. Smith sign, I'll go see him, get his signature, notarize it, get it filed, and we can set a court date, but I need to go later in the week."

"Just a signature means your meeting with him will be quick," she said. "You'll be back in an hour, maybe two. I'd go, but only attorneys can just drop in, and only certain persons can have the contact needed to get a signature."

"Sounds to me like you checked," Martin said.

She stared at him intently.

"I have the Caldwell hearing this afternoon," he said.

"Mr. Martin, are you *unprepared* for that hearing?"

"No. I'm more prepared than I've ever been for any court case."

"Then you can take an hour or two and get this signed," she said.

"I can take an hour or two tomorrow," he said.

"Mr. Martin, you are as prepared as you have ever been, your words. Sitting in your office, brooding, worrying, will not improve your chances of success today. You have a client that has been patiently waiting for you to visit and to sign the brilliant Petition for relief you have prepared on his behalf. I would implore you to use your time wisely, to use your time efficiently, to use the next two hours in a more productive, cost-effective, and logical manner. A successful attorney must use his time in an orderly fashion, not sitting in his office, staring at the wall, pacing, causing himself to feel an increased amount of consternation over a court date to which he has over-prepared," she said.

"I never asked you what relationship you have with Mr. Smith."

192

"No, Mr. Martin you did not," she said.

He watched her face, the corners of her mouth, and realized she was about to smile.

"Okay, you don't have to do that," Martin said to Delia knowing the end result would be him having to leave the office anyway to purchase gastrointestinal medicine if he pushed her any further.

"Do what?" she asked.

"You know. 'fish gotta swim?' I don't have time to battle diarrhea today, Delia."

"Are you feeling ill?"

"No, but I'm getting the impression that fact is tenuous at the moment. I will go to the prison right now, but that doesn't mean you're the boss of me," he said.

Delia Hammond smiled, but not her terrifying, gut wrenching, 'make-you-want-to-claw-your-eyes-out' smile, but a pleasant, warm, and regular smile.

"Mmm Hmm," she said, her usual 'of course dear, anything you say' sound. "Drive safely, see you when you get back."

"WHAT IS IT WITH YOU AND DELIA?"" HE ASKED THEODORE SMITH.

"You look nervous," Smith said to him, ignoring the question.

"I have what might be one of the most important hearings of my career in just a few hours and instead of sitting in my office mentally preparing myself, I am here," Martin said to him.

Martin looked at Smith, his hands shackled in front of him as usual, a blank expression on his face.

"You could have come tomorrow," Theodore Smith said.

"That's what I told Delia," Martin said, almost yelling.

"She insisted," Smith said, a statement more than a question.

"She insisted," Martin said, confirming.

"I tried to argue, but I did not want her to smile at me," Martin said, shivering at the thought. Theodore Smith joined him in that shivering, as both had, at one time or another, experienced Delia's special smile.

"What kind of hearing?"

193

"What?" Martin asked him opening the file and attempting to locate the Petition.

"The important hearing you're going to have today. What is it? Why is it so important?"

"There are people who are watching. There are powerful men who are watching to see what happens, how the judge rules."

"Powerful men?"

"It's the Board of Directors of the illustrious Black Flagg Corporation," Martin said.

"You know why they named it that, right?" Theodore Smith asked.

"Nope."

"It's hidden meaning is that a black flag takes all colors."

"All colors mixed together is brown, not black. I probably should not be telling you this, but they want me to throw that case."

"They want you to lose on purpose?" Theodore Smith asked.

"I was asked to take a dive and stay down for the count."

"I see."

"The irony is that the case is a loser," Sandberg said, "there is no chance that I'm going to win."

"That's optimism," Smith said.

"It is not a lawyer that makes a case," Martin said, "it's the facts that make a case. For the hearing I'm about to have, the law does not support my position, no matter how I try to bend it, or interpret it in my favor."

"What do you do when that happens?"

"Usually I get creative. I search and can find some law to support my position. You know for every law there's ten exceptions and for each of those ten exceptions, there's ten different rules, issues fly out of issues that fly out of issues... Sometimes I even win when the case is a loser. The Petition I'm in Court for today is not something any Judge can grant, however. No matter how dire or emergent I can make it sound, it's against the law."

"Then why did the 'big dogs' at Black Flagg ask you lose?" Smith asked.

"They didn't actually ask me to lose. They asked me not to show up, which is pretty stupid. When they realized I was never

194

going to do that, they asked me to lose on purpose. As to why, there are a lot of moving parts, but it has to do with my client. No matter what, I'm going to try my hardest, but I'm still going to lose," Martin said, sliding the signature page in front of Theodore Smith. "I just need to buy some time, somehow."

"You have to stall?" Theodore Smith asked, signing the Petition Martin had prepared.

"Too many moving parts means that timing is a major factor," Martin said. "My client told me this morning that our opposition might have a change of heart and see things our way."

"That's good news."

"But the hearing's scheduled and everyone's emotions are flared up. There's a lawyer on the other side who won't agree to a continuance. I just need more time, even a little might do.

"What if you were to catch a cold, the case would have to be rescheduled, right?" Smith asked.

"Yes, and that would help, but I don't have a cold. Fairness dictates that I am forthcoming."

"What if you step in front of a bus?" Smith asked, smiling.

"It would have to be an honest mistake and I really don't want to kill myself. If that happens, I won't just come back to life like it never happened. I'm not you, Theodore."

"Good luck with it then," Smith said.

"Thanks," Martin said, putting the signature pages back into the case file.

Smith watched as Martin stood to leave.

"You know, when I first went to jail, my lawyer came with me," Theodore Smith said.

"What do you mean?" Martin asked.

"What happened to me was politically motivated. My lawyer was a young man, full of ideas and righteousness. He saw that my sentence was too harsh for what I had allegedly done, the minor part I played in the events leading to my conviction. He argued with the judge about it."

"That must not have gone over well."

"No, it did not," Smith said, "they went around and around until finally the judge held him in contempt of Court and locked him up. He spent the weekend in jail with me. Timing was an issue there, too."

"How so?"

He locked my attorney up prior to completing the hearing. It had to be postponed because the Court hadn't finished with it and my lawyer was locked up for contempt."

"That' a very interesting story," Martin said, seeing what it was that Theodore was trying to tell him.

"I thought you'd like it," Smith said.

"You're a genius," Martin said to Smith.

"I'm a convict," Smith said.

"Not for long if I have anything to say about it," Martin said, excited to finally have an idea, "I have to go. Guard!"

TWENTY-ONE

THE (CHAUVENIST) MONSTERS' CONSENSUS

NADINE CALDWELL, GENIUS IN THE FIELDS OF MATH, CHEMISTRY, AND PHYSICS INTEGRATING WORLD-CHANGING PRACTICAL APPLICATIONS, working at one of the many subsidiaries of Black Flagg, Incorporated, sat in a chair outside of Marcus Whiteacre's office.

True to form, Nadine Caldwell chewed the tip of her thumb. She watched as Marcus Whiteacre's assistant answered phones, worked on her computer, and occasionally looked up to smile at her. Nadine wondered if the woman (so close to her age) smiled at her because she was polite, or because it was part of her job description. Instead of the assistant smiling at her having its intended effect (which Nadine believed was to acknowledge her presence, a gesture of kindness and goodwill) Nadine found the act to be unsettling but couldn't quite pin down as to why.

No matter the cause or reason, Nadine took her thumbnail out of her mouth long enough to smile back to the young woman and to nod to her, the mandatory acknowledgment in such a situation.

There was a buzzing on the woman's phone, and Nadine watched as she whispered a few words into it, could not hear what the assistant said.

"Are you sure I'm unable to provide for you a cold soft drink or hot beverage such as tea or coffee?" The assistant asked her.

"I'm fine, thank you," Nadine said, lying to the woman. Nadine Caldwell was anything but "fine." She watched as a man, somewhat disheveled, walked out of Whiteacre's office, his manner and facial expression displaying sadness and distress. The man had dark circles around his eyes, and even though the room was comfortable, the man was sweating, had huge, wet blotches underneath his arms. The man met her eyes as she walked by her but said nothing.

"Mr. Whitacre will see you now. Go right in," Whiteacre's assistant said, smiling just a little too brightly and with a tone that had just the tiniest bit of unnecessary joyfulness. It was like she was at her own surprise party and not in the midst of her workday as a secretary. Nadine decided that she hated happy people.

"Sir?" Nadine Caldwell said as she entered the office.

"Mrs. Caldwell, how are you on this fine morning?" he said. The morning wasn't fine. She had court today, and she knew that Whiteacre had to be aware of it. The act of Whiteacre pretending it was a regular day (without an impending legal battle) only served to accentuate the mistrust she had felt when she had spoken to him in the past. To her, his teeth were just a bit too bright, and the way his eyes occasionally squinted made him look like a hungry animal.

"I am well, thank you," she said, (taking her thumb out of her mouth just long enough to tell the same lie she had told his assistant. She sat down in one of the plush chairs in front of his desk.

"It's my understanding that you are taking a half day today?" he asked.

Of course, and you know why. You hired my lawyer, after all, she thought.

"I have an appointment this afternoon," she said, referring to the afternoon hearing. She used the word "appointment" rather than "trial" for fear that the meeting with Whiteacre would take longer than it had to.

Nadine Caldwell watched, chewing her thumb, as Marcus poured himself a glass of water. He indicated an offer to pour her , and she shook her head.

"I'm fine, thank you," she said.

"I've reviewed the latest reports and proposals," he said. "I'm *extremely* impressed."

"Thanks," she said.

"I won't insult your intelligence, Nadine. Your work shows incredible promise. Kinetic transference has been impractical. Using the new, less expensive production methods of graphene, besides the possibilities with data, what would be the frequency of recharge? Once a year, even with maximum output?"

"Not that infrequent, but close, of course depending on usage."

"Astounding," he said.

"I didn't know you are a scientist," she said.

"I'm lots of things. One thing I'm not, however, is a mathematician. I did notice that you've conspicuously left some integrations out of the proposal," he said to her. She watched as he smiled, a jungle cat about to have dinner.

"Yes, sir."

"That, in and of itself is impressive," he said.

"It is?"

"You've given us barely enough to show function, but not enough for our research and development team to reverse engineer."

"Excuse me?" she asked, forgetting to be nervous and beginning to become angry.

"I did say I was not going to insult your intelligence. I would appreciate the same respect," he said. "You had to know that was the first thing we'd do."

She looked at him, met his eyes. He smiled at her again, took a sip of water.

"I apologize. I wasn't acting naive. It's not the scrutiny. It's your honesty," she said.

Aside from her extraordinary intelligence, Nadine Caldwell was also very perceptive. She could see that Marcus always seem to know a great deal more than he indicated.

"I have the calculations," she said, "The design is sound. "

She watched as he stared at her, through her.

"It's well within maximum deviation," she said.

"I figured you had them somewhere," he said smiling at her, "It's like a work of art, an etching from a famous artist, but with the color left out of it."

"I have the colors."

"I'd like you to give me the whole picture," Nadine, "I'm sure it's exquisite."

His tone indicated that he was attempting warmth and perhaps some parental kindness, but all she could see was a carnivorous animal on the hunt. "I bet you keep them in that little brown pocket-size notebook I have seen you with," he said.

"Someone can hack digital devices. Proprietary information can be stolen," she said, suddenly acutely aware that her little brown pocket-size notebook was in her pocket where she usually kept it. She wondered if he had someone watching her. Sitting with Marcus Whiteacre, having what might appear to be a casual conversation, Nadine suddenly realized how easy it would be for someone to merely wrest it from her person, put a foot into her back, and push her out into the street.

On one of their worst arguments, the kind that married couples sometimes have, Phillip, had told her that he could not understand how someone could be "so smart" while at the same time, also be "incredibly stupid." It was one of the few times during their entire relationship that Phillip had called her stupid. She took offense but also was flattered at the depth of worry her husband had concerning the safekeeping of her work.

Keeping her most essential secrets with her, at all times, written down in a little brown pocket-sized notebook was smart in that paper could not be stolen through electronic means. Of course, sitting before Marcus Whiteacre, staring into his alligator smile, she finally saw Phillips's point. She realized that keeping the sum and substance by "old-school" medium also meant that "old-school" methods could be used to take them from her.

Nadine was pretty sure (not wholly) that there had *not yet* been an occasion in which she was in Marcus's presence, while at the same time, had her little brown pocket-size notebook *out* of her pocket for him to see it and know what it looks like.

How did he know about it?

"So true," he said, "I keep a journal myself, putting pen to paper. Of course, I'm an old-timer."

"Sometimes it's easier to write things down," she said.

"I feel that way as well," he said. "In accord with that age-old adage about keeping all eggs in one basket, I'm sure you have the rest hidden in a computer backup somewhere, the importance of keeping one's proprietary information safe and secure," he said.

"Of course," she said.

She suddenly felt afraid that he could see she was lying. It was all in her pocket, everything. She never bothered with a computer backup.

She realized that her husband had been correct about keeping her "proprietary" work safe. She felt a wave of apprehension from the eye contact she was having with Marcus Whiteacre, who, at that moment, was undoubtedly looking right *through* her.

Her confirmation that she only had parts of her work in her pocket and the rest in a computer someplace fell flat. She was immediately cognizant of the fact that she was a scientist, not an actor.

She looked at her wristwatch, and in doing so, realized too late her failure regarding the convention which dictates one does not look at one's wristwatch while meeting with the boss.

"You have plenty of time," he said to her. He watched as she put her hands in her lap as if she had made an obscene hand gesture. "Nadine, I know about your afternoon *appointment.*"

She looked at him.

"If we are going to work together, it is important to be forthcoming," he said, "I consider you to be an asset to the company. It is my business to protect our assets, and to be fully aware of all the facts and circumstances involved."

"I find it unsettling, at the very least, that you call me an "asset" and have taken it upon yourself to pry into my personal life," she said.

"All employees, by definition are assets. As to the personal information, it's hardly personal when legal documents are filed with the court and made part of the public record," he said, "wouldn't you agree?"

He watched as she chewed the tip of her thumb for a moment, staring out of the window behind him.

"I apologize for overstepping my bounds," he said.

She nodded, still chewing her thumb, considered what she would tell him as the conversation was rapidly becoming much more acrimonious than she had anticipated.

"Mr. Whiteacre, I know we've talked about it," she said.

"You'll have to narrow it down."

"About the pregnancy? You said it was a consensus that I cannot have the baby, yet still, devote the time and attention needed for my project."

"You seemed to agree with me at the time. Has that changed?"

"I was enamored. I was flattered that your great company was interested in me, wanted to hear what I had to say," she said. She paused for a moment to realize her habit, took her thumbnail out of her mouth. She watched as he casually took another sip of his glass of water and leaned back in his chair, his eyes never wavering from her.

"Thing is, what you have provided for me here is any workaholic scientist's dream."

"Is there a problem?"

"The problem, Mr. Whiteacre, is that as it pertains to my pregnancy, there shouldn't be a *consensus*, nor any discussion at all. I'll tell you the same thing I told my husband, that is my body and I will be the only person to make a decision regarding whether or not it is with child."

She watched as her words took root in him. It was clear to him that Whiteacre had the same two choices that every living thing has when faced with a conflict, big or small. Marcus Whiteacre knew that humans called it "fight or flight." Marcus preferred to call it "concede or fight," as in his opinion, there were times, especially when one has been cornered, that fighting is untenable and there is just nowhere to flee.

Marcus could apologize to her and perhaps repair the damaged relationship, but he was far too intelligent to engage in an exercise in futility and decided to argue the point.

"Nadine, do you own a car?" he asked.

"I'm pretty sure you know that I do," she said.

"Do you get regular maintenance, oil changes, tune-ups?"

"Sure."

"Why?" he asked.

He watched as she frowned, not because she was considering the question, but because she felt he was patronizing her. He decided he would answer the question for her.

"You get oil changes, scheduled tune-ups," he said, answering the question for her. "If you hear a strange sound coming from the engine, you bring it to a mechanic. You do these things to ensure that your automobile will get you from point A to point B. Running a company, ensuring its smooth operation is no different. When I have an employee who has a legal or a personal problem, and that employee is of particular importance, would it not behoove me to take interest and perhaps conduct that routine maintenance, assist that employee and enable that employee to focus on his or her work?"

"I've never run a company," she said.

"Then you can take my word for it. For any system, be it an automobile, business relationship, or a company, risk management and regular maintenance are necessary for continued survival."

"Risk management?"

"In this case, assisting employees when needed."

"Like hiring an attorney for me," she said.

"Of course. My job includes taking whatever actions I deem necessary to assist you in maintaining focus on your work."

"The Board of Directors had a meeting concerning my pregnancy?"

"Yes, we did, and..."

"You put it to a vote, someone made a motion to the floor, someone seconded, you said 'aye' or 'nay,' and the group believed that I would be an ineffective employee if I went to full term and had this baby?"

"Nadine, don't be naïve. If you are at home, changing diapers, breastfeeding, up all night, you're certainly not as effective as you would be without a child, wouldn't you agree?"

"No, I do not agree," she said, still frowning.

There was a moment of silence that passed between them.

The only thing that Nadine felt she had been naïve about was that she could have this very conversation with Marcus and it would remain professional and not become hostile.

She watched as he sighed deeply, finished his glass of water.

"I take it then that you are going to cancel your hearing this afternoon?"

"No, I am *not* going to cancel the hearing scheduled for this afternoon," she said.

She watched as his face relaxed, relief displayed in his eyes and the lines in his face.

"Oh, that's good, very good," he said. "I was afraid that you changed your mind. I was afraid that you had irresponsibly decided that motherhood was more important than changing the world. If I may be so bold, you do not even need to attend the hearing," he said.

"I don't?" she asked.

"Of course not, as you said, it is *your* body. Instead of going to the hearing, you can have the abortion right now. I can have a car take you, and I have doctors standing by, ready, willing, able, and paid handsomely for services rendered."

"But the hearing..." she started to say. Without a thought, Whiteacre cut her off.

203

"What would a judge do? Hold you in contempt for exercising *your* right to *your* body?"

He watched as she stood from her chair, slowly, much like a camouflaged rabbit trying to decide whether or not to run and risk being seen by the predator hunting it, or to stay frozen, hiding, hoping not to be noticed.

"Is there a problem?" he asked.

"I'm beginning to feel like the family pet turkey during the beginning of November."

"Excuse me?"

"Boundaries," she said. He looked at her. "Most people have boundaries. I might believe it was a matter of course that my pregnancy was discussed at the Board of Directors meeting."

"But?" he asked.

"But having a car waiting, just for me, to take me to doctors who are already paid and waiting, just for me, all previously arranged by you is too much. You have no boundaries, Mr. Whiteacre."

He watched as she rolled her eyes, looked up at the ceiling for a moment, lifted herself up and down by the balls of her feet. "This is something wrong here. There's something about you. I can't quite put my finger on it. I'm so stupid. I should've listened."

"Listened to who, your husband? No offense, Nadine, his intelligence is lacking," Whiteacre said.

"Yes, I will agree my husband is not the smartest person, but I'm not referring to him. I should've listened to *myself,* that nagging voice in the back of my head that ends up screaming at me every time I walk through the doors of this building. Everyone here seems to be just a little *too* nice, a little too friendly, everyone going out of their way for me. It's like every day is Nadine day, and the whole place is happy to celebrate. With the red carpet rolled out for me everywhere I go, unlimited funding, all the money I could want, I should have been suspicious, long ago. The world does not work this way."

"You don't believe that you are worth the red-carpet treatment?" he asked her, "Do you have any idea of the importance of your work? Your discoveries?"

"It wouldn't matter if I had discovered cold-fusion," she said, "you've overstepped."

"It's better than cold-fusion."

"Even so, Mr. Whiteacre, put yourself in my shoes," she said, "wouldn't you be suspicious?"

"Not at all," he said. "I'm here to help you, to support you, to support your work, to ensure the best possible environment for your success."

"Which includes paying for lawyers and abortion doctors?"

"If needed. I understand you have not had the pleasure of experiencing big business, but this is how it works."

"It's an invasion of privacy," she said, "it feels like I'm being controlled."

"I'm not sure why you're upset, Nadine. You told me that you were not canceling the hearing this afternoon, that you were going to go to court today and fight against your husband. This company is not trying to control you. I'm not trying to control you. It's your husband that's controlling you. He's the one who is trying to get a court order to force you to bring the pregnancy to term."

"That is correct, but..."

"We want the same thing, Nadine. You're not canceling the hearing. You're going to go, you're going to win, and then you can have the operation and terminate the pregnancy. I'm telling you, I mean, I am suggesting that you don't even need to bother. Like you said it's your body. Why bother arguing over it in a courtroom? Whether you terminate the pregnancy prior to or after the hearing is irrelevant. Why have the hearing if you're not going to have the baby?"

"Oh, I *am* having the baby," she said, her eyes beaming.

His mouth dropped wide open.

"What?"

"You heard me correctly. Mr. Whiteacre. I came here today to tell you that you, and apparently the Board of Directors are *wrong.* I can work, I can be brilliant, I can change the world, and I can do it and be a mother at the same time."

"But the hearing," he said, his eyes wide in disbelief.

"I am going to the hearing, Mr. Whiteacre, because *no one* will tell me what to do with my body, not my husband, who I love very much by the way, not any judge, not this company, and *not you.* Nobody, no man is going to tell me what I can accomplish. If having this baby is a deal-breaker, if you're going to fire me because I'm having a child, which is a ridiculous result, then I quit," she said.

Nadine Caldwell stared at him.

Marcus stared at her.

He'd played his hand. It was time to move on to another strategy.

The moment lasted far too long before Marcus picked up the phone.

"Nadine Caldwell no longer works for this company," he said, then hung up the telephone.

"My husband was right, then," she said, a statement and not a question. "If this were just about developing my project, we'd *still be talking.* You did all this to box me in, to convince me to have an abortion. As ridiculous as it sounds, my husband is talking to her, isn't he?"

It was Marcus Whiteacre's turn to stare at her, frozen.

"This baby, my daughter, she *is* more than the sum of her parts? She is special?" Nadine asked, holding her belly with two hands.

"I've always hated the word 'special.' It can mean something that is precious, priceless. It is also used to describe someone with a disability, like the 'Special Olympics.' The word 'special' can mean something that is good or bad or something that is in between," Marcus Whiteacre said.

"In this case, it is used to describe my unborn child, who, for some reason, you want to see ended," she said.

He stared at her, now very much the carnivore hunting for prey.

The moment for him to deny any of her allegations had passed.

Fear took hold of her as she realized the great lengths, the money and time expended, the considerable effort that had been made for the sole purpose of terminating her pregnancy.

Marcus Whiteacre had become a statue, staring at her with piercing eyes, unmoving, unflinching, furious.

Unceremoniously, feeling (and then resisting) the urge to run screaming out of the building, Nadine Caldwell walked out of Marcus Whiteacre's office.

As she headed towards the elevator, she heard the familiar "ding" and saw the doors open to reveal several Laszlos who, to her, looked like regular security, various people of different shapes, sizes, genders, and races, all in uniform, coming to the floor. They were undoubtedly coming for her. They were undoubtedly coming for ill purpose.

Nadine Caldwell concluded that is always easier to go down the stairs rather than up, went down the other hallway, hoping that the security officers did not see her efforts at avoiding them.

Running down the stairs as quickly as she could, her footfalls echoing in the stairwell, Nadine heard doors above her open and close. She heard someone high above her yell the words: "she's in the stairwell." She went down one more flight of stairs and opened the stairwell door. She peered into the hallway from the stairwell. Trying (and failing) to breathe evenly, hoping she didn't appear like she felt like she was running for her life, she walked through the crowded and busy office floor. She walked past the cubicles, *people* talking on phones, working on computers, going about their day.

As she neared the elevator, she had a decision to make. She knew there was another stairwell on the other side of the floor. She wondered if she should get on the elevator or head to the other stairwell. It was clear, at least in her mind, that she was in danger. She resisted the urge to imagine what would happen to her if security caught up with her. Confident that the security officers were not trying to meet up with her for the sole purpose of escorting her from the building, she walked past the elevator and into the other stairwell. She went down another flight, stopped at the floor, and listened to the voices of the security officers that were now coming from below and above. Wiping the sweat from her forehead, she went into the hallway of the floor right below the one she had just been on and headed back towards the elevator. She pressed the "down" button, chewed her thumb, and rolled up and down on the balls of her feet. She smiled as office workers walked past her.

She stepped on the elevator. As the doors closed, she saw security enter the floor and run towards her. When the elevator doors opened, several Laszlos were waiting for her; guns pointed at the opening.

When the doors opened, security stared in disbelief at the empty elevator cabin.

"I thought you said she was on the elevator," one of them said. Another security officer went into the elevator, dismayed that it was empty.

"Where did she go?" One of them asked the other.

"How should I know?"

"She must be on another floor, in the stairwell. Go back up. She can't have gone far!" one of them yelled.

Timing being everything, Nadine Caldwell pulled the panel of roofing aside, dropped down into the elevator cabin. Just as the doors were closing, she managed to put her hand into the opening, breaking the infrared sensor beam and causing the elevator doors to open.

Nadine Caldwell ran as fast as she could towards the glass doors of the entrance to the building.

"There she is!" someone yelled.

"Hey, stop!" someone else yelled.

"Mrs. Caldwell stop!" Another security officer called out. She ignored the demands of the people chasing her and managed to get the door of the building open. She ran through the doors, turned to see if they were still following.

As she was looking behind her while running forward, Nadine Caldwell tripped and landed on the busy street, right in front of a moving car.

TWENTY-TWO

WINNING, LOSING, CONTEMPT OF COURT

"MARTY, ARE YOU GOING? YOU NEED TO GO OR YOU'LL BE LATE!" Delia called out.

Martin Sandberg stood in his conference room, transfixed on the opening. Moments prior he had stood before the back wall of his conference room and stared at it. The wall looked like just a wall.

He knew Abraham Cardozo had made it into something very different.

"Open," he had said, barely above a whisper.

Concurrent with the modus operandi of the very best spy movies, the wall had automatically opened, electronic panels which had been invisible, folded back in a mechanical array, LED lights appeared, and the wall opened to reveal a plated, floor-to-ceiling safe. There were several empty shelves, several empty cubbyholes. The entirety of the safe contained only two items: Lassiter's golf clubs and Connor's briefcase.

Martin stood, staring at the insides of the safe. For the weeks leading up to this hearing, he had tried to put it out of his head. He even called Cardozo, hoping he could convince him to come to the office and take the briefcase away. It kept clawing at the back of his mind and was becoming harder to resist.

When Cardozo answered the phone (after Martin annoyingly called three times in a row), Martin had explained the problem. Cardozo, after a moment of silence, had barked: "the briefcase wasn't meant for you. Leave it alone." Then Cardozo had hung up on him.

Before he hung up, Martin thought he could feel Abraham Cardozo smiling on the other end of the phone. Martin could sometimes *hear* when someone was smiling as they talked.

Martin knew that as it currently stood, he was going to lose and Ariel would be ended without anyone knowing who or what she is or what she might do for the universe.

As he stood staring at it, the briefcase appeared harmless, merely sitting on the shelf. Martin stood transfixed, sorry that he had opened the safe.

He could feel its pull. It was the chocolate uncut birthday cake in the kitchen waiting for the party to start. It was the automobile that the indigent auto lover would never be able to drive. It was the bottle calling out to the person struggling in the program. It was the plate of fresh-baked cookies, menacingly cooling on the stove while the person with diabetes struggled to put the delicious scent out of his mind.

As he stood, staring longingly at the briefcase, his back sweating, his shirt stuck to the skin on his back. The air conditioning hit his back, and Martin felt a chill.

"Once you touch it, there's no going back," a voice said behind Martin.

He turned to see Delia standing behind him, a miracle in and of itself, that she had (actually) gotten up out of her seat.

"I know," he said.

"You know what happened to the last lawyer who used Connor's briefcase?" she asked him.

"Except for the original owner, everyone who used it won every case," he said, "just like I need to win this one."

"And as careers blossomed, personal lives were destroyed. Wives had car accidents, children died, buildings burned and lives crumbled," she said.

"Delia?"

"Yes, Mr. Martin?"

"Have I ever told you that you have a way with words?"

"Every day, Mr. Martin," she said.

"I only need to win this case," he said.

"At what cost?" Delia asked.

"I'll put it back as soon as the hearing's over," Martin said.

"You may not be lying to me on purpose, but you know in your heart, Mr. Martin, if you put your hands on it, that will not be the end result."

She watched as he sighed and looked down.

"The alternative is just as bad," he said.

"Maybe not."

"The disaster you know versus the unknown?"

"If you touch that cursed thing, you know what will happen. You may win today, but you will lose everything and everyone. You don't know if you're going to lose today, though."

"I think I do," he said.

Martin Sandberg had no idea how to win the Caldwell hearing and was confident he would not prevail. However, thanks to the recent conversation he had earlier in the day with Theodore Smith, Martin Sandberg had realized that the opposite of winning was not necessarily losing.

The two stood before the safe, mesmerized, eyes open and glazed as if they were watching a fireworks show.

"You know I dislike Mr. Cardozo," Delia said.

"I've seen."

"As you and I stand here, wasting time, staring at that artifact, you have to ask," she said.

She looked at him, but he couldn't break his gaze from the open wall.

"Ask? Ask what, Delia?"

"Why it is that Mr. Cardozo, out of the blue, decided to put a safe in the wall of your conference room."

"He said it was to house artifacts."

"Besides those golf clubs, which are a fluke, by the way, what else is in there?" she asked.

A moment of silence passed.

Delia could feel Martin's epiphany as it if was electric in the air.

Anger soon followed.

He turned to face her. There was a rage in his eyes.

"There it is," she said.

For a moment (or two) Martin wondered if Abraham Cardozo was trying to kill his family by building a wall safe in Martin's office and putting the one thing into the safe that Martin, especially at this point in his life, might not be able to resist. It would be a sickening pursuit of nefarious purposes to put the briefcase that makes all lawyers win, but wrecks their lives, into Martin's safe, knowing that Martin was engaged in the legal battle of his life.

"I've been set up," he said.

"It looks like that to me, Mr. Martin, but what do I know? I'm just a secretary with a pretty smile."

"He wants me to win, but doesn't care if my family suffers? Delia, what's happening here? I mean, what's really happening?"

"If I knew, I'd tell you. All I know is that Mr. Cardozo didn't even bother to put a coffee mug in there and call it the Holy Grail, now did he?"

"No."

211

"He could have at least gone to the Dollar Store and put some knick-knacks in there and told you not to play with the Devil-toys. He couldn't even be bothered to make it look like you were actually holding things for him."

"I don't know what's worse, how stupid he *thinks* I am, or how stupid I really *am*," Martin said, despondent, "it hadn't even occurred to me with all that nonsense about artifacts and whatever, he was putting this briefcase *in my path*."

"Mr. Martin, you may not be the smartest lawyer," Delia said.

"Thanks," Martin said.

"But you *care* the most out of anyone I have ever seen. That makes you the best lawyer," she said.

"Delia Hammond paying me a compliment. Now I know the world is coming to an end," Martin said, finally able to keep his eyes off the briefcase and onto her face. She smiled at him, but it was not one of Delia's extra special "make-you-want-to-go-into-the-center-of-the-lion-cage-at-the-zoo, ring-a-bell-and-yell-'who's-ready-for-supper" smile.

"It's true," she said, "I never met another lawyer who was as caring as you."

"Thanks," he said.

"For a little truth that happens to be a compliment?" she asked.

"That, and at the risk of being sued, I like that smile better than the other one."

"Of course, you do," she said, still smiling her (regular) smile. "You need to say the word and go."

She watched as he sighed, taking one last look at Connor's briefcase.

"Marty?"

"Close," he said.

The safe came to life, and instead of either of them walking away, they chose to watch as the doors to the safe closed, and the wall once again became a wall.

MARTIN SANDBERG SAT AT COUNSEL TABLE, PHILLIP CALDWELL TO HIS RIGHT. Opposing counsel, a young attorney named Wallace Santoni sat at opposing counsel table, notebooks and electronic devices neatly arranged as if the table belonged to him. He seemed as relaxed and comfortable as if he was sitting in his office. Martin knew Santoni. Though Martin had only come across him once or twice, he had felt that Santoni was *off.* Because he was representing the interests of Black Flagg, Inc. (and *not* the interests of Nadine Caldwell in Martin's opinion) Martin realized that his earlier instincts about the young man were justified, at least partly.

Phillip Caldwell, sitting next to Martin, true to form, was sweating profusely. Martin attempted to ignore him, instead fruitlessly trying to focus on the argument he was about to make. Martin's efforts at concentration were pointless. Distractingly, Phillip Caldwell turned at least once every two minutes, looking at the door to the courtroom, waiting anxiously for Nadine to join them in the courtroom. When he was not turning, adjusting, fidgeting, he was looking at his watch, putting a hand through his greasy hair, or squirming in some other manner.

"Can you please sit still?" Martin whispered, even though there was no need to whisper, as this judge had not come into the courtroom as of yet.

"Where is she?" Phillip asked.

"I don't know. Are you sure she's coming?"

"I'm positive," he said.

Martin looked into the young man's face, saw the concern, apparently worried that something had happened to his wife. Martin felt the hearing was an exercise in madness.

Aside from having conversations with what was professed to be the Phillip Caldwell's unborn child, the hearing was odd because Philip and Nadine were not getting a divorce, were still very much in love, and this one matter was the only thing for which they were not of singular mind that is, if Nadine even wanted to go forward. Phillip had told him otherwise but where was she?

Martin looked around the empty courtroom. Aside from Wally at the other counsel table, the clerk, the patiently waiting court reporter, and what Martin was now referring to as "Laszlo Prime" standing in the corner, they were alone.

Martin stared at the bailiff, took an opportunity to look *hard* at him, first straight on, then from the corner of his eye. Martin tried to look past the greasy jet-black hair, the dark, perfectly manicured mustache, and the muscular piston-like arms.

213

From the corner of his eye, Martin was about to see something he thought didn't belong before the bailiff spoke to him.

"Are you about to ask me on a date, Sandberg?"

"What?"

"Quit staring at me, Marty."

"I'll be back in a second," Martin whispered to Phillip. Martin Sandberg walked to Laszlo, stood next to him, instead of the front of him.

"Oh no, you can turn right around and go back to counsel table," he said.

"I'm sorry," Martin said, standing next to him, his hands in his pockets, trying just a little too hard to appear nonchalant.

"I heard about your little meltdown," Laszlo said.

"Are you him?" Martin asked.

"Him who?"

"The one, the real one."

"I'm real, see?" Laszlo said, then gave him a poke. "I'm Laszlo."

"You're Laszlo, I'm Laszlo, everyone's Laszlo," Martin said.

"You know me, Counselor."

"How can I be sure?"

"Because I'm the one who turned you on to coal-fired pizza," he said.

"It's all very disconcerting," Martin said.

"I'd make a joke about birthdays for my family and me being disconcerting, but I don't think you'll find it funny," Laszlo Prime said.

"How many?" Martin asked.

"Six hundred, fifty-four," Laszlo Prime said.

"That's a lot of siblings," Martin said.

"Birthdays can get expensive," Laszlo Prime said.

"I thought you weren't going to make that joke."

"I couldn't resist."

"Ha, ha," Martin said without smiling.

"Didn't I tell you to go back to your table?"

"I thought they were all you," Martin said.

"I heard."

Before the conversation could continue, the door in the corner of the courtroom opened, and Judge Andrew Markowitz sauntered out.

"All rise!" Laszlo yelled.

Martin hurried back to his spot next to Phillip.

"Court is now in session, the Honorable Judge Andrew Markowitz presiding. Please be sure all electronic devices are turned off, if the court is interrupted, I'm authorized to take possession," Laszlo said.

"It seems we are minus a party," Markowitz said, looking at Wallace Santoni. "Mr. Santoni, do you expect your client to attend today?"

"I do, Your Honor. I don't know where she is," Santoni said.

"Mr. Sandberg, does your client have any idea where his wife is?" Markowitz asked. Martin turned to Phillip who shook his head and shrugged his shoulders at the same time.

"We expected her to be here as well," Martin said.

"I am acutely aware that time is of the essence in this particular matter. Are we to proceed without her? Mr. Santoni, do you have authority to waive your client's presence?"

All eyes were on Wallace Santoni, who, without any nervous inflection, buttoned the top button of his coat and gave a fake smile.

"I do, Your Honor, we may proceed without her," he said with confidence.

"Very well, Mr. Sandberg, I have read your motion and accompanying brief."

"Yes, your Honor."

"While I understand that this is an emotional subject for your client, I fail to see any precedent for the relief you are seeking," Markowitz said.

"It borders on frivolous, Your Honor," Santoni said.

They watched as Markowitz sighed deeply, rubbed his temples (as he always did when frustrated) and turned to Wallace Santoni.

"Mr. Santoni, I know you are new to the bar. Allow me a moment to educate you. Unless making a legal objection based on the rules of evidence, 'chiming in' or interrupting a judge, is inadvisable. Do you understand what it is that I'm trying to explain to you?" Markowitz asked.

"Yes, Your Honor, I'm sorry," Santoni said.

"Sit down Mr. Santoni," Markowitz said.

"Now, Mr. Sandberg, tell me why it is you're asking me to rule contrary to the United States Supreme Court?"

"I have an argument prepared," Martin said.

"Yes, and it was probably well thought out, cogent, and organized speech. However, Mr. Sandberg, *Planned Parenthood of Missouri v. Danforth* may be very old precedent, but it is still precedent."

"Yes, Your Honor."

"A potential father, according to *Planned Parenthood v. Casey*, does not even have a legal right to be notified of a scheduled abortion operation."

"We are not arguing the issue of consent," Martin Sandberg said.

"Aren't you?" Markowitz asked.

"The Supreme Court in *Danforth* stated that any law that required a father's consent for an abortion would be unconstitutional, that if a father or husband refused to give consent, that would effectively deny a woman's right, a woman's choice to terminate a pregnancy," Martin said.

"Yes, I've read the opinion. Since it is the mother that carries the pregnancy, the balance naturally weighs in her favor. How is this situation any different? The fetus is several weeks away from viability," Markowitz said, adjusting his small eyeglasses.

"If you've read my brief..." Martin began to say. Judge Markowitz interrupted him.

"Yes, an excellent dissertation on how rights of individuals, especially the fundamental right of parenting has evolved throughout the years. I understand the argument as well concerning this particular pregnancy. We do not give preference. I fail to understand how it is you would expect any judge to tell a woman what to do with her body, no matter who or what is the subject of the pregnancy. Do you have anything to add Mr. Santoni?" Markowitz looked at Wallace Santoni. The young lawyer, still nervous from being chastised moments earlier, appeared as a small animal staring at the massive opened jaws of a predator.

"We agree with the Court's position," Santoni said.

There was a moment of silence where Markowitz stared at Santoni. The young lawyer looked down at his papers, anything to avoid the Judge's disapproving gaze.

"Thank you for that well-reasoned analysis," Markowitz said.

"Do you have anything else to add, Mr. Sandberg?" Markowitz asked Martin.

Martin closed his eyes, knowing that Judge Markowitz was about to rule against him. With his eyes closed, Martin saw her. He did not see her as she was while building the prison cell, in the spaces between his soul and his humanity. Instead, he saw her as she stood on a field of impossible green, lush, beautiful green which was growing in the desert, looking at him as he stood staring, having witnessed firsthand her small and deliberate steps towards saving the world from itself.

A ruling from Judge Markowitz, whether it was legal, fair, justified, or otherwise, in this matter, was a step in the wrong direction.

"Just a moment, Your Honor," Martin asked, "for me to confer with my client?" The judge nodded.

"Listen to me carefully, Phillip," Martin whispered in his ear, "no matter what you see here, no matter what happens, do nothing."

Phillip Caldwell nodded.

"Judge Markowitz, I do not believe you've read my brief. Matter of fact, I don't think you read any of the law you just cited," Martin said.

"Excuse me?"

"If you had, you'd understand what's at stake here."

"I don't care what you think," Markowitz said.

"You better," Martin said, looking at him, staring into his eyes.

"What if I was to tell you that Nadine Caldwell's child will be the next Albert Einstien, Stephen Hawking, Nicola Tesla? What if I was to tell you that the ruling I know you're about to make is going to keep us all from one-day driving hover cars and having a clean Earth?"

"What if her pregnancy is the next Adolph Hitler?" Markowitz asked.

"I know it's not."

217

"I wasn't aware that your license to practice law included the ability to make prognostications," Markowitz said.

"I do not see into the future, so much as like my client, I have met her."

"You've met her? Who?"

"Objection, counsel is testifying," Santoni said.

The argument stopped as both Markowitz and Sandberg looked at him.

"Sit down, Mr. Santoni," Markowitz said.

"I met her, Judge. My client's met her."

"You met an unborn baby?"

"Why do you always interrupt me?"

"What?" Markowitz asked.

"You judges are all alike," Martin said.

"Excuse me?"

"You ask me a legal question, but before I get barely two words out to answer you before you hit me with another question. How is that fair? How is that proper procedure? Hell, how is that how any normal person has a conversation?"

"Mr. Sandberg, you are testing this Court."

"I should hope so. You see, you've failed to keep an open mind, Judge Markowitz. You came here today knowing exactly how you were going to rule. It didn't matter what I said. It didn't matter what I presented to you. I could have God and the Devil down here in this courtroom picking sides for a game of Armageddon kick-ball, and you still wouldn't listen! You have no idea what's truly happening here. You came here today with your mind made up already. Your job is to keep an open mind."

"I'm not going to warn you again," Markowitz said, seething.

"Or what? You'll smack down your gavel and kill another demon? Another angel? Another-who-knows-what? You can't come to Court poised and ready to beat a lawyer down because you know what the motion is and you've already made up your mind."

"Mr. Sandberg!"

"You're clueless! You don't know, and you're never going to know because you don't listen! Why even bother coming to court? A stuffed monkey could do a better job than you!"

As Martin demonstrated his frustration, not only with Judge Markowitz but with everything, the head Laszlo just stood in his usual corner, hands on his hips, smiling.

"Mr. Martin Sandberg, I now find you in contempt of court. You will stop talking! Bailiff, take him into custody," Markowitz said.

Still dumbfounded, Santoni watched as Laszlo Prime casually put handcuffs on Martin Sandberg and began to lead him out of the back door instead of the front.

Martin and Laszlo disappeared out the back door towards the courthouse's holding cells.

"Mr. Caldwell, you now find yourself without an attorney," Judge Markowitz said.

"Yes, sir?"

"It is now incumbent upon me to explain to you how we are to proceed. I could ask you if you are comfortable to proceed without counsel, but seeing as your wife isn't here, either, I feel I have no choice but to continue this hearing until such time as you are able to obtain a substitute attorney. Do you understand?"

"I think so," Phillip Caldwell said.

"Very well, since your attorney has been involuntarily extricated from the proceedings, I have no choice but to continue this hearing. As it stands..."

Judge Markowitz was interrupted.

Anita, Judge Markowitz's assistant suddenly ran into the courtroom. She appeared (uncharacteristically) emotionally distraught. Phillip watched as she whispered something into the Judge's ear.

"I understand," Markowitz said to her, then turned to look at Phillip Caldwell. "Mr. Caldwell, I'm very sorry to inform you that there's been an accident. Your wife has been hit by a car."

TWENTY-THREE

IN THE HOLDING CELL, MARTIN SANDBERG SAT ON THE BENCH CLOSEST TO THE BARS. He was the sole occupant of the holding cell. He might have enjoyed the solitude if the odor wasn't so bad. The unmistakable smell of urine lingered in the air, just strong enough to remind him of where he was. As to how he got there, Martin wondered if he had made a mistake. Since he had been forced to give his wristwatch, (and belt) to Laszlo, he did not know how long he had waited before he had heard someone shuffling down the hallway. This was not the first time Martin had found himself locked someplace and being a realist, he knew it would probably not be his last.

It had been a surprise for Martin, however, to see that the person shuffling down the hall was none other than Judge Markowitz. Martin watched as he pulled a chair from the nearby desk, without speaking, dragged it to the cell, and sat down.

"Did somebody pee on the floor?" Markowitz asked.

"Smells like it," Martin said, eyeing him. Judge Markowitz usually wore an expression that appeared to Martin to be a mixture of frustration and despair. Today, he thought Markowitz looked uncommonly sad.

"Are you all right?" Martin asked him.

"I've put your paperwork through to have you released," Markowitz said.

"Thanks," Martin said.

"I had to hold you in contempt," Markowitz said, "you gave me no choice."

"I know that," Martin said.

"The sentence for contempt is not up to me," Markowitz said.

"I know that, too."

"Normally, if it was bad enough, the worst you could expect is a few hours or the night in lockup," Markowitz said.

"Not in this case," Martin said.

"It's not a regular case. I know it, you know it."

"I'm sorry, Judge."

"For what, Marty?"

"I said some things..."

221

"Why? It makes no difference. No one cares what I have to say," Markowitz said.

"That's where you're wrong," Martin said.

"This was all a mistake," Markowitz said.

"This was about the baby. How far out did you continue the case?"

Judge Markowitz sighed, and to Martin, he never looked more tired.

"There was an accident," Markowitz said, watched in sadness as Martin's eyes grew wide as he suddenly became pale. "That's why she wasn't in court."

Martin approached the bars of his cell and held them in his hands.

"Is she alright?" Martin asked.

"I don't know. Anita told me. I told your client. He ran from the courtroom, presumably to the hospital."

Martin suddenly found it was tough for him to breathe.

"What about the baby? I have to get out of here," Martin said, almost yelling.

"Slow down. I told you I already put through the paperwork to get you out. You're being processed, and someone will come to let you out in a minute or two."

"I need to get out of here now," he said.

"It should just be a minute," Markowitz said, standing. "I think I'm going to go home and maybe sit in my bedroom closet, in the dark, and cry a little."

"Really, Judge?" Martin asked.

"No, another poor attempt at humor on my part," Markowitz said, but Martin knew the truth as he watched Markowitz walk away, leaving him alone in the holding cell.

It took longer than "just a minute" for Laszlo (Prime) to appear at the bars to Martin's cell.

"Great, finally," Martin said.

Laszlo stared at him.

"Are you here to release me?" Martin asked.

Laszlo continued to stare.

"What?" Martin asked. Laszlo handed him a typed, folded paper.

Martin took it and opened it, read its contents.

"That was fast," Martin said.

"You've been at the top of the list," Laszlo said, "They weren't going to drag their feet."

"I don't get this."

"It's not my job to explain it," Laszlo said, stone-faced.

Laszlo watched as Martin sat down, plopped on to the bench, the paper in his hands, his mouth open as he read and re-read the contents.

"I had an argument with a judge," Martin said.

"You were found in contempt," Laszlo said.

"For arguing with a judge. This says..."

"I know what it says, Martin. That's why I brought it to you. They might send me to deliver the sanctions. I want you to know there are no hard feelings. You know, it's not personal."

Martin looked at him, angry. He wondered how much worse it might be if he tried to strangle Laszlo. Being as he was built like a truck, Martin was sure he would not succeed, but the effort might make him feel better.

"It's not personal?" Martin asked.

"That's what I said."

"Next you're going to say you're just doing your job?" Martin asked.

He stared at Laszlo with hatred in his eyes.

Laszlo didn't know what to say to him.

"You can't agree with this."

"It's above my pay grade," Laszlo said.

"That's a stupid thing to say," Martin said.

"No need to get personal."

"This is the very definition of personal. How else would I be? You or some other monster is going to come to my home, bring a few hundred friends for the party and drag me out of this plane of existence. We're not going on vacation, are we?" Martin asked, already knowing the answer. It was on the paper in his hand, now clutched into a fist.

"Which one?" Martin asked.

"What?"

"Which hell? Which hell is it?" Martin asked.

"I don't know, there are so many."

"I'm getting dragged to an undisclosed hell, and my punishment for arguing with a judge is going to be..." Martin

223

stopped, choked. He found that he couldn't say the words for fear of throwing up.

"This was just an argument," Martin said after calming himself.

"You keep saying that."

"I'm going to hell... I can't... It's going to be you?"

"Sandberg, it's..." Laszlo started to argue, but Martin interrupted him.

"I know, I know. It's not *personal.* It doesn't matter how many times you say it, Laszlo. It doesn't matter if you call it 'just business,' tell yourself whatever you have to so you can sleep at night," Martin said, "for having a disagreement..."

"Don't insult me," Laszlo said, interrupting him, his face at the bars, suddenly and abruptly showing his emotions. "You know damned well that this isn't about having an argument with Markowitz. If that were the case, every other person in town would probably be sanctioned right there with you," Laszlo said, voice loud, angry, almost yelling.

Seconds passed while Martin stared at him through the bars as Laszlo paced.

"You did all that on purpose and where did it get you? Nowhere. I swear, Sandberg if you had a brain cell in your head, it would die of loneliness."

"What was I supposed to do?" Martin asked, defiant.

"Your job, Counselor! You do your job, play your part, or the system doesn't work. You thought you'd color outside the lines, render the court *impotent.* 'I'm Martin Sandberg. I don't want to lose so I'll just have myself held in contempt on purpose.' That's not a legal strategy. It made no difference."

"Yes, I think it did."

"No, Martin, it didn't. Nothing's changed except this time you've gone over that line. How'd that work out for you? I hope you're proud."

"At least I'm trying," Martin said.

"No."

"No?"

"I'm going to tell you because I don't think anyone else will and you're far too oblivious to figure it out on your own."

"I'm a captive audience, Laszlo. Have your say and open this cage."

"Martin, you always do what you want, rules be damned. We all have to follow them, that is, except you. You're so self-important you think it's alright to endanger all of us, everyone."

"I didn't do anything to you," Martin said.

"You don't think so? Your kid's dying in a hospital bed? You don't get down and pray by her side like a normal parent, and you don't beg the doctors to save her, that's not the Sandberg way, oh no. The rules don't apply to the great Martin Sandberg, Attorney at Law," Laszlo said, almost growling. Martin watched as he put his face up to the bars.

Martin didn't know Laszlo was harboring such hostility. Martin was sure Laszlo Prime hadn't let him out of the cell because Laszlo was afraid he might hurt Martin.

"Tearing a man-sized hole in the fabric of space, time, and reality is not exactly eco-conscious, Mr. Sandberg."

"I didn't know."

"You didn't know what? That there's be consequences from your little adventure? That that the laws of life and death don't apply where you or your family are concerned?" Laszlo asked.

Martin was silent. He looked away from Laszlo.

Laszlo paced for a moment, seething, silent. He calmed down while Martin looked at the paper in his hands. He looked at it differently than he had a moment ago.

"You're going to pay," Laszlo said, unlocking the cell and tossing a plastic bag containing Martin's belt and other items onto the bench next to him.

"When you do, remember it's not for having an argument with Judge Markowitz. You're going to pay for your arrogance."

A moment passed while Martin stood in the hallway, his plastic bag of personal items under his arm, Laszlo leaning against the wall, presumably waiting for Martin to leave.

"I appreciate your position," Martin said.

"That doesn't matter to me," Laszlo Prime said.

"Nevertheless, I get it. Now here's mine," Martin said, "Not that I care what you think, but for months I did stay by her side, I did pray for her to survive, and I did bargain with the universe to give her back to me. None of that mattered. For my wife? My family? I would use my bare hands and I would break time and space, reality itself, no matter the cost."

"You might have already done that. It's a good thing we're putting a stop to you," Laszlo said, then walked away, leaving Martin alone in the hallway.

MARTIN SANDBERG STOOD AT THE DOORWAY TO NADINE CALDWELL'S ROOM, BEHIND PHILLIP, WHO SAT IN A CHAIR BESIDE HER BED.

"This is this is a mess," Phillip said, turning to see his lawyer standing in the doorway of his wife's hospital room.

"I'm sorry, Phillip."

"Why are you sorry? You didn't run her over."

"I know. That's just something people say, I guess."

"They did an ultrasound," Phillip said, knowing that Martin would be anxious, "The baby's alright."

The relief was palpable.

"Will she wake up?" Martin asked, acutely aware of the bandages around Nadine Caldwell's head, the medical machines working in tandem to noisily keep her and her baby alive.

"No one will say," Phillip said.

A moment passed as both men listened to the beeping and hissing sounds emanating from the machinery surrounding the young woman.

"A woman who was driving a station wagon turned for a moment to look at her kid in the back-seat, I think to pick up a pacifier or something off the floor of the car. She didn't see Nadine until it was too late," Philip said, staring at his wife, his back still to Martin, who remained uncomfortably standing the doorway of the hospital room.

"Mr. Sandberg?"

"Yes?"

"Thank you for fighting for me," Phillip said.

Martin was silent. Uncharacteristically, he was speechless. Phillip turned to him.

"You don't have to say anything," Phillip said, "I know you didn't do any of it for me. I know you were fighting for her, just like I was."

Martin nodded.

226

"A doctor came, well, lots of doctors came," Phillip said to Martin, "This one was a specialist. He told me that he would be able to get Ariel to term and Nadine will give birth by C-Section."

"Even if she's like this?" Martin asked, looking at Nadine Caldwell as she lay on the hospital bed, eyes closed. Martin felt she might be sleeping if you didn't look too closely.

"She's going to be amazing, my daughter," Phillip said.

"See you around," Martin said, but he knew that would not be the case. He was going to be sanctioned and for him it would soon be over.

"I'll keep you posted," Phillip said.

Martin Sandberg quietly left.

Phillip was about to doze when a nurse came into the room.

"Sir?" the nurse said to Phillip, handing him a small plastic bag, "this was found in her pocket."

"Thank you," Philip said, taking the plastic bag from the nurse. As the nurse walked away, Philip took the little brown pocket-size notebook out of the plastic bag and held it in his hands. He opened it, and page by page stared at his wife's incomprehensible writing. It was only a moment before there was a knock on the opened door.

"Mr. Caldwell," a voice said from behind him.

Phillip Caldwell turned to see Marcus Whitacre standing in the doorway of Nadine's hospital room. "I'm terribly sorry to bother you, my name is..."

"I know who you are Mr. Whiteacre," Phillip said, "if you're here to talk to my wife, you are going to be disappointed."

"I'm here to speak to you, Mr. Caldwell," Marcus Whiteacre said, "about *that little brown pocket-sized notebook* you are holding."

TWENTY-FOUR

SMITH V. STATE

MARTIN SANDBERG SAT AT COUNSEL TABLE NEXT TO HIS SHACKLED CLIENT, THEODORE SMITH; THE IMMORTAL SENTENCED TO HIS ENDLESS LIFE IN PRISON WITHOUT THE POSSIBILITY OF PAROLE. They were in Court early, waiting for the designated hearing time, the Judge noticeably absent while the Laszlo stood in the corner, his face clearly demonstrating boredom as he looked at the ceiling, attempting not to fall asleep while standing in the corner.

Martin looked at him. Laszlo did not meet his eyes.

Martin was sure that the last conversation he had with Laszlo was the last conversation he would ever have with Laszlo. Martin's files were on the table in a neat pile, an empty legal pad, and pens in front of him.

"Are you all right?" Theodore Smith asked him.

"Fine."

Theodore Smith, sitting forward so he could see his attorneys face, gave him a look.

"Okay, not so much."

"Do you want to talk about it?"

"Thank you, Theodore, but I'll be all right."

"How long do you have?" Theodore Smith asked him.

Martin looked at him.

"How did you know?"

"News travels pretty fast in prison. You know, a bunch of men packed in like sardines with nothing to do but to gossip all day, everyone knows everyone else's business."

"I see."

"There's that, and the legendary screaming match between you and Markowitz."

Theodore Smith could not resist a smile.

"I wasn't screaming," Martin said.

A moment passed, Smith shifted in his seat, trying to get comfortable, his hands shackled in front of him to a chain around his waist.

228

"Mr. Sandberg?" a woman's voice said.

Martin turned to see a young woman in a business suit standing next to him. She was tall, attractive, with dark hair. She had tiny lines in her face, almost too small to notice.

"Karen Anderson, from Regional State Counsel's office," she said, holding out her hand.

"Pleasure to meet you," Martin said, shaking her hand.

"You as well. I've read your brief."

"Yes?"

"I apologize if it sounds like I'm talking as if you weren't in the room, Mr. Smith," she said, taking the opportunity to meet Theodore Smith's eyes and acknowledge his presence. "The situation here, while obviously unfair, seems to be according to law."

"You'd agree that it's unfair," Martin said.

"How long have you been locked up?" she asked Theodore Smith, "I'm sorry, can I speak to your client?"

"Yes, please," Martin said.

"It's been almost a hundred years," Theodore Smith said.

"You don't look to be a hundred years old, Mr. Smith."

"I won't make a joke about clean living, or about not smoking. You know I'm not the typical convict."

"No, I'm fully aware of the situation," she said, "as it pertains to paranormal proceedings."

Martin and the young prosecutor Karen Anderson watched as Theodore Smith sat forward in his chair, frowning.

"You know *who* I am?" he asked.

"I know you're not human."

"Anything else?" Smith asked.

"Is there something else I should know?" she asked in her most prosecutorial tone.

"No," Smith said, sitting back, his body and face relaxing.

Martin made a mental note (that he was sure he would forget) to ask Theodore Smith what secret he was hiding, besides, of course, the ones Martin already knew.

"Excuse me," Martin said to his client. "I'd like to have an argument with opposing counsel outside of your presence if that's alright." Theodore Smith watched Martin lead Karen Anderson from counsel table.

Karen Anderson followed him out of the doors of the courtroom. They stood in the typical walk-in-closet sized anteroom, designed to insulate the courtroom from the noise and chaos that usually inhabited the hallway of the courthouse, but was (mostly) unsuccessful.

"You know something I don't?" Karen Anderson asked him.

"I was going to ask you the same thing. I don't know who he is, or what he is," Martin said.

"Well, Theodore Smith is only the name he's used for the last two hundred years. It was something else before that."

"Then you know more than I do," Martin said.

"Do you know *what* he is?" she asked him.

"No idea and I felt it was probably better not to ask," Sandberg said.

"I agree that was probably the wisest course of action. I have found, as of late, that the less I know, the easier it is. Either way, I don't see how this court has Jurisdiction to modify or commute the sentence."

"He was given life, no exceptions," Martin said.

"Right."

"It's cruel and unusual," Martin said (while secretly cursing himself for not thinking of something more convincing to say to her.)

"That may be true, but only in its application to the current case. Just because a person has an aversion to prison food, it doesn't mean they should be let out. Just because your client is impossible to kill and lives seemingly forever, doesn't mean he gets special treatment."

"Miss Anderson, my brief explains that Mr. Smith does die. He comes back."

"That's not the crux of the case, in my opinion. Whether he dies completely then comes back like a miracle, or whether his body enters a hibernation state which looks like death, isn't death, but a state in which it repairs itself is irrelevant."

"How do you mean?" Martin asked her.

"The sentence was 'life in prison without the possibility of parole.' He lives, therefore he lives in prison."

"And we don't go any further?"

"Why would we?"

"Surely because the judge who sentenced him had no idea what he was dealing with."

"Even so, the judgment was legal for the law at the time and has to be upheld in this case."

"I'm not arguing that it is illegal. I'm saying that what's happening to him, isn't fair."

"Mister Sandberg," she said, a shine in her eyes as they narrowed, piercing through him, "If you are going to argue that it isn't fair, like a child in the schoolyard having to give up his turn at kick-ball, this is going to be a quick hearing."

"Maybe, but you said it yourself a second ago that you agreed."

"Of course, I can have an opinion as to the fairness of the law, I can agree it's not fair, but I didn't write the bill and pass it through the legislature, and neither did you. It's not my job to determine whether the law is fair."

"It the application, Miss Anderson, it's the sentence being proportionate to the crime. If the usual sentence for each and every criminal was for any convict to be incarcerated in a spider's nest, wouldn't you agree that such a sentence would be an atrocity to a person who suffers from arachnophobia?" Martin asked.

He watched as she sighed, appeared frustrated for a moment, then looked up at him and gave him a pleasant smile.

"Probably like you, I believe that this *whole thing* is idiocy, and when I say 'whole thing,' I mean the *whole* thing..."

"Judge Markowitz calls it a 'great cosmic inside-joke,'" Martin said.

"Very appropriate," she said. "I call it idiocy, you probably call it something else. I don't know when it was or how it came about, but the world is filled with demons and devils, hairy beasts, things with claws and tentacles, and they all come here to have their day in court just like every pissed-off businessman who feels like he got screwed in a contract and people have no idea."

"No, they don't."

"Criminal, civil, family, the law applies to *everyone*, whether you're that pissed off businessman, a devil, or, Mr. Sandberg, a guy who can't die," she said, still looking into his eyes, still smiling pleasantly. Martin felt her stare and smile unnerving, of course not even close to the terrifying, bowel-emptying smile that Delia possessed, but disquieting nevertheless.

"Agree to disagree?" he asked.

"Of course," she said.

"Thank you for at least talking with me and giving your point of view... It's nice to talk to someone else who's like me," Martin said.

"Oh Mr. Sandberg," she said smiling and walking back into the courtroom, "rest assured. I am *not* anything like you."

"IS THIS EVIDENTIARY OR ARE WE JUST HAVING LEGAL ARGUMENT?" Judge Markowitz said, settling into his chair. He looked at Karen Anderson, then at Martin. Though Judge Markowitz had one of the best 'poker-faces' of any Judge he had ever known, Martin could see a momentary flash of emotion when he looked at Martin. It didn't mean that Martin or his client would receive special treatment. It only meant that Markowitz knew Martin was to be sanctioned.

"I wouldn't call it evidentiary, Your Honor, but we might need my client to clear up a few things," Martin said.

"Very well, Mrs. Anderson?"

"I don't have any witnesses, but I agree with Mr. Sandberg in that if we get to a question, calling Mr. Smith to testify might be the only way to clear up some matters."

"Mr. Smith, please stand and raise your right hand... as best as you can, anyway, Markowitz said, realizing that Smith's hands were shackled to his waist.

After swearing (and affirming) to tell the truth, Theodore Smith settled into his chair.

"I have read both of your briefs on the subject," Markowitz said, "Miss Anderson, Mr. Sandberg, both of you did an excellent job outlining the facts and application, and I thank you both for that. When it's done correctly, I don't feel like I'm crawling around in the dark trying to find my glasses. However, I am going to do something I hate to do. I am going to be completely and brutally honest with both of you. I have no idea what to do here. I'm not even leaning in any direction. Usually, I have a notion, an idea, but here, I haven't a clue. I'm hoping that we can all get to the point of sound practical application of the law."

Theodore Smith stole a glance at Martin, who nodded confidently at him, gave him an expression to try and reassure him.

"Mr. Sandberg, you filed the motion, let's hear from you first."

"Thank you, Your Honor. My client, Theodore Smith, has been in prison for almost 100 years. He was sentenced to life without the possibility of parole, back in a time where this was common practice. If you read my brief, you are acutely aware of Mr. Smith's... proclivity to remaining alive."

"Yes Mr. Sandberg, let's not beleaguer the point. I don't mean to derail you, but we should get to the issue," Markowitz said.

"Yes, your Honor," Martin said.

"There's no legal basis for commutation of sentence. Unless you've found one since your motion and brief were filed?"

"No, Judge. There is no precedent on the subject, nothing even close."

"Miss Anderson," Markowitz said, turning his attention, looking at her down his small glasses, treacherously perched at the tip of his nose.

"Yes, your Honor?"

"Am I to assume that it is still the State's position the Court is without jurisdiction to grant relief in this case?"

"That is the State's position. A sentence of life in prison means that if a person is alive, they are in prison. We can all see that Mr. Smith is alive; therefore, he must remain in prison. Not to be morbid, but to be accurate, once Mr. Smith is dead, he may be removed from the prison, and I suppose buried in the cemetery of his choosing. Once Mr. Smith no longer meets the definition of alive, his sentence has been fulfilled."

"Mr. Sandberg, would you care to call your client as a witness?" Markowitz asked. To a practicing attorney, the very question was disheartening. Martin knew that the most likely reason Markowitz was now offering to hear from Theodore Smith was because he was going to rule against him but wanted to give him at least the chance to have his day in Court and say the things he wanted to say. Most Judges and attorneys know that it is difficult to lose in Court, but it is inherently insulting to lose in Court and at least not have a chance to give your side of things.

"Mr. Smith, having been sworn, please give your name."

"Theodore Smith."

"Were you convicted of a crime?"

"Yes"

"Do you agree or disagree with the Court's ruling concerning your conviction?"

"I'm not happy with it. I understand it."

"But do you agree, not with the sentence, that's not what I'm asking you. Do you agree with the finding of guilt?"

A moment passed demonstrating Theodore Smith's reluctance.

"Yes," Theodore Smith said.

"What was your sentence?"

"Life without the possibility of parole."

"And what does that mean?"

"It means I stay in prison until I die."

"Mr. Smith, what is your lifespan?" Martin asked.

"Objection, Your Honor," Karen Anderson said.

"Grounds?" Markowitz asked her.

"The state can stipulate that Mr. Smith's age and lifespan are atypical of the traditional *human* convicted felon. It is not relevant as to how long *Mr. Smith* expects to live."

"Response?" Markowitz asked.

"That's the nexus of the situation here," Martin said.

"So your objection is based on relevance?" Markowitz asked Anderson, finally pushing the tiny glasses back up to the bridge of his nose.

"Amongst other viable grounds," she said.

"Mr. Sandberg, I'm aware we do not know when Mr. Smith's life began nor is there any competent substantial evidence concerning when he will cease breathing, eating, sleeping, and whatever it is that we now define as 'living.'"

"I understand, Your Honor, I'll move on."

"How long have you been incarcerated?"

"Almost one hundred years."

"Tender the witness," Martin said,

"Ms. Anderson?"

"Thank you. Mr. Smith, it appears we all agree that you are alive."

"Yes, ma'am."

"You agree the conviction is valid and you were sentenced to life without the possibility of parole."

"I never said I agreed with the sentence," Smith said.

"Did you have competent counsel?"

"For back then, yes."

"Can you point to any mistake of fact or law which would give the court a legal basis to either overturn the conviction or have the sentence declared illegal or invalid in some fashion?"

"It's not right," Theodore Smith said, "it's... heavy-handed."

"You would agree that many of your peers who are in prison with you would make the same argument about their own sentences?"

"We are here on *my* sentence."

"Understood."

"A person who stole a candy bar shouldn't spend life in prison," Smith added.

"But you committed murder."

"These days, I would have been charged with negligent homicide."

"You weren't sentenced during these days," Karen Anderson said, "while a person who stole a candy bar should not receive a sentence of life in prison, would you not agree that for a person who is charged and convicted of murder, the sentence of life is legal?"

"I would, however, my case is different."

"How is it different?" she asked.

"I haven't been sentenced to *life* so much as I've been sentenced to *eternity*," Theodore Smith said.

Martin watched as Karen Anderson nodded to him, acknowledging the point made.

Martin met her eyes.

"Nothing further," she said.

"I have a question," Judge Markowitz said, "Mr. Smith, I read in Mr. Sandberg's brief that you've died several times while serving your sentence."

"That's correct."

"Can you explain?" Markowitz asked.

"What do you mean, Your Honor, I don't understand."

"How about the last time you died. What happened?"

"The last time was two years ago. One of my *peers* was under the mistaken impression that I stole his orange off his tray at lunch. Though I explained it was not me, I still ended up with a broken piece of plexiglass, his homemade knife, in between my ribs."

"You got shivved over an orange?" Markowitz asked.

"Yes, I got shivved over an Orange."

"Go on."

"Apparently I bled out on the floor. Sometime later, I woke up in a body bag at the prison morgue, where they keep deceased prisoners before transport for autopsy."

"Then what happened?" Markowitz asked.

"I actually sat there for a while before a guard found me, punched me in the back of the head, then put me back in population as if nothing ever happened."

"Does anyone remember?"

"Sir?"

"Did anyone remember that you had been stabbed and that you were killed?"

"As usual, many had seen it, but no one remembered. The guy who stabbed me was in the hole, but no one remembered how he got there or why."

"Not even the guy that stabbed you?"

"He did not remember stabbing me, didn't even remember about the stupid orange."

"Are you sure you died?"

"I think so."

They watched as Markowitz leaned back in his chair. Moments passed, long enough for everyone to realize they were sitting in silence. Finally, Markowitz continued.

"Since I started doing these cases, I wish I could say that this was the strangest," Judge Markowitz said, "but sadly, it is not."

He sighed and took a moment to rub his temples.

"Mr. Sandberg, do you have any questions you wish to ask based on and within the scope of the Court's Questions?"

"Briefly. Mr. Smith, from the moment you were stabbed, how long did it take before you lost consciousness?"

Karen Anderson, Martin Sandberg, Markowitz, even Laszlo watched as Theodore Smith looked at the ceiling, searching his mind.

"I don't know," he said, shrugging his shoulders.

"Do you have a guess?" Martin asked.

"Objection, calls for speculation," Karen Anderson said.

"Overruled. Answer the question, Mr. Smith."

"It couldn't have been but a few minutes," Smith said.

"From the moment you lost consciousness, to the moment you woke up in the morgue, do you know how long that was?"

Again, a moment of silence passed, the participants in the hearing watching while Theodore Smith tried desperately to remember details.

"Maybe a half hour?"

"Nothing further," Martin said.

"Ms. Anderson?"

"Mr. Smith, do you know for sure if you were dead?"

"What a question," Judge Markowitz suddenly blurted out. "I'm sorry. Please proceed."

Anderson nodded.

"Mr. Smith?"

"I know I was unconscious. I know I woke up in a body bag."

"Do you know for a fact that you became deceased?"

"No," Theodore Smith said.

"Nothing further," she said.

"Mr. Sandberg?"

"Nothing further, Your Honor."

"Mr. Smith, thank you for your candor with the court."

"Yes, Your Honor," Smith said, his facial expression one of which a person wears when that person knows a judge is about to rule against him.

"I'll break protocol and ask one more question. If Mr. Laszlo was to retrieve his firearm from his belt and shoot you in the head or heart with it, would you be dead?"

After the question was asked, the tone in the courtroom grew considerably colder.

"Yes?" Smith asked, instead of stated.

"About 30 minutes or so, would you be alive?"

"That is usually the case. I have been hung and shot as well."

Martin Sandberg and Karen Anderson exchanged puzzled glances while they waited for Judge Markowitz.

"Right now, you meet the definition of alive, Mr. Smith."

"What's the definition of alive?" Theodore Smith asked Judge Markowitz.

"The dictionary defines alive as "a person, animal, or plant that is living and not dead." That definition is of little use here. The definition of 'life' is much more helpful."

They could see Markowitz had his dictionary with him on the bench.

"As defined in the dictionary, "life is a physical condition that distinguishes plants and animals from inorganic matter, including, but not limited to the capacity for reproduction, functional activity, growth, and continual change preceding the condition of death.'"

Markowitz looked up from the dictionary and at the participants in the courtroom.

"Without being a scientist, I would paraphrase and say that life includes the exchange of gases, like oxygen, carbon dioxide, biological functions such as lymphatic and circulatory systems working in concert, taking in nutrition, an entity, or being in motion..."

They watched as Markowitz pontificated on the bench.

Martin stole a glance at Theodore Smith, who seemed unusually pale.

He assumed it was because Smith knew he was about to lose the hearing and the grim realization was setting in.

"I would venture a guess that it is much easier to define what is not alive," Markowitz said.

"May I ask a question?" Theodore Smith asked Judge Markowitz.

"Yes, go ahead."

"If I was dead, right now, right here in the courtroom, would this Court, you, Judge Markowitz, be inclined to sign an order declaring my sentence fulfilled, as Ms. Anderson so eloquently put it?"

"I would suppose so, Mr. Smith, yes. "

"Do you promise?" Theodore Smith asked.

Martin suddenly felt like he was going to throw up. The expression on Judge Markowitz's face was similar. Martin looked over at Karen Anderson, who, like he and Markowitz, had suddenly realized something was wrong.

"What did you do?" Martin asked, just long enough to see the frighteningly large pool of blood on the floor, a puddle that was growing at an exponential rate.

"I sincerely apologize for the mess on the floor," Theodore Smith said, "I hid a piece of a razor blade under my skin, and while the hearing was proceeding, I severed my femoral artery."

The courtroom participants looked at him, looked at each other.

"You all look stunned," Smith said.

"Call an ambulance?" Laszlo asked.

"I think that might be prudent," Markowitz said.

"Your Honor, it will be too late. I know you didn't promise, but please. In the nature of what Ms. Anderson called a 'supernatural proceeding' upon my expiration, I beg you to write an order that merely says that my sentence has been fulfilled," Theodore Smith said.

Martin was stunned at how the color was almost completely gone from his face and realizing his time was limited, Martin sat down and quickly began to write on the legal pad.

"Why don't we take a recess?" Markowitz asked.

"No!" Martin yelled.

"No?"

"Here, Judge. Take this, please," Martin said, handing him the legal pad with Martin's barely legible writing on it.

"Ms. Anderson?" Markowitz said. She went to the bench and looked at the pad.

"No objection," she said, "I mean, that's what I said, and we all agree."

"I'll read this out loud for the record. Upon receiving competent substantial evidence, I hereby rule, declare, decree, and order that Theodore Smith, now deceased, has fulfilled his commitment to the state, has served his sentence to full-term, and hereby discharge his body and soul from further obligation in this cause... and right there is where I am supposed to sign and date it?"

"Yes, on the lines I drew," Martin said.

"Mr. Smith, should you expire, I'll sign this handwritten order..." Markowitz looked up at Theodore Smith. "Mr. Smith?" he asked, but it was already too late.

239

MARTIN SANDBERG SAT IN THE ONLY CHAIR IN THE ROOM. He was shivering, holding a photocopy of the handwritten order, signed and dated by Judge Andrew Markowitz. On a table behind him, the figure of a black body bag sat up, gasping for air.

"Hold up," Martin said, running to the bag. Martin unzipped it.

"I meant to unzip that. I forgot. Sorry," Martin said.

Martin watched as Theodore Smith gasped for air. The color quickly returned to his face.

"Amazing," Martin said, "you should go on tour and give shows."

"Except the audience would not remember what they'd seen," Smith said, "What happened?"

"After we all finished wetting our pants, Laszlo checked your pulse, Judge Markowitz actually swore him as a witness, and he testified they you were no longer breathing. Take a look at this," Martin said, handing him the photocopy.

"That's the most beautiful piece of paper I've ever seen," Smith said.

"Markowitz had his assistant make you a copy. I guess he's adjusting to 'Supernatural Proceedings.'"

"'Paranormal Proceedings' is what Ms. Anderson called them," Smith said, wiggling out of the body-bag.

"I could call them something different entirely," Martin said, "Here's the copy he made for you."

Martin handed him the single sheet of paper.

"That was thoughtful," Smith said.

"You were dead. I saw it," Martin said, "while you were dead, Judge Markowitz declared your sentence served to full term. You were incarcerated for life. Your life was over, so he was permitted to sign the order. Even the prosecutor agreed that since you were dead, it was appropriate for the judge to sign the order."

"But I'm alive now," Smith said.

"Let's call it a loophole, and be done with it." Martin said, "I can use the win."

"Agreed. I can't thank you enough."

"Can I give you a ride somewhere?" Martin asked, handing him a brown paper bag with clothes from the "lost and found."

"I think I'd like to walk."

"Understandable."

Martin stayed with him while he dressed and walked with him out into the street. Martin watched as Theodore breathed deeply as if he'd never taken a breath before, standing on the street with his eyes closed, his face towards the sky.

"I don't know what to say, Marty."

"Just tell Delia I did a good job and we'll call it even."

About to part ways, Theodore Smith stopped, turned, and met Martin's eyes.

"I am sorry for what's going to happen you, I mean, since you were, you know, held in contempt."

"I'm trying not to think of it," Martin said.

"Martin... If there was a way for me to go in your place..." Smith said.

"I actually, for a moment, thought of that, too. You would just come back, gasping for air. I wish I could send you and you could tell them that you were me. That wouldn't work, though."

"They would know." Theodore said.

"They would know," Martin agreed, "It has to be me. Theodore, I really appreciate the thought, however," Martin said. Theodore Smith nodded and walked away from him down the street. Martin watched him fade from sight, then headed towards his car.

TWENTY-FIVE

ESMERALDA SANDBERG STOOD AT THE FRONT
WINDOW OF HER LIVING ROOM. She was alone in the home
except for Emily, who was in her room, as her school ended earlier
than her other two children. The different school's release times
created a span of time where she and Emily would be alone
together for a couple of hours every day. Esmeralda usually
enjoyed the "alone mother-daughter" time with her.

Today was different. She had received news that her
husband had been found in contempt and was to be sanctioned.

She stood in silence, staring out of the front window. There
was no sound except the hum of the air conditioning. Esmeralda
Sandberg saw an old white sedan pull into her driveway and
watched as Abraham Cardozo crawled out.

As always when he came for a visit, he was alone. She
opened the door and went outside to greet him.

"Abraham," she said.

"Esme, I'm so sorry," he said, as he closed the car door and
walked to her.

"Come inside, it's very warm outside today," she said.

Cardozo gave her a look, indicating the same concern he
always had when visiting.   "Emily's upstairs, coloring and
playing. It's alright," Esmeralda said, walking to the front door, "I
have something in the kitchen for you."

Esmeralda went into the kitchen, to her refrigerator.

"I have your favorite," she said, "I made it yesterday. This
recipe is always better on the second day. Today it will be even
better."

Esmeralda turned and realized that she was now having a
conversation with herself. She realized that she was alone in her
kitchen, Cardozo had not followed her.

"Abraham?" she asked. from the door to the kitchen, she
could see Emily and Cardozo locked in a death-battle staring
contest.

Silent, hands down at her sides, frowning, she stared at
Cardozo. When he had been following Esmeralda, he had been
forced to stop short, as Emily had suddenly appeared and taken a
position in between him and the kitchen door.

242

Abraham knew there was no going around her and unless she agreed, there was no going past her.

He had tried before.

He would have her permission before being allowed to proceed, or he would leave.

"Emily? I thought you were upstairs coloring," Esmeralda said to her daughter.

Silence.

"Abraham?"

Abraham Cardozo did not respond.

It was as if neither Emily or Cardozo knew that Esmeralda was in the room with them.

Whether it was something physical or something emotional, Esmeralda was not going to have any of it. On this day, upon learning that her husband was in the worst trouble, and Abraham Cardozo actually agreeing to come by to talk with her, Esmeralda quickly lost patience.

"You will go upstairs to your room, *chica.* Mr. Cardozo is my guest and I need to speak with him," she said.

She watched as Emily stood, still oblivious to Esmeralda's presence, locked in her "death stare" with Abraham Cardozo. Esmeralda wasn't sure, (it was so hard to read him) but she thought there was fear in his eyes.

"Now," Esmeralda Sandberg said to Emily, "Now!"

She turned and looked at her mother, frowning, her eyes slits. She gave him one last look as she went up the stairs without speaking. Abraham Cardozo was breathing as if he had sprinted down the street. Beads of sweat had collected on his forehead.

"I'm so sorry, Abraham," Esmeralda said.

"If it is a generous helping of your Ropa Vieja that you have for me, my dear, all is forgiven," he said, the attempt to hide his relief unconvincing. "Sometimes I think you use ancient magic to create such a delicious meal.

She smiled at his compliment.

"I think she still resents me," he said, walking gingerly into the kitchen.

"She spent a thousand years as queen of her very own universe. Now she's here. One day, she will realize that *this* is better."

243

"I think until that day arrives, I should perhaps visit while she is in school."

"Shall I heat it up for you and you can sit at the table?" Esmeralda asked him.

"You should not heat it up," he said.

"No?"

"No, Esme. You're going to want to dump it on my head. I'll take it to go."

"Then at least sit with me and have a cup of tea," she asked, handing him a lunchbox-sized container filled with his favorite dish. He smiled when she gave him the container. He knew the contents would be beyond delicious and it was all he could do to resist the urge to open it and stick his face into it, chomping and slurping.

He sat down. Gingerly, respectfully, he set the container on the table in front of him.

"You look sad, Abraham," she said, putting a mug of tea and a bottle of honey in front of him. He could not help but smile. Esmeralda made the best Ropa Vieja in existence, and she remembered that when he had a cup of tea, he liked the cup to be almost more honey than tea.

"I think you know how your husband feels about me," Cardozo said to her, dumping the honey into his cup.

"You are not his most favorite person," she said, "he calls you an 'officious interloper.' I had to ask him what he meant by that."

"I am officious, and yes, I am an interloper... Your husband is not my favorite person in the world, either. Still, I think it best that we do not mention my little visits."

"He already knows you and I talk, Abraham. If I wanted to feed you like you were a baby and whisper sweet nothings in your ear while you ate the best meal you've ever had, I would not only tell him myself, but I would remind him that he belongs to me, not the other way around. I will be friends with anyone I choose. Martin knows better."

Abraham Cardozo smiled, mostly to himself. He was reminded why he rescued her, defying the nature at the core of his being and, of course, his mandate.

"Still," he said.

"Coming here, visiting me, all of it, Martin and I know you don't have a choice," she said.

"It is my penance," he said.

"I'm sorry, Abraham," she said.

"Nonsense, my dear. Being tasked with keeping an eye on one of the few *of your kind* to ever defy universal law is a pleasure, not a chore," he said.

"But only because I cook for you."

"Oh, so delicious," he said, smiling. He snuck another glance at the container Esmeralda had prepared, hoped she didn't see him.

"I enjoy your visits, anyway," she said.

"I enjoy visiting with you, too, young lady," he said. The smile he had from the thought of his take-home container faded when he met her eyes and realized why she wanted to see him.

When he looked into Esmeralda's face, it was almost too much for him. He felt weak.

A moment of silence passed.

He knew what she wanted.

She knew that he knew.

Both knew Abraham Cardozo was powerless to stop the pending mandate concerning Martin Sandberg.

"I'm sorry, Esme," he said.

"Please, Abraham, there must be something," she said, sitting down at the table next to him.

"There is a price to be paid," Cardozo said.

"Then I will pay it," she said.

"That is not how it works, and I think you know that."

"I wish it did."

He watched as she slumped at the table. He thought she would cry, but she refused to show emotion. It was yet another reason he respected her. He felt that anyone, man or woman, who was comfortable expressing emotion around others, was weak and not worthy enough to share the Earth with him.

She didn't know that Cardozo had an aversion towards seeing another cry. She chose to fight, no matter the battle. It was her way.

"I know what you're thinking," Cardozo said.

"Is that so?" she asked him.

"Indeed."

"Tell me, Perrito, what is it you think you know?" she asked.

"You're thinking that you're going to fight," he said.

"When they come for him, I'll be ready,' she said.

He could see her anger, drifting lightly beneath the surface.

He still had not discovered the source of her power. Maybe the key to Esmeralda Sandberg's power was her fury. It was self-sustaining, after all.

"I see where Emily gets her anger," he said, "and I'm suddenly rethinking the amount of respect I have for your husband," Cardozo said, looking at her. He wondered how it was such a beautiful young woman could be so dangerously angry.

She leaned in, spoke to him, her voice barely above a whisper, her face inches from him.

"With my bare hands, I will crack this world in half to protect my family. I will destroy the ground beneath our feet," she said.

"You have three children, Esmeralda," he said, "you cannot burn the very bridge they are standing on."

He watched as her face softened.

Her fury melted to sadness in front of him. Her eyes glassy, but not crying, she pleaded with him.

"Please, there has to be something."

"You changed reality once. You won't be permitted to break the law again, Esmeralda."

"Then what do I do?" she asked him.

"You tell your husband that you love him. You put your arms around him, and you tell him that it is going to be alright even you know that it is not true... And you keep being the best mother I have ever seen. A child who loses a parent won't ever shed the pain but can learn to live with it. A child who loses *both* parents becomes an orphan."

She met his eyes.

"I fought too hard," she said.

"I know my dear. I know," Abraham Cardozo said, getting up to leave, his container in his hands as if it had been made of gold.

Silently he made his way to the front door.

Emily was standing at the top of the stairs, looking down at him. He fought back the urge to shake.

"Abraham," she said as he opened the front door.

246

"Yes?"
"In the Ropas? it's roasted Poblano Peppers," she said.

TWENTY-SIX

UNDERNEATH THE UNDERNEATH

MARTIN SANDBERG STOOD AT THE FOOT OF
WILLIAM DONNELLY'S HOSPITAL BED, THE MACHINES
HUMMING AND HISSING IN FUTILITY.
Martin looked at William, felt like he could barely
recognize the gaunt figure. He lay still except for the machines
making him breathe and his eyes moving under his eyelids as if he
was in REM sleep.

Martin knew William wasn't dreaming.
He knew William was locked in a death battle with a one-armed
monster and losing. Moments earlier he had asked the resident
how long Will had left. He told Martin that his internal organs
were in the process of shutting down. This meant that soon, the
Libro Del Diablo would belong to someone else and the beast
would begin someone else's destruction, and so on.

He stood over his friend, trying not to imagine the thing
with one arm, holding its severed arm and hitting Will over and
over with it. Though he tried to put the thought out of his head, he
failed. The thought made him shiver where he stood.

"I'm sorry," Martin said. "I know I promised. I could tell
you that the Devil Book wouldn't let me read it, that there's no way
to break a Devil Contract, but you already know these things. I
don't know if you knew I couldn't do it, but I don't blame you for
asking me. I'd ask too," Martin said.

"I came to say goodbye, Will. It looks like I'm going to hell
before you. I'll save you a spot," Martin said to his old friend. He
took one last look before leaving.

Though he thought it was an impossibility, he had to have
a conversation which was much worse than the one he was having
with William Donnelly. Before he was sanctioned, he had to talk
with Esmeralda.

IT WAS ALMOST MIDNIGHT AS MARTIN
AND ESMERALDA SANDBERG SAT AT THEIR KITCHEN
TABLE.
"Do you know where it is?" she asked him. He took a
moment to look at her, then realized what she was asking.

"I left the Devil-Book in my office, but you know it does what it wants. It could be on my pillow or the moon."

She took a moment to look at her husband, kissed him on the top of his head and sat down at the table next to him.

Each had a cup of lukewarm tea in front of them. Martin had taken a sip or two but thought that drinking tea might tarnish the thought of his last meal. Esmeralda had made "Ropas de Viejas," his favorite of all her dishes. Somehow taking the toughest cuts of beef, she was able to make a meal that had just the right amount of spiciness, tenderness and flavor, just enough heat to be perfect. What he (along with everyone else who had the opportunity to partake) said was "cooking magic," Esmeralda said was merely the introduction of roasted Poblano peppers and a crock pot capable of cooking with very low heat.

She made her special rice, homemade queso dip, (and chips) and the obligatory salad, which she knew that Martin would take a few bites of, just to be polite. When the children retired to their rooms, Martin and Esmeralda did the dishes together in silence, Esmeralda washing, while Martin dried. Stolen glances, a look into her eyes, Martin, of course, saw sadness, but he also saw guilt. As he had fallen in love with his wife, he had spent every moment he had getting to know her, the idiosyncrasies, the things that made Esmeralda the person she was. Seeing guilt on her face was the rarest of emotions (for her) and usually surrounded the one act of universal defiance to which both of them had willingly participated.

He knew she felt responsible. He also knew that she was probably the only person on the planet to have the will, the emotional fortitude and just the right balance of power and rage to not only rip open a tear in between life and death but to keep it open. Both had known that time moved differently depending on where one spent his or her existence. Depending on such locations, depending on where someone landed, a moment here could be hundreds of years there. Remembering only bits and pieces, he recalled the time he had spent looking for Emily was much, much longer than it had been for Esmeralda, on this side, desperately holding up the garage door between spaces while supernatural entities watched in both amazement and horror.

He remembered that they had made the decision together. When Emily came back, however, she had brought a few things with her.

By the time the loud, steady piercing hum turned into the familiar beeps of life, Emily Sandberg, queen of her own private hell, was back, uncommon rage included. When a natural resurgence occurred, with situationally correct beings involved, a person on the brink of death might only bring a glimpse of memory as to where they had been and how long they had been there.

The natural order of things was ill-equipped for the side-loaded method for which Martin and Esmeralda had brought their youngest daughter back.

Drying dishes, Martin remembered witnessing the astounding event as his wife caused the world around them to stop while she pried existence apart with her bare hands. Except for the groans of pain, she had done the act in silence. In the past, she had casually explained to him that "deeds of and power were not conducted with stupid words." She had said, "when you defy reality, you don't say abracadabra, Martin. You take everything you have and you bend the universe to your will, not the other way around."

Not understanding what it was she was explaining to him, like a child in school for the first time, Martin understood only a little and decided it was best to leave it that way.

"I can't believe this is happening," she said, looking into her teacup. Martin took her hand, knowing (as most successfully married men) that the most intimate two people can be is when they are sitting at a table, holding hands, communicating.

"I'm sorry," Martin said, "I'm so sorry."

"You're sorry? This is my fault," she said.

"I made the choice. Esmeralda, there isn't anything I would change."

"The Caldwell girl? She had better be worth it," Esmeralda said.

"She is, Esme," Martin said.

"The sad part of all of this, is that I know you, Husband. It makes no difference if Phillip Caldwell's baby is a real live angel, the savior of beasts and men, a ten-foot tall goddess from the great beyond, or a regular human baby destined for a regular life. You would have done anything you could to save her," she said, but Martin wasn't so sure. He didn't know if he would have, but it didn't matter. He was about to die and there was especially no point in arguing with his wife.

Martin could hear the conspicuous ticking of their kitchen wall-clock as they sat in silence for a time. There wasn't anything else for them to say to one another. At 11:50 P.M. he stood. She stood with him.

"Remember, you can't go outside, no matter what you hear," he said, "If you do, you'll be trapped wherever I end up. You have to stay inside."

She nodded.

At first, she said she wasn't going to let him go without fighting by his side. Begging, pleading, and taking the time, effort, and energy, (and using every tool of persuasion at his disposal) she had been convinced to remain with their children. Both agreed that it was better for their children to have at least one parent if they were not going to grow up with both of them.

"I love you," she said.

"Remember," he said, giving her one last hug, "I love you, too."

She watched as he walked outside.

Knowing it was something she couldn't watch, she sat down on the living room couch, put her hands over her ears, and cried quietly to herself.

Martin stood at the end of his driveway and watched as his suburban neighborhood shifted, melted away, shimmered, faded. He watched, amazed as the landscape changed around him, the streetlight above his head and his house the only things that remained from where he was to where he went. The colors changed, the darkness changed, the air changed.

As he stood, waiting, watching, he tried to remember that Owen Hooper had said he was going to lose, his death assured, but he could at least bloody their noses. Martin tried to remember that Owen had told him fighting in this place was more a force of will than a "force of fists."

"You can go down swinging, or you can just go down," Hooper had said.

Martin tried to remember if he had made the conscious decision to fight, but fear took hold as he looked at the horizon and saw them. As far as he could see, surrounding him, he saw thousands.

It took only a moment for him to realize, remember, they were coming to make an example of him.

At the front, Martin thought he might see a reprieve in his old friend, Laszlo Prime. Along with hundreds of demons, all six hundred, fifty-four Laszlos were coming across the dirty rotting plain of existence towards him. He wondered if Laszlo would help him. He wondered if they had been friends. He wondered if it would matter.

As the Laszlos changed before his eyes, he knew that there would be no reprieve from his sanctioning.

He saw underneath the underneath.

Seeing their true form for the first time, he realized the Laszlos were monsters, just like the rest that came to have a party, white, jagged teeth shining from angry smiles in the little bit of unnatural moonlight that peered into the darkest planes of existence.

They were not coming quickly, they were walking, taking their time, the strange sounds they made slowly filling his ears. He turned one last time to look back and realized that his house had faded, he was completely gone and he was alone with them. His family wouldn't have to see or hear what happened next. He thanked the universe for one good thing.

Hands over her ears, staring straight ahead, Esmeralda Sandberg watched as Emily came down the stairs.

Not now, she thought, wondering if the little girl needed a glass of water, or wanted to be tucked into bed.

"Honey?" she asked Emily.

With a nod, and perhaps with a little too much invisible force, Emily Sandberg, the little queen of Hell, pinned her mother against the ceiling of the living room.

Esmeralda felt like she was falling, only upwards, gravity suddenly unconcerned with its usual way of doing things. She was held in place, back flat against the ceiling with a force equal to three times the Earth's gravity.

The feeling was as unusual to her as it was painful.

"Honey, no!" Esmeralda yelled at her, as always, the protective mother.

Emily Sandberg, out of respect for her mother, looked up and met her Mother's eyes. Fear washing across Esmeralda's face as she struggled caused no emotional reaction in the girl, except the ever-present contempt.

Without saying anything, (and without even being near it) without gesture, or even a nod, the front door swung open with a slam. It was as if the door itself was somehow afraid of defying the seven-year-old little girl.

Standing in the driveway, breathing the burned air, waiting to be torn apart by the horde, Martin heard a sound from behind him.

It was sound of the little bell from Emily's tricycle.

He turned to see her just as she was almost to him, her blonde hair blowing in the breeze as she pedaled. She rang her bell again.

Ding! Ring!

For only an instant, Martin forgot what was happening to him as he remembered with love that Emily liked ringing the bell on her tricycle so much, he thought that sometimes it was the only reason she chose to ride it.

The unusual (and terrifying) sound demons made when they were coming to kill someone broke the thought and Martin suddenly realized that his little girl was standing next to him.

"Honey, you have to go back now. Please go back to the house, go inside and find your mother," he said.

Prior to Emily's appearance, his hands had not been shaking. With both refusal and acceptance, out into the darkness, he had brought calm with him. He had mustered everything he had within himself and refused to show fear. He wanted to experience maybe a moment of dignity before they tore him apart.

At the thought of Emily being caught in the middle, the thought of her being harmed, however, Martin suddenly became terrified.

"Please honey, I don't want anything to happen to you. Something's happening. You have to go back," he said, looking behind her.

The neighborhood was gone.

The house was gone.

253

Twilight was the color of burned, dark, red wine.

The only "normal" thing left was the lone streetlight under which he and his Emily were standing.

"Please," Martin said, not to Emily, but out loud to the universe, to anyone who might listen.

Martin suddenly felt heavy.

Wait, what?

Slowly, deliberately, gravity pushed down on him. Legs shaking, he felt himself become heavier and heavier.

He fell to his knees, struggling.

"No," he said, but there wasn't anyone listening to him.

On his knees, staring at the red sky, he pulled with everything he had. Gravity close to four times that of Earth's gravity pulled down on him as he groaned out loud, struggled not to let it bring him down further.

Dark spots began to form in his vision as the pressure caused the worst headache Martin Sandberg would ever have in his lifetime.

He saw Emily step (or skip, he couldn't tell) to where he was stuck, helpless. On his knees, he was eye level to her. He watched as she took a moment to glance at the oncoming horde. He looked into her eyes.

Using her tiny hands, she took hold of his head, one hand just above each ear as she looked deep into Martin's eyes.

"Father," she said.

Martin watched, powerless, as Emily let go of him and walked towards the mass of demons walking in her direction, her light blonde hair blowing in the dank breeze.

Only a few feet away, Martin could see that the demons had been bouncing, moving with deliberation as they made their way towards him in all their horrible glory.

Then it happened.

He thought it was odd the way the mind works when he remembered being at a baseball game as a child and seeing a crowded audience do something called "the wave" when, with just the right timing, people get up out of their seats and sit down and it looks remotely like a wave on the ocean.

It was as if the demons did "the wave." The only difference, however, was that none of them got back up again.

254

Martin could see they were down, pushed to the ground by immense force, just as he was.

The only demon still upright, now a ten-foot tall, hulking monstrosity, (still wearing an ugly thin mustache) holding fast on his hands and knees against the gravitational onslaught, was the Martin's friend, Laszlo Prime. The demon had been stopped while on his way to inflict horrible justice. Martin was sorry he never got to take Laszlo for a pizza lunch as he was sure the conversation would have been fascinating.

Martin watched through the spots in his eyes, struggling to breathe under the strain, as Emily casually walked to the ten-foot high demon Laszlo Prime. On his hands and knees Laszlo was still much taller than she was.

Emily nodded (ever so slightly) and Laszlo's head dropped exactly to her eye level. Martin watched as Emily gently brushed the matted hair from Laszlo's pulsating forehead with a tiny hand, looking into his eyes, much in the same way she had looked into Martin's eyes only a moment earlier. She leaned into him, her face inches from his.

"For eons, until the end of time," she said, "they will sing songs of your suffering."

Martin heard sounds like rocks being crushed. The sound was similar to the way a tree snaps and cracks when it is hit by a bolt from the sky. It was the sound of fireworks in the distance, like repeated gunshots. With their bones cracking, snapping, breaking, as the demons screamed and cried out in agony, groaning, howling, begging, Martin learned something he didn't know before.

Martin learned that demons can die.

He also learned that the sound the demons made when they were being destroyed by his daughter was something that would haunt him for the rest of his life. Their destruction, coal-black smoke filled the red sky as they perished under her power. The sounds of demons screaming filled the air as Emily stood at the front of massacre, her father still on his knees behind her.

Not even the towering Laszlo Prime escaped her wrath.

She took her time with him.

Martin threw up. As he wretched on the ground in front of him, Martin decided he was tired of vomiting.

It was only a few moments, less than five minutes by Martin's estimate, and then it was over. Silence, like the acrid air, was all that was left, except one lone demon lying on the ground at her feet. He was crawling away from her, crying.

Martin watched as Emily walked to him, grabbed him by his ear and dragged him to where Martin was pinned.

Emily brought the demon to within inches of Martin's face.

She held him there, the demon's nose touching Martin's nose.

"This... is mine," she said.

She looked at the demon.

The demon looked confused, looking back and forth between Martin and Emily.

"Mine!" she screamed.

The demon nodded in fear, helpless, half broken.

"You always leave one alive so he can tell the rest," she said, looking at Martin, but both he and the demon knew she was really talking to that lone surviving demon.

Emily and Martin watched as the demon scampered off into the distance.

Martin thought it sounded like the demon was crying but couldn't be sure.

Martin felt the gravity come off him as quickly as it had come upon him, felt lifted, and was again able to stand. His home and the neighborhood around them came back into view.

The light changed. They were back.

He felt weak, exhausted. He struggled to walk, his legs weakened, wobbly, shaking, but managed to walk towards his home.

"Daddy?" she asked him, taking his hand.

"Yes, honey?"

"Would you like to come to my tea party?" she asked him.

"No, honey," he said.

"Okay Daddy," she said.

TWENTY-SEVEN

ABRAHAM CARDOZO SAT ALONE ON HIS FAVORITE PARK BENCH, A SMALL BROWN BAG OF BIRDSEED IN HIS HAND. With the meditative contentment it always brought, (sometimes not without considerable struggle to leave the troubles of the day behind) he made a conscious effort to enjoy the breeze, and the little chirping sounds that the birds made when he fed them.

Closing his eyes, listening to the birds, he had almost reached that calm state when a shadow came across his face.

"No, go away," Abraham Cardozo said to Marcus Whiteacre, who was looming over him, waving his hand as if to fan away a wisp of smoke.

"Abraham," Whiteacre said.

"No," Abraham Cardozo said, interrupting him, "you always have a way of wrecking my day."

"We have to talk," he said, sitting down next to him.

"This bench is specifically designated for those who wish to feed the birds," he said.

He watched with contempt as Marcus pulled a small bag of birdseed out of his coat.

Marcus nodded to him.

"I know the rules," Marcus said, "I know how you love your rules."

"I still want you to go away," Abraham said, stealing one more moment to close his eyes and feel the sun on his face.

Marcus waited impatiently. When it came, he would know the proper moment to attempt the conversation.

His eyes still closed, face lifted to the sky, Abraham Cardozo spoke, breaking the quiet.

"Did you get it?" Cardozo asked, his face towards the sun.

When Marcus did not answer him, Cardozo opened his eyes and looked at him. Abraham Cardozo became acutely aware of Marcus's strange new security officers.

"New security?"

"I've had to make alternative arrangements," Marcus said, motioning for the new security personnel to go far away for him to have a private conversation with his bench-mate.

257

"My last security was better."

"What did Sandberg call them?" Cardozo asked.

"He called them Laszlos."

"What an idiot. Of all things."

"Such a loss," Marcus said.

"Well?" Cardozo asked.

"Here it is," Marcus Whiteacre said, pulling Nadine Caldwell's little brown pocket-sized notebook out of his coat breast pocket.

"That's it?" Cardozo asked. His tone displayed skepticism, but Whiteacre would not lie.

He watched as Marcus nodded, waved away the birds with an aged hand, interrupting their breakfast. He gently set the notebook on the sidewalk in front of them and set it on fire with a match.

Cardozo watched, unamused, as, with a small, steady supernatural breath, Marcus blew on the tiny fire until Nadine Caldwell's pocket-sized little brown notebook was just a pile of ash. Marcus dispersed the ashes with an expensive shiny black shoe.

"Can you imagine?" Abraham asked him.

"I don't want to," Marcus said.

"What if she had..." Cardozo started to muse out loud before Whiteacre angrily cut him off mid-sentence.

"I said I don't want to consider the narrowly avoided, unmitigated disaster that would have happened if Nadine Caldwell's applications came to fruition. Can we please leave it at that?" Whiteacre asked.

"Sorry."

"It's hard to believe that Nadine Caldwell..." Whiteacre said, but this time it was Cardozo's turn to cut him off in midsentence.

"What? Is it so hard to believe that some stupid mouth-breathing human, all by her little lonesome could invent something that could ruin thousands of years of law and order?" Cardozo asked.

"It doesn't matter anymore."

"I'm happy to see that notebook burned, Marcus. You're sure that's all of it?"

Marcus Whiteacre nodded. Cardozo didn't see, as he had turned towards the sun again. He took Whiteacre's silence as an assent. He knew that the last of Nadine Caldwell's treacherous scientific accomplishments was locked inside her head and would probably be there to stay.

A few seconds of silence passed. The birds came back. They were apprehensive but still hungry. Both men tossed seeds on the ground. The tiny birds began resuming their meal.

"How much?" Cardozo asked.

"We settled on fifty million," Whiteacre said, bitterly. Cardozo whistled.

"Phillip Caldwell is not as stupid as I had thought," Cardozo said.

"No, he is not. He was a shrewd negotiator. You know I think he even had a glimmer as to the importance of his wife's discoveries."

"Monkeys typing Shakespeare on a lone typewriter," Cardozo said.

"No, I really I think he might have understood some of it," Marcus said.

Cardozo scoffed. The conversation was annoying him more than he thought it would when he initially saw Whiteacre standing over him.

"I'll have twenty-five million transferred to your accounts by the end of the day," Cardozo said. Whiteacre nodded.

Whiteacre spoke again just as Cardozo was about to feel that familiar twinge of peacefulness he always felt when he sat and fed the birds.

Attempting to hold onto the temporary respite, Cardozo once again closed his eyes and turned his face to the sun.

"I really thought he'd use it," Marcus said, breaking the silence.

"Connor's Briefcase? I did as well," Cardozo said, "if he had, the result would be the same, but at least we would have preserved the entertainment value of watching Martin Sandberg implode."

"We all knew you were going to give it to him," Whiteacre said.

"I didn't give it to him," Cardozo said, "you expected me to hand him Connor's Briefcase and tell him to go forth and conquer? Giving it to him would have been a violation."

"No, you just had a futuristic wall safe put in his conference room. Quite conspicuously, I might add, it was the only thing you chose to put in it. Then, you told him that under no circumstances should he touch it," Marcus said, then watched as Cardozo, still facing the sun, knowingly smiled.

"You might as well have starved the man for three days, put him in a room with a chocolate cake, and told him that he was not allowed to eat," Marcus said.

"Maybe I should have put a chocolate cake in the safe *with* Connor's Briefcase," Cardozo said.

Marcus sat in the silence before the urge to ask the question overcame the apprehensiveness of raising the ire of Abraham Cardozo.

"You should have kicked her in," Marcus said. It came out as a statement, not a question and it came out angry.

Cardozo looked at him, frowning as if he had insulted his lineage.

"I know I did the opposite of what I was supposed to do, Marcus," he said instead of tearing Marcus Whiteacre's throat out. Cardozo had a secret. Keeping it to himself was more important than indulging his ego.

"You'll be paying for that little transgression for some time," Marcus said.

"You have no idea," Cardozo said, "but I just couldn't do it, seeing her there, like that, holding the door open, giving everything, fighting to save her family..."

Abraham Cardozo needed only to look into the eyes of his oldest and dearest enemy to see that the secret wasn't something he would be able to keep, at least not from him.

"Abraham... Falling in love with a human, one that's married, no less?" Marcus asked.

"Don't be stupid," Cardozo said, just a little too forcefully, but he knew it was too late.

"You saw her and with your tongue out, tail wagging in the breeze, you saved the whole family like a good little doggie," Marcus said.

The look of anger in Abraham Cardozo's eyes told Marcus that he probably went a little too far.

"Sorry. That was a bit much," Marcus said.

"You don't need to enjoy it," Cardozo said, "I know the mistake was epic. I should have done my job."

"And now Sandberg keeps sticking his stupid face where it doesn't belong."

"I agree."

"He's a fool," Marcus said through sharpened, gritted teeth.

"A lucky fool."

"I had thought by now his luck would run out," Marcus said, "he's had more than his fair share."

"I wasn't going to say anything, I guess now is as good a time as any..." Cardozo stopped himself. He wasn't ever usually a loss for words, this was no different, but momentarily he was somewhat apprehensive as to what he was about to tell Marcus.

"Yes?" Marcus asked.

Cardozo looked at him, then looked ahead, silent.

"Out with it, Abraham," Marcus said.

"Theodore Smith has been released from prison," he said.

"What!" Marcus Whiteacre screamed.

"It's true."

"Sandberg?" Marcus asked.

Cardozo nodded but said nothing, eyed him as he sat on the bench next to him, seething.

"It's not that idiot's fault he keeps bumping into your little house of cards, Marcus."

"*My* house of cards?" Marcus asked.

As he asked the question, a shadow suddenly cast on them in the shape of a man, much like Whiteacre had cast on Cardozo a few scant moments earlier.

"Are my ears burning?" a familiar voice asked.

They looked up to see him standing in front of them.

Marcus bent to look behind him and see his ineffective security now coming towards them with intent.

"Don't bother. Go back!" Marcus yelled at them. He meant to waive, but it was his fist he put into the air. They backed away.

"Mr. Blackacre, how very nice to see you on such a fine day," Abraham Cardozo said to Theodore Smith, his fake smile beaming.

261

"I am not using that name anymore."

"You are content with the name we gave you? Shall I call you 'Teddy?'" Cardozo asked.

"What do you want, Blackacre?" Whiteacre asked.

"I have everything I want, gentlemen, well, almost. I was strolling through this public park, saw a couple of old friends and thought I'd say hello," Theodore Smith said.

"Enjoying freedom, then? Don't get used to it," Whiteacre said, but the threat fell flat.

"Mr. Cardozo?"

"Yes, Blackacre?"

"Sandberg is your pet mouse, is he not?" Smith asked.

"For now," Cardozo said.

"I would keep him around if I were you. He has potential."

"He's an idiot," Cardozo said.

Theodore Smith laughed.

"That idiot is why I am standing here, in front of my two oldest friends, with nothing in the world but time."

"You've always had time."

"That's not what I meant. My apologies for the misunderstanding. They say it's a dish best served cold, my friends, and I never understood what that meant," Theodore said to them, standing over them, eyes ablaze with fury, "I don't care how it is served, I'll happily devour it off the floor."

They watched in silence as Theodore Smith walked away, smiling.

Marcus waited until he had disappeared from view before speaking again.

"I don't know about you, but I'm ready to kill Martin Sandberg," Marcus Whiteacre said.

"Then I have a surprise for you. A course of action has been proposed," Cardozo said, "you'll be getting a call."

"Go on."

"William Donnelly is going to be overcome soon," Cardozo said.

"And we have another lined up and ready," Marcus said, "so what?"

"Yes, but that particular individual will have to wait," Cardozo said.

Realization showed on Whiteacre's face.

"No. Really? Sandberg will be the next to sign the Grendel Contract?" Whiteacre asked.

"He is next."

At hearing the statement, Marcus smiled so wide Cardozo could see all his teeth.

"Please tell me that you are not making a joke at my expense," Marcus said.

"I wouldn't joke about killing my pet mouse in the most horrendous way possible," Cardozo said, "but Sandberg doesn't know it by that name. Let's stick to 'Libro Del Diablo,'" Cardozo said.

TWENTY-EIGHT

MARTIN SANDBERG WALKED AS QUICKLY AS HIS LEGS WOULD CARRY HIM (which was ever-so-slowly) across the lobby floor of his office. He felt as if he had begun exercising after years of stagnation. Every muscle was sore, weak, and in pain. As he tried to walk, he considered how fighting gravity puts a strain on the muscles.

It was surprising to him that Delia was sitting at her desk. She wasn't filing her nails, playing on the computer, or anything.

"Good morning," she said, refusing to meet his gaze.

To Martin, the deference, Delia's respect was much worse than the oozing contempt she usually had for him.

"Are you alright?" she asked.

"I was about to ask you the same thing," Martin said.

Seconds of silence passed as she watched Martin slowly limp-shuffle towards his office, neither of them answering the other's question.

"I guess I have to unpack," he said.

"I'll help," she said.

"Yeah?" he asked.

The front door to his office lobby opened, and Martin turned to see Abraham Cardozo and Marcus Whiteacre (along with Marcus Whiteacre's new security officers) walk in.

"Now I know the world's coming to an end," Martin said.

He took a moment, blinking, to be sure that his eyes were not playing tricks on him, then turned to keep walking, legs shaking with each step he took.

"We're closed," he said, his back to Delia and the men.

"This will only take a moment," Cardozo said after exchanging glances with Whiteacre.

"Then it will take a moment tomorrow... Go away," Martin said.

"Gentlemen, you heard Mr. Martin," Delia said.

"It's about last night," Abraham Cardozo said.

"Fine, fine. You have five minutes. Everything hurts, and I'm probably not going to hear anything you have to say anyway. I would have stayed home in bed if I wasn't so far behind on my paperwork. You tend to let things slide when you think you're about to be murdered by a horde of demons."

Martin plopped into his desk chair and decided that it never felt more comfortable than at that very moment. Without being invited, the men sat down in the chairs in front of his desk.

"I don't get this," Martin said, "don't you two monsters hate each other?"

"We are of the same mind on a few things," Marcus said.

"I'm thinking, looking at you two, that it's more than a few things, Mr. Whiteacre. I see you have different security people. They can wait outside," Martin said.

Marcus Whiteacre nodded to them. They left the office, closed the door behind them.

"I'd like to resume my suffering alone if it is all the same to you guys," Martin said.

"Martin, there is a matter to discuss," Cardozo said, but Martin cut him off mid-sentence.

"Are they all gone?" he asked Marcus.

Marcus Whiteacre looked at him.

"The Laszlos?" Martin asked.

Neither of them looked at one another.

"The big one at the center of it all. That was my friend, wasn't it? That was the first, and you sent him and his brothers after me."

"We didn't send anyone to do anything," Marcus Whiteacre said.

"I believe you. I was mistaken thinking either of you had a voice in the grand scheme of things. Now I know both of you are middle management."

"Now, Mr. Sandberg..."

"You didn't answer me."

"No," Marcus Whiteacre said, "all of them. Every single one."

The three educated men sat in silence together, dumbfounded, feeling uneasy, unknowing, ignorant, the thought of the previous night foremost on their minds.

Seconds of tense silence passed. The men looked at one another as if they were sitting at a table, gambling, playing cards, trying to decide whether to place a bet.

"I liked him, you know," Martin said, looking ahead past them as if he was alone in his office, "I really liked him."

"Me too," Marcus Whiteacre said.

"We have a matter to discuss," Cardozo said.

"Go on," Martin said, now struggling with a small sealed box containing a bottle of over-the-counter pain medicine. His hands hurt like everything else. It would seem even opening a little cardboard box of pills would be difficult for a while.

"Everyone knows about what happened last night," Cardozo said, watching as Martin unsuccessfully tried to open the box.

"Is that a fact? How about you tell me what happened last night."

They looked at him.

"Both of you are aware, I'm sure, that something can happen, you can see it with your own eyes, you can feel it, but still... Last night? That place? I could even taste it in my brain. It still burns the back of my throat, but it doesn't matter. Why don't you tell me," he said, bitterly, turning the small box of pills over in his hands.

"You know what happened last night, Mr. Sandberg," Marcus said.

"It's like taking a Neanderthal to the movies," Martin said. Marcus Whiteacre and Abraham Cardozo looked at one another, confused.

"The reaction to last night has been emotional," Marcus Whiteacre said, after realizing Martin was not going to explain his "Neanderthal" statement further.

"I know what happened. I know what was supposed to happen," Abraham Cardozo said, taking the box of pills from Martin without objection. As he spoke, he opened the box, opened the bottle and poured a few of the pills onto the desk in front of Martin.

"That's why it was requested that we come here today," Marcus said, sitting forward in his chair.

Martin had the fleeting thought of commenting on who it was that could request the two most powerful men he had ever met to do anything but decided to dry-swallow two pills instead.

He looked at them. They were two little boys who had been caught after breaking the neighbor's window while playing baseball too close to the house. Martin almost wanted to laugh.

"There's a price yet to be paid," Whiteacre said.

Martin met the men's eyes in silence.

"We think we have a solution that would be mutually beneficial," Marcus Whiteacre said as he opened his briefcase and pulled the confounding thing out.

"I was wondering where *that* had gone off to," Martin said as Marcus Whiteacre put the Libro De Diablo on the desk in front of Martin.

"Your old friend, William Donnelly will become deceased in a matter of hours," Marcus Whiteacre said.

"I left that in the trunk of my car. How is it that you've strolled in here with it?"

"It was in my bathroom this morning," Marcus said, his facial expression suddenly appearing very human.

Martin tried to push back the thought of Marcus Whiteacre, standing at a sink, deep in the bowels of hell, brushing his teeth, the Devil-Book sitting menacingly on a closed toilet seat next to him.

"I let him down," Martin said. "I couldn't read it. I couldn't get him into court in time."

"Now you can save him," Whiteacre said.

Martin sat back in his chair.

"You're here to kill me," Martin said.

"Not exactly," Whiteacre said.

"Yes, exactly. Tell me, how many who have signed that are still breathing?" Martin asked.

"One," Cardozo said, his eyes piercing.

"But not for long, Mr. Sandberg," Whiteacre said.

I sign this and Will is ok?" Martin asked.

"Yes, like it never happened."

"And I get ripped apart from the inside out by that thing," Martin said.

"Not immediately."

"I get a little time to put my affairs put in order. That's how it is?"

"As an added bonus, the necessary sanctions for Contempt of Court will be satisfied," Whiteacre said.

"It's a win-win," Cardozo said.

Martin looked at him, eyes beaming, anger and hatred in his eyes.

"Can we stop pretending that this is about Contempt of Court? I know what this is about. This has nothing to do with arguing with a judge or helping the Caldwells. Let's all of us not pretend that we are ignorant."

Cardozo had never seen Martin so angry.

"If you recognize what is happening here, then you know that there is a price to be paid," Whiteacre said.

"You've already told me that," Martin said.

"You owe me," Cardozo said.

Martin scoffed, looked at Cardozo, incredulous.

"I *owe* you?"

"I pulled you and Emily out of Hell," Cardozo said.

"I thought we all just agreed not to pretend we're stupid. I'd be thankful, Mr. Cardozo, if I thought for even a moment you did that for me."

They stared at one another, a test of wills.

"You think I don't know?" Martin asked him.

Whiteacre looked at the two men.

"Whiteacre, you know, don't you?" Martin asked him.

It was true, he knew.

"Know what?" Whiteacre asked, refusing the acknowledgment. Knowing something and admitting that knowledge, after all, is entirely different.

"That Abe here is in love with my wife," Martin said.

The men looked at one another. Cardozo tried to put on his fiercest face.

"Admit it, Abraham. They sent you to find out who had ripped a hole from the hospital to Hell and you took one look at my Esme, holding time and space in her bare hands and you fell in love with her," Martin said.

Abraham Cardozo looked away, the staring contest lost.

He was right, and Cardozo hated him for it, amongst other reasons.

"I've never seen a monster blush," Martin said, satisfaction in his voice.

"Now wait just a minute," Whiteacre said.

"Just a second," Martin said, putting his finger up, interrupting him.

"You didn't do your job. You're the one who needs to pay. You did the only thing you could think of to get your foot in the door with Esmeralda. You played the hero, pulled Emily and me out so she would owe you."

"Stop," Cardozo demanded.

"You'd never seen a woman like her, a human, someone as beautiful as she is powerful," Martin said.

"Stop, Sandberg."

"You failed, Hellhound, you failed because you fell in love and now you have to pay. " Martin said.

"I already paid!" Cardozo growled.

The building shook.

Delia had heard (and felt) the commotion. She stood on the other side of the closed door to Martin's office. She looked at the doorknob for a moment before returning to her desk and sitting down.

"You're mad because she might have feelings for me, too," Cardozo said.

Martin smiled at him.

The act infuriated him further.

Abraham Cardozo considered ripping Martin Sandberg's throat out with his teeth.

"Why are you smiling at me?"

"Because for once, you are clueless," Martin said, "you think I'm going to be the jealous husband? I'll fistfight you, fight for her hand, honor at stake? Mr. Cardozo, I feel sorry for you."

"Wipe that smile off your face," Cardozo said.

"Consider it wiped. Now, the only thing I feel for you is pity."

"You don't get to pity me," Cardozo said.

"Of course, I do. Brother, you and I are in love with the same woman, but what you fail to realize is that every day Esmeralda chooses to be my wife, that day is a gift," Martin said to Abraham Cardozo, "You know as well as me that it's Esmeralda's world, and you and I are just living in it."

Cardozo scoffed but knew he was right.

"Tell me. Would you do it again? Would you do it again for the chance to see her smile because it was *you* that made her happy?" Martin asked.

The silence from Abraham Cardozo gave Martin the answer.

"Me too, brother. The difference between us, Abraham, is that I am still going to leave my socks on the floor and I'm going to leave the toilet seat up at least three times a week."

"I'm not your brother," Cardozo said.

"Either way, I'm not paying. Whiteacre, you can go ahead and have Abraham sign the book."

"You are mistaken," Whiteacre said.

"About what?"

"That is not the price to be paid."

Martin looked at the men. Though the conversation went from uncomfortable to acrimonious, then to hateful, Martin knew that Marcus Whitacre was right.

How many demons died the previous night? How long had it been since a litter was made extinct, like the Laszlos?

Martin recognized the outstanding debt, realized why the phrase "a debt to be paid" was being said over and over.

"You saw what they sent for you," Whiteacre said. "Who or what do you imagine they will send for Esmeralda?" he said.

Martin suddenly felt both cold and hot at the same time, overcome with the epiphany.

"You were right, Mr. Sandberg. This isn't about you arguing with a judge."

"It's about me and Esme. It's about what we did to save Emily. It's about what happened last night."

"We are supposed to be having this conversation with Esmeralda," Whiteacre said.

He looked at Abraham Cardozo, who was looking away and knew it was true.

"Don't do that," Martin said.

"She's the one with the power, Mr. Sandberg. You're just some idiot who walked through a hole."

Marcus Whiteacre's words made the hair on Martin's arms stand. He began to sweat. Fear overcame him.

"Everything you've said is true, Mr. Sandberg. That's why we are here in your office, talking to you, instead of sitting in your living room, talking to the one who wears the pants in the family," Marcus Whiteacre said.

"Come on, Sandberg," Cardozo said.

"Someone has to pay," Whiteacre said, pushing the book towards Martin with his fingertips.

Martin shook his head in disbelief. For just a second, he allowed himself to believe this wasn't happening.

"Martin," Cardozo said, having calmed himself, "Think of Emily."

"Leave her out of this," he said.

"How can we? Look at what you've done to her," Whiteacre said, "by bringing her back your way, you see what you've wrought."

"You don't know if the doctors could have saved her. They might have resuscitated her without you are Esmeralda's intervention. If they had, she'd be your normal little girl, and none of you would be aware of any of this. Of course, we'll never know, will we?" Whiteacre said.

"Please. You have to leave her alone," Martin said. He was begging.

"It's not up to us," Cardozo said.

"If I sign, Esme will be safe? No one will come for her?"

"Yes."

"And Emily?"

"You are getting three for one, Mr. Sandberg. You will rescue William Donnelly and your family will be left alone."

Martin looked at the men.

"How they must hate me," he said.

"You have no idea," Marcus Whiteacre said.

Martin Sandberg nodded his head, looked at the book.

The men watched as Martin opened the book and found the signature page. There were empty spaces beneath the name: "William Donnelly."

They watched as Martin took his letter-opener and cut his hand with it, wincing in pain.

Blood dripped onto the desk next to the book.

Martin looked up at them.

Marcus Whiteacre and Abraham Cardozo were looking at him, confused and somewhat horrified. Both had the same strange facial expression.

Both appeared as if Martin had told a joke that neither of them understood. Both had the same facial expression they would have as if Martin babbled a phrase in an unknown language.

"What on Earth are you doing?" Whiteacre asked.

"What?" Martin asked, "it's to sign the book in blood."

"You use a pen, Mr. Sandberg. We're not savages," Marcus said.

"That's not dried blood?" Martin asked, pointing to the signatures.

"It's black ink. What is wrong with you?" Whiteacre asked.

"Oh," Martin said.

The men watched as Martin found a box of tissues in his desk and cleaned the blood off his desktop. Neither spoke as Martin took a pen from his drawer, took a deep breath and closed his eyes.

In his mind, his eyes closed, he saw the face of the young woman with the white shirt, baggy pants, and tool-belt.

Martin Sandberg wrote his name in the book his wife had so eloquently named the "Libro Del Diablo," and then he was gone.

TWENTY-NINE

MARTIN SANDBERG STOOD IN FRONT OF A WALL THAT HAD NO BEGINNING, NO END, IN ANY DIRECTION. He looked up at the blank sky and saw that the wall went further than he could see. Looking right and left, it was the same. The wall was long as it was high.

He shrugged his shoulders and began to walk along the wall.

He felt the smoothness of the wall with his fingertips as he walked. He walked for what seemed either minutes or hours, he couldn't be sure, then stopped, put his back against the wall and leaned, taking a break.

It was calm to be in a place inhabited by nothingness and a wall. Martin enjoyed the quiet.

"Are you there?" a voice said.

The voice startled Martin, as it felt like a thousand voices at once, but was only one. The voice was deep, angry, but also sad.

"I am here," Martin said.

"She built this for you?" he asked.

"She did," Martin said.

"She built this for me?"

"For us," Martin said.

"It's been a long time since I've seen something new," the voice said.

"For me, it's every day," Martin said.

"You are my new room-mate, then? You signed?"

"I signed," Martin said.

"I'll break free," he said, "as I always have."

"Not this time," Martin said, "but instead of breaking free, maybe we can try something different for once."

"Different?"

"Incarceration is meant to have two purposes. The first purpose is to protect the public from the offender. The rest of the world is safe while the offender is locked away."

The voice huffed.

"The second?"

"The second purpose is rehabilitation. The convicted is rehabilitated so when he rejoins society, he is no longer inclined to offend," Martin said. "In your case, the first purpose has been of such paramount importance, the second has been ignored."

The voice laughed.

The sound was terrifying, maddening, disheartening.

Martin had to fight to keep from screaming.

"You presume to rehabilitate me? You?"

"I know you hate the world."

"There aren't enough specks of dust in the universe with which to count my hate."

"I have to go. I will be back. We'll talk more," Martin said.

There was no answer.

"MR. SANDBERG? MR. SANDBERG? ARE YOU ALRIGHT?" Marcus Whiteacre asked.

Martin took a moment to look both men in the eyes.

"You blanked out for a moment."

"I did?"

"You were staring ahead but not saying anything."

"I'm alright," Martin said.

"For now, maybe," Cardozo said.

Martin had felt the world change as he wrote his name underneath William's, in the space provided.

The men watched as Martin put the book on the bookshelf behind him. Whiteacre looked at him.

"Don't worry," he said, "tomorrow it will either be on my kitchen table or in your bathroom."

"Gentlemen," Martin said to them, just as they opened his office door to leave. They stopped, looked at him. "I'm going to take this as a conclusion to our business dealings. Neither of you is welcome back here to my office."

"Now wait just a minute," Abraham Cardozo said.

"Mr. Sandberg," Marcus Whiteacre said, gently grasping Cardozo's arm, signaling that he wished to speak.

Cardozo pulled away.

"Do you remember your little visit to my Board of Directors?" Whiteacre asked, "Do you remember that you told them you could smell evil on them?"

"I said I smelled their evil and they laughed at me," Martin said.

274

"You called them evil, Mr. Sandberg. They laughed at you because you should already know that good and evil are relative," Marcus Whiteacre said.

Satisfied with himself, Marcus Whiteacre walked out of Martin's office, Cardozo behind him.

THE MEN WALKED INTO THE FRONT LOBBY OF MARTIN'S OFFICE, closing the door to Martin's office behind them. Marcus Whiteacre and Abraham Cardozo seemed to notice the boxes and items strewn about for the first time.

"He didn't think he was coming back," Delia said to them.

In the corner of the room, next to a pile of books, propped up by a collection of boxes was an old set of golf clubs.

"I didn't know Mr. Sandberg played golf," Marcus Whiteacre said.

"He doesn't," Delia said, "some client left them here, I think as payment for legal services. I was going to donate them to auction for the proceeds to benefit the shelter, along with some other things."

"They look like pretty good clubs," Cardozo said, "It's been years since I played a good game of golf."

"Me as well. I used to love going eighteen rounds almost once a week," Whiteacre said.

"May I?" Abraham Cardozo said, leaning in to pick up the golf clubs.

Delia shrugged her shoulders.

"Want to play a round, Marcus?" Abraham Cardozo asked.

"I think that's the best idea you've had in years," Marcus said to him.

Delia Hammond watched as Marcus Whiteacre and Abraham Cardozo walked out of the office, carrying with them the artifact she only knew as Lassiter's Golf Clubs. As the door closed behind them, Delia smiled.

MARTIN SANDBERG STOOD IN THE HOSPITAL ROOM, STARING OUT THE WINDOW AT THE PARKING LOT BELOW. "It's the most amazing thing," he said.

He took a moment to collect his thoughts. Even though the view from the hospital room was just the parking lot, Martin found the rows of cars soothing. He allowed himself to enjoy the moment.

"That one-armed monster ends up getting the best of everyone they've ever stuck him with. Before they started putting him with people, they built a realm just for him. It took him a little while, but he ended up destroying that. It's hard to believe, a whole domain, torn apart by just one monster. They didn't have any other place to put him, that's why they started the contract, had created the Libro De Diablo. I'm going to say they built the contract rather than drafted it. It is a work of art, I mean, from a legal standpoint.

I'm lucky. Most of the time I can't even tell he's there. For a while, I thought Ariel was building that jail cell for me. I don't know why I thought that," he said.

He stopped for a moment to think of her.

"I don't know how I did it, but I went there one night, walked all the way around it. It was the oddest thing, a massive bunker with no windows. I tapped on the wall, put my ear up against it. He was singing, something about walls. He walks around holding his severed arm with the one that's still attached. When he beats on the walls, if I listen hard enough, I can sometimes hear it.

We built the ultimate prison. It's like she knew. You know?" Martin asked, knowing that he would not get an answer.

He listened to the beeps and sounds of the medical machinery, tried to ignore them.

"Phillip's been driving me crazy, but it's okay. He never imagined he'd be a millionaire. I don't know how he soaked fifty million dollars out of Marcus Whiteacre, but he has it and has no idea what to do.

Can you believe he keeps asking me? How in the world would I have any idea how someone should manage such a large sum of money? I found him some reputable financial people. He's hired one of them, but he's still calling me. He says I'm the only one he can trust. I guess he's having trust issues, you know, with all that's gone on. I don't blame him."

Martin Sandberg took a moment to collect himself.

"I don't hear her anymore, not as she was. Sometimes I feel empty. Sometimes I visit Philip, but it's not to visit him. He knows I'm visiting her. I go, and I feed her a bottle, maybe sit in a rocking chair with her, tell her I'm okay. Phillip told me he does the same thing. He said he sometimes finds himself talking to her for hours. Neither of us knows if she understands anything. It makes me feel better to talk to her. I don't know why."

Martin Sandberg, eyes glassy, welling up, turned from the window. He faced the quiet figure of Nadine Caldwell, lying in the hospital bed, eyes closed, the medical machines keeping her alive.

"Your baby is beautiful, Nadine. I don't know if you can hear me, I don't know if you understand any of this... I wish you could hold her. She needs you. Don't get me wrong, Phillip has become quite the baby expert, he's read all the books. He's doing what he promised. He's taking great care of her. However, there is no substitute for a mother. A baby needs a mother. You have to wake up."

Martin looked at her. She looked like she was sleeping, but Martin knew otherwise.

"Phillip says you'll wake up someday. I'd like to meet you properly, instead of talking to you like this. The doctor said that sometimes people can hear. I want to think you can hear me. Talking to you like this may be helping me more than it might be helping you, Nadine.

Will's going to be discharged tomorrow. With the monster gone from him, he's made a full recovery. I know he looks like he's okay, but I wonder about him. Now that he's free from the book, he's ignorant again. If I told him about demons and monsters, he'd laugh at me or try to have me committed. I'm happy for him."

A few seconds went by as Martin listened to the machines.

"I'll come back tomorrow. Thanks for listening," he said.

MARTIN SANDBERG CAME THROUGH THE FRONT DOOR OF HIS OFFICE, CARRYING THE SPECIAL BOX AND THE CUPHOLDER WITH TWO CUPS OF COFFEE.

"I got them," Martin said with a smile.

As he walked into his office, he could see Delia and Theodore Smith hugging. Delia had her eyes closed as she held him tightly.

"Okay, you two. Get a room," Martin said.

"I was about to go," Theodore said.

"No need to leave on my account, Theodore, I have treats."

277

"I have a job interview," he said.

"Good for you," Martin said, "let me know if I can help."

"Thanks, Marty. See you later, baby?"

"See you," Delia said. She tried to act cool but couldn't hide that she was in love.

Theodore Smith left and Martin set the box on Delia's desk.

"Mr. Martin, you never cease to surprise me," she said.

"Take a look at these babies," Martin said opening the box, revealing four carefully crafted cupcakes that were more artwork than something to be eaten.

"Beautiful, just beautiful," Delia said.

"That's what I like to see, you smiling a normal smile, not one of your smiles that makes me want to dress like a Rodeo Clown and run around in traffic," he said.

"Now Mr. Martin, you behave," she said, fake frowning at him, "I don't see another bag or another box. You didn't get yourself anything to eat, Mr. Martin?"

"There are four cupcakes in there," he said.

"I can count."

"I've decided to cut out sugar," Martin said, still smiling at her.

"I'll share. We should celebrate our continuing business," she said, "I was anxious for a while there."

"Me too," he said, handing her one of the cups.

He watched with only minor trepidation as she opened the lid, looked inside the cup, and sniffed.

"Perfect," she said.

He sipped his coffee as she took napkins out of her desk drawer and put one in front of each of them.

"So, what do we have?" he asked her. He watched as she picked up a small stack of message slips.

"We got a call from a man who wants to sue the gypsies for putting a curse on him," Delia said.

"We should pass on that one, don't you think?" Martin asked.

"I agree. We don't need them putting curses *on us*. We have enough problems," she said, crumpling and throwing the slip into the garbage pail.

"Witches involved in a copyright infringement? Something to do with covens stealing each other's recipes?" Delia said.

"Spells," he said, taking a sip of coffee.

"Spells?" she asked.

"You're probably right; it's recipes. Let's pass on that one," he said.

"Haunted car?" she asked.

"No way," he said.

"Cursed car?"

"Nope."

He watched as she threw the slips into the garbage, one at a time.

"Deal with the devil?" she asked.

"Did the potential client say that exactly, that it was a 'deal with the Devil?'" Martin asked.

"That's what he said."

"Pass," Martin said.

"Here's one that's interesting. Wife wants to divorce her husband for giving her a disease."

"He cheated on her, caught an STD?"

"No, she says he bit her."

"Vampire? Zombie? Werewolf?" Martin asked.

"Does it matter?" she asked him.

"Nope," he said, then watched as the slip went into the trash.

"Tenant wants to sue the landlord case? Some kind of tentacle-monster underneath the apartment building, harassing the folks."

"Harassing the people who live there? How so?"

"I don't know," she said.

Looking at his face, Delia realized Martin was interested.

"I may come with you to see that one. I'll call and get an appointment," she said, putting the remaining slips on the table in front of her. The smell of the treats was too much. Without words, they both agreed to eat a cupcake and finish going through the potential clients after.

She handed him a cupcake and he took a moment to look at the intricate flower pattern in the icing. The edible artwork smelled delicious. He was about to take a bite when the front door to his office opened so forcefully that it slammed.

"Of course," Martin said, barely above a whisper.

"You forgot to lock the door," Delia said to him.

Martin turned to see a terrified young man in the doorway.

"Mr. Sandberg you gotta help me," Phillip Caldwell said.

"Good morning, Mr. Sandberg, how are you today? I'm fine, Phillip, how are you? It's nice to see you today," Martin said, longingly staring at his untouched cupcake.

"No, this is serious," Philip said.

Knowing perhaps the only thing in the world that would cause Phillip Caldwell to appear as terrified as he seemed, Martin suddenly felt afraid.

"Is it the baby? Did something happen?" Martin asked.

"They took her!"

"Slow down. Who took her?"

"Children's services! They just came and took my baby!" Philip yelled.

"Breathe," Martin said, relieved that the child was not injured, "we will get her back."

"Please, Mr. Sandberg," Phillip said.

"She's your baby, we will do whatever it takes and get her home," Martin said. Phillip Caldwell nodded.

"We can do this, " Martin said, "tell me everything that happened and let's get to work."

About the Author

Jeffrey A. Rapkin is the son of Angela Rapkin, Ph.D., and Judge Harry M. Rapkin. He has been practicing law since 1996 in primarily South Sarasota County and Charlotte County, Florida. He has worked as a Corrections Officer, government attorney, and is certified by the Department of Children and Families to conduct Assessments and Facilitate the Certified Batterer's Intervention Programs. Rapkin has completed parenting coordinator training and is a Supreme Court Certified Circuit Civil and Family Mediator.

Rapkin has written several nonfiction manuscripts including an instructional manual for attorneys specializing in Restraining Orders and a Family Mediation Guidebook. This is his first work of fiction.

Jeffrey A. Rapkin has been married since 1992 to Virginia M. Rapkin, has three children and a grandson.

Depending on what kind of day he is having, if asked, he will tell you that there are aliens among us, creatures, or both. He's probably joking (except for Bigfoot who he swears is now living in Boca Raton and shops at Wal-Mart at night.)

Jeffrey A. Rapkin, Esq.
Attorney and Counselor at Law

97227141R00157

Made in the USA
Columbia, SC
08 June 2018